THE BLUE DIAMOND

THE
BLUE DIAMOND

A Daughter of Sherlock Holmes Mystery

Leonard Goldberg

MINOTAUR
BOOKS
NEW YORK

First published in the United States by Minotaur Books, an imprint of St. Martin's Publishing Group

www.minotaurbooks.com

Designed by Omar Chapa

Library of Congress Cataloging-in-Publication Data

Names: Goldberg, Leonard S., author.
Title: The blue diamond : a daughter of Sherlock Holmes mystery / Leonard Goldberg.
Description: First edition. | New York : Minotaur Books, 2022. | Series: The daughter of Sherlock Holmes mysteries ; 6
Identifiers: LCCN 2022003291 | ISBN 9781250789594 (hardcover) | ISBN 9781250789600 (ebook)
Subjects: LCGFT: Novels.
Classification: LCC PS3557.O35775 B58 2022 | DDC 813/.54—dc23/eng/20220127
LC record available at https://lccn.loc.gov/2022003291

Our books may be purchased in bulk for promotional, educational, or business use. Please contact your local bookseller or the Macmillan Corporate and Premium Sales Department at 1-800-221-7945, extension 5442, or by email at MacmillanSpecialMarkets@macmillan.com.

First Edition: 2022

10 9 8 7 6 5 4 3 2 1

For Mia and Jackson, two little thieves who have stolen my heart
a thousand times

Contents

God has given you one face, and you make yourself another.

—SHAKESPEARE, *HAMLET*

The blue diamond was amongst the rarest of diamonds, and those deemed flawless were beyond price.

THE BLUE DIAMOND

CHAPTER ONE

The Penthouse Robberies

It was customary for my dear wife, Joanna, to situate herself at the window of our parlor at 221b Baker Street and observe the ongoings down below. On more than a few occasions the view of an individual approaching our doorstep heralded the arrival of a most intriguing case which defied resolution. But on this dreary November morning in the year 1917, it was I, John Watson, Jr., M.D., who was stationed at the window, for Joanna was entirely preoccupied with a large blackboard that stood in the center of our parlor. Upon it were listed the features of sensational robberies which had occurred at two of London's finest hotels, the Fairmont and the St. Regis. Both were known to be frequented by famous, distinguished guests, who expected and received the very best service in every regard, and even the slightest blemish or misstep was quickly corrected and erased from the public's eye. Thus when these exceptional robberies took place within a ten-day period and were reported in depth by all the newspapers, the hoteliers were mortified and implored Scotland Yard to bring about a rapid resolution. Unfortunately, none were forthcoming, and the hoteliers turned their hopes to the daughter of Sherlock Holmes.

"Data! I require data!" Joanna cried out impatiently. "I cannot make bricks without clay."

My father looked up from the *Daily Telegraph* and smiled gently. "That was a favorite quote of your father's, particularly when he was confronted with a most difficult case."

"There is a singular hidden thread here which continues to escape my eye," she continued on, before banging a stick of white chalk against the blackboard. "It will be the common denominator that ties all these features together."

My gaze turned to the blackboard upon which Joanna had listed the characteristics of the robberies that occurred at the elegant hotels.

	THE MAYFAIR	THE ST. REGIS
LOCATION	West London	West London
Suite position	Penthouse (5th floor)	Penthouse (5th floor)
Weather (night)	Fog-shrouded	Fog-shrouded
Item(s) stolen	Ming dynasty vase	Bearer bonds
Ransom note	None	None

"But why no ransom notes?" asked I.

"Because the stolen items can be disposed of at their true market value," Joanna replied. "Bearer bonds are issued by a business such as a corporation or by a government, and are unregistered. The person who holds them owns them, and there is no way to trace or track the buyer or seller. And the Ming dynasty vase in all likelihood has a predetermined buyer, which accounts for the fact it has not shown up on London's black market."

"So the items by themselves represent dead ends, do they not?"

My wife shook her head. "I suspect they represent a key to the puzzle, but it is the lock which remains a mystery."

My attention returned to the street below as an official limousine stopped in front of our doorstep. The driver, holding up an umbrella against the rain, hurried to the rear compartment and opened the door for the two occupants whom I instantly recognized. "I believe we are about to be presented with yet another difficult puzzle," said I, tapping on the window.

Joanna and my father strode over quickly to watch Inspector Lestrade and Sir Charles Bradberry, the commissioner of Scotland Yard, alight from the limousine. Passersby stopped and stared unabashedly at the two notables, as they were no doubt able to identify them from their frequent photographs in London's newspapers. A patrolling constable appeared and motioned for the onlookers to move on, but they only took a step back, for they knew both the men and the famed address they were about to enter.

Joanna looked to her father-in-law and asked, "Watson, in all your years with Sherlock Holmes, were the two of you ever visited by an inspector and commissioner together?"

"Never," my father replied. "On occasion, Lestrade would call on us unannounced, but never accompanied by the commissioner."

"Which indicates we are about to be presented with a case of great importance," she said, stating the obvious before adding an additional clue. "You will note they carry no files or folders, which tells us the crime was recently committed, certainly within the past twelve hours, for no mention was made of it in the morning newspapers."

"I wonder if it is yet another incidence of espionage, which brings with it the direst of consequences," my father pondered.

The same thought crossed my mind, for the Great War on the Continent raged on, with terrible and mounting casualties on both sides. More than a few German agents had been apprehended in London itself, all trying to steal valuable information which could turn the tide of the conflict. Only months earlier we had foiled a plot to kidnap England's foremost cryptographer and transport him to Germany. "God help us if there is another high-ranking traitor involved, for the effect on the country's morale would be devastating."

"That is possible, but unlikely," Joanna argued mildly. "Were that the case, we would not be visited by Scotland Yard, but rather summoned to Whitehall under a cloak of secrecy."

She moved over to the large blackboard and pushed it to the side of our parlor near the workbench, upon which rested an opened monograph on Ming dynasty vases. Joanna had hoped it might shine some light on the robbery we were currently investigating, but thus far it had proved useless. Next to it was a copy of the *New York Times,* which detailed the bearer bonds which had been stolen from the suite of the famous American industrialist Robert Boone Hall. That, too, proved to be of little help.

There was a gentle rap on the door and our landlady, Miss Hudson, showed the two visitors in, then, with a half curtsy, backed out and quietly closed the door behind her. The detectives entered with a firm, hurried step, pausing only briefly by our two-log fire to warm their hands. Both men were tall and middle-aged, but there the similarities ended. Lestrade, the son of the inspector who worked with Sherlock Holmes, was slender of frame and had a pleasant face except for his eyes, which seemed fixed in a permanent squint. Other than a fringe of hair above his ears, he was completely bald, and kept his head covered with a worn brown derby. By contrast, Sir Charles Bradberry was well built and broad shouldered, with neatly trimmed hair and a thick mustache. His expression was stern and determined, his eyes cold and gray with no hint of emotion. Unlike his predecessor, he was widely respected by his officers and the public as well, for he was a strict disciplinarian who would not abide any wrongdoings at Scotland Yard, and those found guilty were either discharged or summarily punished.

Skipping the usual amenities, the commissioner studied the blackboard for a moment before saying, "I am afraid the penthouse robber has struck again, but now he has added assault to his criminal activities."

"Who was the victim?" Joanna asked at once.

"An innocent doorman at the Windsor Hotel who we believe may have witnessed the thief in action."

Joanna gave the commissioner a long, curious look. "The doorman, you say?"

"The doorman," the commissioner repeated. "Who now lies in a coma at St. Bartholomew's."

My wife hurried over to the Persian slipper that held her Turkish cigarettes and plucked one from its packet. She carefully lighted it and began to pace the floor, head down, a stream of pale smoke trailing her. Her lips moved, but made no sound. It appeared that either the occupation or condition of the victim was of particular note. I could not decipher why that was so, for it was entirely possible that an alert doorman had seen some mischief and attempted to intervene.

Joanna stopped in front of the blackboard and studied it at length, drawing one puff after another on her cigarette before adding the word *assault* at the end of the list. Only then did she discard her cigarette into the fire and bring her attention to the commissioner. "Sir Charles, please be good enough to review the characteristics of the initial two robberies which I have enumerated and tell me if they fit with the theft at the Windsor."

In a deep voice he compared the features which occurred at the Fairmont and the St. Regis with those at the Windsor. "All transpired at the West End of London, in the penthouse of each hotel, and on fog-shrouded nights."

Joanna rapidly reached for the chalk and circled the term *Fog-shrouded*. "Last night the fog was quite thick, was it not?"

The commissioner nodded. "It was a pea-souper, with a yellowish tinge caused by the accumulation of sulfur gases."

"Then pray tell, Sir Charles, how does a doorman stationed

at the front entrance of the hotel view a robbery taking place five stories up?"

"Perhaps the doorman was alert to an individual exiting the hotel who was out of place and obviously not a guest," he replied without hesitation. "Say the thief was from the working class and carrying a satchel of tools rather than a suitcase. The doorman confronts him, a struggle ensues, and the poor man is struck by a metal object which causes a skull fracture so severe that the doctors at St. Bartholomew's hold little hope for his survival."

"Was the weapon found?"

"It was seen but not recovered," Sir Charles answered. "Allow me to explain. We believe the attack took place at approximately two AM, for that was the time the injured doorman was discovered by a taxi driver drawing up to the hotel entrance to discharge late-arriving guests. The driver attempted to give assistance and that is when he noticed a metal object near the victim's head. He assumed it was the weapon, but it resided in a small pool of blood."

"Was he able to describe the metal object?"

"He said it was slender and about so big." The commissioner extended his thumb and index finger as far apart as possible. "This would make the weapon five inches in length, but the driver had no idea as to its width. He did remark that it did resemble a railroad spike. In any event, the entrance soon became crowded with members of the hotel staff, a doctor who happened to be a guest, and several ambulance personnel. When Scotland Yard arrived, the area in front of the entrance was being cleaned and the blood washed away. Despite a diligent search by the inspector and his men, no weapon could be found."

Joanna turned to Lestrade. "Were the nearby sewers and garbage bins inspected?"

"Within a two-block radius," he replied. "In addition, the

hotel staff and ambulance personnel who attended the doorman were questioned, and none recalled seeing the metal weapon."

Joanna returned to her Persian slipper and came back with another lighted Turkish cigarette. Again she began pacing, now speaking unintelligibly to herself. The telephone on her writing desk rang loudly. My wife hurried over to it and picked up the receiver, only to immediately place it back in its cradle, thus interrupting the call so that it would not break her concentration. She started pacing once more, speaking as she strode. "The weapon is most important. You must make every effort to find it, even if you must double your search area."

"We shall do so and bring in additional men as well."

Sir Charles asked, "Why is the weapon so important at this juncture?"

"You show me the weapon, I'll show you the man," Joanna replied. "It will also allow us to clearly state that the metal object caused the skull fracture."

"All evidence indicates it did," Sir Charles insisted, and gestured to Lestrade. "The inspector spoke with the surgeon at St. Bartholomew's and can give you their accurate description of the head wound and the type of weapon which would bring about such an injury."

Lestrade opened his notebook and wetted a finger as he went through its pages. "The fracture was high up on the skull, above and behind the eye socket, and appeared to be quite even, like one made with a small hatchet. The blow was forceful enough to cause fragments of bone to be embedded in the brain itself."

"Did the surgeon specifically state that the wound was high up on the skull?" Joanna asked.

"Indeed he did, madam," the inspector assured, again referring to his notes. "It was located well above the eye and near the hairline."

The expression on my wife's face indicated that something was amiss with the inspector's account of the wound.

Lestrade noted the change in her appearance and quickly added, "The surgeon was quite convinced that the injury was the result of a blow from the weapon described by the taxi driver."

My father inquired, "May we know the name of the attending surgeon?"

Lestrade flipped more pages in his notepad before replying, "Sir Thomas Hutson."

"A distinguished physician who is known for his expertise on head injuries," my father noted.

"Who has actually written a thesis on the subject which is considered the gold standard by many," I recalled.

Joanna nodded at the surgeon's qualifications, then summarized the case presented to us. "So we have yet another robbery at a fine hotel, which on this occasion involves a bloody assault. Are these not the salient features?"

"Correct," Sir Charles responded.

"There must be more to it to merit an urgent visit by both the commissioner and an inspector from Scotland Yard."

"There is, madam, for the personage robbed was the Governor-General of South Africa and the item stolen was the famed blue diamond."

Our collective jaws must have dropped at the mention of one of the world's most precious gems, which had been described in numerous newspapers and magazines throughout England. Even photographs of it had been shown, but none could truly reveal its lustrous blue color that made it so unique. The blue diamond was amongst the rarest of diamonds, and those deemed flawless were beyond price. Such was the stone discovered at De Beers Consolidated Mines some five months earlier. It weighed 2,828 metric carats, which made it the second-largest diamond ever found, and only a bit smaller than the celebrated Cullinan Diamond that had a weight of 3,106 metric carats. But it was its blue color, produced by trace amounts of boron that contaminated its crystalline lattice, which dazzled the eyes of every viewer. The gem was so large and unique that once it was cut and polished its value was estimated to exceed a million pounds.

Joanna broke the silence by returning to the blackboard and listing the blue diamond in the item(s) stolen category, along with its estimated worth. She underlined its value and gave the item another long stare before turning to the commissioner. "I assume security was extraordinary."

"It was beyond extraordinary," he replied, then flipped the blackboard over to its blank side and drew a simple diagram with labels.

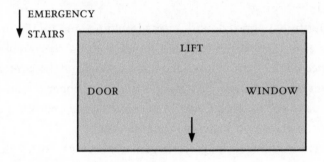

"The entire fifth floor, which I have outlined, was occupied by the Governor-General and his entourage. The floor had eight suites, four a side, a single lift, and only one door out that leads to the emergency stairs. There were ten security agents who were rotated on a frequent basis, with five being on station at any given time. One was positioned outside the Governor-General's suite, marked by the arrow, a second by the lift, a third at the window at the far end of the corridor, and two by the door to the emergency stairs—one in the corridor and another in the staircase itself. No hotel personnel were allowed on the floor after six in the evening, and those permitted prior to that time were carefully scrutinized and searched. As to the Governor-General's suite, there is a single door in, with no possible entrance from the adjoining suites, as well as a set of windows overlooking Fairmont. These windows are kept latched and are checked periodically, particularly at bedtime, to ensure they remain so. For all intents it is a locked room, with no possible way for a thief to enter."

"Well, obviously one did," Joanna remarked, and studied the diagram on the blackboard at length. "Were the floors examined for trapdoors?"

"Carefully, with none being found. In addition, I should mention the floors are heavily carpeted and showed no interruptions or defects. The bathrooms were completely tiled, without breaks or fractures which would allow for a trapdoor."

"And the ceiling?"

"Beautifully engraved, with crown molding, and totally intact. We also went to the roof and found nothing remarkable, then inspected the narrow space above the ceiling and discovered only dust and spider webs. So again, as with the robberies at the Fairmont and the St. Regis, our thief miraculously appears and disappears, carrying off items of immense value."

"It seems odd that such a precious gem was kept in a hotel suite, even with extreme security in place," Joanna wondered aloud. "I would think that a bank vault would have been more in order."

"But not under the current circumstances," the commissioner explained. "The Governor-General arrived only yesterday for a meeting of the Imperial War Conference, which brings together King George with the leaders of the various colonies, such as South Africa, Australia, New Zealand, and Canada. These meetings are of particular importance, for they deal with the vital contributions of the colonies to His Majesty's war effort, which includes troops, weapons, supplies, and vital raw materials. The conference will take place this weekend, but the Governor-General was granted an audience with the King this morning, at which time the blue diamond was to be presented to His Royal Highness as a symbolic gesture of the resolve and never-ending alliance of the colonies to the Crown. With this schedule in mind, a somewhat brief stay at the Windsor under heavy security was deemed appropriate."

"I can thus assume that the presence of the blue diamond in London and its purported use as a gift was known at the higher levels of government," said Joanna.

"And by the various newspapers to whom the information was given, but with the caveat that it not be disclosed until after the presentation was made. It was believed that public knowledge of the gift would be a clear demonstration of the closeness of those involved in the war effort, as well as being a morale booster at a time when one was much needed."

"So it would appear the information was known by many."

"I am afraid so."

"And the information no doubt reached the ears of our most accomplished hotel thief."

"That, too, appears to be the case."

"I take it the penthouse at the Windsor remains tightly sealed off."

"Until further notice."

"And that the Governor-General and his entourage have vacated."

"With such an obvious breach in security, they had no choice but to do so immediately. And of course the audience before the King has been postponed." Sir Charles sighed resignedly to himself. "And at this point it seems we have so little to go on yet again."

"So it would appear."

"I know it is premature, but do you have any helpful suggestions?"

"Only that I be allowed to inspect the penthouse before it is scrubbed clean."

"Lestrade will see to it."

"And I would like to interview the taxi driver who discovered the victim and the Scotland Yard detectives who were first on the scene."

"Lestrade will see to that as well," the commissioner said, and turned for the door. "Please inform us of any noteworthy findings."

Joanna waited until the pair had departed, then gleefully rubbed her hands together. "Now there is a rather tangled piece of work, is it not?"

"But yet again with virtually no clues," I remarked. "Or data as you call them."

"Oh, dear John, it is one of your few flaws that you tend to look for answers rather than asking the important questions."

"Which are?"

Joanna held up three fingers. "First, why would an accomplished thief, who can magically enter and exit a heavily guarded suite, decide to leave via the front entrance at two in the morning when he is certain to be noticed by the hotel staff? Surely, he would know that a reservation clerk, porter, front doorman, and perhaps even the night manager would be present in the main lobby at that time." She paused before smiling at our silence. "Good, for it appears you have no reasonable answer, which raises the distinct possibility that the thief did not exit via the front entrance."

"Then how did he leave?" asked my father.

"That remains a mystery."

"Perhaps he departed via a side or rear door," I suggested.

"If that were the case, he would not have encountered or fought with the front doorman," Joanna rebutted.

My father slowly packed the bowl of his cherrywood pipe with Arcadia Mixture as he gave the matter further thought. "It may be that the thief exited by a side door which he closed noisily and that prompted the doorman to investigate."

"And the thief just happened to be carrying around an object that resembled a railroad spike?" Joanna challenged. "Which is the second question which cries out to be answered."

"Then let us assume that it is some form of weapon which he kept hidden in the event of need," my father proposed.

"Assuming that assumption is correct, how could a spikelike weapon inflict such a terrible wound behind the eye socket near the hairline?" Joanna asked, and turned to me. "John, please hold an imaginary weapon tightly in your hand and attempt to bring about a wound to my skull in that particular area."

I attempted to maneuver and discovered it was virtually impossible to inflict such a powerful blow to the area between the frontal and temporal bones of the skull. "It cannot be done in a face-to-face fight."

"Precisely."

"Your point being?"

"We have a thief exiting where he should not have, carrying a peculiar weapon which is most unlikely, and inflicting a wound with it that is impossible to execute. All of which brings into question the commissioner's contention that the thief departed via the front entrance where he encountered a suspicious doorman that resulted in a brawl during which time the thief used an odd weapon to deliver a grievous head wound in a location that we now know the weapon could not have possibly reached with force."

"So pray tell, what exactly did transpire outside the entrance to the Windsor at that early-morning hour?"

"That is what has to be determined," said Joanna, walking to our bedroom. "And now I shall change into attire more appropriate for catching a most clever thief."

CHAPTER TWO

The Windsor

The front entrance to the Windsor Hotel revealed no evidence that a crime had been committed, for all the bloodstains had been washed away and a new uniformed doorman was in place to greet arriving and departing guests. Nevertheless, Joanna carefully inspected every step of the footpath, finding only a trace of faded blood at the very edge. Next, she followed the façade of the building until it reached a side alleyway, at which point she signaled for my father and me to follow but remain behind her. We came to a row of windows which were tested and shown to be locked, then proceeded to a wide door near the rear of the structure which opened easily and led to an expansive kitchen where a chef and his assistants were busily at work around a long cutting board. The air was filled with the aroma of freshly baked bread mixed in with the appetizing scent of exotic spices. A variety of fowl were hanging from hooks on the far wall.

Joanna strolled over to the chef, who was seasoning nicely marbled filets of beef with cracked black pepper. A short, stout man, he was wearing a hat characteristic of his profession and seemed unbothered by our sudden appearance.

"I am the daughter of Sherlock Holmes," my wife introduced herself.

"I know who you are, madam," the chef said genially. "And the gentlemen accompanying you must be the esteemed Watsons who prove to be so helpful in your adventures."

"They are, and they do."

"How may I be of service?"

"I am here investigating the crime which occurred here earlier this morning."

"Dreadful business," he said sorrowfully. "Is there any news on the condition of our poor Henry?"

"I am afraid his condition remains grave," Joanna answered honestly.

"So sad."

"Indeed, quite sad. All are praying for his recovery," she consoled as the chef made the sign of the cross. "Now, as to the purpose of my visit. I noticed that your door which leads to the alleyway was unlocked and would allow for early entrance into the hotel. Is that usually the case?"

"Only during working hours, so we can have easy access to the rubbish bins outside. After ten in the evening, the door is locked and remains so until six the following morning."

"Surely, some staff stay throughout the night in the event there is a late order for room service."

"One of my assistants is available from eleven to six for precisely such an occurrence."

"And was such an order placed last night?"

"Allow me to check." The chef hurried over to a shelf and reached for a large ledger which he opened and briefly studied. Returning to his place by the cutting board, he reported, "No orders were received after midnight."

"I take it that during that period the door to the alleyway remained locked."

"That is a strict regulation, madam, and if breached the person responsible would be dismissed." He glanced over to the assistants who had gathered in to listen to the interview. They all seemed to nod knowingly at the restriction and the penalty for breaking it.

"Thank you for the helpful information," said Joanna, and led the way out, but not before checking the simple lock on the door, first by gross inspection, then with her magnifying glass.

The outer side showed a bit of rust, the inner polished brass. "No scratch marks," she reported.

Closing the door behind us, I waited until we were well away from the kitchen before asking, "Were you examining the lock to determine if it had been picked?"

"I was."

"But why? If the thief exited via that door, he could have easily unlocked it from the inside and thus had no reason to pick the lock."

"Assuming he did leave via the kitchen door, he might have used a pick to relock the door from the outside and in this manner cover the route of his exit."

My father joined in, "But my dear Joanna, with an assistant chef stationed in the kitchen throughout the night, how could the thief have exited unnoticed?"

"The assistant chef, after working a long day, would be required to sit alone in a quiet kitchen and wait for the telephone to ring. Perhaps he dozed off for much-needed sleep, knowing no one would be the wiser, for the sound of the phone would instantly awaken him and allow him to perform his duties without delay."

"But there were no chairs or cots in the kitchen."

"But there was a cutting board, seven feet or more in length and three across, which he could have laid upon, using his rolled-up chef's hat as a pillow."

I nodded at a personal memory. "Much like a weary intern napping on a gurney during a lull in the emergency room."

"Exactly," said Joanna, returning my nod.

"So you believe he may have in fact exited via the kitchen."

"I believe the opposite, for the evidence says otherwise. In particular, a clever thief would never take a route that brought him to the front of a lighted hotel entrance when he could have raced in the opposite direction down a dark, fog-shrouded alley-way which would have allowed him a perfect, unnoticed escape."

We departed the kitchen area and took a sharp right turn which led to the rear of the hotel. Standing there was a large lorry from which four workers were in the process of unloading a mammoth bathtub. Our eyes went to the double doors of the hotel, which were opened widely.

"It will be a tight fit!" Joanna called out to the workers.

"Yes, ma'am," replied the burly leader of the group. "But we shall be careful and squeeze it through."

"Into a storeroom, I assume."

"Where it will not stay for long, for it is to be installed im-mediately." The worker signaled his men to place the bathtub down, then wiped perspiration from his brow using his sleeve. "We heard that a rather stout maharaja from India is about to arrive."

"I would imagine it will be moved quickly, for the storeroom is no doubt crowded as is."

"Oh, it is, ma'am, with stacks of furniture and bathroom fix-tures, along with large containers of linens and uniforms and what have you."

"I shall like to take a look."

The worker hesitated as his brow furrowed in suspicion. "Well, ma'am, you will require permission from the hotel man-agement to enter."

My father stepped forward and spoke in an authoritative voice. "We are with Scotland Yard, and you can confirm our association with the constable at the entrance if you wish."

"There is no need, sir," the worker acquiesced, and quickly stepped aside.

On entering, Joanna examined the double door's inner lock-ing mechanism, which consisted of thick metal hinges on each side which could be secured together by a hanging Chubb lock. The storeroom itself was quite large, with seemingly every inch taken up by rows of furniture that were covered with sheets to protect them from dust and stain. Behind them were porcelain bathroom fixtures and large, closed boxes that were labeled with black markings.

It was a second set of double doors which led into the hotel itself that briefly drew Joanna's attention. Like its duplicate facing the alleyway, the doors were opened and had a locking mechanism which consisted of thick metal hinges and a Chubb lock. After finding little of interest, Joanna guided us into the staircase where canvas had been laid down, no doubt to guard the floor against dirty footprints that might be left behind by the workers carrying the giant bathtub to its final destination.

As we stepped away, I glanced back at the doors and their locking mechanism, then commented, "I do not believe our thief could have come this way unless he was a master lockpick."

"Based on what, may I ask?" Joanna inquired.

"The Chubb lock," I replied.

"A most astute observation, John," said she, with a warm smile.

"But it was so obvious."

"Nonetheless, astute, for it imparts important information to us," Joanna explained. "With the Chubb lock being so difficult to pick, it would require an hour or more for even a master lock-pick to open it, and our clever thief certainly could not afford that amount of time, for he no doubt was working on a very tight schedule."

"He would have to be in and out in a matter of minutes," my father interjected.

"And equally as important, Watson, if the thief did come this way, how did he manage to enter the heavily guarded penthouse without being noticed?"

On our return to the front of the hotel, we were greeted by Inspector Lestrade, with a tip of his brown derby. At his side was a lean and trim man who was introduced as Detective Sergeant Harry Stone. With his strawberry-blond hair and rosy cheeks, he seemed far too young to be a detective sergeant, but the set of his square jaw and his penetrating dark eyes indicated he was a man not to be underestimated.

"Sergeant Stone here was the first to arrive at the crime scene, which unfortunately was in a state of mayhem," Lestrade went on. "I think it best he give you the particulars."

The young detective stepped forward and began a detailed description without referring to notes. "The footpath was quite crowded, with individuals continually moving in and out of the entrance. Most of the bystanders appeared to be hotel staff attempting to lend a hand, whilst others were curious onlookers. Just beside the door was the badly injured doorman, who was being attended to by a doctor who happened to be a guest at the hotel. The bandage that had been applied to the doorman's head was soaked through with blood, which no doubt indicated the severity of the wound. I quickly secured the area and questioned those who had gathered around the victim. There were no witnesses to the attack."

"Did you discover a weapon?" Joanna asked at once.

"None was seen, madam, but it is possible that its presence was obscured by the dim lighting and puddles of running blood. I waited for the ambulance personnel to come and fetch the victim before undertaking a more thorough investigation. There was no weapon to be found beneath the doorman's body or under his beefeater hat, which must have been dislodged during the struggle."

"I take it the entire area was carefully searched."

Stone hesitated before answering, as if pausing to accurately compose his answer. "It was, madam, but please keep in mind it was quite dark and foggy, which limited our vision. Even with torches, the lighting was dim, particularly in the nearby alleyway. At daybreak we again searched the two-block area, including the rubbish bins and sewers, but could not find the weapon."

"So the weapon supposedly seen by the taxi driver seemed to somehow vanish," Joanna concluded.

"So it would appear, madam."

A black taxicab drew up to the entrance and came to a stop with squealing brakes. Out alighted a small, thin driver with graying black hair and a noticeably humped back. Hat in hand, he hurried over to Lestrade and asked in a deep cockney accent, "You wanted to see me, guv'nor?"

Lestrade nodded briefly. "Our investigation has been joined by the daughter of Sherlock Holmes, who wishes to question you."

The driver took a nervous step back and bowed awkwardly, obviously awed by my wife's presence. He kept his head down in the position of submission.

"I have only a few questions for you," Joanna said in a soft voice. "Please try your best to remember, for your information could be of help to us."

"Yes, ma'am," the driver answered in a tone so low it was difficult to hear.

"First off, let us have your name."

"Jack Hawkins, ma'am."

"And how long has Jack Hawkins been driving a cab?"

"Over three years, ma'am."

"I would imagine during that time you had more than a few interesting experiences, some of which are best left untold."

"Indeed I have," he replied, with a quick smile that revealed a number of missing teeth. "Even on the west side, where not all rides are uneventful."

I marveled inwardly at my wife's ability to put witnesses at ease, particularly those from the working class, who as a rule are reluctant to speak with the authorities, for fear it will somehow involve them. Inquire of their occupation, Joanna had recommended, for it elevates their status and provides a topic about which they believe they know more than you. Now the driver was informing her on the various routes through West London and the time required for each. "So the ride from Belgravia where I picked up the fare to the Windsor would take no more than fifteen minutes," he said, nodding as if to confirm the information.

"Not a very expensive ride," Joanna noted.

"True enough, ma'am, but the guests at the Windsor are quite well-to-do and often leave a generous gratuity."

"Thus you expected the night to end in a most pleasant fashion."

"That I did, but I could not have been more wrong," Hawkins stated. "I could not sleep a wink last night because of the gruesome sight I saw."

"Now, it is here that I need you to be very precise," Joanna urged. "The memory may be very disturbing, but an exact description could prove most helpful. Please begin with your arrival at the Windsor."

Hawkins took a deep breath, as if steadying himself. "I came to a halt at the hotel's entrance and hurried around to open the rear door for my passengers. It was then that I saw poor Henry laying on the footpath, faceup with his hat off. I rushed to his side, for I feared he had somehow tripped and struck his head. That was the moment I saw the terrible wound."

"Can you tell us the location of the wound?"

"It was right here," Hawkins replied, pointing with his index finger to an area behind his temple. "And it was spurting blood, like from a fountain. I do not know why, but I held my hand over the wound in an attempt to stop the bleeding, but it was of no use. Then I ran into the hotel and cried out for assistance."

"Who was the first to arrive at the entrance?"

"A porter, then the desk clerk who was the one that summoned a doctor that happened to be a guest."

"Did you then return to your taxi?"

"No, ma'am. I stood guard over poor Henry until the ambulance arrived."

"Was there any unusual feature about the doorman other than the terrible head wound?"

Hawkins closed his eyes briefly as he thought back. "I saw no other bleeding sites, but Henry had a very odd look on his face."

"One of terror?"

"No, ma'am. It appeared the entire left side of his face sagged, with his lips drawn far down and his mouth opened."

"I take it the head wound was behind the right temple," my father surmised.

"It was, sir."

My father and I exchanged knowing glances, for the sagging face indicated a facial palsy, which was a sign of cerebral damage. The blow to the head had no doubt crushed the skull and permanently injured the brain. I gazed over to Joanna, who nodded subtly, for she was a former nurse and was thus aware that injury to the right brain caused left-sided palsy.

"Very good," Joanna praised the driver's accurate account. "Was it while standing guard that you noticed the weapon?"

"I accidentally stepped on it, ma'am."

"Did you pick it up?"

"No, ma'am, for it was covered with blood."

"Please describe it for us in exact detail."

"It seemed to have a length about so," Hawkins recounted, and extended his thumb and index finger, much as the commissioner had done earlier. "It seemed to gleam a bit, like metal would, but then again that could have come from the blood that covered it."

"Did you believe it to be a knife?"

Hawkins shook his head. "I thought it looked more like a railroad spike, for the middle was thicker than one might see in a knife. That, plus the handle was not that of a knife."

"How did it differ?"

"It appeared to have a hole or indentation in it which would allow for a better grip, I would say."

"At that point, you must have moved away from it."

"I did, ma'am, so I could keep a close eye on Henry."

"Then the ambulance arrived. Yes?"

"Some minutes later it did, and they carted poor Henry off on a stretcher."

Joanna's eyes narrowed a moment. "Could they have taken the weapon along with the injured doorman?"

The driver shrugged his shoulders. "It might have happened."

"But it did not," Stone interjected, stepping forward. "I later questioned the ambulance personnel and they neither saw nor collected the weapon."

"Well done, Sergeant," said Joanna, and came back to the taxi driver. "What of the passengers in your cab? Could they have moved the weapon or pushed it aside?"

"I think not, ma'am, for the woman had experienced a fainting spell no doubt brought on by the terrible sight, and her husband was attending to her."

Joanna furrowed her brow in thought, as if she was attempting to mentally re-create the crime scene. Her gaze went from the footpath to the entrance, then back to the footpath itself before returning to the taxi driver. "I would like you to envision the crowd which had gathered around the injured doorman. Were any of the faces out of place and obviously not staff or guests of the hotel?"

"None come to mind, ma'am."

Joanna paused at length, now tapping a finger against her

chin, which was a sign she was attempting to fit the pieces of the puzzle together but with little success. All the while she kept her eyes fixed on Hawkins, who must have considered her stare one of accusation.

"I swear I have told you the truth, ma'am," he said anxiously.

"I believe you have," Joanna assured him, bringing her mind back to the interrogation. "Unless any colleagues have more questions, you may be on your way."

With our silence, Lestrade gave the taxi driver a wave of dismissal and watched him hurry away to his taxicab. Then Lestrade asked my wife the question which had crossed all of our minds. "Is the weapon truly of that much importance, madam?"

Joanna nodded firmly and gave the inspector the same answer she had given earlier to the commissioner. "You show me the weapon, I'll show you the man."

"And what may I ask makes you so certain of that?"

"The weapon and its oddity," she replied, and turned to the entrance of the hotel. "Now, let us inspect the penthouse itself."

The refined lobby of the Windsor had the features one would expect in one of the world's finest hotels. Glittering glass chandeliers shined down on fashionably attired guests who were seated in exquisitely upholstered chairs, whilst uniformed waiters silently moved about and served them tea from elegant china. The reception desk, with its mahogany counter, was well off to the side and unobtrusive, so as not to interfere with guest activities. We entered a brass lift which had more than enough room for the five of us, and seemed to carry the scent of fresh flowers although none could be seen. On exiting at the penthouse, we were greeted by a half salute from a uniformed constable who was stationed just outside the lift. Another uniformed constable was positioned at the exit to the emergency staircase. The floor appeared to be otherwise empty. Lestrade led the way into the large suite which had been occupied earlier by the Governor-General of South Africa.

In the center of the drawing room stood a tall, well-built man, middle-aged, with neatly trimmed blond hair, high cheekbones, and thin lips sealed together in a fashion that kept his face expressionless. But his pale blue eyes remained fixed on us as if searching for some concealed article. With obvious respect, Lestrade formally introduced Maj. Eric Von Ruden, the Governor-General's head of security. The bulge on the left breast of the officer's jacket indicated he was armed.

He bowed stiffly to Joanna, saying, "I have heard of your talents and can only hope you can assist us to recover the blue diamond."

"I shall do my best," said Joanna, and immediately began pacing the heavily carpeted floor, pausing intermittently to stomp with the heel of her shoe and listen for a returning echo. Next, she examined the paneled walls of the room, tapping on them as she searched for evidence of a concealed exit. She then carefully inspected the ceiling, with its intricate carvings and crown molding, but could find nothing of interest.

"I can assure you, madam, that every square foot of the suite has been pored over for trapdoors and secret entrances and none were discovered," Von Ruden informed her. "We even used stethoscopes to listen for hollow spaces after striking all surfaces, but could detect no sounds of such a space."

"I am certain your search was very thorough," Joanna said, "but I have always found it best to conduct my own investigation, which ensures that nothing has been overlooked."

Von Ruden's face reddened a bit as he obviously found Joanna's directness and insistence to perform her own search somewhat degrading. Here was a man sure of himself and unaccustomed to being superseded by a woman. Well, Major Von Ruden, thought I, welcome to the world of Joanna, the daughter of Sherlock Holmes.

Now my wife was busily occupying herself at the large

window that overlooked Mayfair's most prestigious streets. It possessed a brass latch with a horizontal handle, which when pulled down unlocked the currently locked window. She carefully examined the latch, then the windowsill and its entire frame using her magnifying glass. The inner edge of the frame seemed to draw most of her attention.

"I can assure you that window, along with all the others, was locked at the time of the robbery," Von Ruden volunteered.

"The latches are quite solid and well placed," Joanna noted, now opening and closing the lock with apparent ease.

"And thoroughly tested before the Governor-General was permitted to occupy the suite."

"As would be expected," said she, kneeling down to inspect the underside of the sill and the space beneath it. Joanna was about to rise when she spotted an object of interest on the carpet. She searched for it and held it up to the light for closer inspection. We all moved in nearer to view a dark thread which had been knotted into a small circle. "A thread in which the ends have been tied together."

"It most likely comes from the Governor-General's wife, who performs embroidery as a hobby," Von Ruden suggested. "The patterns are quite intricate and the threads often form loops."

"My wife does the same," Lestrade interjected. "She enjoys embroidering names onto pieces of clothing and occasionally ends up with bits of unusable thread."

The telephone on a small writing desk rang and the chief of security hurried over to answer it. He moved to a far corner and spoke in such a low voice it was impossible to decipher the nature of the call. Whilst he was distracted, I watched Joanna covertly drop the circle of thread into her purse. The detective sergeant's keen eyes also observed my wife's sly move.

Von Ruden came back to the group and announced, "I am afraid my presence is required elsewhere."

"Before you depart, could you give us a brief summary of what transpired in the penthouse once your staff was notified of the disturbance at the front entrance?" Joanna requested.

"I shall give you the same account I gave to the good inspector," Von Ruden began with a strong South African accent in which *good* was pronounced "goodt." "At exactly two eighteen I was told of the incident at the hotel entrance. My entire staff was immediately placed on heightened alert. All exits were carefully checked, all members of the entourage awakened and made certain of their well-being. I myself awakened the Governor-General from a sound sleep and it was shortly after that we discovered the blue diamond was missing."

"Where was the gem kept?" Joanna asked.

"In a thick velvet case that was situated on a lamp table beside the Governor-General's bed."

"Unattached to any object, I take it."

"Unattached."

"Please proceed."

"At first we wondered if perhaps the diamond had fallen off the lamp table," Von Ruden continued on. "Perhaps the Governor had flailed his arm during sleep and dislodged the gem. But this was not the case, for it was not to be found on the floor or anywhere else in the suite after a most intensive search. It was obvious the security of the penthouse had been breached, and for that reason the Governor and his entourage were forced to quickly dress and pack their belongings so they could be moved to a safe, undisclosed location. As I mentioned earlier, the entire penthouse was searched side to side and top to bottom, but no evidence of a secret entrance could be discovered."

"Very good," said Joanna. "I do have a few more questions, however."

Von Ruden glanced impatiently at his timepiece. "I have a most important meeting to attend."

"We are almost done," Joanna told him. "Please be good enough to give me the exact time the Governor-General and his entourage retired for the evening."

"Shortly after ten."

"Who was the last person in the corridor?"

"The Governor's private secretary, who had just exited this very suite."

"And the time?"

"Again, shortly after ten."

"From that moment on, was anyone, excluding the security staff, seen in the corridor?"

"No one."

"Did the door to the lift even open?"

"It did not, madam, nor was anyone seen or heard in the emergency staircase."

"Thank you for the most excellent summary," Joanna said. "I have no further questions."

With a quick nod, the director of security turned and hurried for the door.

Lestrade waited for the sound of footsteps to disappear before asking Joanna, "Do you have any idea how the thief entered?"

"Not as yet, but the game is early."

"Early or not, the clever thief has left us no clues."

"Oh, there are clues, Inspector, waiting to be discovered."

On that note, Joanna led the way into the expansive bedroom, with its four-poster bed which remained unmade. She lay down on the edge of the bed near the lamp table and extended her right arm as far as it would go. Her reach was a good twelve inches from the table. "Von Ruden was grasping at straws," she stated, referring to the possibility that the Governor-General had flailed an arm in his sleep and dislodged the blue diamond from the lamp table. Next, she knelt on the floor and, asking for Lestrade's torch, searched beneath the canopied bed.

"Anything?" Lestrade inquired.

"Dust and spider webs."

Joanna then examined the window, along with its latch, frame, and sill, and found nothing of interest. Close to the window was a writing desk and chair, which she inspected, looking I suspect for more loose thread, but discovered only a small, cracked button. The walls and carpeted floor revealed no evidence for a trapdoor or hidden entrance, so we moved on to the tiled bathroom, where the only item of note was an oversized bathtub that still had a damp bottom.

With our search completed, we took the lift down to the main lobby, which remained somewhat crowded with elegantly attired guests milling about. One of the guests recognized Joanna and declared in a clearly audible voice, "I believe that is the daughter of Sherlock Holmes." Heads turned immediately in our direction and the hum of the muted conversations increased noticeably, all wondering about the reason for her presence. News of the great theft had not been divulged, but soon would be and shortly thereafter become the talk of London.

As we exited the hotel, a uniformed doorman tipped his beefeater hat and wished us a very pleasant good afternoon. I nodded back and wondered if perhaps the critically injured doorman had similarly greeted the individual who had managed to steal the blue diamond. The thief must have entered via the front entrance and found his way to a secret hiding place which would give him access to the Governor-General's suite. But where was that hiding place?

On the footpath and away from the doorman, Lestrade shook his head unhappily. "I am afraid we have, as our American colleagues would say, dug a dry hole."

"Perhaps," said Joanna, glancing up to the penthouse and the roof above it. "But it was of interest that the robbery occurred at the Windsor less than twenty-four hours after the guests had been registered. Please speak with the managers at the St. Regis and the Fairmont and determine the time their guests arrived and the time the robberies occurred."

Lestrade scribbled a quick note to himself. "May I inquire how that would be helpful?"

"It could be another common denominator which ties the robberies together."

"And you believe this information will somehow lead us to the thief?

"That is my method, Lestrade," she replied. "First, you must gather up all available clues; concern yourself with fitting them together later."

"Speaking of clues, madam," Stone said, stepping forward. "What was it about the piece of thread that so drew your attention?"

"Its unusual appearance."

"Which was?"

"It was tied into a circle," Joanna replied, and, using her folded umbrella, hailed a passing taxi.

CHAPTER THREE

The Twinkling Lights

My father's frailty reappeared just before nine that evening. He was dozing in his comfortable chair in front of a cozy fire when he suddenly awakened short of breath. Gasping for air, he sat up abruptly and took a number of slow, deep inhalations before his respirations returned to normal. The episode lasted only a half minute or so, but was yet another sign of his advancing age and in particular his weakening heart.

I hurried to his side and took his pulse, which was rapid but strong and even. "Are you now better, Father?"

"I believe so," he replied, and inhaled deeply without difficulty to reassure me. "It was simply a brief spell."

"Which are happening all too often," said I worriedly. "Have you been taking your cardiac medication on a regular basis?"

"I must confess I discontinued the digitalis leaf several days ago, for my vision had become bothered by a yellow hue, which is a sign of the drug's toxicity," he confirmed. "But I shall restart it immediately."

"Please do."

"And I shall retire early, for a good night's sleep always improves my condition." With effort he arose from his chair and, after bidding my wife and me a pleasant evening, retired to his bedroom.

Joanna waited for my father to close the door behind him before speaking in a quiet, anxious tone. "I am concerned that these bouts are occurring with such frequency."

"As am I."

"Perhaps lowering the dose of digitalis leaf will remove its toxicity, yet allow the drug to maintain its beneficial effect."

"That thought crossed my mind as well, and I shall ask my father's cardiologist if such a reduction in dose would be appropriate."

"Please do at your earliest convenience."

My wife's concern was every bit as great as mine, for she cared deeply for my father, not only as a wise and trusted friend, but as the last, true link to her own father. And like Holmes, she depended on him to be a sounding board for her theories and assumptions. He was and would always be her Watson.

The telephone rang loudly, interrupting our silent thoughts. Joanna reached for the receiver and greeted the caller, "And good evening to you, Inspector Lestrade."

She pressed the phone to her ear and listened intently, as if not wanting to miss a word. "Twinkling lights, you say? . . . High up and at the very front . . . Then off altogether? . . . Yes, yes. We shall be there shortly."

Joanna placed the receiver down and explained the nature of the call. "For unknown reasons, there is now a cluster of twinkling lights high up on the face of the Windsor in an area near the penthouse."

A flood of questions came to my mind, but before I could inquire Joanna held up a hand and hurried to the Persian slipper for one of her Turkish cigarettes. After lighting it, she began to pace the floor of our parlor, head down, as she listed the strange details of the twinkling lights. "There are four or five of them in no particular arrangement, which blink intermittently and at times seem to disappear altogether. They cannot be seen at a distance, for their intensity appears relatively weak."

"Do sparks arise and descend from them?" I asked, no longer able to hold my patience.

"An excellent question, John, but the answer is no, indicating the source of the lights is neither small fires nor damaged electrical wires."

"I take it you believe these twinkling lights may somehow be associated with the robbery."

"That was my initial inclination, but there is a problem with that conclusion, for the lights were not present last night according to the manager of the hotel."

"So you are of the opinion it is a curious, but unrelated, finding?"

"I am of the opinion that it is another unexplained finding

which requires careful investigation, for such clues are the ones that all too often turn out to be the most important."

"Then let us be on our way to the Windsor," said I, arising from my chair and reaching for my hat.

"Should one of us stay here in the event Watson has yet another frightening episode?" Joanna asked at once.

"Allow me to look in on him before we decide whether that will be needed."

I tiptoed into my father's bedroom and found him snoring lightly and sound asleep. He had removed his smoking jacket and slippers, and, with his pulse and respirations being slow and regular, I thought it best not to awaken him for a change into his sleepwear. I tiptoed out and quietly closed the door behind me.

"He is asleep and quite comfortable," said I. "There is no need to keep watch on him."

Ten minutes later we boarded a carriage for the short ride to the Windsor. Although the mystery of the twinkling lights was of keen interest to us, it was overshadowed by our concern for my father's health. We wondered if I should suggest to the cardiologist that we limit my father's activities and allow him to rest more. Perhaps it might be wise not to involve him in the more taxing investigations, particularly those which required long walks or trips up multiple flights of stairs. These measures might help, but my father would have none of it, for our criminal investigations were his life's blood and the reason for his very existence. To discontinue or even limit his involvement would surely break his spirit, which was the very last thing we wished to do.

Our carriage drew up at the entrance to the Windsor where Lestrade, Detective Sergeant Stone, and the night manager awaited us. The manager, introduced as Richard Hopkins, was a man of slender frame, with carefully groomed dark hair and a mustache so thin it could have been drawn with an eyebrow pencil. He was obviously not pleased with our presence, for it caught the interest of arriving and departing guests.

"There, you can clearly see them," Lestrade told us, craning his neck to the maximum and pointing to the uppermost floors of the hotel. "Notice how they flicker, as if being turned off and on."

"But there are no such lights on this building," Hopkins noted. "Nor any exposed electrical wiring."

"Are you certain they were not present last night?" Joanna asked, reaching into her purse for a miniature Zeiss monocular scope.

"I am positive, madam," Hopkins assured. "As part of my routine, on my arrival I carefully inspect the front and sides of the hotel to determine if there are any irregularities. There were none."

"So you were not the very first to notice the blinking lights."

"I was not, madam. It was a couple returning from an evening stroll who reported the sighting to the registration desk."

"But you yourself did not see them on your earlier arrival at the hotel. Correct?"

"Correct, madam. All was dark except for the lights in several of the rooms on each floor," he replied. "Were twinkling lights in play, I would have surely seen them, as would the doorman who accompanied me on my inspection tour."

"So," Lestrade summarized, "we have flickering lights that mysteriously turn on in mid-evening, and continue to do so with intermittent interruptions."

"We considered calling the Metropolitan Fire Brigade, but they have no ladders capable of reaching the top floors," Hopkins informed. "Thus we phoned Scotland Yard in view of the theft which occurred early this morning."

"And we responded promptly for the same reason," Lestrade added. "However, from this vantage point, the lights appeared unrelated to the robbery."

"So it would seem," Joanna said, and, bringing the monocular scope to her eye, began her investigation of the flickering lights. She moved the scope slowly up and down, then side to side, before commenting, "I count five lights beginning at the third floor and extending up to the penthouse. They appear to be arranged in a single, vertical row, with all of equal intensity. If my sighting is correct, the uppermost light ends in the middle of the penthouse next to a window. Would that be the location of the suite previously occupied by the Governor-General?"

"It is, madam," Hopkins replied.

"It seems most unwise to have such clearly visible lights high up, with the bombing raids occurring on such a frequent basis," Joanna continued on.

Lestrade chimed in hurriedly, "Are you suggesting they might be used as a target for German bombers?"

"Just a thought." My wife downplayed the possibility.

"Well, it might nonetheless merit—" The inspector broke off his sentence as the lights suddenly dimmed, then disappeared from sight. "Now they are gone, much like they are being controlled by a hidden switch."

We collectively gazed up at the front of the hotel and waited for the supposed switch to turn back on. Gradually the topmost lights began to flicker, soon followed by the others.

"Someone is playing tricks," Lestrade grumbled.

Joanna gazed up at the night sky and studied it briefly before a faint smile crossed her face. "That someone is God, who is moving the clouds about, so they intermittently allow moonbeams to shine through. What we are observing is the result of moonlight being reflected off carefully placed objects."

"What objects?" Lestrade queried, with a puzzled expression.

"That is what we must determine," Joanna answered. "And the sooner the better."

"I am afraid the search will have to wait until morning when perhaps the Fire Brigade can devise a method for reaching the objects."

"No, no," Joanna insisted immediately. "It must be done now, while the objects continue to reflect light and can be easily located."

"But how?" Lestrade challenged. "It would be far too dangerous to lower a man from the roof in the darkness. One misstep could spell disaster."

Joanna pondered the problem at length, shaking her head at one possible solution and nodding ever so slightly at another. Then, with a sudden move, she brought the monocular scope to her eye and studied the flickering lights once more. "The lights appear to be in close proximity to the windows."

"But too far away for a man leaning out to reach," Lestrade estimated. "It would not be possible."

"It would if the man was properly equipped," Joanna said, nodding firmly to herself before turning to the hotel's night manager. "Does the Windsor have a maintenance man on duty?"

"Twenty-four hours a day in case of real need," Hopkins replied.

"I take it he repairs and replaces windows which have been damaged."

"He does."

"And on occasion I suspect he must have to work on the exterior of the window and its frame."

"That occurred not long ago when a flock of large birds lost their way and crashed into a window on the fourth floor," Hopkins recalled. "The entire frame splintered, sending shattered glass down onto the footpath below. So severe was the damage that the entire window had to be replaced, and that required Stoddard to work on the exterior while suspended from the window opening."

"He must have been secured by thick ropes," Joanna surmised.

"I could not discern the presence of ropes from a distance," the manager said honestly. "But surely they were attached to him."

"Not by themselves," Stone interjected. "An experienced worker would insist upon being wrapped in a harness before climbing out of a window four stories high."

"Have you seen such an apparatus in use?" asked Joanna.

"On numerous occasions, madam, for my father was a carpenter and roofer by trade," Stone replied. "When I was a young lad, he would often take me along to his work sites, for my mother was ill and not always able to look after me. I would watch him strap on a harness-vest and descend without fear from high places. I considered him the bravest man in the word, madam."

"And he raised a most observant son," Joanna praised before returning to Hopkins. "Is your maintenance man currently in the hotel?"

"He is in the penthouse repairing the damage caused by the Governor-General's security team as they searched for a hidden entrance into the suite, which of course was not discovered."

"I should like to have a word with him," Joanna requested.

"Of course. This way, then."

We walked through the vacated, eerily silent main lobby and boarded the brass lift which now carried the aroma of sweet cigar smoke. Hopkins attempted to excuse its presence by telling us that guests at the hotel were encouraged not to smoke in the lift because some were bothered by the odor left behind. Joanna assured him she was not in the least annoyed by the pleasant scent, with its creamy layers of cocoa, roasted almonds, and subtle spices, which was characteristic of the H. Upmann cigars that were far and away the best of the Cubans. The hotel manager was amazed at my wife's knowledge of cigars, but this was not the case with Lestrade and myself, for we were aware she had acquired Sherlock Holmes's remarkable ability to identify a given tobacco by its ash or scent. That talent had proved most helpful in leading us to the culprit in the case of *A Study in Treason*.

We stepped out of the lift at the penthouse level and found Samuel Stoddard, the maintenance man, painting the wall next to the suite occupied earlier by the Governor-General. There were deep niches and scratches in the panel which were obvious to the eye.

"Stoddard, Scotland Yard is in need of your services," said Hopkins. "Do your best to accommodate them."

"Of course, sir." Stoddard stepped back, wiping his palms on his paint-splattered overalls. He was a short, muscular man, with heavily calloused hands that seemed oversized for his frame.

"Do you have your harness apparatus available?" Joanna asked.

"I do, ma'am," he replied. "I keep it stored in an equipment closet off the staircase."

"Please fetch it, for you will soon have need of it."

"May I ask what this need is?"

"There is an object just outside the window of the suite which was robbed early this morning. It is most important that we examine that object."

"Can it not be reached by leaning out the window?"

"It appears to be far more than an arm's length away."

The maintenance man gave the matter further thought before asking, "How large is this object?"

"We believe it will fit in your hand."

"And how am I to recognize its position in the darkness?"

"It glows, much like a blinking light."

"Will it be hot to touch?"

"We think not."

"I shall wear protective gloves just in case."

He hurried away down the corridor, like a man on a mission, and disappeared behind the door to the emergency staircase. We heard the creaking sound of another door being opened.

"There is a worker who knows his business," Joanna commented. "Note the pertinent questions he asked."

"But he neglected an important one," Lestrade disagreed mildly.

"Which was?"

"Whether the object is firmly attached and will require special tools to remove it."

"A man of his experience will take that into account."

As if on cue, Stoddard reappeared wearing a bulky, weathered harness that covered his entire torso, shoulder to hip. Around his lower waist was a tool belt that held a variety of heavy-duty hammers, pliers, and chisels. In his hand was a coiled-up, thick rope of considerable length.

Upon entering the spacious suite, Joanna asked the maintenance man, "What will serve to anchor your rope?"

"The legs of the bathtub, ma'am."

Stoddard quickly went about his preparations, like a man who had performed the task a hundred times over. He passed the rope through a metal loop on the harness and tested it in place, then tied the other end of the thick rope to the front legs of the large, porcelain bathtub. Finally, he fitted his hands with leather gloves, which, he explained, were known to best resist sparks and heat.

Backing his way out the opened window, he slowly descended into the dark night. We listened intently for the sound of a tool chipping at the stone façade, but none was forthcoming. The rope extending out the window moved a bit farther down, then went side to side, but remained silent.

"Is he having difficulty locating the objects?" Lestrade asked with concern.

"That should not be a problem," said Joanna, and pointed out the window at the sky. "A half-moon is out and its beam should be reflecting off the objects."

"Then why is it taking so much time?"

"He has obviously encountered an unforeseen obstacle."

The rope suddenly tightened as Stoddard began his ascent. As he reappeared, we all noticed that his hands were empty except for the rope they were holding. His harness was likewise empty, and his tool belt contained only metal tools, with no evidence of a strange object.

Pausing to catch his breath, he reported, "There were no objects to be seen or felt."

"But you must have seen the flickering lights," Joanna pressed.

"I did, ma'am, but they did not arise from an object."

"From what, then?"

Stoddard shrugged his shoulders. "I could not be certain of the source, except to say the light came from a hole in the stone façade. That was true for several of the flickering lights, ma'am."

"How deep were these holes?"

"No more than a few inches, and at their base was only stone."

"Strange business, this," Lestrade remarked. "Perhaps an investigation by the Fire Brigade will be more revealing."

Joanna tapped a finger against her chin, weighing the maintenance man's findings and trying to somehow fit them into the puzzle of the flickering lights. She seemed lost in thought for a long moment before saying, "Holes in stone do not emit light, flickering or otherwise."

"I can assure you these do," Stoddard insisted.

"And at the base of the holes was only stone, you say?"

"I believe so, ma'am. But my sense of feel may have been hindered by the leather gloves I am wearing."

"That might be the case," Joanna agreed, then added, "I

should tell you that the source of the lights is of great importance to us and could help us solve the riddle of the robbery. With that in mind, would you be willing to have yet another look at the holes which emit light but this time with your hands ungloved?"

"That will be no problem, ma'am."

"Excellent," Joanna encouraged. "I am particularly interested in what lies at the base of the holes from which the light appears to arise."

With a nod, Stoddard again exited via the window and descended into the dark night. The sky was now thick with moving clouds which allowed only glimpses of the moon to shine through. The dimness was certain to make Stoddard's task even more difficult. Several minutes passed before the rope tightened and the maintenance man lifted himself back into the suite.

"I tested three of the holes, ma'am," he reported. "There was only hard stone at their bottoms."

"Did the flickering lights reappear when the moon briefly showed itself?" asked Joanna. "In particular, did the lights always seem to arise from the holes?"

"They did, ma'am, but there was something unusual about the lights on my second trip down. In a few places the illumination was on the brick itself near the hole."

Joanna's eyes suddenly widened. "As if it were painted on?"

"More like a smear, ma'am."

My wife quickly drew the curtains and turned off all the lights in the suite, which caused everything to go pitch black. "Now, Stoddard, hold up your hands for us."

He promptly did, and his fingers glowed in the darkness.

"I say!" Lestrade cried out, stunned by the revelation.

"Fluorescein," Joanna stated. "It was the fluorescein which reflected the moonbeams and produced the flickering lights."

"But to what end?" inquired Lestrade, who proceeded to

touch the maintenance man's hand with his index finger, after which he raised the digit and watched it gleam in the blackness. "What purpose could it possibly serve?"

"To show the burglar the way."

"Are you saying our thief somehow climbed up the stone façade and silently entered the Governor-General's suite?"

"I am."

"But where is the proof?"

"Please have the taxi driver, Jack Hawkins, at the front entrance of the Windsor tomorrow morning at nine sharp," Joanna replied. "He will provide the proof for us."

"How so?"

"With his keen eye," said Joanna, and, turning on the lights, departed the suite.

CHAPTER FOUR

The Proof

My father appeared much improved when he came to breakfast the following morning. He was neatly attired in a gray Harris Tweed suit and his color was good and his spirits high as he strolled to his comfortable chair where the early-edition newspapers awaited him. There was actually a bounce to his step.

"You seem fit this morning, Father," I commented.

"A good night's sleep and resuming my cardiac medication proved to be the best remedies," said he.

"Was the digitalis leaf taken at full dose?"

"I decreased it to half strength, which will hopefully control my heart arrhythmia yet avoid its toxicities."

Joanna and I exchanged knowing glances, for my father, who was an excellent physician with over thirty years' experience before retiring, had more than enough insight on how to treat his bouts of cardiac arrhythmia, which went under the name of supraventricular tachycardia. Nevertheless, I planned to speak with his cardiologist to make certain he agreed with my father's self-treatment.

"Dreadful," my father remarked, shaking his head at the terrible news on the front page of the *Guardian*. "We cannot continue to sustain the magnitude of these losses."

He was referring to the grievous number of casualties the allies had suffered at the Third Battle of Ypres. At last report, over two hundred thousand were killed, wounded, or missing in the horrendous action which had taken place in the Flanders region of Belgium. That was the cost of a hard-fought so-called victory, for a war that showed no signs of ending.

For better or worse, the eye of the reader was distracted by the news of the spectacular blue diamond robbery, which occupied the other half of the front page. Detailed descriptions of the precious gem and its estimated worth were given at length, as were the opinions of ill-informed criminologists on how the theft may have been accomplished. Of particular note was mention of a five-thousand-pound reward for information leading to the return of the diamond.

"A five-thousand-pound reward should be a most enticing sum," my father said, lowering the newspaper.

"But not enough for these thieves," Joanna countered. "For to execute such a carefully planned venture was quite expensive in itself."

"Why so costly?"

"Because so many people had to be involved."

"How do you know this?"

"Because Joanna believes she has uncovered the secret entrance into the penthouse," I answered for her.

"Pray tell how—" My father's next question was interrupted by a gentle rap on the door, followed by the entrance of Miss Hudson bringing with her a quite full breakfast tray.

She set the table with nicely prepared eggs, bacon, and haddock before pouring tea and quickly departing, for she would shortly leave for the markets at Covent Garden where she would purchase the poultry, vegetables, and fruit upon which we would dine over the coming week.

Once the door closed, my father requested in a rush, "Now, my dear, I require the particulars on this secret entrance which so mystified everyone."

"It is based on assumptions."

"Which, in your case, are invariably correct."

"I thought you were a stickler for proof, Watson," Joanna teased.

"I thus take it your assumptions are weak."

"As are most assumptions until proved," she replied. "For now, let us enjoy Miss Hudson's sumptuous breakfast, then be on our way, for the proof awaits us."

"I demand at least a hint," my father insisted.

"All is based on flickering lights which were noticed high up on the façade of the Windsor," my wife acceded.

"What!" My father's brow went up. "Like those on a Christmas tree?"

"More or less." Joanna described the fluoresceinated holes which appeared to flicker because of the intermittent moonlight. She detailed their depth and position, as well as the fluoresceinated smears next to them. "For obvious reasons they could only be seen at night."

My father gave the matter long thought before suggesting, "Perhaps they were a signal of some sort."

"You are close, Watson, but not in the manner you think,"

Joanna said. "Now, we must attend to our breakfast before it becomes cold, and hurry to the places where the proof exists."

"*Places,* you say?" I inquired.

"Places," she repeated.

Twenty minutes later our taxi stopped in front of a large shop which carried the name Piccadilly Outdoors. Joanna hurried in and returned shortly with a small, neatly wrapped package. It was quite narrow and less than a foot in length. She held the package on her lap and nodded slowly to herself, saying, "Was it not my father who stated that 'It has long been an axiom of mine that the little things are infinitely the most important'?"

"Which he clearly demonstrated over and over," my father noted.

"And which we are about to demonstrate yet again."

"I take it we must wait to see the package unwrapped," said I.

"You do indeed," Joanna replied. "And you will soon learn the reason why."

Our taxi drew up to the entrance of the Windsor where Inspector Lestrade, Detective Sergeant Stone, and a very nervous Jack Hawkins awaited us. Hawkins removed his cap out of respect as his eyes darted back and forth between the three new arrivals.

Lestrade glanced at his timepiece and said, "You are a bit behind time, madam, and I had begun to fear you would not show."

"I was delayed, for I had to make a purchase," Joanna explained, then looked at the cockney cabdriver. "I have only one question for you, Mr. Jack Hawkins, and once it is answered, you can return to your duties."

"Very good, ma'am," he replied anxiously.

My wife turned her back to him and carefully unwrapped the package, which revealed a metal, spikelike object that she laid on the pavement. "Examine this item, Hawkins, and tell us if you have ever seen it before."

The cockney cabdriver leaned down and, after a brief inspection, jerked his head up. "That is it! That is the weapon that hurt poor Henry."

"Are you certain?"

"No doubt, ma'am. It was covered with blood earlier, but washed clean it is the same."

"Thank you, Hawkins," she said, and waved him on his way with a hand gesture.

Once he was well gone, Joanna picked up the metal object and held it on high for all of us to see. The spikelike item was approximately five inches in length, tapered yet thick, with a sharp point at one end and a sizable hole at the other. "This, gentlemen, is a piton, which is used the world over by mountain climbers," she announced. "The sharp end is hammered into the mountain so that a rope can be passed through it, which secures the climber and saves him in the event of a fall."

"So these pitons were drilled into the stone façade to allow our thief to climb up to the penthouse," Lestrade said, envisioning the ascent. "But why the fluorescein?"

"To mark the position of the pitons, so they could be seen and removed by the thief on his descent," Joanna replied. "Of course it was quite foggy the evening of the robbery, but that presented no problem to our thief, for there was blurred light from the lamppost below which reflected off the fluorescein and caused it to flicker ever so faintly. Thus only the thief who was just feet away would notice it."

Lestrade tilted his derby to scratch his head. "But why take the time and effort to remove the pitons after he had the blue diamond in hand? Should he simply not have been on his way?"

"He did not wish to leave an important clue behind."

"And what makes the piton such an important clue?"

"It tells us the thief was an experienced mountain climber."

"How many of these are in England?"

"A limited number, I would think."

Sergeant Stone entered the conversation with a question which I myself was about to ask. "Assuming your deductions are correct, they do not explain how the thief, after ascending to the penthouse, was able to open a latched window. A piton would have been of no use in that instance."

"But a thread would," Joanna elucidated. "You will recall the length of thread with a knotted loop at its end, which was discovered beneath the windowsill. It was placed earlier around the handle of the latch, and when pulled down caused it to open, and when pulled up allowed it to close."

"But perhaps the piece of thread was not used for that purpose," Lestrade challenged. "We were told that the Governor-General's wife was an embroiderer and that may well have been the source of the thread."

"That is most unlikely, Inspector, for embroidery thread is far thinner and thus weaker than the ordinary type utilized in sewing," Joanna rebutted. "The thieves would use the stronger, thicker thread for obvious reasons and this was the sort I came upon under the windowsill."

"And even the sturdier variety ruptured under the intense pressure of opening and closing the latch, which is why a piece of the strand was found in the carpet," I noted.

"With the rupture occurring near the loop as one would expect," Joanna appended. "I actually performed a similar experiment at my workbench and confirmed the presumption. It was quite simple to set up. I took a long length of sewing thread and tied a sizable loop at one end, then inserted the loop around a brass handle which could be moved up and down. I next passed the free end of the thread through a crack in a piece of wood, and began pulling back and forth on the thread, which caused the brass handle to shift up and down. On the fifth movement the thread split apart at the point where it rubbed against the opening in the wood, which was close to this loop. This of course simulated the mechanism that the thief used to open the window to the Governor-General's suite. The locale of the rupture was identical in both instances."

Stone nodded at the explanation, then said, "That is why you were so interested in the window frame. You were searching for a thin crack through which the ordinary thread could be inserted."

"And one was clearly present."

"But who placed it there?"

"Yes, indeed. Who?"

Lestrade eagerly joined in again. "Are you saying there is an insider involved?"

"Unless you can provide me with a better explanation."

"We shall have to question everyone who had access to the penthouse."

"Starting with the maids and porters," Joanna suggested. "For they would be the ones most likely to be bribed."

Lestrade and Stone exchanged firm nods, indicating that such an investigation would be instigated shortly.

My father reached for the piton and held it in a menacing position. "A removed piton would also serve as an ideal weapon in a street brawl, particularly if the victim was already down when the blow was delivered."

"That being the case, the doorman never stood a chance," I concluded.

"I do not believe there was ever a struggle between the thief and the doorman," Joanna disagreed. "It does not fit."

"Why so?"

"An experienced thief would never leave via the well-watched front entrance," she replied. "It was unnecessary and far too risky."

"How then did the terrible head wound occur?"

"That is what we are about to learn," Joanna said, and, after signaling to a waiting taxi, gave the driver instructions to take us to St. Bartholomew's Hospital.

As we entered the cab, the wind picked up and brought with it an Arctic chill. Nevertheless, I cracked open the rear window, for my wife was lighting a Turkish cigarette, whilst my father was slowly packing the bowl of his pipe with fresh tobacco. Those were signs that both were rethinking the clues which lay before us. My father's expression indicated that he considered one or more of the findings troublesome.

He took several puffs on his pipe, then turned to Joanna and in a soft voice said, "I fear, my dear, that you have dismissed the thief's exit from the front entrance too easily."

"Pray tell how so?"

"Because it would have been a simple matter for the thief to adorn himself in fine attire and depart the hotel without attracting the doorman's attention. He would have been thought of as being a guest, perhaps out for a late-evening stroll."

"But, Watson, you are assuming the thief actually exited the Windsor."

"Why would he not? He has the precious jewel in hand, and the more distance he places between himself and the hotel the better."

"You are neglecting one very important fact."

"Which is?"

"The thief was a guest of the hotel or at the minimum conspired with another guest to commit the robbery."

My father shook his head in puzzlement. "I am afraid you have lost me."

"Allow me to reconstruct the crime, Watson. The lowest of the fluoresceinated pitons was positioned on the third floor, whilst the highest was at the level of the penthouse, which tells us the thief climbed out of a third-story window to begin his ascent. Thus he must have been a guest or coconspirator of a guest at the

Windsor. There was no need to run or draw attention by leaving the hotel at such a late hour when he would surely have been seen by either a porter or doorman. The smart move was to vacate his suite the next morning, which I believe he was scheduled to do, for a guest on the third floor would hardly be considered a suspect. That is the way I would play it."

I nodded at my wife's conclusion. "You have said in previous cases that to find the trail of a criminal, place yourself in his shoes, and follow the path he would take."

"Spot-on, dear John, for we are dealing with a most clever thief whom we will identify on our return to the Windsor," said she. "You show me the list of guests who checked out the morning after the theft, and I will show you the thief."

"Then we have him."

"Hardly, for he no doubt registered under a false identity." Joanna took a deep, final puff on her cigarette and discarded it through the opening in the window. "I am surprised the Watsons have not asked me the most disconcerting clue, that being the apparent absence of flickering fluorescent lights on the façades of the St. Regis and the Fairmont, which were similarly burglarized. Since they were not observed, how can we use the lights as a common denominator for the secret entrance into the hotels?"

She gave us a moment to provide an answer, and when one was not forthcoming she continued on. "This finding or lack thereof was of concern to me as well until I reviewed the newspapers I collected which detailed the weather conditions surrounding the three robberies. Therein I found the explanation which solved the dilemma of the missing lights. At both the St. Regis and the Fairmont the crimes were also committed on a quite foggy night, so the lights would not have been visible from the ground level. The following morning, however, there was a heavy downpour accompanied by a swirling wind, with gusts up to twenty miles an hour. I am of the opinion the rainstorms washed away the fluorescent stains from these two hotels. No such deluge occurred the morning and day following the burglary at the Windsor, and thus the fluorescence remained."

"And the fluorescent smears on the façade alongside the piton holes were made by the maintenance man as he moved his hand back and forth," my father concluded.

"Very good, Watson, for in the darkened hotel room I saw fluorescent stains on his fingers as well as on the palms of his hands."

As we approached St. Bartholomew's, I turned my attention to the possible reasons for our upcoming visit which was to explain how the doorman was so grievously wounded by the metal piton. But how could examining the doorman and his wound give us any explanation other than it was made by the piton which was no doubt in the thief's possession? The size and shape of the penetrating injury would show that it was made by a pointed object. We might even find metal fragments in the wound itself. As an associate professor of pathology at St. Bart's, I had seen numerous skull wounds from various objects, and those made by sharp metal weapons left a distinct marking. Thus I expected Joanna would wish me to carefully examine the doorman's injury and tell her of my findings. I would soon learn this was not to be the case.

On arrival at the side entrance, I held the door for Joanna and my father, saying, "To the surgery ward, then."

"Later," Joanna responded. "But first, let us go to the department of pathology, where I would like you to retrieve an undamaged skull."

"For what purpose?"

"To prove a point."

We hurried down to the subterranean level of the hospital and entered the office of the director of pathology, a position I now held since the untimely death by suicide of the former director, Peter Willoughby. On seeing us, my meek but ever-efficient secretary rose from her desk. "May I be of help, Dr. Watson?"

Waving her down, I replied, "Not at the moment, Rose. I have stopped in for a skull which we require the use of."

"Shall I call Benson?" she asked, referring to the head orderly.

"There is no need. The one in my office will suffice."

I led the way in and over to a hanging skeleton which was believed to belong to one of England's most notorious highwaymen. With care I detached the skull, which was normal in every regard except that it lacked teeth.

"Where to now?" asked I.

"The rear of the building," Joanna replied.

On departing the office, we were meet by Benson, who had the unique talent of showing up when he was needed without being called.

"Is there a problem, sir?" he asked, gazing at the skull I was holding.

"None. The skull is for a study we are about to undertake."

"Then I shall go about my duties," said he, turning to walk away before pivoting back to us. "By the way, sir, I am afraid you have a bit more work on your hands. The doorman from the Windsor has passed on."

"Where is the corpse?"

"In the morgue, sir."

"Have it placed in the autopsy room at once."

"But, sir, it has not been properly prepared for autopsy."

"We will only be examining its exterior."

"The head, then?" Benson surmised.

"The head wound," I specified. "And be certain to leave its bandage on and untouched."

As we climbed the stairs to the ground level, my father remarked, "So now the thief carries the charge of murder."

"Involuntary manslaughter at best," Joanna corrected.

"May I ask what evidence brings you to that conclusion?"

"The evidence soon to be provided by the skull in John's hands."

On exiting the building we were met by a bone-chilling wind and a darkening sky which indicated a rainstorm was about to occur. We held on to our hats as the wind gusted and brought with it slivers of sleet. I could not help but wonder if the inclement weather would interfere with whatever experiment my wife had in mind, for it was apparently designed for the outdoors. My father and I followed her to the rear of the building, where Joanna came to a stop and gazed up.

"It is four stories in height," said she. "And from my past experience as a nurse at this hospital, I would approximate the height of each floor to be twelve feet or slightly more."

"Each measures twelve feet," I confirmed.

"Thus, from roof to ground, we are dealing with a fall of fifty feet if one includes the thickness of the roof. Correct?"

"Correct."

"And the Windsor Hotel consists of five stories, each with a similar height," Joanna went on. "Let us assume the piton becomes loose and detached at the midpoint of the thief's climb, which would have been the fourth floor. Thus its descent to the footpath below would measure forty-eight feet. With these approximations, we can say the fall of the piton and the height of St. Bart's measure near fifty feet? Agreed?"

"Agreed."

"Then let us proceed with the experiment," she said, and walked over to the downpipe which originated at the gutter on the edge of the foot and descended to the ground, where it discharged collected rainwater. "Now, John, I would like you to position the skull at the opening of the downpipe, and tilt it in such a fashion so that the area just above and behind the eye socket is snug up against the opening."

I performed the task in short order and backed away. "Done," I reported, dusting off the knees of my trousers.

"Very good." Joanna reached in her purse and handed me the metal piton, with specific instructions. "Please go to the roof and find the opening where the downpipe connects to the gutter. I would then like you to place the piton, sharp edge down, into the opening and allow it to fall freely."

I hurried back into the building and took the slow-moving lift to the fourth floor, and made my way to the roof via the emergency stairs. The cold wind was gusting and sleet was beginning to cover the surface, which rendered it quite slippery. I carefully stepped along the edge of the roof until I reached the end of the gutter where the opening to the downpipe was situated. Inserting the piton into it, sharp edge pointing downward, I released my grip on the metal spike.

Not waiting to hear the results of the experiment, I departed the roof and took the stairs down to the ground level, enjoying the warmth of the enclosed space, which was short-lived. Outside, the temperature had dropped even further, but my father and Joanna seemed unbothered by it. She was holding up the human skull, which had a piton deeply embedded in it.

On my approach, Joanna handed me the skull and requested, "Your assessment, please, John."

The evidence was quite clear. The metal piton was firmly inserted into the area of the skull called the pterion, which is the thinnest part of the skull where the parietal, frontal, and temporal bones join together. It is located just above and behind the eye socket. Thus the lethal blow to the doorman's head was delivered by a falling piton.

"What do you make of it, John?"

"An object falling thirty-two feet per second per second can cause severe injury, and in this case, lethal damage."

"What else does it tell us?"

"That there was never a struggle between the thief and the doorman."

"Spot-on."

"So the thief was never at the entrance or even near the injured doorman."

"That is a step too far," said Joanna. "For in all likelihood the thief or his coconspirator was on the footpath near the gravely injured doorman."

"Based on what, pray tell?"

"The missing piton."

It required a moment for the crime scene to play itself out in my mind. "He came down to fetch it!"

"Precisely," Joanna agreed. "The thief became aware of the disturbance at the entrance, probably at the very onset. He had seen the piton detach or it may have actually slipped from his grasp. Imagine if he witnessed the piton striking the poor doorman's head and inflicting obvious severe injury. The thief would race down to the entrance and blend in with the onlookers, waiting for the opportune moment to remove the bloody piton from the crime scene."

"But why take the chance of being discovered?" my father interjected. "Would he consider it that important?"

Joanna nodded firmly. "Oh, yes, my dear Watson, and for two very good reasons. First, as I mentioned earlier, he would wish his method of entry into the penthouse to remain a secret. The piton would tell us the thief is a mountain climber, which narrows down the list of suspects significantly. And secondly and perhaps even more importantly, the thief's fingerprints would be on that piton. He would be determined not to leave it for Scotland Yard to find."

With that explanation and the sleet now falling heavily, we rushed into the hospital and down to the autopsy room where the body of Henry the doorman awaited us. He was a large man, thick of frame and tall in height, with a pleasant expression even in death. The dressing around his forehead was soaked with clotted blood.

"Please tell us his exact height," Joanna requested.

Carefully applying a tape measure, I replied, "Six feet and a quarter inch."

"Quite tall, then."

"Quite. But why the interest in his height?"

"If he were exceptionally short, say five feet or so, I could envision an attacker coming up beside him and inflicting such a wound with a piton," she replied. "But with a victim of more than six feet, such a blow could never be landed with force."

"Which is further evidence that a falling piton was responsible for the wound," I commented. "There can be no other cause."

"That was the point I wished to make. Now, please remove the dressing."

I placed on rubber gloves and unwrapped the blood-soaked bandage, below which lay a wide, cleft-like lesion filled with massive clots. "The piton no doubt penetrated into the brain itself."

"Which in all likelihood brought about his death," my father added.

"That along with severance of the middle meningeal artery which is located just below the pterion of the skull." I removed much of the blood clots, which allowed us to visualize the torn artery. "He had no chance to survive."

"All because of a piton that accidentally slipped," my father noted. "And it is now gone, along with the thief's fingerprints, which are lost forever."

"Perhaps not," Joanna said. "They may still be waiting for us to discover."

"But how do we go about finding them?"

"By returning to the Windsor at the appropriate time," she answered, and led the way to a waiting taxi outside St. Bartholomew's.

CHAPTER FIVE

Fingerprints

With the assistance of Inspector Lestrade, it was arranged for the investigators associated with the penthouse robbery to meet at the Windsor just after dark that evening. The miserable weather had persisted, with a cold, torrential rain now pouring down in sheets. After depositing our umbrellas with a porter, we decided to first visit the small office of the night manager, Richard Hopkins, who quickly rose from behind his desk to greet us.

"Have there been important developments?" he asked eagerly.

"Not as yet, but there may be one in the making," Joanna replied, glancing around the office, for its neatness had caught her eye, as it had mine. Everything on his desk was perfectly placed, with papers and folders carefully stacked and equidistant from one another. The three chairs we seated ourselves in were arranged in a straight line, with an exact foot separating them. The ashtray before us was ornate and contained a single, used cigarette, with cold ashes next to it.

"We have a request regarding your guest list," Joanna began. "I require the names of the guests who occupied suites on the third floor of your fine hotel the night of the robbery."

Hopkins reached for a large ledger, which rested on a shelf behind him, and quickly thumbed through its pages. "Here we are," said he. "There are ten suites on the floor, but only six were occupied on that particular night."

"Is that number of unoccupied suites not unusual?"

"Quite so, but on occasion the reservations are so scheduled that for a brief period we have a block of vacated rooms."

"So I take it the suites were occupied the following morning."

"They were, madam."

"Please proceed with the list."

"As I mentioned, there were six in all." The hotel manager read from the ledger and gave details of each. "Suite 301 was occupied by Sir Charles Gregory and his wife, he being a long-standing member of Scotland's parliament. Suite 303 was taken by Mr. Ty Cobb, a baseball player of some fame. In suite 305 was Monsieur Claude Duval, a minister in the French government, and his wife, who appeared quite ill."

"Are you aware of the nature of her illness?" Joanna asked.

"Of that I am unsure, although she was visited by Dr. Isaac Walton, a physician from St. Bartholomew's who we were instructed to show in immediately."

"Sir Isaac is an esteemed specialist in neuromuscular disorders," my father noted.

Hopkins nodded at the information. "She was in a wheelchair, sir."

"Her illness may have been the purpose of her visit," my father suggested.

"So it would seem," said Joanna. "But tell us, Mr. Hopkins, do you know the position the minister holds in the French government?"

"I was not so informed, madam, but I am inclined to believe it was of considerable importance, for he had a chauffeured government limousine at his disposal."

"Pray continue," Joanna requested, but I could see from her expression that she was docketing that particular bit of data for future use.

"The fourth suite was reserved by A. J. Kronenberg and Son, a renowned Swiss jewel firm, which is well known to us. They send buyers to London on a frequent basis, for our city is of course a center of the diamond trade."

"Was the Kronenberg suite centrally located?"

"In what regard, madam?"

"Was it located directly below the suite occupied by the Governor-General?"

"It was, but on the third level," Hopkins answered, obviously not seeing the importance of his responses.

"I take it the Kronenberg representatives were in their middle years."

"They were somehow younger," he replied. "I would say in their late thirties."

"Did you recognize them from prior stays?"

"I did not, which is not unusual, for they tend to register in the morning, while I am the night manager."

"How often do they in fact visit the Windsor?"

"At least three times a year, with reservations being made far in advance by their office in Geneva, to which the expenses incurred are forwarded," Hopkins appraised before turning the page in his ledger. "The fifth suite was registered to Emil Hirsch and his wife, who are here for the wedding of their daughter, and the final suite was taken by a pair of elderly sisters from Canada."

"Well done and rather complete," said Joanna. "But there is one final piece of information I require. Did any of the occupants you named check out of the hotel on the morning following the robbery?"

"They all remained, even the Kronenberg representatives, who were scheduled to depart, but delayed their departure by a day."

"Was a reason given for their delay?"

"No, madam, but such changes are not uncommon with our business guests."

As we rose to leave, Joanna glimpsed the used cigarette in the ashtray. "Ah, a Benson and Hedges, a brand I, too, prefer."

"I find an occasional smoke calming."

"Well then, thank you for your time," said she, turning to leave, then quickly turning back to the hotelier. "One last question comes to mind. Were the six occupied suites you listed all facing the front of the Windsor?"

"All but one, for that is the preferred location."

"Was the unoccupied suite situated near the center of the floor?"

"It was at the very end, madam."

"And kept locked, I would think."

"Securely so."

Joanna reached hesitantly for the door, as if another question was coming to mind, but she decided not to pursue it at the moment. "Please remain in your office, for Inspector Lestrade may wish additional information."

The main lobby was crowded with guests because of the inclement weather which showed no sign of letting up. We made our way through the guests, many of whom appeared to be milling about, and held our conversation until we approached the lift.

In a quiet voice, my father commented, "The Kronenberg representatives are rather interesting suspects, are they not?"

Joanna nodded slowly. "The theft originated from the third floor beyond any question, but a master thief would have signed out of the hotel that morning; yet all occupants remained. By all logic, he should have checked out early the next morning, so as to place as much distance as possible between himself and the crime scene. It is thus a finding that defies explanation other than our very clever thief is thinking one step ahead of us and doing the unexpected."

"Is he that clever?"

"Apparently so," said Joanna, before remarking, "It would be a mistake to underestimate this formidable foe."

"May I propose an unfounded speculation?" my father offered. "It revolves around the centrally located suite of the Kronenberg representatives."

"*Unfounded* does not necessarily imply *false,* Watson, so pray tell let us hear it."

"The Kronenberg representatives may have been legitimate jewelers, but perhaps their overwhelming greed led them to construct or perhaps participate in the robbery of the blue diamond," my father construed. "Being esteemed jewelers of international repute, they might well have known all about the precious gem and its eventual travels to London, and thus could have planned the theft far in advance. Once the diamond was in their possession, the Kronenberg representatives decided to stay put, realizing that a hasty departure might cast suspicion on them."

"Excellent, Watson," Joanna congratulated. "And I must admit the very same thought crossed my mind. However, there is a major flaw associated with that scenario which I should bring to your attention. First and foremost, what would the Kronenberg representatives do with this huge diamond, whose size was only outweighed by the Cullinan stone? Keep in mind that its immense value could only be attained once it was cut and polished. Now, who would perform that very delicate task? There are very few capable of it, and all are located in Antwerp, which is currently under German control. Furthermore, were this famous blue diamond to suddenly appear in Antwerp or anywhere else for that matter, word would spread like wildfire around the world and its origin be investigated, which would lead to the thief, who would be arrested or spend the rest of his life running from the law. What I am saying is that no reputable diamond cutter would ever see or touch the blue diamond at this time in history."

"Which indicates that the Kronenberg representatives are not the most likely of suspects," my father concluded.

"Unless the Kronenberg representatives are not the Kronenberg representatives," she replied.

The lift door opened and we entered, discontinuing our conversation in the presence of the lift operator. But Joanna's last statement on the Kronenberg representatives stayed in my mind. Legitimate or otherwise, if they were involved in the theft, they would have needed the assistance of someone within the Windsor to arrange for the location of their suite as well as for the perfect timing. They could not have done it by themselves. I leaned close to Joanna's ear and whispered, "An insider was involved."

"Obviously," she whispered back.

The operator brought the lift to a smooth stop and we exited at the penthouse level where Lestrade and Major Von Ruden, the South African director of security, awaited us. Standing just behind them was Henry Overstreet, who was Scotland Yard's fingerprint expert.

Lestrade greeted us with a tip of his derby, saying, "I trust you have had the opportunity to requestion the night manager."

"We have," Joanna replied. "Unfortunately, the information he provided was of limited value."

"So we are no closer to the identity of the thief than we were this morning," Von Ruden said unhappily.

"That is not entirely true, for we now have a partial picture of the intruder," Joanna recounted. "You see, we can state with certainty that he is an experienced mountain climber, and this bestows on him certain physical characteristics. He is young, lean, and trim, with shoulders too broad for his frame and perhaps calloused hands from holding rough ropes."

"Those features are so common they would hardly be worth pursuing," Von Ruden scoffed.

"Concentrate on his age," Joanna directed. "He is between the ages of twenty-five and thirty-five, and thus his relative youth would stand out at the Windsor, whose guests are far older and for the most part well into their senior years."

"Such an individual would stick out like a sore thumb in the lobby here," Lestrade opined.

"Indeed he would," Joanna went on. "I would thus suggest that all the hotel staff on duty the day and evening of the robbery be asked if they spotted an individual with the characteristics I just mentioned. In particular, focus on the staff present at or around the time the doorman was injured. And if by chance they did notice such a relatively young individual lurking about, they should be asked if they had even seen this person before."

"That is quite a long shot, but nevertheless one worth taking," Von Ruden agreed. "But surely the fingerprints you spoke of would be far more revealing."

"Assuming they can be found," Lestrade chimed in.

"Oh, they shall," said Joanna without inflection. "But first, I require the following information. Has the penthouse remained locked down since the robbery?"

"Completely, with no one other than the investigative team allowed in," Lestrade responded.

"Please name the individuals other than the Governor-General and his wife who have been in the suite since the time of the robbery until now."

"Only myself and my second-in-command, Adolph Smits, from the South African security unit," Von Ruden answered promptly.

"I can vouch for Detective Sergeant Stone and I having crossed the threshold of that suite," Lestrade replied.

"Excellent," Joanna approved. "I will require fingerprints from each of those named, including those from Stoddard, the maintenance man."

"For what purpose?"

"You will shortly see."

Joanna led the way into the darkened penthouse. After the entire group was inside, she closed the door tightly and drew the curtains, leaving only a narrow opening for the moonbeams which were peeking in between the clouds. For a moment the drawing room went dark; then small flashes of fluorescein began to appear, most of which seemed concentrated on the window and its sill.

"There!" my wife exclaimed, and pointed to the window with her magnifying glass. The group followed her over and watched as she leaned in to study the flickering spots of fluorescein. "I can see nicely defined fingerprints."

My father and I moved in to inspect the glowing fingerprints using Joanna's magnifying glass. When my turn came, I examined not only the sill, but the glass panes as well, for both showed clear prints made by fingers and palms. Some were quite distinct, whilst others were poorly defined. More than a few could surely be used to identify a given individual.

Joanna turned to Overstreet and requested, "Please be good enough to collect the visible samples."

"You of course realize that all of the fingerprints may not have come from your robber," said Overstreet.

"I am aware, for some of the investigators may have unwittingly touched the fluorescein stains and thus left behind their own fingerprints. That is why we should gather the fingerprints from all who entered the suite after the robbery. We shall depend on Major Von Ruden to obtain the prints of the Governor-General and his wife."

"You must know that even if we discover unidentifiable fingerprints, we have no prints from a suspect to match them against," Lestrade cautioned.

"That may not be necessary, for the fingerprints alone could serve as yet another mechanism to identify the thief."

"How so, may I ask?"

"In a rather straightforward fashion," Joanna replied. "First, we must establish that the unidentified fingerprints found in this suite most likely belong to the thief. Then we shall ask Mr. Overstreet to carefully inspect the suite on the third floor directly beneath this one, for that is where the thief began his climb. He should pay particular attention to the prints on the windowsill and glass panes. Once we have found the match, and I believe we shall, we will know with complete certainty that the individual who occupied the third-floor suite is our thief."

"But how will this assist us?" Von Ruden asked, with a puzzled expression. "We still have no picture of the thief."

"But the sketch artist at Scotland Yard may well provide us with one," Joanna replied. "We should begin by questioning every staff member who serviced the occupants of the suite, including the maids, porters, waiters, desk clerks, and hotel manager. Each will be interviewed by the artist and asked to recall in detail the faces of the occupants of the suite. From their recollections, the artist will present us with a fairly accurate depiction of the thief."

"Is he that skilled?" Von Ruden asked.

"Quite so," Lestrade assured. "In the past we employed the method of anthropometry, in which the artist depended solely on certain obvious facial features such as the brow thickness or jaw shape. Now, a skilled sketch artist, using detailed descriptions from witnesses, can produce a likeness of the suspect that is often spot-on." He turned to Overstreet, saying, "We shall begin our inspection of the third-floor suite straightaway."

"Very good," Joanna said as she took our arms and guided us out of the suite and down the corridor to the lift.

"Who would have possibly thought we could solve this case so rapidly?" my father asked.

"Be careful with your prediction of success," Joanna warned. "But we will shortly have the face."

"That may be wishful thinking, Watson, for a clever thief would only show us the face he wants us to see."

My father sighed unhappily. "He may be using a disguise."

"That would be the smart move," said Joanna as the lift door opened.

CHAPTER SIX

The French Minister

"Lestrade is following in his father's footsteps," grumbled my father, placing down the morning newspaper.

"How so?" asked I.

"He garners all the credit from Joanna's marvelous deductions, much as his father did with Sherlock Holmes."

I glanced at the bold headline in the *Daily Telegraph* which read "Glowing Bandit Sought." The article beneath it took up a full two columns. "Lestrade must have described the fluoresceinated fingerprints at length."

"And the fluoresceinated holes in the front of the Windsor which the thief used to hoist himself up and guide his way down," my father added, and looked over to my wife. "Does it not bother you when the inspector claims all the credit which in fact belongs to you?"

Joanna shrugged her shoulders at the notion. "Lestrade serves our purpose, and for that helpful function I allow him to bask in the limelight."

"But he does it time and time again, like a warrior displaying stolen valor."

"In the end, then, when the case is solved, shall I seek public acclaim?"

"Not a bad idea, I would think."

"But, my dear Watson, I already have that and see no need for excess."

A smile was crossing my father's face when the telephone beside him rang. His expression suddenly turned serious, for, as I noted earlier, early-morning calls tended to bring unwelcome news. My father reached for the receiver and his greeting told us he was speaking to Inspector Lestrade. He spoke briefly, using monosyllabic questions of *Who?*, *When?*, and *Where?* "Of course, we shall be there shortly," and he ended the call.

Placing the receiver into its cradle, he turned to us and said in a somber voice, "I am afraid there has been another break-in at the Windsor."

"Which floor?" Joanna asked at once.

"The third, and in particular the suite occupied by the French minister and his wife."

"Which items were stolen?"

"A diamond-emerald necklace, with a matching bracelet and brooch."

"And their value?"

"Lestrade did not say."

"A critical clue," Joanna said more to herself than us, and dashed to the wall rack for her coat. "We must hurry before Scotland Yard muddles up the evidence."

Outside, the weather had finally cleared, although overcast skies persisted, with the threat of rain ever present. Our taxi ride to the Windsor was slowed by the still-flooded streets, but the interval gave us time to consider the purpose of the most recent break-in. On the surface it appeared to be the jewelry, in which case the gems would have to have astonishingly high value. Joanna's reasoning went as follows. The purported thief already had in possession a blue diamond worth many millions, bearer bonds which could fetch a million or more, and a priceless Ming dynasty vase sought by collectors the world over. With such a treasure in hand, why bother with jewelry most likely worth far, far less? Why take the chance of being caught for such relatively small gain? Our clever thief would never behave in such a fashion. Which raised the possibility we were dealing with two different thieves. Thus the importance of knowing the true value of the diamond-emerald matching set.

A light drizzle was again starting as we arrived at the entrance of the Windsor. Hurrying through the lobby, we could not help but notice Scotland Yard detectives, with their notepads and pencils, interviewing guests who seemed bothered by the inconvenience. Off to the side near his office, Richard Hopkins stood, wringing his hands and obviously distraught over the unwelcome disturbance that now enveloped the hotel. A second breaking and entering with the theft of a valuable item implied that none of the guests or their belongings were safe. More than a few rooms were certain to be vacated prematurely.

"Let us have a word with the hotelier," Joanna said sotto voce, and walked over to Hopkins, who straightened his posture as if to dispel the worry on his face.

"I do not understand how yet another burglary could have occurred," he complained to us. "Security guards were stationed on each floor at the emergency exits and at the lift in the lobby. And I personally viewed the exterior of the building hourly, searching for any unusual lighting in the rain, but seeing none."

"But was not the rain replaced by a heavy fog in the early morning?"

"It was, which was my downfall, for I was distracted by the lights in the nearby windows which may have overpowered the weak fluorescein illuminations."

"Which floors were the lights on in the early-morning hours?"

"Both the third and fourth floors, for the thunder and lightning of the rainstorm must have aroused some of the guests from their sleep."

"Most unfortunate," Joanna said, and glanced over to the registration desk. "How many of your rooms have been vacated this morning?"

"None as yet, but it is before eight and the day is young yet."

"Let us hope there will only be a few."

Hopkins nodded weakly, knowing full well that was not to be the case.

"I shall need the names of all those who do vacate, particularly the ones who do so prematurely," Joanna instructed, and waited for the hotelier to nod his response.

An empty lift awaited us and once again it carried the scent of fresh flowers. The noise and vibrations of the ascending lift covered my whispered question to Joanna.

"Do you believe the night manager's position is now in jeopardy?"

"I would not be surprised," said she.

"But he did have seemingly adequate precautions in place."

"To no avail, and the hotel owners will wish to blame someone and thus replace him, if only to reassure future guests."

On reaching the third floor we were greeted by Inspector Lestrade, who skipped the customary amenities and proceeded to give us the details of the most recent break-in.

"The French minister and his wife retired to their beds at half ten, with the windows left open, for both require cold night air to sleep well. Shortly after one, the minister was awakened by his wife's labored respirations, for her muscle disease can impair her breathing. He attended to her, propping her up on pillows which alleviated the difficulty. After using the bathroom, he returned to bed and slept soundly until six, which is the time he usually arises. Shortly thereafter, he noticed his wife's jewelry was missing from its opened velvet case."

"Be good enough to describe the jewelry in detail," Joanna requested.

"There was a necklace, with matching bracelet and brooch, all studded with small diamonds, with a nicely cut emerald in their centers."

"Expensive, then?"

"Quite so, for it was insured for ten thousand francs, which of course is the equivalent of four hundred English pounds."

Joanna nodded subtly to my father and me, for it was obvious that the possessors of the blue diamond, which was worth millions, would not risk all to steal an item valued at four hundred pounds. An experienced master thief would never even consider it. My wife gave further thought to the recent theft before coming back to the inspector. "Tell me, Lestrade, were other items missing?"

"Only some official papers which were thought to be secure in a locked attaché case."

"Was the lock broken or picked?"

"We suspect not, for the briefcase itself was taken, indicating the thief was unable to open it."

"And what was the nature of the papers?"

"The minister would only say they were official and that it was most important they be found and returned immediately."

"I would think the minister is most concerned over the loss."

"Very much so, and his wife is equally upset, for the jewelry pieces are family heirlooms which have been passed down through the generations."

"I should like to speak with them."

"This way, then."

We approached the minister's suite, but did not enter, for Joanna wished to examine the outer surface of the lock with her magnifying glass. After careful inspection, she announced, "There is evidence that an attempt was made to pick the lock."

"But surely the robber entered via the opened window which gave him easy access," said Lestrade.

"But it was possible, perhaps even likely, he tried to pick his way in. That mode of entry would be quicker and easier, which would appeal to any worthwhile thief."

"I should mention that security guards were stationed at the exits to the emergency stairs on each floor."

"Who were no doubt positioned in the staircase itself, so as not to upset the guests."

"Why is that of importance?"

"Because it raises the distinct possibility that the thief occupied a suite on the third floor and could move about in the corridor without being noticed."

"Which would be further evidence that the thief is amongst the hotel guests who we considered to be so distinguished," said Lestrade, with a brief frown.

"Which is a stark reminder that criminals come from all levels of society and even those in the loftiest ranks can be tempted when the reward is great enough. As my father once noted, greed is a strange transformer of the human character."

The floor to the suite opened and Detective Sergeant Stone stepped into the corridor, pausing to quickly strip off his rubber gloves. He gave my wife a courteous half bow and said, "It is good to have you on board again, madam."

"Let us hope I can be of service."

"I hope so as well, for thus far there are few clues at our disposal," Stone said, as he pocketed a stick of white chalk and turned to the inspector. "I have marked off the entire area surrounding the window and its sill, so it will remained untouched."

"See that it stays that way, for Overstreet will arrive shortly to lift fingerprints from it," Lestrade directed.

"Have you examined the window for fluoresceinated finger-prints?" asked Joanna. "Now would seem to be an ideal time, with the dimness persisting outside."

"Unfortunately, we must leave all the lights on for the pres-ent, for the minister is constantly hurrying between rooms to render care to his ill wife," Lestrade explained. "Once we have completed a careful search of the entire suite and Overstreet is with us, we shall darken the drawing room and look for fluores-ceinated fingerprints."

"Very good," said Joanna, and entered the suite with slow, deliberate steps. She gazed around the drawing room, ceiling to floor, before paying particular attention to a French antique chair near the door. "Was this the position of the chair when you just arrived?"

"Yes, but it was tilted back a bit on its legs," Lestrade replied.

Joanna next moved to the window which was partially opened no more than a few inches. "Was this the extent of the opening on your arrival?"

"It was much wider, but a light rain was falling and wetting the carpet, so we closed it to its present position. Is that important?"

"Only if you touched it with ungloved hands."

"My gloves were on, madam," Stone informed.

"Well done," said Joanna, dropping to her knees to test the dampness of the carpet. "It is wet under the sill, but dry a few steps away, which tells us the entry did not occur until after one when the torrential rain had diminished and the thick fog set in."

"Had it occurred earlier, the thief would have been drenched and tracked water across the length of the parlor," my father added.

"And might have even left footprints in the soaked carpet."

Joanna rose and, with her handkerchief, gripped the edge of the window and easily pulled it wide open, just as the thief would have done from the outside.

Claude Duval, the French minister, entered from the bedroom and closed the door softly behind him. He was a short, stout man, balding, with round spectacles which seemed too small for his face. Unshaven, he had obviously taken little time with his attire, for his shirt was without a tie and unevenly buttoned. Lestrade made the introductions in a formal manner.

"It is an honor to meet you, Minister, but not under these most unpleasant circumstances," said Joanna.

Duval returned the courtesy with a slight bow and responded, "The honor is mine, madam, for I have heard of your talents and hope that you can bring the stolen items back to us."

"I shall try my best, but I require more information and in particular a description of the stolen items."

"The jewelry included a necklace, bracelet, and brooch, all of which had an emerald in their centers that was surrounded by half-carat diamonds. The entire set had been placed in a velvet holder for the night."

"And their location?"

"On a nightstand next to our bed, and lying atop my attaché case."

"Please describe the case."

"It is made of fine cordovan leather, with a double brass lock."

"I take it the attaché case was locked?"

"But of course, and it could only be opened with a special key which I keep on a chain and always close to me."

"May we know the contents of the case?"

The minister hesitated, his face closing. "It contained official papers, madam."

"Of considerable importance, then."

"They are official papers, madam," he repeated sternly, ending that topic of conversation.

"Then we shall leave it at that," Joanna said, and glanced over to the chair by the door. "Am I correct in assuming you had tilted that chair against the doorknob to prevent the door from being opened even with a key?"

"Yes, madam. It is a precaution I always take when traveling."

"Claude!" his wife cried out from behind the closed door to their bedroom.

"If there are no further questions, I must attend to my wife."

"Of course, Minister."

Joanna waited for Duval to depart and close the door tightly behind him, then turned to Lestrade and in a quiet voice requested, "At your earliest convenience, have the commissioner contact the Secret Intelligence Service and have them answer the following two questions: Is this the Monsieur Duval who is the current French minister of war, and, if so, does he have meetings set up with His Majesty's War Cabinet?"

"May I tell him the reasons for this request?"

"Simply say that the answers may well change the entire calculus of the penthouse robberies."

Duval returned from the bedroom, carefully closing its door behind him. "My wife's breathing becomes a problem when she slips off her pillow."

Our thoughts were interrupted by a gentle rap on the main door to the suite, after which Henry Overstreet entered, with his fingerprint kit by his side.

"Ah, excellent timing, Overstreet," said Lestrade. "We shall extinguish all the lights and show you the position of the fluoresceinated fingerprints." He hurried over to the wall and switched the lights off, then drew the curtains, which turned the room pitch black. We waited patiently in the darkness, but the air remained absolutely black, for no fluoresceinated markings appeared.

"Not even a glimmer of fluorescein," Lestrade said dishearteningly.

He switched the lights back on and gave Stone instructions to lean out the window and look for fluoresceinated fingerprints on the outer window frame when the lights were again extinguished. Stone did as instructed, but saw only the dimness.

"Very clever, this thief of ours," Lestrade pronounced, as the lights in the drawing room came back on.

"Yes, very clever indeed," Joanna agreed, staring at the window at length, studying it like a canine would. For a moment, I saw a faint smile cross her face. "Well then, we shall be on our way, for there are other avenues which require investigation."

As we walked down the deserted corridor to the lift, I asked my wife, "What so drew your attention to the window in the minister's suite?"

"I was struck by the curious finding which Lestrade spoke of."

"But he stated there were no fluoresceinated prints on the window."

"That was the curious finding," said she, and left it at that as the lift arrived.

CHAPTER SEVEN

The Mountain Climber

As we approached the Diogenes Club on Pall Mall, my father's face brightened, for it brought back memories of his happier days with Sherlock Holmes. It was here, in this very club, that

Holmes had introduced his brother, Mycroft, to my father. On our drive over, my father had recounted how Holmes considered his brother to be his superior in both observation and deduction, and further believed that Mycroft could have been the world's greatest detective, but he had neither the ambition nor energy to pursue such a profession. Despite his brilliance, Mycroft seemed entirely satisfied to earn a livelihood auditing books in some obscure government department, for he had an extraordinary faculty for figures. Holmes was of the opinion that his brother could have outwitted a dozen Moriartys with ease. In my own mind, I wondered how well Mycroft would hold up in a contest with the Great Detective's daughter.

We entered the club through impressive mahogany doors and, on introducing ourselves, were escorted down a wide corridor that was eerily quiet. There was glass paneling on one side, behind which was a large and luxurious room where sat a goodly number of gentlemen who were reading journals and newspapers, with each member being entirely separated from the others. The club manager showed us into a small chamber, with plush leather chairs and a narrow, glazed window that overlooked Pall Mall. Arising to greet us was the gentleman Joanna had arranged for us to meet. His name was Sir Alan Faraday, and he had once been England's most renowned mountain climber. He looked every bit his previous role. Tall and trim, with prominent shoulders and silver-gray hair, Faraday had a rugged, handsome face that was heavily lined from excessive exposure to the sun and wind. He came over to us with a decided limp that was only partially abated by the use of his walking cane.

"And so I have the pleasure of being in the company of the daughter of Sherlock Holmes and the Watsons," he said warmly.

"It is our pleasure, Sir Alan," Joanna responded.

Faraday gestured to the leather-bound chairs and waited for us to be seated, before laboriously lowering himself onto a couch which allowed him to stretch out his damaged leg. "Now pray tell, how I can be of help to you."

"We need to make use of your expertise in certain aspects of mountain climbing."

"Such as?"

"Let us begin with the physical features of an experienced climber," Joanna replied. "I have been led to believe that the majority of climbers are, like you, lean and trim, with prominent shoulders. Is that correct?"

"For the most part those characteristics fit, but keep in mind that holds true for active climbers. As the years pass by, weight comes on and the shoulder muscles lose their prominence."

"It is an active mountain climber who holds our interest, for he would be the one involved with the robberies at the Windsor," Joanna specified. "Are you familiar with those events?"

"All of London is."

"And you have no doubt read of the thief and the fluorescein-ated clues he leaves behind."

Sir Alan chuckled softly. "You are of course referring to the Glowing Bandit."

"I am and in particular his nighttime escapades," Joanna went on. "Here we have a rather daring thief who ventures out into a drenching rain or dense fog to scale the front of a hotel's façade which has no protrusions or ornaments to hold on to. This act obviously requires considerable climbing skills. Now, who among English mountain climbers—using ropes, pitons, fluorescein, and what have you—could accomplish such a feat? In my view, it would require someone with a fair amount of experience."

"Most assuredly," Faraday agreed. "An amateur, even a

foolish one, would never attempt it. The climb would depend in large measure on the correct placement and spacing of the pitons, and on how far to hammer them into the stone. And how reliable the stone was to secure the piton when the weight of the climber pulls mightily against it. The list would go on and on, with each phase being as important as the one which preceded it. The feat you described would be risky, even for an experienced climber, for a single slip could cost the individual his life."

"Please be good enough to give me the names and whereabouts of English climbers who in your estimation would be up to the task."

Sir Alan gave a show of consideration before responding. "There are three who come to mind. First would be Elliot Aimes, who was once one of the best climbers in the world, but now suffers from dementia and resides in his daughter's home in Bristol. I saw him last a few years back and he did not recognize me, yet we were once the best of friends. The next candidate would be William Howe, but it cannot be him, for he is badly crippled and is now confined to a workhouse for the infirm and destitute. The third climber capable of such a feat would be Philip Walker, who is younger than the others and far more fit. But as good a climber as he is, he has a far darker side. In a fit of rage, Walker bludgeoned his wife with a metal stoker which caused severe damage and eventually her demise. He is currently serving a well-deserved sentence of ten years at Pentonville."

Joanna's brow went up. "Are you certain he remains in prison?"

"Quite so, for he writes me frequently to proclaim his innocence," Faraday replied. "I received such a letter from Pentonville only last week."

"So obviously it cannot be one of those three," Joanna reckoned, before pondering the dilemma further. "Of course one such climber could easily be brought in from the Continent."

"Where experienced mountain climbers abound."

"Which country would offer the best and widest selection?"

"Switzerland by far, particularly during wartime."

Joanna, my father, and I exchanged quick, knowing glances, with the same thought racing through our collective minds. The Kronenberg representatives! The alleged jewelers from Geneva who reserved the suite directly below that occupied by the Governor-General.

Sir Alan looked at us oddly. "Did I say something amiss?"

"To the contrary. You said something spot-on." Joanna arose from her chair and pointed to a small table that rested beneath the glazed window. "May I use your telephone?"

"Of course."

She hurried over to the telephone and rapidly dialed a number which connected her to the operator at the Windsor. "The hotel manager's office, please."

A few slow moments passed before she spoke again. "Ah, Mr. Blair, then. I take it you are the daytime manager at the hotel. . . . Good. This is Joanna Watson. . . . Yes, yes, Sherlock Holmes's daughter, and I wish to know if the Kronenberg representatives continue to occupy their suite. . . . They vacated early this morning," she repeated, then asked, "Will their expenses promptly be sent to their headquarters in Geneva?"

Joanna smiled at the response. "They paid the bill in cash, you say. . . .

"Yes, yes," she added. "Most unusual."

After thanking the hotel manager for the information, Joanna placed the receiver down and proclaimed with certainty, "We have our thief."

CHAPTER EIGHT

The Suicide

We started off early the following morning, for Joanna required
further information on the Kronenberg representatives—or
should I say alleged Kronenberg representatives—which only the
hotel manager at the Windsor could provide. It was clear the evidence against the jewelers was entirely circumstantial and would
never stand up in a court of law. Nevertheless, my dear Joanna
was not the least dissuaded by this impediment, for she reminded
us of Henry Thoreau's famous observation that "Some circumstantial evidence is very strong, as when you find a trout in the
milk." That aside, it was of the utmost importance to prove that
the Kronenberg agents were involved in the robberies, for they
represented the loose thread which could unravel the complex
mystery before us.

As we passed by Marble Arch, my father pondered, "Could
jewelers also be such experienced mountain climbers?"

"It is possible, particularly so if they began in their early
years," Joanna replied. "Goodness knows Switzerland has more
than enough mountains to practice on."

"But those facts alone are not sufficient to form such a strong
suspicion of their involvement."

"Not by themselves," Joanna agreed, "but when combined
with the manner in which they paid for their hotel stay, it points
the finger of guilt directly at them."

"It is not unlawful to pay for one's charges in cash," my father
argued.

"But it does not fit the situation," Joanna rebutted. "Here we
have guests from a renowned Swiss jewel firm, who are known to

the hotel and customarily have their expenses forwarded to Geneva. Now suddenly they pay in cash, which cannot be traced or followed. Business travelers would never do this, when they know their expenses are covered by a controller at their head office." She paused to study my father, for he was obviously not convinced. "Allow me, Watson, to bring this matter to a personal level. Say you, as an expert on a given disease, have been invited to present your research at a medical conference in Paris. You have been told they will cover all of your traveling expenses and have arranged with a hotel to do so. Would you insist on paying in cash at the end of your stay? I think not. So I ask you, what would be the purpose of paying in cash?"

My wife's question was met with silence from both my father and me. Why indeed pay when your hotel fare is already covered?

"Because the guests do not want their expenses forwarded to Geneva, where it will be refused, for no such travel arrangement was made by them," Joanna answered the question. "That, you see, would immediately raise suspicion of them and a search for their whereabouts would be undertaken by police here and on the Continent. Admittedly, it would require some days for the deceit to be uncovered, but even with a head start the thieves would remain on the run, with their accurate descriptions posted everywhere."

My father nodded at her assessment. "And had you not inquired, their payment in cash would have gone unnoticed, for the expenses incurred would have been satisfied and the hotel would not have to forward the bill and wait for reimbursement."

"And no one would have been the wiser," I added.

"But we still require confirmation from the Kronenberg home office in Geneva," my father noted.

"We shall have it soon," said Joanna as we approached the Windsor. "For I phoned the hotel manager last night and asked that he contact the Swiss jewelers on this very matter."

Much to our surprise, Inspector Lestrade was positioned at the entrance to the hotel and appeared to be giving instructions to a uniformed constable, who promptly hurried off to a nearby alleyway where he stood guard to discourage passing onlookers.

Lestrade tipped his derby in a most brief fashion and asked, "How did you learn of the suicide so quickly?"

"Whose suicide?" Joanna asked at once.

"The hotel manager Hopkins, who apparently leaped to his death from the roof late last night."

We were stunned at the news and it required several moments for us to process the startling development. What would lead to such an event? was the initial thought that went through our collective minds. Perhaps it was the prospect of dismissal because of the recent sensational robberies or perhaps he had already been made redundant.

"Did he leave a note behind?" Joanna asked, as if reading my mind.

"He did indeed," Lestrade replied. "It was placed on the typewriter for all to see and read *I have ruined my good name beyond repair.*"

"In his typewriter, you say?"

Lestrade nodded his response. "And pulled halfway up so as to surely be noticed."

"Was it signed?"

"Initialed, with a somewhat scribbled *H*."

"Not very neat," my wife muttered to herself.

"What is that, madam?"

"Nothing of consequence," said she, but the narrowing of her eyes indicated she thought otherwise. "Please give us every detail of the suicide."

Lestrade reached for his notepad and began thumbing through its pages. "Mr. Hopkins was last seen at around midnight by a porter in the main lobby. He seemed his usual self as he went about his duties to make certain all was in order. The lobby was quite busy at the time, for the opera at Covent Garden had let out late. In any event, at half six this morning a kitchen worker decided to take a breather and stepped out into the alleyway to do so. It was then he noticed a leg sticking up in the space between the large garbage bin and the wall. He naturally investigated it further and found that it belonged to the crushed body of Mr. Hopkins."

"Crushed to what extent?" Joanna asked.

"The side of his head was mashed in down to his brain and his rib cage was severely dented."

"When you arrived, had the garbage bin been moved?"

"It had not, for the staff was wise enough to leave everything in place until Scotland Yard was called to the scene. Only then was the bin pulled away from the wall so the body could be examined."

"Can you give us an estimate of how close the bin was to the wall?"

"It was quite close, no more than a few feet, for the body seemed crammed into the space. I suspect the force of the plunge drove the body into that confined space."

"So it would appear," said Joanna. "At this point, I think it best we allow my husband to examine the corpse and provide us with a more detailed description of the injuries induced by the fall."

"Very well, madam," Lestrade agreed, and led the way past curious onlookers who were not discouraged by the presence of the constable at the entrance to the alleyway. As was her custom, Joanna took slow, deliberate steps, with her attention fixed on the pavement rather than on the garbage bin ahead. It had rained the night before and there were numerous muddied footprints, many with other prints superimposed upon them. Nothing seemed out of order until we reached the garbage bin, with the body of Richard Hopkins lying beside it. As Lestrade had described, Hopkins had suffered a crush injury to the parietal bone of the skull, which exposed convoluted brain tissue. The thorax of the corpse was likewise crushed in to such an extent that it caused the entire body to be bent. Once I completed my examination, I moved to the inner edge of the garbage bin, upon which there was an obvious bloodstained area that held scattered pieces of bone and brain tissue, indicating the site where the hotel manager had landed with great force.

After detailing my findings to the group, I stepped aside to allow Joanna to perform her inspection. She seemed most interested in the puddle of blood behind the garbage bin and, using a nearby twig, measured its depth. Standing on her tiptoes, she next gazed into the bin itself, which was empty but carried the odor of rotting food.

"The bin was carefully examined and no body parts were seen," Lestrade informed. "It appeared clean in every regard despite its unpleasant aroma."

"No blood, then?"

"None was noted, which suggested he hit the bin head and chest first before plunging onto the pavement where he bled as he died. So all the pieces seem to tie together, but give us no exact reason for his suicide."

"I am afraid that will await deciphering his final note," my father said. "Perhaps there is evidence for the ruination in his office."

"We searched and could not find even a clue to account for such misery."

"I should like to have a quick look at his office, Inspector," Joanna requested. "If only to satisfy my own curiosity."

"This way, then."

We hurried out of the alleyway and entered the main lobby

of the hotel, which was now crowded with guests, all of whom seemed to be talking simultaneously, which filled the air with the loud hum of conversation. The noise quieted as we moved through the throng, but we could feel their eyes following our every step. A uniformed constable was stationed outside the entrance to Hopkins's office, and he opened its door for us.

As before, everything was neat and in perfect order. The desk was uncluttered and all of the items atop it were equally spaced apart. The ornate ashtray contained used cigarettes and cold ashes, with a writing pad next to it that contained an empty top sheet. But it was the typewriter on a small side table which drew our attention. Within it and pulled up from its carriage was the suicide note, upon which was typed:

I HAVE RUINED MY GOOD NAME BEYOND REPAIR

H

The *H* was poorly written and somewhat lopsided. "Thus it is clear Mr. Hopkins intended to take his own life and left a final note to indicate his intentions," Lestrade concluded. "In my experience, suicides in the better class almost always involve insurmountable debt or overwhelming shame. We shall shortly have to have a chat with the widow and take a keen look at their finances. Hopefully an answer to this tragedy will be reached and we can close this most regrettable matter."

"Perhaps the recent robberies, which brought such disrepute to the Windsor, caused a deep depression which consumed him," my father suggested.

Joanna moved over to the ashtray on the desk and, using a pencil, separated the two used cigarettes from their ashes. "We have two different brands, one being Benson and Hedges, the other Player's."

"Is that of significance?" asked Lestrade.

"Only in that Mr. Hopkins's preferred brand was Benson and Hedges."

"Perhaps he had a visitor earlier in the evening."

"Yes, but who?" Joanna's gaze went to the writing pad, from which she detached the blank front sheet and held it up to the light, searching for indentations. With a graphite pencil she gently traced back and forth over the sheet and produced a single line of numbers. "A phone number, I would think," she elucidated, and, reaching for the telephone, began to dial. After the briefest of conversations, which ended with, "Wrong number, please forgive," she placed the receiver down and came back to the group to inform, "It was the St. Regis Hotel."

After opening the desk drawers, which revealed no items of interest, Joanna picked up the large guest ledger on a nearby shelf and thumbed through its pages. "Ah, here we are. Not only are the guests from the Kronenberg jewelers underlined, but there is also an asterisk by their names followed by the number three-oh-five." She then examined the following pages before remarking, "I do not find similar markings by other guests."

The door to the office opened quietly and in walked a tall, nicely attired man, with thinning gray hair and a narrow, worried face. To those of us unfamiliar with him, he introduced himself as Jonathan Blair, the daytime hotel manager.

"Forgive me for not returning sooner, but there were other matters which required my immediate attention," he apologized.

"Understandable," said Joanna. "I trust you recognize me."

"I do, madam, for the inspector told me to expect your arrival."

"Very good," she went on. "I have a number of questions for you, the answers to which could be most helpful. Let us begin with the ledger which lists the needs and requests of your guests."

The hotel manager moved in closer, his eyes fixed on the ledger, his senses now obviously alerted.

"I am particularly interested in a pair of your most recent guests, the Kronenberg representatives. I take it you were aware of their most recent visit."

"I was."

"Did you recognize their faces from earlier visits?"

"No, madam, which is not unusual, for they send different individuals as their representatives, depending on the matter at hand."

"So the last to visit may not have been the actual son."

"I suspect not, for Kronenberg and Son is the name of the jewelers, and not necessarily that of the representative."

Joanna nodded at the information which she was already quite aware of. "In reviewing the ledger, I see there is an asterisk by the name, with the number three-oh-five beside it. Please explain their relevance."

"The asterisk denotes a special request and the number next to it is a preference for a particular suite."

"Do you recall if a reason was given for that request?"

Blair shrugged his response. "It varies, madam. Some prefer a given number out of habit or superstition, others because of the view from the suite. I do not remember a reason for the request, for we do not require one."

"To the best of your recollection, have prior Kronenberg representatives asked to be placed in suite three-oh-five?"

"No, madam, they have not."

"And finally, Mr. Blair, last evening I spoke with Mr. Hopkins and asked that he phone the Kronenberg home office in Geneva and inquire if they had indeed sent their representatives to the Windsor. Please be good enough to contact your hotel telephone operator and determine if such a call was placed."

"She will return to her duties at seven this evening, at which time I will—"

"No, Mr. Blair, I wish to have the answer *now,* for it is of the upmost importance. You should place that call to Geneva while Scotland Yard is still here."

"Very well," and he quickly moved to the telephone. "It will require some time to make the connection."

"We shall be on the roof while you gather the information." Joanna turned for the door, then in an instant turned back. "I neglected to ask if you smoked cigarettes, and if so is there a brand you prefer?"

"I enjoy an occasional Dunhill, madam."

"A smooth tobacco."

"Very much so."

"We shall be off to the roof, then."

On departing the manager's office, we spotted Major Von Ruden hurrying across the main lobby toward us. Beside him was a tall, broad-shouldered man, in his middle years, who was introduced as Lt. Adolph Smits, second-in-command of the South African security unit. His sharply chiseled, handsome face was marred by a deep scar that ran along his left jawline.

Von Ruden was taken aback for a moment at the presence of our group. He quickly gathered himself before saying, "So you, too, were summoned to the Windsor by Mr. Hopkins."

"In a manner of speaking, we were," Lestrade responded dryly.

"I presume you received the same urgent message as we did."

"Which message is that, pray tell?"

"A phone call received by the operator at the St. Regis, in which Hopkins insisted on our presence in his office this morning on a matter of great urgency."

"Did he give specifics?"

"None whatsoever," Von Ruden answered. "It appeared that Mr. Hopkins wished to inform us of the details in person."

"I am afraid that will not be possible, for Mr. Hopkins took his own life early this morning."

Von Ruden's face showed genuine shock, whilst Smits's remained stoic. Collecting himself, the major asked, "Was a reason given?"

"Only in a note which stated he had ruined his good name," Lestrade replied. "Do you have any idea what set of circumstances would bring Hopkins to such a drastic end?"

"I can only surmise that it had to do with the theft of the blue diamond."

"That might well turn out to be the case," Joanna agreed, now studying the stoic Smits head to toe. "Did the message ask that both you and your second-in-command come to his office?"

"It was meant only for me," Von Ruden answered. "I have Smits along to follow up on any clues, for I must leave shortly to escort the Governor-General to Buckingham Palace, where he has an audience with His Majesty King George."

"I was under the impression that the Imperial War Conference was not to convene until later this week," said Lestrade.

"That is correct, Inspector," Von Ruden concurred. "The Governor-General's visit is a private audience."

"I see," said Lestrade, obviously moved by the gravity of the upcoming meeting. "We are on our way to the roof to finish up this apparent case of suicide, and you can join us if you wish to do so."

"I must return to the St. Regis to ensure that all security measures are in place, for the Governor-General will depart within the hour. I trust you have no objection to Lieutenant Smits serving in my stead and reporting back to me if any clues regarding the blue diamond are uncovered."

"None whatsoever."

"You should know that Smits, prior to joining our unit, was a member of the Johannesburg Metropolitan Police, where he specialized in diamond theft."

"Well and good," Lestrade approved as he and the departing major exchanged tips of their derbies.

Joanna turned to Smits and asked, "Lieutenant, am I correct in assuming you dealt primarily with polished diamonds while serving with the Johannesburg police?"

"That is correct, madam," Smits replied, with a strong Afrikaner accent. "On occasion, however, we were called in by De Beers to investigate a missing uncut diamond."

"How exactly does one go about tracking a large, unpolished diamond?"

"If you are referring to one that is sizable and of the blue variety, it can only be entrusted to the world's finest diamond cutters, who are all situated in Antwerp."

"But much of Belgium is currently occupied by the Germans, so such a transaction would be nearly impossible for a British thief, would it not?"

"Unfortunately, madam, money still flows easily between warring countries."

"Unfortunate, indeed," Joanna remarked, and turned to Lestrade. "Let us follow the final path Mr. Hopkins took to the roof."

"To the lift, then," said the inspector.

"I believe he traveled otherwise," Joanna contended. "Hopkins was last seen by a porter in the lobby, and not by the security guard stationed by the lift. Thus the hotel manager must have taken the stairs, and so should we."

The staircase, like the interior of the lift, carried the aroma of freshly cut flowers, in the event the guests were forced to use them. The stairs and the platforms at each floor were scrubbed clean, with not a speck of dirt to be found. Joanna led the way up slowly, head down, eyes fixed on the spotless surfaces. As we approached the third-floor platform, the air took on the odor of a strong disinfectant. A large door off to the side had the label MAINTENANCE attached to it, and just outside the door were scuff marks on the sparkling clean floor. Joanna knelt down and attempted to remove them with vigorous rubs of her handkerchief. The scuff marks persisted.

Lestrade followed my wife's efforts with interest and commented, "We are of the opinion those marks were made by the maintenance man as he dragged heavy equipment from the closet."

"An important finding," said Joanna.

Lestrade basked at the compliment. "There is a rather massive vacuum cleaner within the closet which may well have caused it," he added.

Joanna opened the unlocked door and we all peeked in. There was indeed a large vacuum cleaner with rubber wheels that stood amongst mops, brooms, dustpans, and sizable containers of bleach and disinfectants. Various tools and tool kits and two harnesses lined a side wall.

My wife attempted to lift the vacuum cleaner by its handle and had difficulty doing so. "It is quite heavy," said she, now pushing the cleaner back and forth on its wheels. "Yet it moves easily."

"Some of the truly large vacuum cleaners have a locking mechanism on their wheels," Smits interjected. "If the brake was engaged, it would leave drag marks as it was pulled out of the closet."

"Which I suspect was the case here," Lestrade agreed.

We ascended the last two flights to reach the unlocked door to the roof, which opened with a squeal, indicating its hinges were well rusted. The roof itself was carefully inspected and gave no evidence that a man had leaped to his death from it only hours earlier. Joanna spent considerable time examining the damp surface, looking I believe for signs of Hopkins's exit, but none could be found.

Our group returned to the main lobby via the lift, and parted company, with Smits hurrying away to join the South African security unit, whilst Lestrade strode over to a pair of Scotland Yard detectives who were comparing notes.

Joanna watched their departures, but rather than proceed to the front entrance, she guided us back into the hotel manager's office, where Jonathan Blair was placing the telephone down. He was shaking his head, obviously confused.

"It makes no sense whatsoever," Blair said, trying to solve the riddle. "Why would guests who were not representatives of the Kronenberg jewelers register under that name?"

"I take it their Geneva office did not make the reservations," Joanna asserted.

"Their last reservation was four months earlier, and only a single representative was sent," he answered, then repeated himself, "It makes no sense whatsoever."

"It does to some," Joanna said, and, without further explanation, led us through the lobby and out the main entrance.

While waiting for a taxi, she gazed up to the very top of the Windsor and seemed to study it at length.

"What do you see?" my father asked.

"I see very dark waters which are far more evil than I anticipated."

CHAPTER NINE

The Autopsy

The crushed body of Richard Hopkins lay on the autopsy table at St. Bartholomew's, with his lifeless eyes staring up at the bright lights overhead. Benson, the orderly in charge, had straightened the bent corpse out as much as possible and, now satisfied with his efforts, moved back to view the remains.

"Most jumpers do not come from the Mayfair district," he commented. "The better class usually prefer poison or a gunshot to the head."

"Given the circumstances, perhaps those modes of suicide were not available to him," I opined, watching the orderly push a stand of instruments nearer to the autopsy table.

"Well, I can assure you, Dr. Watson, his act was most inconsiderate, for it will surely result in a closed-casket funeral, which most families dread," Benson said in an emotionless voice, and, with a brief nod, exited the autopsy room.

"An interesting observation on suicide by your orderly," my father remarked, giving the matter further deliberation. "But I view it from another angle, in that one would have thought that Hopkins, with his long and devoted service to the Windsor, would have chosen a way other than leaping off the roof, which will only add to the notoriety that now engulfs the hotel."

"I do not believe the choice was his," Joanna asserted.

"Whose, then?"

"The individual who murdered him."

My father's brow went up. "Do you have proof in this regard?"

"I am hopeful that dear John will provide that with a careful autopsy."

I must admit that at this juncture I was totally unprepared for Joanna's revelation. "Are there any clues in particular I should pay attention to?"

"His fingernails."

Despite the hint, I began the autopsy at the anatomical locale farthest away from the point of interest. It was my long-held belief that when one started with the obvious it detracted from the subtle. Thus I commenced with a study of the corpse's feet which showed immaculate toenails, as would be expected in such a neat individual. There were no bruises, lacerations, or open fractures on the lower extremities, which was in contrast to the thorax. His rib cage was crushed in, with multiple rib fractures, the sharp edges of which had penetrated the chest wall. There no doubt would be considerable hemorrhage within the pulmonary cavity.

My attention turned to the fingers, but on gross examination I could see no evidence for broken bones or other proof of trauma. However, the fingernails showed a most unexpected finding. Although they were neatly trimmed, there appeared to be a collection of dark material beneath the nails of the second and third fingers of both hands. It was a classic sign of a struggle.

"He fought!" I exclaimed, and inserted a slender probe beneath the nails to extract what appeared to be black strands. Placing them on a white surface, I studied the material with a magnifying glass and could clearly make out dark threadlike fibers. "He was clawing away at some article of the attacker's clothing."

"Which most likely were thick leather gloves," Joanna surmised. "I suspect Mr. Hopkins was being strangled from behind."

"Let us prove it beyond a doubt." I quickly moved to the victim's eyes and pulled down the lower lids to expose the conjunctivae, which showed the presence of small hemorrhagic spots called petechiae. These telltale spots are often seen in those who died from asphyxia, and are caused by an acute increase in cephalic venous pressure. In strangulation, the venous return from the head to the heart is obstructed, which increases the vascular pressure in the eyes and results in conjunctival hemorrhages.

"He has multiple petechiae in the conjunctiva, which is strong evidence for strangulation, but they can also be caused by severe head injury, from which he obviously suffered," I diagnosed.

"Then we must proceed to the neck where the hyoid bone awaits study," said Joanna.

"Indeed." I reached for a scalpel and made a vertical, midline incision just above the larynx which brought the horseshoe-shaped hyoid bone into view. "It is shattered, which is an indisputable sign that the victim was strangled to death."

My father stepped in for a closer inspection and nodded his confirmation before turning to Joanna. "Like your father, you saw what we saw, but thought what we failed to think."

"It is the difference between seeing and observing, Watson," she explained. "The clues can only present themselves. It is up to the observer to determine their nature."

"Pray tell which of those natures did we overlook?"

"I am afraid a goodly number," said Joanna, and began with the findings at the garbage bin outside the kitchen at the Windsor.

One by one she went through the clues whose meanings were evident to her but so unclear to others. "First was the tight space of only a few feet between the wall and the bin into which the body was crammed. Jumpers do not simply drop over the edge of a roof; they leap, and such a move carries them a minimum of five feet away from the structure. Next was the small puddle of blood beside the corpse. Crushing head injuries hemorrhage profusely, but only if the victim is alive. The already dead bleed very little, as was the case with Richard Hopkins, who left only a small puddle of blood on the pavement. Then there was the suicide note in the typewriter. Why bother to type it when there is a large writing pad on your desk which is certain to be seen? And do you think an exceptionally neat man like Hopkins would sign with a nearly indecipherable *H*? Certainly not. He would clearly sign his name, which would require him to remove the note from the typewriter and then, for some unfathomable reason, reinsert it. Finally, we have the scuff marks on the floor outside the maintenance closet on the third floor."

At this point, I interrupted. "But they surely could have been made by the huge vacuum cleaner."

"Initially I, too, considered that possibility, but soon discarded it," Joanna went on. "Dragging the heavy vacuum cleaner, with its wheels locked, could have produced those marks. However, on closer examination, the width of the wheels was an inch at best, whereas the scuff marks measured far greater, much like those left by resisting heels. Moreover, the wheels of the cleaner were not locked and turned easily, and thus I think we can justifiably conclude that this was their customary status in the closet."

"But what was Hopkins doing on the third floor in the middle of the night?" asked my father.

"An excellent question, Watson, and even more importantly, who was he with?"

"The murderer."

"Of course, but why?"

After considerable thought, both my father and I gestured with opened palms, indicating we had no answer, for the clever murderer had seemingly left no clues behind except for the ill-defined scuff marks.

"I can postulate, if you would like," Joanna offered.

"Please do," my father urged.

"I suspect the murderer was invited in by Hopkins to share some newly discovered evidence," she envisioned.

"But why share?"

"Perhaps to confirm the presence of the evidence."

My father gave Joanna a most puzzled look. "In the maintenance closet?"

"Here it becomes murky," she went on. "For it is possible that the murderer thought Hopkins was somehow interfering with or about to disrupt the scheme behind the theft of the blue diamond. In order to silence the hotel manager, the murderer persuaded Hopkins to show him the evidence in the maintenance closet."

"And while Hopkins was in the process of opening the closet door and had his back turned, the visitor throttled him."

"Then carried the body to the roof and dropped the dead Hopkins over the railing."

"But your machinations prior to the murder are purely supposition," my father challenged. "You presume that it was the murderer who lured Hopkins to the maintenance closet on the third floor, but have no proof to back up that presumption. It is just as likely that it was Hopkins who persuaded the murderer—"

"Excellent, Watson!" Joanna interrupted abruptly. "Perhaps it was Hopkins who did the tempting."

"But why would this act be so important?"

"Because it would indicate that Hopkins himself was involved in the theft and there was some item of evidence which indicated he was."

"But the closet was searched by us and others, and nothing of note was found. As you will recall, everything was clearly visible and the light within was quite good."

"The inner light!" Joanna proclaimed, as a sudden revelation came to her. "It was there directly before our eyes, but we did not see it."

"What?"

She did not answer the question, and instead hurried over to the light switch on the wall. "John, please turn the corpse's hands to a palms-up position."

I moved back to the autopsy table and followed her instructions, all the while wondering what evidence the surface of the palms held. The skin itself was smooth and cold and free of any blemishes. "I see nothing unusual!" I called out.

"If my supposition is correct, that is about to change!" she called back, and switched off the lights.

The autopsy room went black except for a sliver of light that crept in from the corridor and shined through the bottom edge of the door. But the faint radiance was bright enough to reflect a fluorescent glow from the corpse's fingertips.

"I say!" my father cried out.

"He must have been handling a container of fluorescein liquid," I surmised. "But to what end?"

"It was not a container, but a clue that Hopkins had come upon," said Joanna, as the lights were switched on and the fingertips lost their glow. "It was a most important clue which I believe revealed the nature of the theft."

"Which was?"

"We must return to the maintenance closet at the Windsor, for therein lies the answer."

At Joanna's request we remained silent during our taxi ride through the west side of London, for there were pieces to the puzzle which continued to elude us. In particular, which clue was so revealing that it merited murder? And to complicate matters, it had to be present or perhaps hidden in the maintenance closet. In my own mind's eye, I again went over the contents of the closet, which included mops, brooms, dustpans, cleaning and disinfecting agents, along with tools, tool belts, and harnesses hanging on pegs on the wall. Then there was the huge vacuum cleaner which was used to sweep all the suites, including those occupied by the imposters who registered as representatives of the Kronenberg jewelers. Certainly the clue was not contained in the collection bag of the cleaner, for its contents would have been discarded by now. It seemed to remain a puzzle within a puzzle.

I glanced over to my wife and watched her nodding with confidence to herself. "Do you know where the clue is located?"

"No, but I know how to find it."

On our arrival at the Windsor, we went directly to the lift, having decided there was no need to involve the hotel manager in our search. The mood throughout the staff and guests in the main lobby appeared quite somber, for most were no doubt still dwelling on the suicide of an individual they either knew or recognized. On our ride up, we noticed that the lift operator had a slender black band on his upper arm, which in all likelihood represented a sign of mourning.

We alighted from the lift and hurried down the eerily silent corridor. All of the doors were closed, the air still despite the slow-turning fans overhead. Stepping out into the staircase, we immediately noted that the scuff marks outside the door to the maintenance closet had been scrubbed away. A bad sign, I thought, for the closet itself may have been tidied up or perhaps scrubbed as well, which would have unintentionally removed the clue we were looking for.

"Should we simply go over the space inch by inch?" my father inquired.

"No need," Joanna said, and guided us into the spacious closet, closing the door behind the three of us. The entire closet went dark, other than a narrow streak of light which shined through a crack on the side of the door. As if by magic, a large harness and coil of rope hanging from the wall lit up with a fluorescent glow.

"The fluoresceinated harness and rope," said Joanna in a quiet voice. "That was the clue Hopkins came upon."

"Could the dye not have been placed there by Stoddard, the maintenance man who so ably assisted us?" asked I.

"Most unlikely, for he only came in contact with traces of fluorescein on the outer wall," Joanna elucidated. "You will note that the harness and rope are heavily stained, whilst the fingers of Stoddard's gloves show only traces of the dye, indicating his exposure was minimal."

"But would not Stoddard have been wearing that harness when he was in the suite with us?" my father pondered. "Surely, we would have seen the fluoresceinated harness light up after the drawing room went dark."

"*If* he had been wearing it," Joanna countered, and opened the door to allow light to flow in. "Please study the wall again, Watson, and tell me how many harnesses you see."

"Two! There are two of them!"

"But only one is heavily stained with fluorescein," Joanna pointed out. "With that in mind, pray tell who would have used it?"

"The mountain-climbing thief."

"Precisely."

"But why would the robber choose to secure the harness and rope he employed in the maintenance closet?"

"They required a place to hide their climbing equipment," she explained. "A large, bulky harness and a thick coil of rope would not fit in a gentleman's suitcase, and even if they could be squeezed in, there was always the chance it might be noticed or somehow discovered by the cleaning staff."

"But why two harnesses?" asked I. "It would seem that one would suffice for the thief's needs."

"A very good question, John, for which there is only one apparent answer," Joanna responded. "Please observe that one of the harnesses is weathered and old, with multiple cracks in its leather and frayed shoulder straps. That no doubt was the one Stoddard was accustomed to wearing and that he outfitted himself with to search the façade for us. It showed very little fluorescein staining, for much of the dye had been washed away by the rain before Stoddard began his climb. By contrast, an experienced mountain climber like our thief would never trust his life to such faulty equipment. Thus he brought along his own harness, which became heavily stained while he was scaling the hotel wall."

"But why does the thief's harness carry so much stain?" I inquired. "He only required a minimum amount of dye to paint the pitons, and thus the fluorescein should have been limited to his hands."

A knowing smile came and went from Joanna's face. "You are overlooking the fact that most individuals who work in aprons or harnesses often wipe their hands on them to remove excess liquids. And of course the fluorescein on his harness would not have been seen by those below because our thief was continually facing the wall while he went about his business."

"What makes you so certain there was excess dye?"

"The fluorescein smears on the bricks adjacent to the pitons."

I nodded at Joanna's deduction, but one important question remained to be answered. "But pray tell, how did he manage to bring a bulky harness into the hotel without being noticed?"

"Oh, there were a number of secret entrances, such as a route from the darkened alleyway to the staircase via the storeroom, the locks to which could have been opened by Hopkins."

"Which explains the fluoresceinated fingerprints in the Governor-General's suite," I recalled. "But why were such prints not found in the suite occupied by the French minister? Surely, our thief would have used the same equipment."

"A most important observation, the meaning of which Lestrade conveniently overlooked and for which there can only be one explanation," said Joanna. "On his second climb the thief must have been wearing gloves. And that, my dear John, is the curious finding on the window which by all measures should have revealed fluoresceinated fingerprints, yet did not show even a hint of a glow."

"But where are these gloves?" my father asked.

Joanna pointed to a pocket in the stained harness, into which a pair of rubber gloves were partially stuffed. "As he climbed into the suite, he no doubt placed those on."

"Our thief appears to be gaining in cleverness," I commented.

"I suspect it is the mastermind rather than the thief whose cleverness is increasing," said she. "The thief is merely a pawn or worker in the scheme of things and is being controlled by an individual who is very much aware of every floor, suite, and closet at the Windsor."

"And that individual is most assuredly a part of the hotel's inner circle," my father added. "Or could have been Hopkins himself, who was perfectly positioned to set such a plot in motion."

"But why was he murdered?" I asked.

"Perhaps it was a falling-out among thieves," my father suggested.

"My thoughts exactly," I agreed. "So it would seem that Hopkins may well have been involved in the theft of the blue diamond. That being the case, the fog engulfing this mystery appears to be lifting, does it not, Joanna?"

"To the contrary," said she, "for the fog you speak of is growing even thicker and brings with it far more questions than answers."

CHAPTER TEN

The War Document

After signing the Official Secrets Act, which bound us to keep secret all matters revealed and committed to us, we were escorted into the office of the commissioner of Scotland Yard by Inspector Lestrade. The stern stance and voice of Sir Charles Bradberry indicated the gravity of the situation.

"I will omit the usual amenities, for we have not a minute to spare," said he, gesturing us to our seats. "You should be aware that when we request information from the Secret Intelligence Service, it must go through channels and often requires days for them to respond. On submitting your questions, however, the reply came within hours, along with the insistence you sign the Official Secrets Act. I wish to make clear that not a word of their response is to be discussed or spoken outside this room. Are we understood?"

The commissioner waited for our collective nods before continuing. "First, allow me to inform you that Monsieur Duval's position in the French government is so sensitive he traveled to London under the guise of accompanying his wife here for medical purposes. His wife is of course ill and requires care by specialists, but at this time there is no need for additional medical attention, although we wish the Germans to believe so. Nevertheless, even if his wife's health had taken a sudden downturn, the Huns would surely assume that Duval would meet with his British counterpart while in London."

Bradberry walked over to a large window and gazed out at a bright, sun-filled day that was in contrast to the dark mood in his office. He drew the blinds, as if to shut off the world from the words he was about to speak. "Now, as to the purpose of his visit. Under tight security, the minister was scheduled to meet secretly with His Majesty's War Cabinet to coordinate the future maneuvers of the Allied forces in Flanders, where our victories have been so costly."

My father, a former army surgeon, who still bore a wound from the Second Afghan War, could not help but interrupt. "Please do not tell us the plans for such maneuvers were in the minister's attaché case."

"I am afraid they were, Dr. Watson."

The enormity of the theft could not be overestimated. Britain had suffered massive casualties during the Third Battle of Ypres in the Flanders region of Belgium, and the counting continued, with little chance of slowing. Every city, town, and village in England grieved for their losses, and now no doubt another offensive was either under way or in the late planning stage. Were this information to fall into German hands, the result would be catastrophic.

"We must have that document back and the sooner the better," the commissioner commanded. "Needless to say, Scotland

Yard is employing its full force around the clock to reach this end, but thus far we have been unsuccessful. In this regard, I hear from Lestrade you remain deeply involved in the theft of the blue diamond and have made some progress. With your talents in mind, His Majesty's government would like you to devote every effort to retrieve the minister's attaché case and the document it contains."

"I take it Scotland Yard believes the document remains in England for the moment," said Joanna.

"That is our belief, for the important portions of the plans are written in code and the thieves may not yet realize what they have in their hands."

"Unless of course it was the Germans who arranged for the theft," Joanna argued mildly.

"We think otherwise," Bradberry countered. "The penthouse thieves up to this juncture have stolen immensely valuable items which can easily be disposed of on the black market. Thus, in our view, they are rather common robbers, with particular skills, who show no allegiance to anything other than their own greed. And this presumption is now confirmed, for only this morning we received a ransom note, demanding one hundred thousand pounds for the return of the blue diamond."

The arrival of the ransom note did in fact change the entire complexion of the crimes. Now it was abundantly clear that the thieves had no true loyalty to any country or cause. They were only interested in money, and in this instance an enormous amount of it. Thus the ransom note gave us insight into the character of the thieves, but little else. Joanna apparently thought otherwise.

"May I see the note?" asked she.

"Of course," Bradberry replied, and handed her a letter-sized sheet of paper. "It was examined for fingerprints, which it does not carry, and has no watermark, making it impossible to trace."

Joanna held the ransom note up to the light, for my father

and me to see. It was written on a plain white sheet, with large block letters roughly scribbled in black ink. There was no date or signature. It consisted of only two lines, which read:

£100,000 FOR THE BLUE DIAMOND
INSTRUCTIONS TO FOLLOW

Joanna studied the ransom note at length, first without, then with her magnifying glass. "It is an old trick, but one that has some merit."

"What are you referring to?" Bradberry asked at once.

"The block letters are uneven and tend to tilt upward," she replied. "And in many places the hand of the writer is rather unsteady."

"An uneducated person, then," the commissioner deduced.

"Possibly, but more likely the writer is using his nondominant hand, which alters the letters in such a fashion that makes it difficult to assign them to a given person or technique. Nonetheless, there are certain features which stand out. These include the odd shape and slope of the letters, the irregular spacing between the letters, and the differing amount of pressure applied to the paper by each letter. Putting all these findings together, I would conclude that the ransom note was written by a rather clever fellow, using his nondominant hand."

"Your findings are most interesting," the commissioner noted. "But unfortunately, they do not bring us any closer to resolution."

"But the note itself can buy us time, if we play our cards correctly," Joanna informed. "And at this moment that is our most precious commodity, for given enough time it will lead to the clever devil's downfall."

"Do you have some basis for this opinion?" asked Bradberry.

"The mistakes he is making, despite his apparent cleverness."

"Certainly not his handwriting charade you described."

Joanna waved away the notion. "No, Commissioner, it is the botched suicide of Richard Hopkins."

"And how does one botch a suicide?"

"By leaving clues behind which indicate that the victim did not take his own life, but was murdered."

Almost in concert the brows of Bradberry and Lestrade went up, but it was the commissioner who asked, "Is there proof of this?"

"Indisputable."

Joanna described in detail the note in the typewriter with a scribbled *H* for a signature, the all-too-narrow space between the garbage bin and wall where the body was discovered, and the small puddle of blood which oozed from the victim's head, which should have been much larger. She asked that I tell of the conjunctival petechiae and shattered hyoid bone found at autopsy which confirmed that strangulation was the cause of death.

Bradberry tapped a finger against his cheek as he assimilated the new information and gave the matter more thought. "He must have come across a clue of considerable importance, which he unwittingly presented to the perpetrator."

"That is one possible scenario, but there are others which require further investigation."

"Thus the suicide note was a total ruse."

"So it would seem, but the note itself may have some value. The *H* in the word *THE* in the ransom note should be compared to the signature *H* in the suicide note. I believe you will find they are identical, informing us that the mastermind behind the theft and the murderer who took Hopkins's life are one and the same."

The commissioner nodded at my wife's conclusion, then added, "I should have questioned the man's suicide when I learned he had recently come into a handsome inheritance of twenty-five-hundred pounds. An individual who comes into that kind of money does not suddenly decide to end his own life."

Joanna's eyes narrowed. "When did this most fortunate inheritance occur?"

"Some months ago," Bradberry answered. "The bank manager was told by Hopkins to expect a transfer of twenty-five hundred pounds from a bank in Switzerland, where a beloved uncle had passed on."

"Does that money remain in Hopkins's account?"

"Only fifty pounds does, for the remainder was placed in a family trust."

"A wise move."

"Indeed, for they have a handicapped son who is looked after at Allenby House, where Hopkins's wife is employed as a nurse and where she can have close, daily contact with her disabled son."

"And her husband's death is yet another burden for the poor woman," Joanna said sympathetically. "Has Scotland Yard had the opportunity to speak with her?"

"We thought it best to allow more time to pass before talking with the grieving widow."

"Perhaps I should be the one to speak with her, for I, too, was once a sad widow and know the terrible pain she must now be enduring."

"We would be most grateful for you to do so."

Joanna nodded her acceptance, as a hint of melancholy came and went from her face. "Now let us return to the problem at hand and in particular our need for more time to untangle this complex web. And the ransom note gives us the opportunity to prolong our silent conversation with the perpetrators."

"How so?"

"In all likelihood the perpetrators will wait several days to send a follow-up ransom note, for they believe the delay will make us even more anxious and eager to submit to their demands. When the instructions for the payment arrive, I suggest you respond by informing them that more time is required to collect a vast amount of money. A deferral of two additional days would seem reasonable."

"What if they refuse?"

"They won't when you tell them that the ransom is now in the process of being gathered by the De Beers Consolidated Mines, which is working with a consortium of banks who requested the delay."

"That may buy us two days at the most."

"Which is good enough for a start, yet we shall need more time. Therefore, when the money is supposedly at hand and the perpetrators are so informed, they should be told that De Beers insists that the stone they profess to have is in fact the blue diamond. Make them describe some feature of the gem which will assure that it is genuine."

"And what feature might that be?"

"Consult with De Beers and have them give you a characteristic of the diamond which can be seen and measured by a nonexpert. For example, the width in inches of the deepest groove or valley would do nicely."

"That should gain us a total of six or seven days," Bradberry estimated.

"And gives us the time necessary to set a well-concealed trap for them," I added.

"That is wishful thinking," said Joanna. "For this will not be a straightforward trade, but one done through a series of intermediaries who will be impossible to follow."

"Are you referring to the black market?"

"That is where the deal will be done for all the stolen items."

"All?" the commissioner asked quickly. "Are you saying that

the bearer bonds and Ming dynasty vase, as well as the blue diamond and war document, will be handled by a black marketeer?"

"Of course, for any stolen item which is of high value and is well known cannot be offered on the open market," Joanna answered.

"But the bearer bonds can simply be sold to any buyer without identifying the seller," my father argued. "Is that not true?"

"Yes and no. In order to redeem bearer bonds, the bond certificates must be presented to the bond agent who handles redemption on behalf of the issuer. The agent then pays the bearer who must provide a name and address to which the cheque is sent."

"So the bond agent actually sees the seller."

"Unless it is accomplished through an intermediary."

"Such as the black market."

"Precisely, Watson. And the same holds true for the Ming dynasty vase, particularly if a predetermined buyer is already in place at an agreed-upon price."

"Can we expect to see the war document on the black market as well?" Bradberry asked worriedly.

"That is most unlikely, Commissioner, for once the thieves realize what they have in their hands, they will immediately know who will offer the most for it."

"The Germans," Bradberry grumbled under his breath.

"Who would pay any price for those plans."

"Would they be so bold as to offer the war document back to the French or British, as well as to the Germans, at an astronomical price, of course?"

"I think not, for the chance of being apprehended would increase greatly, and the fact that they had proffered the plans to the enemy would subject them to a charge of treason, for which they would surely face the hangman's noose."

The commissioner took a deep breath and exhaled resignedly.

"So I take it you feel the best path to the war document is via the blue diamond."

"At this juncture it is our only path."

"And if we reach a dead end after the seven–day delay?"

"Then I am afraid that both the diamond and the document will be lost forever."

We were about to rise when the commissioner gestured us back into our seats. "There is one more piece of information I must share with you, which unfortunately you will find most distressing. Last night in a heavily wooded area of Surrey, a South African criminal was discovered by Scotland Yard and ordered to surrender immediately. Rather than do so, he killed himself with a gunshot to the head. His background was quite sordid in that he participated in the Maritz uprising in South Africa some years back, an event orchestrated by the Boers to bring about freedom from their British rulers. The failed insurrection was led by a Colonel Salomon Maritz, who fled to Europe after his defeat. Not so fortunate was one of his lieutenants named Frederick Becker, a particularly violent fellow, who was captured and given a lengthy prison sentence. Five months ago Becker escaped from Paardeberg Prison, and there was evidence he subsequently made his way to London. We were on alert for his presence and eventually tracked him down to a secluded cottage in Surrey. That is where he took his own life after vowing he would never return to prison."

"A somewhat interesting fellow," Joanna remarked. "But what is so distressing about his presence and death in Surrey?"

Bradberry reached into an open drawer for a small slip of paper which he slid across the desk to us. It read:

221b Baker Street

+O +++

"There is no question he meant to do you harm," the commissioner stated.

"Oh, he planned to do much more than harm," said Joanna darkly, studying the coded note with her magnifying glass. "It would appear this man was an assassin sent to dispose of the occupants residing at 221b Baker Street. That is attested to by the three crosses accompanying our address. The meaning of the other symbols awaits further study."

"Perhaps some foe is holding an old grudge," my father ventured.

"Or a new one."

"Such as?"

"A thief who is guilty of murder," Joanna responded. "I would wager ten guineas it is the mastermind behind the theft of the blue diamond who feels us nipping at his heels and about to reveal his identity. Thus he and his associates hired an assassin to remove the obstacle to their fortune."

"But the assassin they sent will surely not be able to do so from his grave in potter's field," said my father.

"They will send another."

"A distinct possibility," Bradberry agreed. "Perhaps it would be wise for me to post a constable at your front door around the clock."

"A constable on our doorstep would only force the assassin to perform his dastardly act elsewhere," said Joanna, shaking her head at the offer. "It is best their assassin remain in the open, believing we are unaware of his plans."

"You place yourself in great danger," he warned.

"We have no choice if we are to apprehend the assassin and put his threat to rest," said she, and pushed her chair back. "And Commissioner, please be good enough to contact your counterparts in South Africa and request that they send a complete dossier on Frederick Becker."

"Is there any particular aspect of Becker's past which you are interested in?"

"The acts of violence he committed," Joanna replied, as we again began to rise.

The commissioner quickly motioned us back into our seats. "I must ask you to remain while we await the arrival of Captain Vernon Carter-Smith."

The name drew our immediate attention, for he was the most secretive of men, who was rarely seen and about whom little was known. Vernon Carter-Smith was said to be a co-founder of the Secret Service and was in large measure responsible for the capture of twelve German spies at the beginning of the Great War. Following his brief exposure in the newspapers of 1914, he seemed to have disappeared, never to be mentioned again.

"May we inquire as to his current position?" asked Joanna.

"He is director of MI5," Bradberry informed us. "While most are familiar with the Secret Service, few are aware of its MI5 section, which stands for *Military Intelligence,* with the number five indicating it is the branch which deals with domestic matters. Needless to say, they are a highly selective group involved with the most sensitive of matters."

Joanna gave the description momentary thought before saying, "They were no doubt the special unit who recently uncovered a nest of German spies in Croydon and had them promptly hanged at the Tower of London."

"One and the same."

My father and I exchanged knowing glances, for it was now clear that the affair of the stolen war document went far deeper than we could begin to imagine.

As if on cue, the door opened without a preceding rap and in walked a man of average height and frame, with thinning gray hair and pale blue eyes that were partially obscured by horn-rimmed spectacles. His general appearance was unremarkable in every way and would go unnoticed by most, which of course were the ideal features for a man who worked in the world of shadows.

"I have taken the liberty of introducing you prior to your arrival," said Bradberry to the director of MI5. "I believe you are familiar with Mrs. Joanna Watson and the good Drs. Watson."

"I am," Carter-Smith replied, in a voice that was meant not to be interrupted. "I take it you have sworn an oath to the Official Secrets Act, but I must emphasize that not a word of our conversation leave this room, for the outcome of the Great War may hang in the balance. Am I clear?"

"Quite," Joanna answered for the three of us.

"Let us begin with the dreadful news from the front," he went on. "The Third Battle of Ypres has finally come to an end with devastating Allied losses, which now number over three hundred thousand killed, wounded, or missing. Despite the cost, the battle in the fields of Flanders was of little strategic gain, for our troops failed to advance to the German submarine base at Bruges, from where their U-boat fleet is threatening Britain with defeat. Needless to say, our men are demoralized and war-weary, and now facing manpower shortages."

I swallowed hard, for it was obvious that the news from the front was even more desperate than the newspapers had reported. It seemed likely that all Belgium would soon fall and give the Germans an unimpeded path to the English Channel.

"To worsen matters, our intelligence has learned that the Germans are very much aware of our weakened position, and are planning to mount a powerful offensive in the early summer, which is called Operation Michael. They will employ heavy artillery, gas, and infantry to overwhelm our troops and drive them into the sea. With complete control of Flanders, the enemy will have an ideal springboard into France and eventually over to England."

"Can nothing be done to stop their advance?" my father spoke out involuntarily.

Carter-Smith nodded slowly, but without conviction. "Perhaps, but all depends on recovering the war document stolen from the French minister, for it contains a clever plan to trap the German army and inflict staggering losses upon them. You should know that the document is coded and carries the title 'Backs to the Wall.'"

"Not a very encouraging title," Joanna commented.

"It was meant to be," the director of MI5 explained. "The heading was typed in English to mislead the reader, while the remainder of the document is coded. Upon deciphering it, however, the Germans will learn that the Allied forces plan to engage the enemy army near the city of Amiens in northern France. Here our troops will give ground and retreat as if in defeat, thus making it appear that the Germans have punched a large hole in the Allied line. That will be the intended consequence, for once the Germans have progressed well inside our position, the British Expeditionary Force will mount a counteroffensive, with several of its divisions on the periphery advancing and outflanking the German forces, thus closing the trap and inflicting the heaviest of losses on the enemy. The battle at Amiens might well be the most decisive battle of the war."

"Bravo!" my father cheered. "Give the Bosch a stinging defeat they will long remember."

"But first we must regain possession of the document, for otherwise all is lost."

Joanna wrinkled her brow in thought before inquiring, "I take it that MI5 has not uncovered any clues regarding the whereabouts of the war plan?"

"Not as yet, and thus we, as well as the entire War Cabinet, would welcome your assistance. I was instructed to give you every detail of the coded document, in hopes it will provide some pointers we have overlooked."

"I am afraid you have presented us with a tangled knot," said Joanna, and, after more thought, added, "Is there not some loose thread hanging from this knot?"

"One perhaps," Carter-Smith replied. "We are aware of wireless messages being sent from London to U-boats in the Channel, and are doing our very best to track down the source of the radio signals."

Joanna nodded at the importance of the new information. "They would have to arrange for the document to be transported out of England and into German hands."

"Precisely so, which is the reason we are monitoring the wireless messages so closely." The director of MI5 took a deep, unhappy breath. "It is of particular note that the most recent deciphered transmission contained the words *Backs to the Wall.*"

"They have the document!" I blurted out.

"Or are in the process of buying it," Joanna ventured. "However, its purchase would require a large sum of money, which even the best of spies do not have on hand. Thus the intercepted message could be a request for such funds, in British pounds of course."

"That is our belief as well, which indicates the document is still on English soil," said Carter-Smith.

"Most likely, but it will not remain here for long." Joanna reached in her purse for a Turkish cigarette and, after lighting it, began pacing the floor in the commissioner's office. Back and forth she went, head down and mumbling to herself, all the while ignoring the men in the large room who were watching her every step. It required multiple trips across the office before she abruptly stopped and turned to the director of MI5. "There is a major problem which needs to be overcome, assuming we gain possession of the document."

"Which is?"

"How can we be certain the document has not been photographed by the Germany spy?"

"Why would he do so?"

"Because it is what I would do were I in his stead," Joanna said, sending a puff of white smoke into the air. "Think how clever it would be for the spy to purchase the war plan and photograph it, then return it to the thief with instructions to sell it to us, which of course the thief would be delighted to do, for it would double his profit. Were that to occur, we would be led to believe we were the sole possessor of the document and proceed with the confrontation at Amiens to trap the enemy. The Germans would be prepared for it and deal us a crushing blow, in essence turning our proposed trap into a disaster."

"It would be a catastrophe, from which we would never recover."

"But hold on a moment," my father interrupted. "How likely is it for a spy on the move in a foreign country to have such bulky photographic equipment?"

"It need not be unwieldy or cumbersome, Dr. Watson," Carter-Smith informed. "There are now miniature cameras disguised as pocket watches, which can take pictures through the stem where a rapid-fire lens is located. The film can be loaded in daylight and is capable of up to twenty exposures."

"I say!" my father exclaimed. "Would the Huns have such a device?"

"All spy agencies have them, including our Secret Service, where it has already been put to good use."

"So even if we capture the spy with the document, he may have already transmitted its contents," I said worriedly. "We would never know."

"There is a way around it," Joanna suggested.

"Which is?"

"Capture the spy and persuade him to tell us exactly what he has and has not done."

Carter-Smith shook his head at the notion and said, "It has been my experience that German spies are quite tight-lipped and refuse to utter even a syllable of information. That was the case when an offer of life was given to the recently captured spies while they awaited the hangman's noose."

"Did you repeat the offer while the spies were standing on the gallows having the black hoods applied?"

"We did not."

"That was the opportune moment," Joanna said, as she extinguished her cigarette and reached for the door. "I have seen the black hood break down the strongest of men."

CHAPTER ELEVEN

Security Measures

Upon our arrival home, we immediately set in place all necessary security measures, for the note handed to us by the commissioner indicated that violence would soon come our way. With this in mind, we hired a nearby locksmith to affix a sturdy metal hinge to the door to our rooms, which would be secured by a Chubb lock. Next, a tripod with a monocular telescope on top was positioned by the window overlooking Baker Street; this device would allow us to detect individuals who were surveilling our residence. Whilst I was drawing the curtains to conceal the telescope, my father brought in his Webley revolver that had remained quite serviceable from his bimonthly visits to the practice range. Yet he repeatedly checked its chambers and made certain the weapon was fully loaded before resting it in a shoulder holster. In the midst of all this activity, Joanna phoned the commissioner and asked that he arrange for detectives to be assigned to keep a close watch on her son, Johnny, who was a student at Eton. The lad had been kidnapped in one of our earlier adventures, and that terrifying experience still weighed heavily in our memories.

Now, with all the security measures assembled, we attended to the last, most important task and summoned Miss Hudson to our rooms. The kind woman's eyes widened as Joanna informed her of the dire threat we were facing.

"Oh, dear," said she in a hushed voice, clearly understanding the seriousness of the situation. "Are we all at risk, then?"

"Very much so," Joanna replied. "Thus it is of the greatest consequence that you follow our instructions to the letter, for our lives as well as yours may well hang in the balance."

Our landlady's face showed concern, but no obvious fright, for this was the brave woman who in the dark of night stepped out into Baker Street and shook her fist angrily at the overhead German aircraft that were dropping bombs on a nearby district. "Shall I write down your instructions?"

"There is no need, for they involve your usual tasks, but done in a somewhat different fashion," said Joanna. "First and foremost, you must keep the doors locked at all times, particularly the one to the tradesman entrance. You should accept deliveries from only those you recognize."

"I know all the tradesmen by name."

"Excellent, but if the delivery is made by someone you do not recognize, have him place the package or box at the doorstep rather than allow him to enter."

"How long should I leave it there?"

"Until you are certain the deliveryman is well gone, and you can accomplish this by peering through the kitchen window."

"Easy enough to do."

"And under no circumstances are you to admit any unannounced visitors, particularly those who have even a hint of a foreign accent that might suggest a German background."

"Bloody Huns," she muttered under her breath.

"Finally, I thought it wise to have the locksmith return later and apply a padlock to the tradesman entrance, for which only you will have a key."

"Shall I draw the blinds on the ground floor?"

"Leave a narrow opening, so you can see out while others have difficulty looking in."

With the instructions being given, Miss Hudson departed in a firm, confident stride, like a woman on a mission. As with most Londoners, she had a deep loathing for the Germans, particularly for the nighttime bombing raids on civilian targets.

At last we were able to enjoy cups of freshly brewed Earl Grey tea whilst resting around a cheery, three-log fire. The day had been filled with so many unexpected twists and turns that we only now were able to fully consider and connect the various findings.

"The coded note being carried by the apparent assassin is quite worrying," said my father.

"And revealing," Joanna noted. "For it indicates the perpetrators feel we are close to solving the riddle and uncovering their identities."

"But we obviously are not," my father stated, now packing the bowl of his favorite cherrywood pipe. "There is not a single clue which beyond any doubt points to a given individual."

"It is not a singular clue, Watson, which should draw our attention, but a continuation of seemingly unrelated findings, which at this juncture are apparent to the mastermind."

"But not to us."

"Not as yet, but all will become clear as more clues are uncovered," Joanna went on. "For now, however, let us concentrate on the clues we have uncovered. Everything points to the perpetrator as being closely associated with the Windsor, where two major thefts have occurred. We can say with some confidence that the thief knows his way around every turn and corner of the hotel, and is aware of who is occupying a given suite and for how long."

"But what of the thefts at the Fairmont and the St. Regis?" asked I. "How could someone at the Windsor be so familiar with the other hotels?"

Joanna waved away the contradiction. "The hotel managers at the finest hotels, like their concierges, form a clique and trade information on their guests, including the status and wealth of those occupying the penthouse, where the highest levels of society would stay. You see, John, to them it is a badge of honor to serve personages of such high standing."

"So you are limiting the suspects to the hotel managers such as Hopkins?"

"Oh, if it was only that simple, for the rich and famous draw everyone's interest, from the chambermaids to the lift operators to the registration clerks. Take for example that the deliveryman at the rear of the Windsor knew that the oversized bathtub was being installed for the arrival of a very stout maharaja from India. Now pray tell, how did he come by this information?"

"He was told by a hotel employee," I answered promptly. "And it could have been any of the staff at the Windsor."

"Exactly, dear heart. A chambermaid could have peeked into the ledger in Richard Hopkins's office and seen who was soon to arrive. And imagine her excitement when she learned that the

Governor-General of South Africa would be a guest, to be followed by a minister from France. I can assure you she could not wait to gossip the news to her coworkers."

"So it might have been anyone who unintentionally let out the information."

"Or someone who was bribed to do so, which brings us to the most fortunate and recent inheritance that came Hopkins's way."

"But it came from a deceased uncle in Switzerland," I argued.

"Who happened to have an account in a Swiss bank, from which the tidy sum could be transferred and never traced because of their strict banking laws. How very convenient for the suddenly prosperous Richard Hopkins."

"But you would have to prove that such an uncle never existed, and that might well be impossible to do."

"I do not have to prove anything, for the obvious suspicion alone is enough for now, in that Hopkins was in the perfect position to be part of the team which committed the theft of the blue diamond—a team that may have no longer required his presence."

The lighted pipe nearly dropped from my father's lips as he leaned forward to ask, "Are you telling us that Hopkins was murdered because he was a member of this criminal enterprise and not because he had uncovered an important clue?"

"Bravo, Watson, for that remains a distinct possibility. Perhaps he was initially bribed, but discovered something that he thought considerably increased his worth to the group and demanded a larger share of the ransom."

"But why not just pay him an additional twenty-five hundred pounds, which is a small fraction of the sum being asked for in the ransom note?"

"Because blackmailers have a nasty habit of coming back again and again, insisting on larger and larger payments," Joanna explained. "It is very difficult to satisfy greed, and the murderer would no doubt be aware of this."

"The finger of guilt now seems to be pointing directly at Richard Hopkins," said my father.

"It did from the onset." Joanna arose out of her overstuffed chair and strolled over to the Persian slipper for one of her Turkish cigarettes. After lighting it, she started to pace the floor, leaving a trail of pale white smoke behind. "The clues were right before us, beginning with the curious finding in the French minister's suite. You will recall that the window failed to reveal any fluoresceinated fingerprints, when by all accounts they should have been present."

"Which could be explained by your earlier observation that the thief was wearing gloves."

"But why on the second robbery and not on the first?"

"He must have been warned," my father replied. "That is the only possible explanation."

"Excellent, Watson," Joanna praised. "You have outdone yourself again. But pray tell who did the warning?"

"It could have been any number of individuals."

"Actually, the number is quite limited," said she. "You must pay particular attention to the timing of the two robberies. Keep in mind that it was on the evening *following* the blue diamond heist that we discovered the fluoresceinated fingerprints in the Governor-General's suite. Yet only hours later did the same thief enter the French minister's suite and abscond with the war document, leaving no prints behind. So how could he have possibly known about the fluoresceinated fingerprints and be warned to wear gloves on his subsequent outing?"

My father answered, "Certainly not from the newspaper stories of the Glowing Bandit, which did not appear until the next morning's edition."

"Which leaves us with the individuals who were in the Governor-General's suite the night the fluoresceinated fingerprints were discovered." Joanna discarded her cigarette into the fireplace, then held up a hand to count off the possible suspects on her fingers. "There were five of us in the suite at that moment—John, myself, Lestrade, Hopkins, and Stoddard, the maintenance man. You were not present, Watson, for you were a bit under the weather. So, of the five of us just mentioned, who would have been the most likely to pass on the finding of fluoresceinated fingerprints, which necessitated the use of gloves on the thief's second outing?"

"Hopkins!" my father and I answered simultaneously.

"And there is another piece of evidence—admittedly circumstantial—which points in his direction," Joanna continued on. "It was John's astute observation in the storeroom that its doors were secured with sturdy Chubb locks that would have required an expert to pick open. All of which tells me the thief did not exit through the storeroom nor via the kitchen where an assistant chef was stationed until morning. Thus he must have remained in the hotel."

"We previously assumed that was the case," said I, not understanding the relevance of my wife's reasoning.

"We also assumed that the thief came down to the lobby and out the main entrance to retrieve the bloodstained piton," said Joanna. "But we can now see in retrospect that such a retrieval would have been foolhardy. Under no circumstances would the thief take the chance of being seen in the lobby or near the injured doorman. The smart move would have been to remain in one's suite as far away as possible from the incident."

"You cannot be certain of that," I argued mildly.

"It is what I would have done had I been in the thief's shoes," Joanna responded. "Keep in mind that the unseen is the unsuspected. It is an axiom that even the dullest of thieves adhere to."

"Then who went to the front of the Windsor to fetch the bloody piton?"

"The individual who was told of the thief's misadventure and who could easily pass through the lobby to the crime scene without arousing suspicion."

"Richard Hopkins, the hotel manager," I replied with the obvious answer.

"Who unfortunately is now quite dead and cannot provide us with the information we need."

"Which I am afraid brings us to another dead end," my father replied.

"Not necessarily, Watson, for it is often the trail rather than the destination which gives up the most important clues."

Our conversation was interrupted by the loud ring of the nearby telephone. My father answered the call and spoke briefly with Inspector Lestrade, then, placing his hand over the receiver, informed us, "There is promising news and not-so-promising news."

"Start with the former," Joanna requested.

"The fingerprints in the Governor-General's suite match those found in the Kronenberg suite, thus proving that the supposed jewelry representatives were the thieves."

"And the not-so-promising disclosure?"

"The sketch artist was unable to compose a picture of the thief because the witnesses gave varying and often-conflicting descriptions of the imposters. So it appears we will be deprived of a most helpful clue."

Joanna made a show of concentration before saying, "There

were two representatives and the witnesses may be confusing one with the other."

"Is there a way to separate the two?"

"Have the lift operator interviewed, for he in all likelihood saw the pair repeatedly and up close, and might be able to give more accurate descriptions," she replied. "It is a long shot, but one worth taking."

My father relayed the suggestion to Inspector Lestrade and, placing the receiver down, grumbled unhappily, "For every step forward, we seem to take one back."

Outside, there was the loud sound of screeching brakes, followed by the noise of metal being crunched. We hurried to the window to view a motor vehicle which had strayed off the street and crashed into a lamppost on the footpath. Apparently, there were no injuries, for the driver was inspecting the damage done to the front fender. Despite the relatively benign accident, my pulse was racing as adrenaline flowed through my veins, for such unexpected interruptions reminded me of the danger we were currently facing. My wife's and father's facial expressions told me that their senses as well had been brought to a heightened alert.

"I continue to think of the three crosses on the assassin's note," I thought aloud. "They are certainly meant to be grave markers for us."

"That is obvious," said Joanna. "What is far less clear is the meaning of the circle and multiple, disarranged dashes at the bottom of the note."

"Do you have any idea what these curious symbols designate?"

"They represent further instructions, I would think."

"But to what end?"

"To our demise," she said darkly, and retreated to her workbench, where her magnifying glass lay atop the assassin's note.

CHAPTER TWELVE

The British Museum

The following afternoon we arrived at the British Museum for a meeting with Sir David Shaw, a distinguished curator in charge of ancient Mesopotamian script and language. Sir David and my father served together in the Second Afghan War, and their friendship had allowed us to impose on him in the past for assistance in decoding complex messages. Unimpressive at first sight, the curator was tall and stoop shouldered, with reddish-gray hair and a hawklike nose upon which rested the thickest spectacles I had ever seen. But behind those heavy lenses was a brilliant mind, the owner of which had been knighted by Queen Victoria for his wartime skills in deciphering top-secret coded messages, some of which were so sensitive they would never be allowed to see the light of day.

As we moved through the great hall, we passed a throng of visitors surrounding the Rosetta stone, which many believed to be the most informative rock ever found. A guide was telling the group the fascinating story behind the stone, which had been described to us in detail by Sir David in one of our earlier meetings. The Rosetta stone was discovered in Egypt by soldiers in Napoleon's army whilst they were digging near the town of Rashid, which translates as *Rosetta*. Carved into the four-by-two-foot stone were three distinct scripts. The upper text was Egyptian hieroglyphs, the middle written in demotic Egyptian, and the lower in ancient Greek. Because all three of the scripts read essentially the same, the stone provided the key to unlocking the deep mystery of Egyptian hieroglyphs. As we ascended the stairs to the second floor, I could not help but compare Sir David to the Rosetta stone, for both had the unique ability to take coded symbols and translate them into the spoken word. My father had once told me in one of his reminiscing moments that the curator's decoding of the enemy's message had saved his regiment from suffering massive battlefield losses.

We entered Sir David's undistinguished office, which was small and crowded, with little room to spare. Every inch of the walls was taken up by books, ancient artifacts, and framed photographs from archaeological expeditions. Even his desk was cluttered with papers and notes held down by clay tablets with unrecognizable script written upon them. He greeted us warmly and gestured us to three uncomfortable wooden chairs.

"I hear you had a code that is proving somewhat difficult," said Sir David.

"*Most* troublesome indeed," my father emphasized. "But I must preface the conversation we are about to have with the following restrictions. The note you will shortly see involves an assassin, of whom we have the misfortune of being the target. The details and circumstances of the case we are currently involved in cannot be discussed or even spoken of in any way, form, or fashion. I can only say that the events to which the assassin is attached reach the highest level of His Majesty's government."

Sir David tilted his chair back, happy to engage and not the least bit dissuaded by the imposed limitations. "One of those for-your-eyes-only, eh?"

"I am afraid so."

"I trust I will be allowed to examine the entire message, for not to do so might present difficulties which cannot be overcome."

"Here is the complete note," said Joanna, opening her purse for the folded slip of paper which she handed to the curator. "As you will see, it consists of an address and two sections of symbols which, except for the crosses, cannot be deciphered."

Sir David arose and stepped over to a small blackboard behind his desk. Adjusting his thick spectacles, he studied the message at length before copying it in enlarged form with white chalk.

221b Baker Street

+O +++

"The address is quite simple, for it belongs to the Great Detective's daughter," he began. "But it also gives us information about this assassin. We can say with some degree of confidence that he is not from London or even the British Isles, and thus one must conclude he is a foreigner."

"May I ask how you reached that conclusion?" my father inquired.

"It is quite simple, Watson," Sir David elucidated. "The name and address of both Sherlock Holmes and his now famous daughter are well known throughout the city and the country itself because it has been published over and over in the stories chronicled by you and now your son. A foreigner would not be aware of these adventures. Furthermore, it would not be a challenge for a British citizen to memorize the name and number of the address, but it might slip the mind of a foreigner who was unfamiliar with the streets of London. You see, it would not do for your assassin to forget his targets' address."

The three of us nodded to one another, for the next assassin to be assigned would most likely come from South Africa, like his now dead compatriot in Surrey. Earlier in the day Lestrade phoned to tell us that an informant had revealed that Frederick Becker was a member of a clan of international assassins based in Johannesburg. We of course remained silent, remembering our solemn oath to the Official Secrets Act.

"Now let us move down to the second line of the coded message and concentrate on the four crosses and circle," the curator continued. "It consists entirely of symbols, which I am afraid increases the difficulty of the decoding process. Most secret messages rely on letters and numbers to transmit their meaning, as you no doubt recall from our prior discussions. For example, numbers can be used to designate a given letter, with the number one representing the letter *a,* the number two a *b,* and so on. That is obviously not the case here. Nor do we have any letters to work with, which complicates matters, and leaves us to deal with large crosses and a complete circle. Now pray tell what do you make of the crosses?"

"We believe they represent grave markers for the three of us, which of course indicates the purpose of the assassin's mission, for someone wishes us dead," Joanna answered.

"An obvious explanation," Sir David agreed. "But there are four crosses in the code. What is the meaning of the first cross attached to the circle?"

"I suspect it is directed at my son, Johnny," Joanna replied, as her face suddenly hardened.

"A distinct possibility, but a bit too conspicuous, which is always a flashing warning sign in any code. Such added symbols are at times inserted simply to confuse or mislead the decipherer."

"Nevertheless, with even a hint of danger to my son, I have requested Commissioner Bradberry to assign detectives to watch our Johnny while he continues his studies at Eton."

"A wise move and one that is understandable, but for the present you must push that concern aside and think like the individual who constructed the code and hired the assassin. His primary objective is to destroy you and the Watsons, for therein lies the threat you apparently pose. Here, the lad would be of no consequence."

"But why then a fourth cross?"

"Why indeed, and why is it separated from the other crosses by a circle?"

"It must have special significance," my father surmised. "Otherwise, it would not have been inserted among the crosses."

"Perhaps it is not meant to be a simple circle," Sir David prompted. "Might it not signify a naught or null, indicating that some function the assassin customarily performs was to be omitted?"

"Involving a cross?" I wondered aloud. "That makes no sense whatsoever."

"But it does if one envisions the cross attached to the circle as a marker of graves which is to be omitted," Joanna said quickly, assigning a new meaning to the symbols. "That being the case, I suspect the assassin was instructed to bury us at some undisclosed site, which in essence ensures that we disappear from the face of the earth."

"And what purpose would that serve?" asked I.

"We would be listed as missing and Scotland Yard would be forced to use at least a portion of their manpower to search for us," said she. "We would become the headlines in all of London's newspapers, which would take the focus off the penthouse robberies."

"Now you are thinking like the code maker," the curator noted. "And that is an essential ingredient if one is to break the code."

"But that brings us no closer to the identity of the assassin or the method he plans to use," my father interjected.

"Perhaps that information is hidden in the third portion of the note, which consists of multiple broken lines of varying size." The curator used a stick of white chalk to count the total number of apparent dashes that seemed so disarranged. "At first glance, I wondered if the dashes might be Morse code, but that requires the presence of dots as well, which are notably absent. Thus we can exclude that possibility. Next, I counted the number of individual dashes in the cluster and came up with the sum total of fifteen. It is a number which may bear directly on the threat you are facing."

"How so?" my father asked at once.

"It is a simple deduction, if true," Sir David responded. "To begin with, you do agree that the assassin has been given instructions to commit this most unpleasant act."

"Most assuredly."

"Which leaves us when and how, does it not?"

"It does."

"Then perhaps the number fifteen is a date by which or on which the act was to be carried out."

My father nodded grimly. "The fifteenth of the month is only five days away."

"And that may be the significance of the number fifteen," said Sir David. "But there are numerous other possibilities, such as the method of execution, which is described in a readily accessible book like the Bible. I am afraid it is a quite long list of possibilities."

"I believe you are telling us, Sir David, that the deciphering of this message will involve a prolonged, tedious process," Joanna concluded.

The curator nodded so firmly that his thick spectacles almost dislodged from his nose. "Quite so, for the codes without numbers or letters are the most problematic. We have only symbols to work with, and symbols alone resemble hieroglyphs, which history has taught us are the most difficult codes to break. I am afraid it will take considerable study to solve this riddle."

"Can you estimate the amount of time which will be required?"

"It is impossible to say."

"You are surely aware that we desperately need this code deciphered," Joanna urged. "And we have such little time to do so."

"I shall give it my best," Sir David said in a voice that carried little optimism.

As we arose from our seats, Joanna inquired, "I have been told that the British Museum has in its possession a very fine collection of Ming dynasty artifacts."

"It is the most outstanding collection in all England," Sir David noted.

"I take it the artifacts are looked after by a curator."

"One with an astonishing knowledge on the subject," he replied. "Margaret Howe is a world-renowned expert on the Ming dynasty and has been with the museum even longer than I."

"Would it be possible for us to meet with her during our visit?"

"That should not present a problem," Sir David said, turning for the door. "Allow me to determine if she is in and has a bit of free time in her schedule."

Once the curator had departed from his office, my father said in a hushed voice, "That was not a very promising conversation, I would say."

"He has given us some important clues, Watson," Joanna pointed out. "In particular, we must focus our attention on the randomly arranged dashes, for I believe they will tell us how and when he plans to send the three of us to our graves."

"But I had that in mind prior to our meeting with Sir David," said my father.

"As did I, but like the master code breaker advised, we must now direct *all* our efforts on those disarranged dashes, for therein is the specific information we must acquire in order to avoid a most unpleasant ending."

"Are you certain of those conclusions?"

"Not so much with the date as with the method of execution, and that is by far the most critical piece of knowledge we require."

"But the circle and crosses could somehow relate to the method of execution as well."

"I believe you are spot-on, Watson, for any symbol, even one of lesser consequence, might yet provide us with useful information. It is for that very reason that I have once again asked Miss Hudson to scour every inch of our storeroom in an effort to find my father's monograph on secret writings, in which he analyzed one hundred and sixty different ciphers."

"It could prove most helpful," my father concurred, as he recollected Sherlock Holmes's brilliant monograph on deciphering codes. He had never seen the treatise, but he had no reason to doubt his dear friend's word that it had been written and bound into a volume. In an earlier case which involved a most difficult code, we had imported Miss Hudson to search everywhere for the monograph, but unfortunately she was not successful.

Sir David returned and gestured for us to follow him. "Margaret would be delighted to meet with you, for she knows of your adventures as chronicled by your husband."

"Excellent," said Joanna, obviously pleased. "I am most eager to meet with her as well, for her knowledge of Ming vases may prove to be invaluable."

"This way, then, but be forewarned that her sharp brain is equally matched by a sharp tongue."

Sir David ushered us down the corridor to a corner office which was considerably larger than his. Most of the space was taken up by a long, rectangular table upon which rested scattered, broken pieces of blue-and-white porcelain. The woman behind the makeshift desk was quite small, no more than five feet in height, with a slender frame and gray-brown hair that was severely pulled back into a tight bun. Her sharp features and thin lips gave her a rather stern look, but her voice was most welcoming.

"So I have the honor of meeting the daughter of Sherlock Holmes and her colleagues, the Watsons," said she, waving us to the far side of the table where we would stand, for there were no chairs in the office.

"You do indeed," replied Joanna.

"I should tell you first off that I hold detectives in the highest regard and had done so long before I heard of you and your esteemed father," Margaret Howe went on. "Did you know there was a detective in ancient China who was revered and acclaimed, much like dear Sherlock?"

"Tell me more," Joanna requested, her interest piqued.

"His name was Judge Dee, a magistrate and statesman of the Tang court. He was quite upright and shrewd, and seemed capable of solving the most difficult criminal cases. However, Judge Dee tended to deal in the supernatural, which I suspect Sherlock Holmes would find most unappealing."

"He had no truck with ghosts and witchcraft," my father volunteered.

"Nor do I," asserted the curator. "Well then, let us proceed to business."

Sir David turned for the door, saying, "I must excuse myself, for I have important matters to attend to."

"What? Has Mesopotamia suddenly arisen from the desert sand?" she asked playfully.

"Only in my dreams," Sir David replied as he departed, closing the door behind him.

Margaret Howe smiled to herself, clearly fond of Sir David, then returned her attention to the artifacts on the table. She reached for a broken piece of porcelain and moved it next to another piece, then gently pushed the two together into a good fit. "I take it you are here regarding the theft of the Ming dynasty vase from the Fairmont," said she, attempting unsuccessfully to match two additional pieces.

"How did you come to that conclusion?" Joanna asked.

"Oh, simple detective work," she replied. "David told me of your interest in the Ming dynasty collection and I have read in the newspapers of your involvement in the penthouse robberies. Two plus two still equals four, even to an antiquated curator who spends most of her time trying to construct a badly shattered vase."

"Your reconstruction seems to be coming along nicely."

The curator shrugged. "Some days are better than others, but I push on, for this particular vase originates from the first period of the Ming dynasty, which renders it immensely valuable. This vase in pristine condition would bring in excess of one hundred thousand pounds at auction."

"And what value would you assign to the vase stolen from the Fairmont?"

"Being it, too, is from the first period, it would fetch a similar amount."

"Pray tell what makes such vases so valuable?"

"Their rarity, together with their magnificent artwork and exquisite coloring," Margaret described. "Even with modern technology, the blue color cannot be reproduced."

"Are all Ming vases blue?"

"They come in four colors—blue, green, red, and white. But the blue is the most sought after and often the most expensive."

My father leaned in to carefully inspect a piece of blue porcelain, then asked, "Is there some special feature to blue pigment?"

"All the colors tend to hold up well, but particularly the blue," Margaret detailed. "It was produced by painting cobalt oxide from Central Asia into the porcelain, then covering it with a glaze called Yingqing. The end result was a dazzling, brilliant blue. You might be interested to know that the stolen Ming vase was noted for its stunning blue color, which had not lost its luster despite the passage of many centuries."

"So it appears you have heard of this porcelain vase," said Joanna.

"Not until its theft from the Fairmont."

"But the articles in the newspapers did not describe its unusual features."

The curator hesitated, as if to choose her next words. "I heard it from another source."

"The black market, then," Joanna stated in a nonaccusatory tone. "Which is the reason for our visit."

"I assure you I am in no way involved in the theft," Margaret said defensively.

"I am certain you are not," Joanna went on. "Nevertheless, experts in various forms of art often hear rumors or even gossip of a unique work of art that is being offered up for sale in dark places."

"That does occur on occasion," Margaret admitted.

"And on occasion, experts are called in to verify the authenticity of the item."

"I have never been asked to do so, and if asked I would never consent."

"But I think you are aware of a particular art dealer who has done so in the past and would do so again."

Margaret hesitated once more, longer this time, as she pondered the appropriate response to give. "I have never been associated with this individual, nor am I certain that he is the one you are seeking."

"His name," Joanna insisted.

"Oliver Anders."

"I need details on the man and his background."

"He comes from an aristocratic family of considerable wealth, so why he involves himself in this sordid business is beyond me. On the surface he is respectable in every regard, with a thriving antique business which deals primarily in Oriental art. That being the case, it is said by some that he plays both sides of the street, not only providing an expert opinion on the authenticity of an item, but also a list of clients who would be interested in and capable of purchasing the item in question."

"He is a bit of a rogue, then."

"Let us say his principles are not of the highest value, but he nonetheless is a most fascinating character, with some rather unusual features."

"Such as?"

"He is a most superstitious fellow that at times brings chuckles from his colleagues," Margaret replied, pausing to allow a smile to come and go from her face. "Every day without fail he strolls from his gallery near Trafalgar Square to St. James's Park, where he feeds the swans, but will not do so unless at least one of the flock is black. Would you care to hear the story behind this superstition?"

"Indeed I would."

"It seems that some years ago Oliver's gallery had taken a severe downturn, with bankruptcy close and creditors banging on his door. Well then, one afternoon following lunch he walked over to St. James's Park and, using bread crumbs, decided to feed the swans from the shore of its magnificent lake. Apparently, the collection of birds included both black and white ones. In any event, when Oliver returned to his gallery he was met by two customers who purchased some very expensive items. Dear Oliver wondered if the feeding of the swans had brought him good fortune, so he strolled back to St. James's Park the following day to feed the colorful swans again, and lo and behold on returning to the gallery he found a group of wealthy American tourists who were eager to buy ancient artifacts. Thus, he was absolutely convinced that the swans were his good-luck charms, and the superstition was born."

"As with most superstitious individuals, does he follow the exact same regimen on each visit?"

"To the very letter, in that the swans must be both white and black, and must be fed from the same location near the Blue Bridge over the lake. If that particular spot is taken by a visitor, Oliver will wait until it is vacated."

"So this superstition must be working quite well for him."

Margaret nodded her answer. "According to those who know Oliver best, his gallery continues to thrive, which begs the question why such a successful dealer would resort to such sordid activity."

"Greed," Joanna answered simply.

"No doubt, for I have heard his fees are often enormous and must be paid promptly when the stolen item is put up for sale."

"Does he receive a commission for his efforts regardless of whether the sale is completed?"

"All those who are involved do so, but the payment is well concealed."

"How so?"

"Rather than cash, the individual will sell a mediocre work of art to an undisclosed buyer at a grossly inflated price. The dealer's commission is thus hidden with the purchase."

"Very clever."

"Indeed." The curator returned her attention to the artifacts on the long, rectangular table and began moving selected pieces of blue-colored porcelain toward one another. "I trust my name will not be mentioned as a source of this information."

"You need not be concerned," Joanna responded, reaching for the doorknob. "For to the best of my recollection, this conversation never took place."

Chapter Thirteen

The Widow

We waited an additional day before visiting Allenby House, an impressive redbrick building that was situated in a nicely wooded area of West Surrey. It was surrounded by an expansive green lawn which had kept its color despite the onset of winter weather. As we rode up to the main entrance, we were greeted with waves from children in wheelchairs, most of whom were being attended to by uniformed caregivers. Alighting from our taxi, we could clearly see the terrible effects of the diseases the little ones were afflicted with. Most striking were those with cerebral palsy, whose spastic muscles bent their extremities and bodies into contorted forms. Others, with normal physiques, were obviously mentally deficient and made high-pitched sounds as we approached.

At the reception desk we were given directions to the visitors' room, which was located at the end of a long corridor. As we passed multiple closed doors, again the high-pitched sounds with no apparent meaning came to us. I could only hope they were not the pitiful cries of distress.

Nearing the door to the visitors' room, Joanna warned us in a hushed voice, "We must be careful here and in no way indicate that we are aware of her husband's involvement."

"What if she brings up the possibility?" I whispered back.

"She will not, for widows go to great ends to protect the good names of their deceased husbands."

"But what if she herself is involved?"

"We will find that out soon enough."

Joanna quietly opened the door and led the way into a small, windowless room, with comfortable but weathered furniture.

Seated at a round, polished table with a vase of flowers atop it was a stunningly attractive woman, with straight blond hair that fell directly to her shoulders without a strand being out of place. She had distinctly Teutonic features, with a pale complexion, narrow nose, and deep blue eyes that were reddened from grief. Beside her in a large pram was a cyanotic toddler, who stared out into space and seemed unaware of our presence.

After the introductions, Anika Hopkins began to gently rock the pram, which brought forth a sound of happiness from the child. "My little boy suffers from a congenital heart defect, which accounts for his blue coloring," she explained. "His circulating blood does not carry enough oxygen, and this worsens his already severe mental deficiency. He never causes trouble, for my dear son is a good boy, and will not interfere with your questioning."

"This must be a most difficult time for you," Joanna said in a sympathetic tone.

"I shall manage," Anika replied softly.

"I am certain you will," Joanna encouraged. "Has the hotel offered you any assistance?"

"Not as yet."

"Perhaps they will be generous for your husband's long and devoted service."

"Let us hope."

The toddler next to her began to utter a sound of discomfort, his tiny arms now flailing about. His mother once again gently rocked the pram and murmured a reassuring, "Shhh, shhh."

I could not help but study the young child who exhibited the classic signs of a severe heart defect. His skin color was deeply cyanotic and there was bulbous enlargement at the ends of his fingers, all of which were the result of chronically low blood levels of oxygen. And his respirations were far too rapid as he attempted to compensate for his obvious hypoxia. Death would not be long in coming.

The toddler finally quieted and Anika brought her attention back to Joanna. "It was kind of you to inquire about our financial status, but I believe we can make do with my husband's recent inheritance."

Joanna feigned surprise. "I take it the inheritance was sizable, was it not?"

Anika narrowed her eyes suspiciously. "May I inquire why you are investigating this aspect of Richard's life?"

"We must unfortunately look into the financial status of all unexplained suicides, for overwhelming debt can drive an individual to such an unpleasant end."

"That certainly was not the case with my dear Richard, for the inheritance was so generous it allowed us to establish a trust fund which ensures that our young Scotty will always be cared for."

"Will there be enough to attend to your needs as well?"

"Quite, for in addition to the money we received, there will be more to come from the sale of yet another valuable asset."

"I hope you yourself will not be burdened with the task of selling this asset during this most difficult time."

"Oh, no, for the ancient vase remains in Switzerland, where it will be sold at auction, with Richard's share being transferred to our account at Lloyd's of London."

"Perhaps it would be wise for you to hire an appraiser to examine the item, so you will be confident of its true worth."

"Richard had considered having that done, for we know so little about Oriental vases, but we were assured that the auction house in Geneva was most reputable."

"That should give you some comfort, for such antiques can vary a great deal in value," Joanna remarked, knowing full well that no such vase existed. "You would surely wish to protect your additional and no doubt substantial return."

"I am afraid it may not be substantial, for Richard's share

of the sale is only ten percent," Anika corrected. "But it might nonetheless add nicely to my son's trust fund."

"Let us pray it does," said Joanna, squinting an eye as if puzzled. "You mentioned the auction would take place in Geneva. Why there rather than London?"

"Because Richard's uncle resided in Switzerland for a good many years and that is where his estate will be settled."

"Well, in any event, I am pleased to hear that you and your little boy will have a secure future, thanks to the generosity of a kind uncle," said Joanna. "I take it that your husband and his uncle were close."

"That is the strange part of this totally unexpected inheritance," Anika replied. "For Richard had no knowledge of a wealthy, long-lost uncle."

"Had he never heard of him?"

"Never."

"Well, good fortune can come in many different forms."

"As Richard can attest—" The widow stopped in mid-sentence to correct herself. "As Richard would have attested to."

"It will require time for your husband's passing to truly set in," Joanna empathized. "For I, too, lost a husband early in our marriage, and was left alone with a baby boy."

"How long does the terrible grief last?"

"Until the great pain begins to subside."

Anika nodded sadly. "It is by far the greatest pain I have ever endured."

"It will pass," Joanna said comfortingly, and reached over to touch the widow's hand before changing the subject. "I notice from your pronunciation of the word *greatest* that you must be from South Africa. Is that assumption correct?"

"It is, for I was born and grew up in a suburb outside Johannesburg."

"And what brought you to London?"

"I wished to train as a pediatric nurse and was fortunate enough to find myself a position at the Hospital for Sick Children."

"Do you have family in London who could come to your assistance at this dreadful time?"

"There is no one living here, but I do have a stepbrother from Johannesburg who is currently visiting London and of whom I am quite fond," Anika said, her mood brightening somewhat. "He holds a most important position there, as head of security for the Governor-General."

"Oh, yes, Major Eric Von Ruden, a most impressive man I met while investigating the theft of the blue diamond," Joanna recounted, keeping the surprise out of her voice. "He is proving to be very helpful to Scotland Yard as they delve into this mystery."

"He has been most consoling to me, for he is kind of heart as well."

"So it would appear that you and your stepbrother are close."

"Quite so."

"Was he also close with your husband?"

"Indeed he was, for Eric served as best man at our wedding."

Joanna nodded slowly at the new information, measuring her next words before saying, "He must have been genuinely moved by your husband's death."

"He took it badly, although one would never know it, for dear Eric rarely shows emotion," said Anika. "I suspect that stoic demeanor comes with his profession. Yet Dolphie nearly came to tears on hearing the news."

"Dolphie?" Joanna asked. "I am unfamiliar with that name."

"Oh, surely you met him, for he is Eric's most competent deputy and carries the rank of lieutenant."

A faint smile crossed Joanna's face as the recollection came to her. "You are referring to Adolph Smits, whom I encountered briefly."

"He is called Dolphie by his friends, which is a rather large group that included Richard and myself."

"Close, were they?"

"Close enough for him to serve as a groomsman at our wedding."

Joanna leaned back and tapped her fingers together as she attempted to assemble all of the new information into a coherent picture. I suspected that the same question was at the forefront of both our thoughts, and this turned out to be the case. "With London and Johannesburg being so distant from one another, how did your husband establish such a close friendship with Major Von Ruden and his top lieutenant?"

"Richard served as hotel manager at the Dorchester in Johannesburg for several years before coming to the Windsor," she replied. "It was there and then we met, and he eventually became acquainted with Eric and Dolphie. My husband and Dolphie became the best of friends, for both had a deep interest in sports and, upon their retirement, planned to open a sports equipment shop. They had even chosen a location for their venture, and they would supply it with goods for rugby and football and various mountain activities."

Joanna leaned forward to ask, "Mountain activities such as hiking and skiing?"

"Of course, but mainly for climbing, for both were climbing enthusiasts and took to the slopes as often as possible."

The stunned expression on our faces obviously unsettled Anika Hopkins, for she quickly asked, "Have I mentioned something untoward?"

Joanna recovered from the startling information far more rapidly than I or my father, for she managed to show a look of disbelief and said, "I had no idea that there were mountains in South Africa that would attract climbers."

For the first time a hint of a smile came to Anika Hopkins's face. "Most people have that impression, but two hundred and fifty miles south of Johannesburg is the Drakensberg range, which has mountains that reach heights of over ten thousand feet. Dolphie is truly an expert climber and has reached those peaks on a number of occasions. Richard, on the other hand, was only a beginner when he received the offer to come to London and manage the Windsor."

"Did your husband actually attempt to scale such a high peak?"

"Oh, no, for that would be far too dangerous. He was satisfied to climb much smaller mountains, but always under Dolphie's guidance of course."

"Does Dolphie continue to climb?"

"Quite often, for I am told he will shortly journey to Kenya to scale Mount Kilimanjaro, whose summit approaches twenty thousand feet."

"With his move to London, did your husband continue to climb?"

"His interest remained, but the time required and the cost of such ventures were too steep for our current status in life," Anika replied. "But I believe he truly yearned to return to the heights, for he kept all of his climbing equipment in excellent condition."

"Fully equipped, was he?"

"Very much so, for our storage room was filled with neatly placed harnesses, ropes, and a goodly supply of pitons." A sudden thought appeared to come to the widow, for she nodded absently to herself. "I suspect that Dolphie would very much like to have Richard's climbing items, perhaps as mementos of their times together."

"I am certain he would."

Anika stared at Joanna, as a wary expression came to her. "Why all these questions about my husband? Had he done something wrong?"

"Not to our knowledge," Joanna lied convincingly. "But Scotland Yard leaves no stone unturned when it comes to totally unexpected deaths, particularly when the individual was the manager of a famous hotel where two sensational robberies had occurred. Of course the note he left behind indicated there was some unbearable event which caused him to take his own life. Might you be of help in that regard?"

"I have no idea, for he lived an upright and honorable life, and there are many who would vouch for him in that regard."

"That is good to know," said Joanna. "And you should carry that comforting memory with you always."

"I will, and thank you for those kind words."

"And you no doubt are beginning to think of the future, are you not?"

"Everything is so much in flux," said she, with her voice cracking for the first time.

Her child began to cry once again, as if he could sense his mother's deep sorrow. Anika gently rocked the pram and waited for the toddler to quiet. "Perhaps we will return to South Africa."

"That may be a wise decision," said Joanna. "Whatever road you decide to take, our best wishes go with you."

"Thank you again for your kindness."

As we departed, I could not help but gaze back at the grieving widow patiently rocking the pram of her terribly ill little boy whose life was to be so short. A mother's love has an endless depth, thought I, looking away from the tragic scene.

Stepping out of the entrance to Allenby House, Joanna commented sotto voce, "I had no idea that mountain climbing was such a favorite among South Africans."

"Of particular interest was the fine collection of climbing equipment that was being maintained by Richard Hopkins," I noted quietly. "It would have presented no problem for him to take his personal paraphernalia and place the items in the maintenance closet for use by the imposters who registered as representatives of the Swiss jewelers."

"Hopkins may have actually done some of the climbing himself," my father ventured.

"I think that most unlikely," Joanna said. "Better to have an expert do the deed rather than an amateur, for the inexperienced climber could make a costly mistake, particularly in the darkness."

"So it *had* to be imposters who made the ascent," I asserted.

"Or someone capable of scaling Mount Kilimanjaro."

A bell sounded loudly, and virtually all the wheelchairs and ambulatory patients turned for the entrance to Allenby House. Many of them had happy smiles on their faces, suggesting the bell signaled the time to gather for lunch. One mentally handicapped youngster was clapping his hands at the prospect of the upcoming repast.

We strolled across a well-manicured lawn, and headed toward a heavily wooded area that formed the easternmost boundary of the institution. The plentiful leaves on the trees as well as those on the ground were no longer green but rather the glorious autumnal colors of gold and orange. As we entered the woods, the temperature seemed to drop noticeably, bringing a chill to the air.

"So it would appear the entire venture was first conceived in Johannesburg, with the plan itself to be carried out in London," said Joanna, pulling up the collar of her coat. "You will recall that the blue diamond was discovered at the De Beers mine less than a year ago, with the Governor-General's journey to London being scheduled shortly after the discovery. Thus it was most likely then that Richard Hopkins was brought into the fold."

My father nodded at Joanna's conclusions. "Indeed, for only with Hopkins in place could the plan be set into motion."

"It was a well-designed crime, driven by greed, which they believed to be perfect," said I.

"'The best-laid plans of mice and men often go awry,'" Joanna quoted a line from the poem "To a Mouse" by Robert
Burns. "Although I suspect that it was not so much greed on
Hopkins's part, but rather a desire to make certain his little boy
would be well cared for after he and his wife were gone."

"But surely he knew the lad's life-span could now be measured in months," I thought aloud.

"Oh, he must have been told so by the doctors," said Joanna.
"But deep down he no doubt continued to hope for some sort of
miracle to occur."

"Much as his wife now believes that the child can survive the
sea journey to South Africa, which is far beyond wishful thinking," I added.

"Hope reigns eternal."

"But not in this—"

Our conversation was interrupted by a loud gunshot which
echoed through the forest. We were startled motionless for a moment before the old soldier in my father's blood took hold. He
hurriedly pushed us into a strand of thick trees which provided
excellent cover from all directions. In the stillness we pricked our
ears, but neither heard nor sensed the close passage of a bullet. Yet
we continued to wait in silence, listening intently for a second
sound or for the footsteps of the individual who fired the initial
shot. My father had his Webley revolver in hand and pointed at
the thickest portion of the woods. Another minute went by, with
the forest remaining eerily quiet. Then the second shot was fired,
and we breathed a sigh of relief, for the sound was that which
came from a shotgun, a weapon used by hunters and not assassins.

My father holstered his revolver, but kept his hand on its grip
in the event a rapid withdrawal was necessary. We moved slowly
through the thick foliage and came to a clearing where stood a
hunter appropriately attired in a shooting jacket and Wellington

boots. By his side was a medium-sized brown-and-white hound who eyed us carefully.

The hunter waved to us cordially with one hand, whilst the other held the shotgun that was broken open, with its barrels pointing downward and clearly free of cartridges. Around his waist was a brace of grouse.

"Good hunting, eh?" my father called out.

"Can't grumble," the hunter replied. "Are you here visiting the Allenby House?"

"We are, for an acquaintance has a tiny lad who is a patient here."

"Rest assured he will be well looked after, for the Allenbys are most generous and most charitable."

The hunter went on to tell us how the Allenby family had established the institution in memory of a son who was born with multiple congenital abnormalities and required constant care. Not only did the family donate the land, but they built the facility itself, then placed it all in a charitable trust which provided for its long-term upkeep. "The Allenbys are loved and cherished by every man and woman in the district, and woe unto the individual who utters a bad word about them," he added, with great solemnity.

"Do you know the family?" asked my father.

"I do indeed and it is my honor to call them friends."

"So I take it they allow you to hunt?"

"They do, with the only restriction being that I limit myself to the hour between noon and one, when the little ones are having their lunch and will not be bothered by the occasional gunshot."

"The family seems most concerned with the comfort of the children."

"That, my dear sir, is an understatement."

"Well then, we shall be on our way and wish you good hunting."

"And a most pleasant day to you as well," the hunter responded, and, with a quick whistle to the hound, started across the open field.

We strolled back through the thick woods and did not speak until the Allenby House was again in sight. Even then, we spoke in low tones, with the three of us all thinking the same thought.

"A rather unnerving episode," said I. "We would have been such easy targets."

Joanna nodded at my assessment as she signaled to our taxi, waiting at the front entrance to the institution. "That was a most unpleasant reminder of the ease with which a skilled assassin could have silently approached us and gone about his business."

"We were easy targets indeed," my father remarked. "A high-powered rifle, holding a clip with multiple rounds, could have taken the three of us out in short order."

"We must be more cautious and avoid being seen in the open," Joanna warned. "But we cannot allow ourselves to be forced into seclusion, for we must continue our investigation regardless of the risk if we hope to survive."

"Which only increases the urgency to decode the assassin's note," said my father. "It is for this reason that I contacted Sir David this morning in hopes of receiving a bit of optimism. Unfortunately, the code remains undecipherable, even to the eye of a renowned expert."

"Were there any hints whatsoever?" I asked.

"Only that the symbols of mixed, randomly arranged dashes were either a most complex code or a simple one."

"Which did he favor?"

"Both."

We strolled on, watching colorful birds take flight as slender squirrels searched for nuts to store up for the coming winter. An owl perched on a high branch peered down at us, no doubt sizing us up and wondering about our presence. But despite the welcoming bucolic scene, the threat of an assassin waiting for an opportune moment to strike continued to weigh heavily on our minds.

"Let us hope Miss Hudson can find Holmes's monograph on secret writings, for there may lie the esoteric answers to the code," said my father, breaking the silence.

"Did you ever see a page or two of the monograph while he was composing it?" Joanna asked.

"I did not, but I clearly recall the case which prompted him to write it," my father replied, and proceeded to describe the circumstances in detail.

Sherlock Holmes and my father were involved in an adventure which carried the name "The Dancing Men." It centered around a most difficult code which appeared to show figures of dancing men in various stances. Both Holmes and Sir David were baffled by it, although the Great Detective was later to decipher the code and that led to the resolution of the mystery.

"Are you certain the monograph was dedicated in large measure to symbols?" Joanna inquired.

"Oh, yes, for the figures of the dancing men absolutely fascinated Holmes and Sir David, for both at first wondered if the figures were related to those seen in Egyptian hieroglyphs, which of course was not the case."

"What did the dancing figures represent?"

"Letters, with the most commonly observed figure indicating an *e*, which is the most frequently used letter in the English alphabet. Then came *a* and *t* that were based on the same premise."

As my father concluded his past adventure with his dear friend and colleague, I detected a glint in his eye and so I asked, "Father, there must be times when you wish for Sherlock Holmes to reappear, such as he did after his purported death at the Reichenbach Falls?"

"I do indeed, but then I am comforted by the fact that Holmes left behind a most wise daughter to take his place."

A half smile crossed Joanna's face, but it quickly faded. "Thank you for the well-meant compliment, but the solution to this complex case continues to elude the ever-wise mind you have attributed to me. At this point the only certainty we have is that Richard Hopkins was involved and a necessary component in the theft."

"Do you not hold him in large measure responsible?" said I.

"Richard Hopkins was in all likelihood a pawn, much as were the climbers posing as jewelers," Joanna replied, watching the taxi approach. "It is the mastermind who controlled him that must be uncovered and dealt with."

"What makes you so confident that there is a mastermind at the helm?" my father inquired.

"Because it is apparent that a most clever individual is pulling a variety of strings in a coordinated fashion," replied Joanna. "Thus he has to be very familiar with those strings."

"Which points the finger of guilt at someone very near the inner circle," my father concluded.

"Oh, there is more to it than that, Watson."

My father gave the matter considerable thought, but had no answer.

"You must think in terms of the blue diamond theft, in which success depended on detailed knowledge of the Governor-General's schedule."

My father's eyes abruptly widened. "It must be a member of his entourage."

"Obviously," said she, as the taxi driver opened a rear door for us.

CHAPTER FOURTEEN

Sherlock's Monograph

On our return to 221b Baker Street we found Miss Hudson standing amongst stacks of dust-covered boxes in the hall outside our storeroom. She had her hands on her hips, and a most determined expression on her face.

"No luck, then?" my father asked.

"None thus far, Dr. Watson, but if the monograph you described exists, I shall find it," said she.

"I am certain you will," my father encouraged.

"Do you by chance recall its cover?"

"I do not, but you will recognize it, for within its pages will be a strange set of symbols and markings."

"Such as the markings in the great pyramids in Egypt?"

"Quite similar, I would think."

"I shall look for that in particular."

"Please give it your best effort, for much depends on the monograph."

"I will not rest until I find it," Miss Hudson vowed. "I can, however, take a moment to prepare a kettle, if you would like."

"Perhaps later," my father refused gently. "But do carry on."

We waited for Miss Hudson to march back to her appointed task, then entered our parlor and went straightaway to work on the code. Joanna quickly wetted a cloth and cleared the standing blackboard, and with white chalk copied the coded message on the board, leaving generous spaces between the lines for our interpretations.

221b Baker Street

+O +++

"I notice that you have included the first line of the message," my father commented. "But surely we already know its meaning, in that it informs the assassin of our address."

"Perhaps it means more," Joanna suggested.

"Such as?"

"Such as the place where our executions are to take place."

"With a rifle shot through the window, then?"

"That method would be most unlikely, for our drawn curtains show just a narrow opening and at best he could dispatch only one of us with a high-powered round."

My father pondered our presumptive executions at length before asking, "Do you have any idea how the assassin plans to go about this dastardly act?"

"The answer lies in the following two lines," Joanna responded, and pointed to the second line of the code. "Let us first focus on the closed but empty circle, for therein is the key to the multiple crosses. Although we came up with a plausible meaning earlier, I am not convinced it truly signifies burial without markers. That is simply one possibility and far from being a certainty."

"But surely the crosses are grave markers for the three of us," said I.

"But why is there a fourth cross preceding the circle?" Joanna queried. "And what is the significance of it being separated from the other crosses?"

"Perhaps it has no meaning and is meant to distract us," I proposed.

Joanna shook her head at my proposal. "That circle somehow

connects the crosses to one another and until we understand its meaning we cannot decipher the second line."

"Nevertheless, your notion that it tells the assassin to dispose of our bodies in a manner that ensures they are never found is clever enough to be worthy of consideration," said my father. "I can see the headlines in the newspapers shouting to their readers, 'Search for Sherlock's Daughter Continues.'"

"I have not discarded that possibility altogether, but the mechanisms for performing such a disappearance are truly difficult. Our assassin not only has to kill us, but somehow collect the bodies and transport them to an undisclosed location where they will remain hidden for all time. That is quite a formidable task, I should think." Joanna waved away that consideration before walking over to the Persian slipper and extracting a Turkish cigarette. She lighted it with care, then proceeded to pace the floor of our parlor, occasionally stealing a glance at the blackboard whilst muttering, "The circle, the circle carries an important clue."

Our collective thoughts were interrupted by a sharp rap on the door, which opened widely and allowed a proud Miss Hudson to enter with a dust-covered book that she raised up high for us to see.

"I discovered it in the very last box atop a folder entitled 'The Dancing Men.'"

"Well done, Miss Hudson!" exclaimed my father.

"It is always a pleasure to be of service," she replied as a blush came to her face.

"Did you peer inside it?"

"I did indeed, Dr. Watson, for my curiosity took hold of me and I wanted to determine if it contained the symbols that you described."

"And?"

"There were a number of pages with the most unusual figures

from top to bottom," Miss Hudson replied. "Why, the dancing men by themselves took up an entire page."

"Spot-on!" My father hurried over for the monograph and after a quick study made a request to the landlady. "Perhaps now, Miss Hudson, would be a most excellent time for a fresh kettle of your fine tea."

"I shall see to it," said she, departing and closing the door behind her.

My father placed the monograph on our workbench and motioned to Joanna. "You should do the honors, my dear, since these very pages were the singular work of your esteemed father."

The monograph brought about a totally unexpected response from Joanna. She approached the book with a look of obvious reverence, for here was an item her father not only wrote, but whose pages he no doubt touched on numerous occasions. And the thought must have crossed her mind that the Great Detective had, in a manner of speaking, appeared one final time to assist the daughter he had never met.

On her opening the monograph, Joanna's face returned to its usual neutral expression, for the detective in her had again come to the forefront. Slowly she began turning pages whilst my father and I eagerly peered over her shoulder. The initial sections were dedicated to cryptograms which consisted of letters and numbers, and how each could be used to decipher or construct a code. We next came to the pages designated solely to symbols, which appropriately enough began with the dancing men. There were three long rows of figures that showed men in various dancing positions. Below each was a letter of the alphabet that each individual figure represented.

"Such a difficult code," Joanna remarked.

"Which delighted your father and required several days of study to decipher," my father recalled. "Yet to Holmes it was not some great accomplishment, but merely a complex puzzle that needed to be understood if the case was to be brought to resolution."

"The messages must have been quite long to allow for such decoding," Joanna commented.

My father shook his head. "As a matter of fact, they were rather short, but there was a goodly number of them which arrived over the course of several days. Holmes had to compile all of them for study, and that was why the answer did not come to him immediately."

Joanna turned to the following page that contained rows of squares and triangles, some of which were empty, whilst others possessed single dots and dashes in their centers. Their meanings varied from pain to anatomical parts to war, with a few noted to be of Aztec or Egyptian origins. Nowhere to be seen was a cluster of randomly placed dashes, which comprised the third section of the assassin's note.

As we proceeded to the next page, Joanna cried out with delight, "Ah, circles!"

Before us was a list of a dozen or more circles, each with a concise definition beside it. The ones with dots in their midst signified a group or gathering, with the number of dots indicating relative size. The circles devoid of markings designated eternity or under some circumstances a void. We were more than a little disappointed, for none fit or offered an explanation of the circle surrounded by crosses.

On the succeeding page was the final listing of circles. One showed multiple dashes radiating from its surface that could be interpreted as being central or most important. The very last line showed a circle with a small cross at its very bottom:

"It has some semblance to the circle in the assassin's note, but it is upright and not nearly close enough to be of relevance," my father remarked, and adjusted his reading spectacles. "What meaning did Holmes attribute it to?"

"'It is a symbol used by geneticists to indicate the female gender,'" Joanna read aloud from the small print.

"That offers us little information," said I dispiritedly.

"To the contrary, John, it unlocks the mystery of the second line," Joanna informed us, rubbing her hands together at the revelation.

"How so?"

"You are studying the symbol in its upright, vertical position," she elucidated. "Lay it on its side and tell me what you see."

I did and immediately blurted out, "A female lying in repose!"

"Yes, and that female represents the daughter of Sherlock Holmes lying quite dead," said my wife. "Thus the second line of the assassin's instructions denotes me as the primary target, with you two to follow. This explains the rather clever yet simple code of a circle with three crosses attached."

"By Jove, Joanna! I believe you have it," my father lauded warmly.

"But what I do not have is the method by which we are to be dispatched."

There was a loud rap on the door and Miss Hudson hurriedly entered, but without the kettle of tea she had promised. "I have discovered an unusual package at the tradesman entrance," she reported in a rush. "Perhaps you should have a look at it."

"Most assuredly," replied Joanna, and dashed out of the parlor, with my father and me only a step behind.

We raced down the stairs two by two, asking for information as we went. The question which immediately went through my mind was how could a delivery meant to be opened by Miss Hudson carry a deadly threat to the Watsons? I could not come up with an answer, but the expression on Joanna's face told me she could.

"What was so unusual about the package?" asked Joanna.

"That it came with a thick string around it," Miss Hudson replied.

"Do you have any idea as to its source?"

"I was expecting a delivery of beef since our supply is quite low, but I do not ever recall it being fastened with a tight, thick string."

"I take it you were not present when the delivery was made."

"I was not, which makes me believe it came while I was searching for Mr. Holmes's lost monograph."

"And who as a rule makes the delivery?"

"Eddie, the son of our butcher, who is always quite prompt and would not be expected to leave the delivery on the doorstep."

We hurried into the kitchen, where I opened the window to the alleyway and gazed out at a cardboard box, measuring approximately two by two feet, that rested on our doorstep. It had no markings or attached sales slips, and was tightly secured by a thick string. I came back to Joanna and my father to describe the box in detail.

"Was the string confined to the box or did it extend to the door?" asked Joanna.

"There was no attachment to the door," I replied.

"And no other object near it?"

"None."

With that information, Joanna slowly opened the door and studied the well-secured box at length before lifting it and bringing it to the kitchen's cutting board.

"A long knife, if you please, Miss Hudson," she requested.

Our landlady reached for a knife of considerable length and, after handing it to my wife, stepped back behind her. "What do you believe is in the box?" Miss Hudson asked nervously.

"That is what we are about to determine," said Joanna. "Now, all stand away in the event there is a spring-loaded weapon of some sort which suddenly jumps out from the opening. And if you hear a hissing sound, run from the room as fast as you possibly can."

The three of us backed away, and inched ourselves closer to the kitchen door, with our ears pricked for an unusual sound.

With care, Joanna sliced through the tight binding and watched the folding edges of the box fall harmlessly aside. Using the knife and keeping her distance, she reached into the box and removed several layers of wrapping. The aroma of freshly cut beef began to fill the air.

"A false alarm," Joanna stated, after peering into the container.

"It is still possible that the assassin tampered with the package, which was left unattended," my father suggested. "Perhaps he left a hidden calling card in the form of a deadly poison within the beef."

"The very same thought crossed my mind, Watson, but I think it most unlikely because of several findings," said Joanna, and turned to our landlady. "Tell me, Miss Hudson, to the best of your knowledge was our butcher ever a seafarer?"

"In his younger days he was," she replied immediately. "According to Eddie, his father served in the Royal Navy and was discharged early after suffering a serious knee injury. But how in the world could you have possibly known that?"

"By the knot in the string which secured the package," Joanna answered. "It is called a bowline knot and has been used for centuries by seafarers, for it's easy to tie, yet quite secure when placed under tension."

I nodded at the obvious conclusion. "Thus, had the assassin opened the knot, it is highly unlikely he retied it with a bowline knot unless he was a seafarer, which we can reasonably assume he was not."

Joanna nodded back at my assessment. "In addition, you will note that the large order of beef remains precisely sectioned into portions by sheets of paper, as one would expect from an experienced butcher, but not from an assassin poisoning all the slices."

"All good points," my father agreed. "But an expert assassin might be clever enough to cover all these tracks."

"That, too, crossed my mind, and thus I think it wise to discard the beef, which will rid us of any worry."

"I can prepare a nice lamb roast with mint sauce in its stead," Miss Hudson offered.

"Excellent," Joanna approved. "We shall look forward to it."

"I am so sorry to have needlessly frightened you," Miss Hudson apologized.

"Not at all, dear lady, for your action was indeed appropriate and you should be commended for it," Joanna praised. "Please continue to be vigilant, for the danger is very real."

We ascended the stairs slowly and quietly, relieved that the threat turned out to be imaginary. But it was also a reminder that literally every step of our existence was at risk, and that even our secured rooms offered limited protection. I could not help but wonder if we should reconsider Commissioner Bradberry's recommendation that a constable be placed at our doorstep around the clock. I decided to bring forth the idea when our nerves were more settled.

As we entered our parlor, my father asked a question which was also on my mind. "Joanna, have you ever encountered a spring-loaded knife?"

"Only in my reading," she replied. "But I place that form of weaponry far down the list of possibilities, for it would injure or dispatch only one of us, which is not the manner with which an assassin would go about his work. Killing just one, you see, heightens the alertness of those remaining. Our assassin has been instructed to do the three of us in simultaneously, which I believe is the reason the three crosses are so close together in the code."

"Was the hissing sound you mentioned in the kitchen meant to serve that purpose?" I asked.

"It was and again I learned of it from my reading," Joanna answered, then went on to describe how a madman in Rome had sent a large, unexpected gift to an individual who had dishonored the sender's mother and father to such an extent that they had taken their own lives. The present was concealed in a tightly secured box that was delivered to the family of the man who had brought so much pain to the sender. When the box was opened, a needle punctured a balloon within and a thick vapor of deadly cyanide gas was released, killing all those nearby instantly. And so the aggrieved man had taken his vengeance, for which he was hanged, reportedly with a smile on his face.

"But how could the assassin have known we would gather around the box when it was delivered?" my father inquired. "It could just as well have been opened by Miss Hudson alone in her kitchen."

"It is best not to underestimate how clever our assassin may be," Joanna advised. "For he would rightly assume that an unmarked box delivered to our doorstep would arouse the interest and suspicion of the entire household. Thus the three of us would open the box carefully no doubt, but anyone within feet of it would end up very dead."

"But disposing of our bodies would be no simple matter," I interjected. "And that, too, is an integral part of his plan."

"That would present no difficulty to the assassin," Joanna countered easily. "He could continue to surveil our rooms, watching for any signs of activity or perhaps for delivered goods to pile up at the tradesman entrance. He could then break into the kitchen, find the bodies, and arrange for a large lorry to back into the alleyway and fetch the remains."

My father sighed resignedly. "Can he be that clever?"

"Oh, yes, and that resourceful," she noted. "For example, where pray tell do you believe he might have come up with the idea for a punctured balloon releasing deadly cyanide gas?"

"Probably from the same article you read about the murderer in Rome."

"Or he himself may have invented a similar device and used it before," Joanna proposed. "Again, we should not underestimate this assassin, for we are involved in a high-stakes game and our thieves will be willing to pay for the very best of assassins."

"Who continues to have the advantage," my father grumbled. "And we seem no closer to evening the playing field."

"Which is why we must devote all of our attention to the third section of the assassin's note," Joanna said, and moved in nearer to the blackboard, with the entire coded message written in enlarged form. Pointing with a stick of chalk to the cluster of dashes, she counted off their number, which was fifteen in all. "Here again is the most—"

A shrill whistle sounded outside, which caused a chill to run up and down our collective spines. We raced to the window and, parting the curtains, watched a constable passing by on a bicycle as he shouted loudly, "Take cover! Take cover!" It was an immediate warning that German bombers were approaching, now no more than minutes away. Reaching for our topcoats, we dashed down the stairs and into Miss Hudson's kitchen, where large timbers had recently been installed to brace against explosions.

"Let us huddle close to the timbers, which will be the safest place," Miss Hudson directed, her voice calm despite the peril we were about to face.

We hurried to the reinforced wall and listened intently for the dull drone of overhead bombers, which had been absent for the past week because of foul weather, with heavy cloud cover. But today the skies cleared and were followed by a full-moon night, which gave the German pilots an unobstructed view of the entire city. Our ears remained pricked, but all they encountered was an eerie silence.

"Did you draw your curtains tightly?" Miss Hudson asked in a whisper.

"We did," Joanna replied. "And the fire in our hearth was barely more than a glow."

"Let us hope others followed suit."

Our landlady was referring to the measures necessary to bring about a complete blackout which concealed targets the German pilots were searching for. In every neighborhood curtains had to be drawn and fires reduced to a minimum or extinguished altogether, so they gave off little or no light. But blackouts were often to no avail, for the initial wave of bombers usually dropped incendiary bombs that caused massive fires which lighted up the city for the oncoming second wave. The silence continued and I wondered if we had time to sprint to the Baker Street Underground station, which was only blocks away and would provide the safest of shelters. But this notion was quickly rejected when I heard the thunder of far-off explosions. Then came the hum of bombers overhead and we pressed ourselves against the timbers, and waited for the hell that was sure to come.

The thunderous explosions grew closer and closer, which caused the oven and icebox to noisily rattle. Dishes and glasses fell to the floor and shattered into pieces. Joanna and I held on to each other tightly, wondering if these were to be our last moments together on earth. A split second later there was a deafening blast which shook the entire kitchen so violently that layers of plaster were torn from the ceiling and rained down on us. My ears were ringing as another bomb exploded and yet another, but the latter, although quite loud, seemed farther away. We waited anxiously for the explosions to be far off in the distance, and then waited even longer in the event there was to be a third wave of bombers.

Finally, we stood and, catching our breaths, turned on the lights, only to find the kitchen had a ghostlike appearance, with everything covered in a fine, white dust. Miss Hudson, ever the housekeeper, paused to sweep up the broken glass, then followed us out into the alleyway. We thankfully noted that the exterior of our building, as well as those structures surrounding us, had no apparent damage except for the one nearest ours that showed cracks in the masonry, some of which had fallen to the ground. As we gazed out into the distance, it appeared that half of London was ablaze, with flames spurting into the air like eruptions from volcanic mountains. The inferno was so intense it literally lighted up the landscape of the city. A truck from the Fire Brigade raced by, its bell clanging, which made me wonder how many had been killed in the raid and how many more were trapped helplessly beneath the burning rubble.

Miss Hudson stared out at the ghostly sight and said in a sharp voice, "We should give the bloody Huns a double dose of their own medicine."

"Which should be promptly delivered," my father added, as another truck from the Fire Brigade roared by.

CHAPTER FIFTEEN

St. James's Park

On our ride to St. James's Park, we were forced to take a circuitous route, for a number of streets along our way were deemed impassable because of bomb craters and stacks of rubble. As we drove by one house in particular, it reminded us of the stark realities of war. The front of the dwelling had been blown away, exposing all of its rooms, one of which was a library, with all its furniture in disarray and most of its books on the floor, although a few remained on their shelves. An elderly couple was picking through the ruins, attempting to salvage what little they could. The man was stunned, the woman crying.

Throughout our entire journey, Joanna repeatedly glanced back over her shoulder to make certain we were not being followed. Only when she was satisfied we were not under surveillance did she instruct the driver to turn off onto the Mall, a processional road that linked Buckingham Palace to Trafalgar Square. We continued on until the taxi was ordered to stop at the entrance to St. James's Park.

As we strolled through the tall, stately gates, I was once again impressed with the beauty of London's oldest royal park. It consisted of fifty-seven well-manicured areas of expansive lawn and trees too numerous to count, all of which seemed to be centered around a large lake, with water so calm a ripple could not be seen. Over the magnificent lake was the iron-span Blue Bridge, which offered visitors a spectacular view of Buckingham Palace. In the distance we could see a man standing near the bridge feeding a gathering of swans who announced their presence with loud, hoarse trumpets. They, like the individual handing out food, ignored our approach.

Drawing closer, we could clearly make out the individual stationed beside the iron-span overpass. He was a tall, slender man, with aristocratic features and golden-gray locks that curled at his collar. His dark suit, with its chalk stripes, was perfectly fitted and expensively tailored.

"Suppose he chooses not to see us?" whispered my father.

"He will not be given that option," Joanna whispered back.

My wife slowed the pace to steal a final glance at the lawn we had just traversed. "All seems clear."

"But surely the assassin would not carry out his plan at noon in a royal park crowded with visitors," my father noted.

"It is not the assassin I am concerned with at the moment, but those who may be watching Oliver Anders."

"Pray tell why would he be under surveillance?"

"Because he is a rogue whose associates might not consider him to be trustworthy," Joanna replied. "This is particularly so when there is a priceless Ming vase involved."

We approached Oliver Anders, who continued to pay us no notice, nor did the feasting swans, with their long necks gracefully curved into S's. As Margaret Howe had predicted, the flock of snowy white swans contained a few black ones as well.

"I require a moment of your time, Mr. Anders," Joanna introduced.

Oliver Anders quickly turned to us, obviously caught off-balance. He studied us carefully before saying, "I believe you have the advantage, madam."

"I am the daughter of Sherlock Holmes, and the two gentlemen by my side are the Watsons."

"I—ah—I," Anders stammered, his face losing color. He paused to audibly clear his throat and collect himself. "What may I ask is the purpose of this unannounced visit?"

"We require information," said Joanna simply.

Anders hesitated, weighing his response. "Perhaps I should contact my barrister."

"Feel free to do so, and have him meet with us in Inspector Lestrade's office at Scotland Yard, or if you prefer we can all gather at your gallery."

"I think it best we talk here," Anders said quickly, then dusted off his hands and waited for the swans to swim away. "What is this information you seek?"

"Everything you know about a very valuable Ming vase

which I believe you were called upon to certify its authenticity and estimate its worth."

"Is there a particular Ming vase you have in mind?"

"The one recently stolen from the Fairmont."

Anders stiffened noticeably, his lips moving but making no sound as he attempted to come up with a response which denied his involvement.

"Tell us all and we will no longer be of concern to you," Joanna said, then added a warning. "Withhold or fabricate your answers and I can assure you that you will find yourself being asked the very same questions in an interrogation room at Scotland Yard."

"I will not incriminate myself," Anders blurted out.

"Are you guilty of a crime?"

The art dealer hesitated once more before saying, "Not to my knowledge."

"Then let us proceed," said Joanna, taking a quick glance over her shoulder. "First, I need to know what makes Ming vases so valuable."

"Not all are," Anders said authoritatively. "It is those from the first Ming period which are so highly sought after."

"And which of their traits make them so desirable?"

"The smoothness of their surface, together with their pure whiteness and translucent quality," Anders replied, now clearly in his element.

"Their whiteness, you say?" Joanna quizzed. "I was under the impression that most Ming vases were entirely white, except for the colorful figures drawn on them."

"Allow me, madam, to give you a bit of history on the coloring of Ming vases," the art dealer chatted freely, as the worry left his face. It was one of Joanna's hidden talents to put an informant at ease by asking innocent questions directed at the individual's particular area of expertise. She believed it gave them the feeling of superiority, which was often untrue because she had studied the subject at length prior to their meeting. Anders waited for a strolling couple to pass by before speaking again. "The first Ming dynasty vases were often made of mixed blue-and-white porcelain, but as time went by and the Arab world became their primary clients, the pictures of carpets and textures became more numerous and colorful. Much later on, the vases returned to a rather complete white background, with delicate blue designs and lettering, and those have become the most desirable."

"I take it the Ming vase from the Fairmont was of the latter variety."

Anders nodded. "Of the very first quality, or so I am told."

"There is no need to play games, for the ground rules have been established and I will adhere to them," Joanna pledged. "With that in mind, let us return to the stolen Ming vase. I am informed that under most circumstances there is a predetermined buyer for such an item. And I was further told that such a buyer existed for this vase."

"He did exist, but unfortunately he was a member of the Russian royal family and, having been caught up in their revolution, was summarily executed by the Bolsheviks. Thus the vase now finds itself on the open market."

"The black market," Joanna corrected.

Anders remained silent, which for all intents and purposes was an affirmative response.

"Tell us how you went about the appraisal of the ill-gotten vase," Joanna pressed.

"I had no idea it was stolen," Anders insisted.

"Would you be willing to swear to that under oath?"

Anders again remained silent, but this time his response was an obvious *no*.

"You may as well be straight with us, for Mr. Freddie Morrison will either back up or refute your assertions."

All resistance left the art dealer, as his posture slouched noticeably at the mention of a syndicate boss known to deal in stolen art. Anders quickly glanced around and spoke in a hushed voice, like a man trying to conceal his guilt. "I drove to a hotel across the Thames where Mr. Morrison and one of his associates awaited me. The room was well lighted and they made no attempt to hide their identities. On a table in the center of the room was the magnificent Ming vase I just described to you."

"Was he satisfied with your estimate?"

"So it seemed."

"Were you paid for your services on the spot?"

Anders shook his head. "Other avenues of payment were arranged."

"And were later done satisfactorily?"

"Quite so," Anders replied before a look of concern crossed his face. "I trust you will not mention this meeting to Mr. Morrison."

"There will be no need," said Joanna, and gestured dismissively with her hand. "I believe our conversation has come to an end."

Oliver Anders gave the hastiest of nods and hurried off like a man escaping from certain danger.

"What do you think, Joanna?" asked my father.

"I think we are being followed, Watson," she responded in a most casual fashion, keeping her eyes fixed on us. "I thought I might have seen him earlier, but now I am certain."

"Do you believe he is the assassin?" my father asked at once.

"That is unlikely," Joanna replied. "This fellow is either not that skilled or he is making an obvious attempt to be seen."

My father reached into his jacket, his hand now on his Webley revolver. "If he begins to approach us, I shall confront him."

I quickly moved to the side of Joanna which blocked the watcher's view of my wife. "Please look over my shoulder and tell us how close he is now."

"Fifty yards or so," said she.

"Does he have anything in his hands?"

"Nothing."

My father eased the weapon about in his shoulder holster, saying, "Let me know if he makes a sudden move."

"He is walking toward us, with no attempt to conceal his presence," Joanna reported. "He appears to be taller than most, with no topcoat against the chill. His hands remain free by his sides. Now he is at twenty-five yards."

We waited, with the three of us on high alert, as the man came closer yet.

"Well, this is certainly a surprise," said Joanna. "For the man approaching us is Adolph Smits, the second-in-command of the South African security unit."

My father and I turned to watch the officer strolling toward us at a slow, steady pace. He kept his hands by his sides, but there was a definite bulge in the left front of his jacket, indicating he was armed. And his lack of a topcoat was to be expected, with his position as a trained security guard, for such a garment would interfere with a quick draw of his weapon.

"Good afternoon, Lieutenant Smits," Joanna greeted. "To what do we owe this honor?"

"I have information to share," said he in a neutral, unhurried tone.

"At the direction of your Major Von Ruden?"

"At the direction of your Commissioner Bradberry."

In an instant, the lieutenant had our complete and undivided attention. We stepped in closer yet so as not to miss a word.

"Let us move further away from those gathered on the Blue Bridge," Smits advised, turning his back to the structure.

"Certainly we cannot be overheard from that distance," my father remarked.

"Not by ears, but perhaps by a lip-reader with a set of bin-oculars."

Smits was showing himself to be a high-level security officer down to his marrow, thought I, remembering that someone assigned to protect the Governor-General had to be constantly on guard and could not afford to overlook even the most unlikely of possibilities. His actions also emphasized the importance of his message.

"Were you contacted by the commissioner himself?" asked Joanna.

"It was I who called the meeting, for I was of the opinion that the information I had received was accurate," Smits replied. "Both Major Von Ruden and Inspector Lestrade thought otherwise and only agreed to the assembly at my insistence."

"Did you threaten to take the information to the commissioner without their approval?"

"I did, and I believe that was the reason they finally acquiesced," Smits answered, as he watched my father remove his hand from his concealed weapon. "I must say during my presentation the commissioner did not appear to be overly impressed and seemed to agree with Von Ruden and Lestrade, who considered the information to be unreliable. But I was later to receive a note from the commissioner instructing me to transmit the intelligence to you and allow you to determine its merit."

"So there was at least a portion of the information he considered relevant."

"That would be my impression."

"Pray tell continue, giving me every particular."

"I should begin by telling you that during my time with the Johannesburg Metropolitan Police I kept a number of reliable sources in place, one of whom contacted me with the knowledge I am about to impart to you."

"Were these sources paid for their information?"

"Only if it was proved accurate."

"Do we know if this intelligence is indeed accurate?"

"That is to be determined."

"And what makes you believe your source is on the mark?"

"Because to me all the details fit, yet to others they do not."

"A puzzle within a puzzle, or so it would seem."

"Not if one reads between the lines."

"Proceed then, omitting the comments of Lestrade and Von Ruden."

"My source is a diamond thief par excellence who has been arrested on a number of occasions, but never convicted, and currently lives a life of luxury," Smits commenced. "He was so very good at his former trade that he at times served as a consultant to De Beers when there was a major theft which defied resolution. They of course called him in with the theft of the blue diamond, which explains his detailed knowledge on the subject. In any event, it has come to his attention that an enormously valuable diamond will in the near future be transported to Antwerp, where it will be cut and polished by the Royal Asscher Diamond Company. The details of the contract are now being finalized as to the number of gems to be produced and how they are to be distributed."

"But why then is it being ransomed here in England?" I asked at once.

"There are two possibilities," Smits replied. "Either it is camouflage to divert our attention or it is a backup plan if the diamond cannot be transported."

"I favor the latter," said Joanna. "Why settle for one hundred thousand pounds when the cut and polished gems could bring a million or more? Thieves are universally greedy and they always go for the largest return. Moreover, our thieves are in no hurry, for they have now agreed to extend the deadline by two days to allow De Beers to gather the hundred thousand pounds. Clever thieves would never consent to such an obvious ploy and would demand prompt payment, for they realize the longer they wait in hiding, the greater the chance they will be discovered."

"But Antwerp is under German occupation," my father countered. "How would the blue diamond reach the cutters?"

"Which is the exact point raised by Von Ruden and Lestrade," Smits answered. "They believe the risk to transport the blue diamond is far too great, and they are of the opinion that the supposed venture is a hoax and not worthy of consideration."

"Not an unreasonable conclusion," Joanna seemed to agree. "Why take a great risk when one can have an assured hundred thousand pounds in hand?"

"For two reasons," Smits elucidated. "First is pure and simple greed, which affects us all, but diamond thieves in particular. This is their one big score which will never come their way again, even if they live a dozen lifetimes. And the second reason I believe they will take the risk is the reliability of my source. He has never failed me in the past and would not do so now."

"What makes you so confident of this source?"

"Because he owes me the irreparable debt."

"Which you will not go into."

"That is correct," Smits said, his face closing.

Joanna carefully weighed all the conflicting features before stating, "I take it the commissioner is not fully convinced of the plan to transport the blue diamond to Antwerp."

Smits smiled thinly. "I think, madam, he wishes you to investigate the matter and persuade him one way or the other."

"I shall look into it at my earliest convenience."

"The sooner the better, madam."

"I have one final question," she requested, as Smits was turning away. "Are you familiar with an assassin named Becker?"

"There are more than one of him."

"I was unaware."

"It is a family business which is passed down from one generation to the next," Smits informed us. "There are five of them at last count."

"Four," Joanna countered, and told of the death of the South African assassin in Surrey.

"Good riddance, but I fear that yet another has taken his place."

A chill went down our spines at the reminder that a skilled assassin was stalking us.

"They are trained to be assassins from their earliest years," Smits continued. "They rarely fail, and if they do so on the first attempt, they soon return to complete their mission. They are as dedicated and cold-blooded as they come, and it is believed they receive their final training in Corsica, which is the breeding ground for the world's most talented assassins."

"A nasty bunch by any measure," Joanna remarked. "Do you happen to know their favorite method of killing?"

"They seem to favor high-powered rifles and secretly administered poisons, but they can be quite inventive if need be," Smits replied. "At times they will set up deaths which appear accidental, such as a motor vehicle bursting into flames because of a petrol leak. But it is always the unexpected, for that is the trademark of a skilled assassin."

"Is it fair to say that you encountered the Becker family while a detective in Johannesburg?"

"On several occasions."

"Were you ever aware of any code or symbols they might have used in their messages?"

"I am afraid not, madam."

"Most unfortunate," said Joanna, as a hint of disappointment crossed her face. "We do, however, thank you for your time and information."

"Then I shall wish you a pleasant afternoon and be on my way."

We watched Smits head out to the expansive lawn and waited for him to be well out of hearing distance before speaking.

My father sighed resignedly. "I fear we continue to find ourselves in a lurch."

"And that lurch is made worse by the fact that all of Smits's assumptions are based on contacts of dubious merit," said I.

"You raise an excellent point, John, for assumptions based on secondhand information from dodgy characters are often misleading," Joanna noted.

"Do you believe we are being misled?" my father asked.

"I believe the individual we just spoke with is a member of the inner circle who also happens to be a skilled mountain climber and an expert in diamond thievery. And that same individual might well find a million pounds irresistibly tempting."

"Are you saying that Lieutenant Smits may be involved in the theft of the blue diamond?" I asked, surprised by her presumption.

"That possibility crossed my mind," Joanna replied.

"But why then was he so willing to share and discuss all of his information with us?"

"Perhaps he was attempting to learn how close we are to the truth."

"Goodness, Joanna!" my father interjected. "Do you consider everyone a suspect?"

"Until they are proved otherwise," said she, and, taking our arms, began to stroll back to the main gate.

CHAPTER SIXTEEN

A Clever Deception

After carefully inspecting the locks securing the windows and doors on the first floor, we adjourned to our parlor, where we relaxed in front of a glowing fire and enjoyed snifters of nicely aged brandy. Outside, a chilly frost had set in, which made the warmth of the fireplace even more inviting.

My father was packing the bowl of his well-worn pipe as a gust of Arctic air suddenly howled down Baker Street. "I suspect this foul weather will keep the German bombers on the ground tonight."

"Thankfully so, but it will also provide our assassin with excellent cover," Joanna pointed out. "We should keep in mind, Watson, that distractions can often form the basis of deception, which is a feature assassins depend on."

"But surely it will be difficult for him to carry out his entire plan, with disposal of our remains and what have you, under these circumstances."

"Skilled assassins are not as much concerned with difficulty as they are with opportunity."

"But his instructions call for our dead bodies to disappear."

"Which is based on a decoding we are unsure of."

My father raised his brow in surprise. "Do you not believe he intends to dispose of our remains?"

"That may be so, but by what method?"

"Unfortunately, the answer to that question continues to escape us."

Joanna studied my father at length over the rim of her snifter before saying, "Do you believe history tends to repeat itself?"

"I do."

"Then perhaps we can learn how the skilled Corsican assassins of yesteryear disposed of their victims."

"Is there a manual on the subject?"

"Not as such, but one can discover a great deal by delving into the historical accounts of Corsican-trained assassins, which I took the liberty to do this afternoon."

"And what method did they use?"

"They weighed down the body with stones before dumping it

overboard into the depths of the Mediterranean, usually a goodly number of miles off the Corsican coast."

"That would be most difficult to perform in the English Channel."

"But not beyond their means."

There was a brief rap on the door and Miss Hudson peeked in. "I am sorry to disturb you at this late hour, Dr. Watson, but there is a gentleman who wishes to see you on a most urgent matter. He presents himself as Mr. David Shaw."

"Sir David!" my father exclaimed excitedly.

"Has he been knighted?" Miss Hudson asked in a most reverent tone.

"By Queen Victoria herself."

"Oh, dear!"

"Please be good enough to show him in."

Miss Hudson scurried out, not bothering to close the door behind her. We could hear the footsteps hurrying down the stairs, as she no doubt prepared herself to greet the distinguished visitor.

"He has broken the code!" my father cried out.

"Let us pray," I hoped, turning to my wife. "What say you, Joanna?"

"We shall see."

Miss Hudson ushered the visitor in with a flourish, then performed a half curtsy before departing, and silently closing the door.

Omitting the amenities, Sir David said, "I am sorry to intrude on you so late in the evening, but I may have unveiled the third portion of your code." He walked over to the fire to warm his hands, then continued in a voice of obvious enthusiasm. "During my drive home only minutes ago, I noticed sleet beginning to fall and be blown about by the wind. The scattered pieces were suspended in midair and took on a pattern of interrupted lines, some of which were large, while others were quite small."

"Like the arrangement of the broken lines in the coded message," I interjected, unable to hold back my thoughts.

"Yes, except it wasn't your code which came to mind, but that of an ancient Aztec hieroglyph I had studied years ago." Sir David moved to the blackboard and began to draw a symbol which consisted of a large circle surrounded by a multitude of radiating dashes.

"It resembles a sun that is emitting its rays," my father surmised.

"Your impression will change after I have added a few more details." The curator next sketched a figure in repose within the circle itself. "What this ancient hieroglyph showed was a live victim being dissected by warriors with sharp knives. It illustrated the enemy's body being dismembered, with the various parts divided up and eaten by the conquerors. This form of nourishment was believed to impart the enemy's powers to those who ingested the dissected flesh." At this juncture, he paused to give us time to assimilate the new information.

Joanna rapidly interpreted the strange symbol. "So you are of the opinion the assassin plans to kill us and then dismember our bodies."

"But surely does not plan to eat us," I ventured.

"But there are plentiful carnivores in Sussex and Kent who would be more than happy to perform that task for him," Sir David apprised.

"Or those parts could be nibbled on by fish in the English Channel," Joanna added.

"Possibly," the curator agreed mildly. "But wild animals would make a much more thorough job of it and leave only scattered bones behind."

"All well and good," said Joanna. "But it still does not tell us the method of our execution, and that now remains the singular and most important riddle of the message."

"I continue to be troubled by the concept of dismemberment," I contended. "To dismember a body is no simple task and
requires a great deal of effort, even with heavy instruments such
as saws and hatchets and the like. Then the body parts have to be
collected and transported to some distant site away from prying
eyes. And keep in mind the assassin would be confronted with
three victims, which renders his task even more time-consuming
and arduous. I cannot conceive of a highly skilled assassin performing in such a fashion."

"Nor could I," Sir David conceded.

"Then the notion of dismemberment seems most unlikely,"
said I.

Sir David gestured with his hand in a dismissive motion. "I
am afraid, young Dr. Watson, that you are considering the term
dismemberment in the manner of a pathologist or anatomist. You
envision arms and legs being sawed off and secured in thick cloth
sacks for later disposal."

"What other definition do you have in mind?"

"You must place yourself in the place of the assassin who
wishes to perform his task and dispose of the remains in a most
rapid and thorough way. There are, for example, meat-grinding
factories on the outskirts of London which are closed at night,
but could be secretly opened for the appropriate bribe. One pass
of a body through a heavy-duty grinder and I assure you a total
dismemberment would be complete."

"That is too gruesome to think of," my father commented.

"But not too gruesome to have actually occurred," Joanna
informed us. "Sir David, I believe you are referring to the Bou-
vier case in Paris, in which a wife arranged for her husband's
mistress to be disposed of in such a thorough manner."

"Your recollection is correct," the curator said. "But alas, the
poor woman's face could be partially reconstructed, which led to

the wife's downfall. Nevertheless, when it is done correctly the victim disappears forever."

"And there are waste incinerators which would also serve the assassin's purpose," Joanna offered for consideration.

"And the list goes on," Sir David told us. "But the purpose of my visit is not to set forth the gruesome possibilities, some of which no doubt have already crossed your minds. I am here because I believe we have deciphered enough of the code to determine the circumstances under which the assassin will strike. There can be no question he plans to kill the three of you collectively at the very same time. The crosses, which are close together in the message, indicate such is the case."

"I should tell you, Sir David, that we have uncovered the meaning of the blank circle with a cross preceding it," Joanna interjected, and explained it represented the genetic symbol for a female. "She is obviously lying in repose and is connected to the three following crosses."

"Well done," the curator complimented. "Putting all the symbols together confirms my belief that the three of you are programmed to die simultaneously, with your remains disappearing from the face of the earth. The *how* remains an enigma, but not the *when*. He will make his move when the three of you are together in a space to which others are not privy. Your deaths will have to be done quickly and with a method that allows for your remains to be collected and transported to a hidden locale where you will decompose in one fashion or another. With all this in mind, I would strongly suggest you avoid wide open areas where you are alone and from where the sound will not carry. Furthermore, I would not travel to the countryside by coach or motor vehicle, for accomplished assassins are not bothered if they have to kill the driver or anyone else who unintentionally crosses their path."

"Sir David, it would seem your knowledge of assassins extends

far beyond the coded message we presented to you," Joanna remarked.

A faraway look came and went from the distinguished curator's face as he nodded. "I learned about them in Afghanistan,
which breeds a particularly nasty brand of assassins who, unlike
their Corsican counterparts, delight in cruelty."

"What makes you believe our assassin is from Corsica?" Joanna asked at once.

"Because you are high priority and are known to be very
clever," Sir David replied. "Those who wish you dead would
hire only the very best of assassins, which of course emanate from
Corsica. Am I off the mark with that assumption?"

"You are unfortunately very much on the mark."

"Then be most careful and measure your every step," he warned.
With a tip of his derby, the knighted curator bade us good night and
departed, but the solemnness of his visit remained behind.

The three of us exchanged knowing glances as our collective
minds went back to the visit we paid to Allenby House, and in particular to our stroll into the heavily wooded area where we encountered the armed hunter. Should anyone at the facility have heard the
sound of gunfire, they would have assumed it was the hunter shooting grouse and given little attention to the sudden blasts. And since
there are known to be more than a few carnivores in the forests of
Sussex, disposal of our remains would not have required transport
to a distant location.

"It was a foolish move on our part to take that stroll after
visiting Richard Hopkins's widow," Joanna summed up our feel-
ings. "We would have been easy prey."

"And an excellent lunch for the larger carnivores," said I.

"Perhaps we should continue this investigation from our
rooms here at 221b Baker Street, at least for the time being," my
father suggested.

"I am afraid that will not do, Watson, for the evidence we require is well beyond these confines," said Joanna. "But your point is well taken, and I believe we can reduce our risk by limiting our travels to places where people tend to assemble."

"Easier said than done," I noted.

"We have little choice, for our only hope to survive is to bring this matter to a complete and final resolution. Then our executions will have no purpose."

"But the assassin still may not withdraw," my father warned.

"He will when his method of payment no longer exists," Joanna responded, rising from her chair to stretch her back. "By the way, Watson, pray tell how is it that Sir David is so well versed in assassins?"

"During the Second Anglo-Afghan War, David served as an intelligence officer and was not only a first-rate code breaker, but an excellent interrogator. He was particularly good when it came to assassins, for he was fluent in their language and was knowledgeable about the history and methods of assassins throughout the world. Thus the captured killers were of the opinion that they and the interrogator belonged in the same cult and spoke freely in his presence. David once remarked to me that Afghan assassins held their Corsican counterparts in the highest regard and yearned to reach their level of excellence." My father paused to study the bowl of his pipe before carefully lighting it. "I can assure you David is very much aware of the danger we face, and that is why he hurries to give us every bit of information he can decipher from the note which instructs our Corsican-trained assassin."

"We certainly appreciate Sir David's tireless effort," said Joanna. "But I am of the opinion that he, like we, has been overlooking the most important feature of the message, which is its simplicity."

My father gave Joanna a puzzled look. "I am having difficulty following that line of reasoning."

"We are making the message too complex," she elucidated.

"There are three sections to the coded message and we are attempting to decipher each before bringing them together to establish the assassin's instructions."

"Hold on a moment," my father interrupted. "We know that the first line with the Baker Street address tells the assassin where we live and perhaps where the executions are to take place."

"But by which method?"

"We cannot be certain."

"So we now move to the second line, which dictates our executions, but we remain unsure as to where and how," Joanna went on. "Then we proceed to the third line, with its radiating dashes, which continues to be a puzzle."

"But suggests our remains are to be dismembered."

"Again, we are guessing and making the code far too complex, and that does not advance our cause," said she. "The more I think of it, the more I believe that the message does not consist of three parts, but only one. In a single glance, it informs the assassin of where, who, and how."

"Pray tell what brings you to that conclusion?" I asked.

"Because that is how I would send the message to an assassin," Joanna replied simply.

"Is that based on your intuition?"

"It is based on the historical account of Corsican assassins I read earlier today," said she. "And on that note I shall retire for the night."

Once the door to the bedroom closed, I spoke to my father in a hushed voice. "I am afraid I do not agree with my dear wife on the decoding matter. It would seem that an assassin's note should be more complex, perhaps even giving him alternatives."

"Here you must be careful, my son, for alternatives are never as well planned as the original, and tend to be prone to errors."

"But I thought assassins were thought to be so very clever."

"At killing they are, but not necessarily at thinking."

"Have you evidence in this regard?"

"Think of the message the assassin had in his pocket when he was cornered and killed. He must have already had his instructions well in mind, one would think. So why carry around an incriminating note that a decipherer could decode?"

"Careless," I opined.

"Or the behavior of someone who is not very bright, which is yet another reason Joanna believes the instructions to the assassin are straightforward and not riddled with complexities." My father gave me a gentle smile and reached over for his latest copy of the *Lancet*. "And now back to my medical journal, where I am provided with more answers than questions. Although I must say the article dealing with the treatment of gout was not nearly as informative as I had hoped."

"A new therapy, then?"

"Supposedly, but there are unpleasant side effects which no doubt limit its use."

In an instant my father went from being an inquisitive detective to being a careful, measured physician. With thirty years of medical practice behind him, he knew one had to be skeptical of new treatments for old diseases. And this seemed to be the case with an extract from a Chinese herb that appeared to reduce the inflammation in those suffering from an attack of gout. The extract appeared to bring relief, but caused considerable gastrointestinal discomfort, with hemorrhaging occurring on one occasion.

"Not very promising, I would think," my father concluded.

"So I take it you would continue to treat such patients with colchicine?"

"It is tried and true."

"But is it not also associated with gastric problems?"

"To some degree, but those can be ameliorated when the drug is ingested with food."

"Then you would not recommend the new treatment?"

"Not until it is shown to be superior to colchicine and its side effects minimized."

I rose to place another log on the fire, but stopped before the hearth and sniffed the air as my nose detected a peculiar odor. "Do you smell something burning, Father?"

He, too, stood and sampled the still air in our parlor. "It is not from the fireplace, for it seems to have a burnt-petrol quality."

"Nor is it from the outside," I determined, glancing over to the closed window behind the partially drawn curtains. After only a moment's hesitation, I dashed over to the door and opened it, and was promptly met with a plume of noxious smoke. "Run for Joanna!" I shouted to my father, slamming the door shut. "And obtain three handkerchiefs wetted heavily with water!"

I raced to the coatrack for a scarf, which I jammed into the space beneath the door to prevent more smoke from entering the parlor. Pricking my ears, I listened for the sounds of Miss Hudson scurrying about, but heard only silence and wondered if the dear woman was deep in slumber and unaware of the danger.

Joanna and my father rushed from the bedroom, with wetted handkerchiefs at the ready. They stopped at the closed door for a brief moment to sample the air and nodded to each other, with my wife saying, "It has the aroma of cooking oil on fire."

"Burning grease!" my father confirmed.

"To the kitchen, then," I directed at once, reaching for the doorknob as we covered our noses and mouths with wet handkerchiefs. "And stay low, for the smoke will rise and be less dense near the floor."

We hurried into the hall, our postures bent at the waist, and found our way to the staircase in the thick smoke. The dense haze burned at our eyes and blurred our vision as we slowly descended into the darkness of the ground floor.

"Shall we awaken Miss Hudson?" my father asked worriedly.

"Let us find the source of the fire first and determine if it can be extinguished," I advised, coughing forcefully as the air became even more polluted.

We entered the kitchen and nearly stumbled over the body of Miss Hudson. In an instant my father attended to her as I switched on the light. It remained quite dim in the kitchen, but I could hear Miss Hudson moaning and wheezing as she regained consciousness.

"Her pulse is rapid, but strong," my father pronounced. "We must move her to the outside as quickly as possible."

Joanna raced to the tradesman entrance and opened it widely, which allowed a plume of smoke to escape and partially clear the room. I gripped Miss Hudson by her shoulders and slowly backed away, dragging her heavyset body toward the alleyway. At the doorstep my foot caught on an unseen obstruction and I stumbled backwards onto the wet pavement, causing me to land on my buttocks. A fraction of a second later I heard a rifle shot ring out, followed by the sound of a bullet whizzing by my head. Crawling frantically on my hands and knees, I quickly reentered the kitchen. The alleyway suddenly became flooded with light as a heavy motor roared to life before grinding into reverse and disappearing into the black night.

"Are you injured?" my father asked, helping me to my feet.

"The shot missed, but not by much," I replied, dusting the wet dirt off my trousers.

Joanna rushed over and gave me the tightest of embraces, then kissed my cheek, but only after examining my face and neck. "You seem to be in good form," said she, smiling with obvious relief.

"Never better," I assured her, as my pulse gradually slowed from my close encounter with death. "The bloody assassin was waiting for us to step outside."

Joanna nodded. "He planned to do you first, and when the two of us rushed to your aid he would complete the executions.

All to be done on a stormy night, which would conceal the sound of his rifle."

"And he had a lorry ready to carry off our remains as well," said I. "We were most fortunate and, in a manner of speaking, owe our lives to Miss Hudson."

We looked over to our dear landlady who unwittingly caused my stumble which resulted in the assassin's bullet passing harmlessly by. She was now sitting up and holding a damp cloth to the back of her head.

"John had a most fortuitous mishap," my father agreed.

"Indeed, for the assassin's deception almost worked to perfection," said Joanna, and pointed to a metal barrel which contained oil-soaked rags that were smoldering and gave off the noxious fumes we had detected earlier. "He overcame Miss Hudson and set the fire, knowing we would rush to the kitchen and seek shelter in the alleyway where he and his high-powered rifle awaited us."

"How did he gain entrance into the kitchen?" my father queried. "The door lock could not be opened from the outside."

Joanna gestured to the lock. "It was pried off its hinges."

"From the inside obviously," my father noted. "That does not tell us how he entered."

"He made his way in through the window," Joanna explained, and moved over to a glass pane which had a circular section removed. "I would think he used a glass cutter which allowed him to reach in and unlock the window. Then he went about the business of detaching the door lock, so he could drag in a barrel of oil-soaked rags to start his fire. Miss Hudson must have heard the commotion and rushed in to investigate, for which she paid a most unpleasant price."

"With a rather vicious blow to her occiput," my father diagnosed. "Fortunately, there is no evidence of a fracture."

Miss Hudson was now sitting in a chair, still holding a damp cloth to the rear of her head. "I believe the bleeding has stopped, Doctor."

"Very good," my father said.

"But the headache remains."

"It will for a while yet, but with time it will subside."

"And the dizziness?"

"That, too, will disappear."

Miss Hudson unsteadily got to her feet and with our assistance returned to her bedroom. My father made certain she was comfortably tucked in her bed and promised to check on her periodically to assure a complete and uneventful recovery.

We reentered the kitchen and rolled the smoking barrel into the alleyway, but only after dousing the smoldering rags with a bucket of water. The door was secured by propping up a sturdy wooden chair under its doorknob.

As we slowly ascended the stairs to our parlor, my father grumbled under his breath, "This assassin is most menacing, making us unsafe even in our own rooms."

"No, Watson," said Joanna, helping him up the final step, "we are quite secure in our rooms, particularly with your Webley revolver always at the ready. The danger lurks when we venture outside 221b Baker Street."

"But surely you have not changed your mind and are now suggesting we spend the foreseeable future confined in our parlor watching the world pass us by."

"To the contrary, we will continue as before and get to the bottom of this most bothersome matter quickly, for that alone will secure our survival."

"And exactly how shall we proceed?"

"By following the money," Joanna replied succinctly. "But now, let us brew a fresh kettle and settle our nerves in front of a warm fire, for we have a most busy tomorrow awaiting us."

CHAPTER SEVENTEEN

The Syndicate

All that was required was one phone call and we were granted an immediate late-morning audience with Mr. Freddie Morrison, the head of London's most notorious crime syndicate. Reaching for our coats and scarves, Joanna did not reveal the reason for Morrison's prompt response, only telling us that we would learn of it soon enough. It would be just the two of us, however, for my father decided not to join us and to instead remain at 221b Baker Street, where he could periodically look in on Miss Hudson, his major concern being the possibility of an intracranial hemorrhage as a consequence of the head trauma she had suffered. As we hurried down the stairs, Joanna continued to dwell on our landlady's condition.

"I would think that bleeding into the cranium would bring forth instant symptoms and not be delayed," she queried.

"That occurs only when the bleeding is into the brain itself," I explained. "On occasion the hemorrhage takes place between the brain and the dura, which is its covering. The blood may then form a clot, which can cause pressure and result in symptoms days or even weeks later."

"Let us pray that is not the case," said Joanna, as our four-wheeler splashed through puddles from the early-morning downpour.

"If such a subdural hematoma does exist, it can be surgically removed."

"Which is not the most pleasant of remedies."

"It carries some risk," I admitted.

We rode on in silence, now passing the stately landmarks of Westminster before crossing the Thames and entering the industrialized section of South London. As we neared the Angel pub, I found myself wondering if the ever-clever Freddie Morrison would somehow recognize us from our visit a year earlier, at which time we presented ourselves as a wealthy South African couple interested in buying a stolen masterpiece. Our disguises were so convincing that we even passed the scrutiny of Miss Hudson, who believed we were elderly friends departing after stopping by to see my father. My concern was that the once-deceived Freddie Morrison would not be eager to do business with us yet again.

"Have you considered the possibility that Mr. Morrison will somehow recall us from our prior visit?" asked I, breaking the silence.

"It will not matter, for he will be enticed to participate in our pursuit of the Ming vase," Joanna replied.

"How so?"

"By speaking of treason, which can be quite motivating."

Our carriage arrived at the front entrance of the Angel pub, which for all the world appeared to be a simple neighborhood drinking establishment. But sights can be deceiving, for from behind its doors emanated some of London's most notorious and violent crimes.

Alighting from our carriage, Joanna instructed the driver, "You are to park next to the tobacco shop on the opposite side of the street and wait for us there."

"What if I am ordered to move, ma'am?"

"Tell them that Mr. Freddie Morrison wishes you to stay in place."

We walked down a narrow alleyway which was littered with trash and carried the aroma of spoiled garbage. From within the pub we could hear the sound of loud conversations and occasional outbursts of laughter. Just ahead of us, a burly man wearing a leather jacket over a turtleneck sweater stood guard.

"The same security as before," I said sotto voce.

"Except now he is armed," Joanna noted, gesturing subtly with her head to the obvious bulge beneath the left side of his jacket.

"Do you believe that is solely on our account?"

"His type does not discriminate."

The guard carefully measured us and, without a word, opened the door to a busy kitchen. It was as if time stood still for a moment, then rapidly reverted to a year earlier when we made our first visit. Several cooks were preparing dishes of shepherd's pie and Welsh rarebit, whilst two slightly built Asians were washing and drying dishes, and speaking in a totally incomprehensible language. We were ignored, with no one even bothering to glance our way. On leaving the kitchen area, we were joined by a new guard who ushered us through a noisy, crowded pub where we received a few curious stares, but little else. At the end of the bar was a nicely decorated Christmas tree, for it was already late November and the joyful holiday was not far off. Our usher opened a door to our right, and we entered a plain office that was filled with tobacco smoke. From behind an uncluttered desk, a heavyset man wearing a nicely tailored suit stood and motioned us to the two chairs in front of him. He was well groomed and could have passed for a businessman except for the deep scar that ran from his ear to his upper cheek.

We were not yet in our seats when Morrison bellowed out, "What is this nonsense about treason?"

"I can assure you it is not nonsense," Joanna replied calmly.

Morrison stared at her, the anger obvious on his face.

Joanna was unmoved by his intimidating glare. "I take it your man remains outside the door, and clearly within hearing distance."

"So?"

"Please have him excuse himself."

"Why should I do that?"

"To prevent him from becoming compromised."

"Which implies that I am about to become compromised."

"That depends entirely on how you play your cards, Mr. Morrison," Joanna said evenly. "The SIS wishes for only you to hear our conversation."

Morrison's face turned to worry at the mention of the Secret Intelligence Service, who were known to deal harshly with those attempting to harm the Crown.

"It would be in your best interest to remove the guard at the door," Joanna advised, her voice a touch harder now.

Morrison hesitated for a brief moment before calling out, "Ralphie, take a walk about!"

"Good," Joanna approved. "Let us proceed with the business at hand."

"I am not a German spy!" Morrison protested loudly, slamming his fist down on the desk.

"But the very last thing you would want is to be closely associated with one."

"I have never done so."

"But you are about to, and trust me when I tell you that carries grave consequences."

"What the bloody hell is this all about?" Morrison asked, becoming even more exasperated.

"First, let us set the ground rules. If you answer all of our questions truthfully, you will never see or hear from the SIS. Should you withhold information or fabricate your replies, you most certainly will."

"Get on with it," the syndicate boss spat out. "And you may wish to begin with the purpose of this visit."

"I require knowledge on a most valuable Ming vase which is or shortly will be in your possession."

Morrison was instantly on guard. "I know of no such vase."

"That is your first lie and hopefully will be your last, for questioning before the SIS can be most unpleasant."

Morrison sighed resignedly as the resistance disappeared from his face. "I will not admit to any guilt."

"Then speak in a third-person fashion."

"Which will not be a confession and cannot be construed as one."

"Obviously."

Morrison cleared his throat, as if preparing for a formal presentation. "Let us say a friend of mine was approached by someone claiming to have in his possession a most valuable Ming vase, which he wished to put up for sale."

"On the black market."

"I believe he did request that."

"But of course the vase would have to be appraised and certified that it was genuine."

"Of course."

"And how was that accomplished?"

"According to my friend, a meeting was arranged at a local hotel, and those gathered included my friend, the appraiser, and the possessor of the vase."

"Were there no guards?"

"In the corridor outside the door."

Joanna stared at Morrison for a long moment, as if waiting for a more thorough response.

"And two more in the lobby," he added quickly. "One cannot be too careful when dealing with such a precious item."

Joanna nodded in agreement. "With the vase being so treasured and fragile, I suspect great care was taken in his presentation."

"Oh, indeed it was, madam," Morrison replied. "I was told it was brought into the room inside a sturdy piece of luggage, which was only slightly larger than an attaché case and made of a metallic material."

"Was it luminous?"

Morrison shrugged. "My friend didn't say."

"Pray continue."

"In any event, the vase itself rested in a central, heavily padded section of the case, which prevented it from moving about and being damaged. The other two sections were equally well padded, but empty."

I held my expression even, but we had just uncovered a most important piece of information. Three separate and heavily padded sections! One for the vase, another for the blue diamond, and a third for the war document. There was no doubt in my mind as to the purpose of the heavily padded sections. But why then were two of the compartments empty? The answer came to me immediately. Only the vase was up for sale, and thus there was no reason to display the diamond or the document.

"Did your friend notice any other unusual features of the carrying case?" Joanna was asking.

"Only that it was quite expensive in that every inch was lined with heavy-duty cotton gabardine, like you see in trench coats."

"So the Ming vase was exceptionally well protected."

"Indeed, and meant to stay in place."

"But surely the vase had to be lifted out by the appraiser."

"Oh, it was, and most carefully, before being positioned under the brightest of lamps for reasons my friend was not told."

"It was placed there for accurate appraisal," Joanna elucidated. "There are a number of features that determine the value of a Ming vase, but perhaps the most important is its translucency, which can only be ascertained using an extremely bright light, and thus the purpose of the lamp. This particular vase was given the highest mark in that category."

I smiled inwardly to myself, for in an instant Joanna had

made Freddie Morrison aware that she was well knowledgeable about Ming vases and any information he provided had best be spot-on or there would be consequences. The expression on his face told us he had gotten the message.

"Give us the appraised value," Joanna requested.

"One hundred thousand pounds."

"Rather steep, I would say,"

"As it seemed to the buyers who were contacted."

"Was there any interest at all?"

"Not at that exorbitant price," Morrison replied unhappily. "Even one of the wealthiest men in Asia, a shipping magnate from Hong Kong, who is usually an eager buyer, backed away."

"And with the war raging on the Continent, I suspect the list of European buyers must be quite limited."

"It is almost nonexistent, madam."

"Yet the rather stubborn seller refused to budge, eh?"

"Not a shilling, but such stubbornness is not uncommon in South Africans."

Joanna's eyelids went up briefly, then returned to their neutral position. "South African, you say?"

"His accent was quite distinct, or so I was told."

"Perhaps he was using it as a disguise to mislead those present."

"No, madam, he was definitely South African and from its capital, Pretoria."

"Was your friend that accomplished at reading accents?"

"Not him, but my man Ralphie, who was born and raised in Pretoria," Morrison explained. "Ralphie was standing guard for my friend and heard the seller's voice through the door, and later told me that the man's accent indicated he was from Pretoria and nowhere else, for people from the capital speak with an accent which distinguishes them from those from all other cities."

"Did your friend describe the seller from Pretoria?" Joanna asked in a nonurgent manner, but she involuntarily leaned forward, for here was the clue which could unravel the entire mystery of the blue diamond.

"He did not see his face, for the seller had arrived first and stood well back in the shadows," Morrison replied.

"But a moment ago you told us there was a bright light in the hotel room," Joanna challenged the answer.

"There was, madam," Morrison said at once. "But according to my friend, it was an electric lamp on the table next to the Ming vase. It could be bent and positioned so that it shined down directly on the vase, which left the remainder of the large suite in shadows."

"Could your friend make out any of the seller's features?"

Morrison shrugged. "He was of average height and frame, or so he appeared to be in the dimness. His voice certainly did not belong to the ordinary thief."

"Was he educated?"

"So it would seem, but he wasn't aristocratic if that is what you are asking."

Joanna's next question was phrased to determine if Ralphie, the guard outside the door, might have gotten a look at the seller. "Who departed the suite first?"

"My friend did, along with the appraiser, followed by my man Ralphie," the syndicate boss replied, then squinted an eye, as if thinking back. "When they left the hotel, Ralphie and my friend had the feeling they were being shadowed, perhaps to make certain they were well gone."

"Very good," said Joanna, pushing her chair away from the desk.

"Before you depart, madam, I hope you will be good enough to answer a question for me," Morrison requested.

"That depends on the question."

"What in the world does the Ming vase have to do with treason and the SIS?"

"I shall give you a partial answer, but it is to go no further than this room. Understood?"

"Fully, madam."

"The SIS believes those who stole the Ming vase also made off with an important document, which the Crown wants back."

"May I know the nature of that document?"

"I will say no more, nor should you," said Joanna, ending the conversation.

"May I assume I will not be visited by the SIS?"

"That is a reasonable assumption," Joanna replied, rising out of her chair. "If by chance your friend is contacted again by the seller, you are to inform us immediately. And should such a sale be in the making, it would be in your best interest to call us without delay and before there is any transfer of funds."

"I shall," Morrison vowed, then quickly appended, "but what if the seller reappears to renegotiate a price?"

"Then have Ralphie detain him, which will put both you and him in good standing with the SIS."

We departed the Angel pub unescorted and strolled out in the cloudy midday. Joanna signaled to our carriage across the street and watched it make a slow U-turn, with traffic being halted by Ralphie, who appeared out of nowhere.

"Was there a reason you mentioned the missing document to Morrison?" I asked, as a light rain began to fall.

Joanna nodded. "He is a clever fellow, and if he hears even a whisper about the document, he will connect them to treason and notify us faster than an eye can blink."

"The prospect of a noose around one's neck can be very motivating."

"Quite so."

"And I could not help but notice your considerable interest in the metal carrying case Freddie Morrison so aptly described."

"That was because it was most informative."

"Yes, indeed, for its three sections are meant to transport the Ming vase, blue diamond, and war document, and thus we can be certain the same individual was responsible for stealing and eventually disposing of all three."

"Oh, it tells us a great deal more than that," Joanna said, as we ran for our carriage in the sudden downpour.

CHAPTER EIGHTEEN

Adolph Smits

Much to our surprise, on our return to Baker Street we found Miss Hudson in her kitchen busy at work preparing a freshly delivered goose for the oven. Despite my father's protestations, she insisted on resuming her duties, yet again displaying a stiff upper lip. By her side was the largest Alsatian I had ever witnessed. The hound must have weighed at least eighty pounds, and did not move an iota as she warily studied the recent arrivals.

"I take it you have recovered," said Joanna to our landlady.

"Fit as a fiddle, as they say," Miss Hudson responded.

"No headaches, then?"

"A minor ache."

"And the dizziness?"

"Gone."

"Excellent," Joanna said, turning to the giant hound. "Please tell us of your new friend."

"This is Dolly, who belongs to my good chum Bertie," Miss Hudson replied. "Bertie and his wife had to travel to the Hebrides to attend a dear aunt's funeral and asked me to look after their sweet dog, who I must say will provide us with additional protection."

"She does not appear to take well to strangers," my father noted, keeping his distance from the Alsatian.

"That is easily remedied," Joanna told him. "Miss Hudson, do you still have some slices of cold lamb from an earlier dinner?"

"I do."

"Three small portions, if you please."

Our landlady fetched the half slices of lamb on a platter and handed them to Joanna, who promptly distributed the pieces to my father and me, keeping one for herself. "Now we shall give the hound a peace offering."

We each fed Dolly the cold lamb, which she rapidly consumed before looking up at us for more.

"That will do for the time being," Joanna informed the dog, and gave her a gentle scratch behind the ears. "Now that we have established our bond with the Alsatian, she will consider us friends."

The hound leaned in closer to my wife, who applied more scratches to Dolly's ears.

"How often should we give her these tidbits?" I asked.

"Only after we return from one of our outings," Joanna replied. "Should we follow that plan, she will always be waiting for us at the door, and she will become most unhappy if someone attempts to come between us and her."

"A formidable obstacle," I remarked.

"It was unfortunate that Dolly was not here last night to greet the intruder," Miss Hudson said, and fed the hound a final scrap of lamb from the platter.

For a brief moment I envisioned the giant Alsatian lunging for the assassin's throat and taking him down. It was not an unpleasant thought.

"Well, then," Miss Hudson broke into my daydream, "it is back to our fresh goose, who will shortly find itself inside a hot oven."

"I must insist you rest," my father advised strongly. "Surely, you realize that the healing process is not yet completed."

"Just a few more minutes," Miss Hudson requested. "For without my special basting, the goose will not be nearly as tasty."

"A glaze of honey and spices, I would hope," Joanna chimed in.

Our landlady nodded happily as she basted the goose with her appetizing recipe. "It gives the bird a most crispy and delectable exterior."

"I require your word that you will rest once the goose is in the oven," my father demanded.

"You have it, Dr. Watson."

"And should your symptoms recur, you must notify me immediately."

"Yes, yes," she replied absently, reaching for more of her recipe.

My father sighed resignedly, and joined us as we departed the kitchen and started up the stairs to our rooms. He waited until we were well out of Miss Hudson's hearing distance before speaking.

"She is a strongheaded woman, and I shall have to look in on her shortly to make certain she is following my instructions."

"Do you believe her symptoms will return, Watson?" Joanna asked concernedly.

"They may well if she does not rest appropriately," my father replied. "The blow she received no doubt bruised her brain and that requires time and rest to heal."

"Perhaps we should bring in someone to assist her," I suggested.

My father shook his head immediately. "The kitchen is her kingdom, and she will not allow trespassers."

We entered our rather chilly parlor, for the fire had burned out long ago, leaving only cold ashes behind. I reached for logs to start another, whilst Joanna lighted her Bunsen burner to brew a

kettle of Earl Grey tea. As was his habit, my father walked over
to the window and parted the curtains just enough to allow him
to peer out onto Baker Street and determine whether anyone was
watching our rooms.

"Nothing," he declared, "except that the sudden downpour
is over and the sun is attempting to show itself."

"Make a mental note of all you see, particularly of individuals
who seem to be walking back and forth without stopping into
any of the shops," Joanna instructed. "You should be most interested in a man that you have noticed before."

"Specifically if he glances up at our rooms."

"He is too clever for that, for he will note that the curtains
are closed and understand the reason why."

"Then why does he surveil?"

"To follow our exits and wait for the most opportune moment to strike."

My father gave Baker Street a final study before retreating to
his overstuffed chair by the fire and reaching for his cherrywood
pipe. "I take it your visit to see Mr. Freddie Morrison was not
very productive."

"To the contrary, Watson," Joanna replied, and began listing all the points of interest we encountered during our visit to
the Angel pub. She described the rather unique carrying case in
detail, with emphasis on the three heavily padded sections it contained, two of which were empty. "Pray tell what do you make
of that?"

"They are meant to protect three separate items, most likely
the Ming vase, the blue diamond, and the war document."

"Bravo, Watson! But it goes much deeper, for now we know
that the diamond and vase are for sale, but the war document is
not. Why?" she prompted. "Why would the document, which
when deciphered be worth far more than the diamond and vase
combined, not be placed on the black market?"

"Because it has not been decoded?" I surmised.

"Are you certain of that?" Joanna pressed, and waited for an answer which was not forthcoming. "But for the sake of discussion, let us say that the document has not been decoded. Who would still be intensely interested in the contents of a briefcase stolen from France's minister of war, who happened to be visiting London just prior to a meeting of the Imperial War Conference?"

"The Germans!" my father and I shouted out simultaneously.

"Yes, for they are clever enough to discern its value sight unseen."

My father gasped. "The Germans have already purchased the document and are awaiting its transfer."

Joanna nodded at my father's conclusion. "And that is the reason it is not on the market, and it also explains the mention of the war document by name in the wireless message picked up by MI5. They believe that message was being transmitted by a German spy to a U-boat in the Channel, and so do I."

"I fear we find ourselves in a dreadful position," said my father.

"Which is the reason we must quickly discover the location of the blue diamond, for by its side lies the war document."

"Tomorrow will not be soon enough," my father agreed, slowly packing the bowl of his pipe. "Which brings to mind the telephone call I received earlier from the commissioner's office. The ransom has long been secured by De Beers, but the thieves were told their measurement of one of the stone's features was off by a fraction of a centimeter, which of course was not the case. They were instructed to remeasure with a more accurate instrument, such as calipers. This ruse should buy a few more days, but no more."

"Were the thieves perturbed by yet another delay?" asked Joanna.

"They readily agreed according to the commissioner."

"Something is off here," Joanna said, and walked over to the Persian slipper to extract a Turkish cigarette. After lighting it, she began pacing the floor, head down, her brow furrowed in thought. She muttered to herself, discarding one notion whilst concurring with another, before finally concluding, "They are working on their timetable, not ours."

"How did you gather that, may I ask?" my father inquired.

"Because, as noted before, it is in their best interest to bring the ransom to a rapid finish, for any delay goes against them and increases their chances of being apprehended," Joanna answered. "That is the manner in which accomplished thieves would think, and our players surely fall into that category."

"But what then would be the purpose of such a delay?"

"If I were to surmise, I would believe it had to do with a predetermined escape plan."

"And the unique construction of their carrying case would indicate they intend to travel a considerable distance with their stolen items," I added.

The phone sounded, and Joanna hurried over to pick up the receiver on the second ring. "Yes?" she answered pleasantly, then listened with a most serious expression before asking a rapid list of questions. "So the attempt was unsuccessful? . . . Badly wounded, you say? . . . No sign of the assassin, then? . . . Yes, yes, Inspector. We shall arrive via Admiralty Arch."

Placing down the receiver, Joanna relayed the contents of the phone call from Inspector Lestrade. "There has been an assassination attempt on the Governor-General of South Africa," she reported darkly. "He is unharmed, but Lieutenant Smits, who stepped in to protect the Governor-General, has been grievously wounded and is being rushed to St. Bartholomew's. The attempt was made by rifle from some distance, and an intensive search is currently under way for the assassin."

"Certainly it cannot be our assassin who is responsible," my father thought aloud.

"Do not exclude that possibility, Watson," said Joanna, and, after casting her cigarette into the fireplace, dashed for the coat-rack. "We must hurry, John, while the good Dr. Watson will remain to look after Miss Hudson."

We were able to hail a four-wheeler in short order for the ride to Trafalgar Square where the South African High Commission was situated. As we passed Marble Arch and continued on by Hyde Park, I quickly put together the few pieces of information we had at our disposal and came to a rapid conclusion. We were no doubt dealing with a German assassin who was sent to deliver a terrible blow to the Allied forces by killing the Governor-General of South Africa. That picturesque dominion, which was more than five thousand miles away, stood steadfast by England in the Great War and had provided thousands upon thousands of the bravest troops, as well as unlimited supplies of the raw materials required for armament production. The assassination of their beloved Governor, a valiant soldier in his own right, would surely have a crushing and demoralizing effect on the entire South African contingent. "The bloody Germans," I muttered under my breath."

"Then, you believe they are responsible?" said Joanna.

"Don't you?"

"There is room for doubt."

"Why so?"

"History," Joanna responded. "Of course there is a long list of state leaders being assassinated, but I defy you to name one that was killed by a professional hired by the opposing government. It has not occurred in modern times, for I believe there is an unwritten and unholy agreement not to assassinate opposing heads of government. Politicians and generals, yes, but not presidents or prime ministers."

"I have never heard or read of such an agreement."

"But it makes logical sense, does it not? Simply put, 'if you assassinate my prime minister, I will make every effort to assassinate yours. In essence, if you sign my death warrant, I will sign yours,' and let me assure you that presidents and prime ministers wish to live a long life, much as everyone else."

"Why then are they so closely guarded?"

"To protect them from fanatics and the mentally disturbed, not from professional assassins."

"So you have real questions regarding Germany's involvement in this dastardly act."

"I do, and I have yet another question which I have been unable to answer."

"Which is?"

"Why are we being summoned to the scene of this attempted assassination?"

Our carriage arrived at Admiralty Arch, but could proceed no farther, for the entire Trafalgar Square was sealed off by long lines of constables standing shoulder to shoulder. We approached the square on foot, but were halted by a uniformed policeman, who upon recognizing Joanna allowed us to continue on. Other than the multitude of detectives from Scotland Yard and members of the South African security unit, the square was empty and eerily quiet. Even the ever-present pigeons had decided to vacate the area.

Inspector Lestrade was standing next to Nelson's Column and, on seeing our arrival, beckoned us over with a wave. "Thank you for coming so promptly."

"As requested," said Joanna, glancing past the monument to the steps of the National Gallery and beyond to the crowd of tourists behind a wall of uniformed constables. "It appears you have the situation well in hand."

"But with no sign of the assassin," Lestrade said dourly.

"As a rule, they are quite skilled at escaping."

"Without a trace thus far, I should add."

"Do you know the general location from which the shot was fired?"

"We are certain of the building, which our senior detectives are now searching room by room."

"When the site is found, I hope they have been instructed not to forage about until we have had a look."

"They have been ordered not to touch or move any item."

"Very good," Joanna approved. "And now, Inspector, please inform us why our presence is required at the scene of this attempted assassination."

"It was the commissioner himself who requested your presence, for he believes an association may we exist between you and this event," Lestrade replied. "We appear to have two professional assassins in our midst, one devoted to your demise, the other to the death of the Governor-General. The commissioner further believes that both assassins are connected to the war effort, and wishes for the two to be promptly tracked down and any hidden agenda revealed before they are executed as foreign agents. He is of the opinion that your assistance would be invaluable in bringing the pair to a swift and just end."

"I suspect he has some idea on how this happy ending is to be brought about."

"He does indeed," Lestrade went on. "He would like a perfect trap set when the transfer of the blue diamond occurs, with of course the assassins being enticed to be present or nearby."

"He is asking for the impossible," Joanna said at once. "The exchange of money for the gem will be carried out by neutral parties, with the ransom deposited in an escrow account, no doubt in a Swiss bank. The funds will only be released when the diamond has been authenticated and transferred back to the rightful owners."

"The commissioner is well aware of the procedure for transfer," Lestrade responded. "Nevertheless, he has confidence you can come up with a unique plan which will allow us to repossess the blue diamond without giving up a shilling."

"A tall order."

"But one he feels you are quite capable of."

"Let us begin with the problem at hand, then," Joanna said, with an expression that made me believe she already had the concept of such a plan in mind. "I need the particulars of this assassination attempt."

"We should have Major Von Ruden supply you with the details, for he was an eyewitness to the entire event," said Lestrade, and signaled to the head of the South African security unit, who was standing on the other side of the Nelson Column and scanning the surrounding buildings with oversized binoculars. It required another set of hand signals to catch his attention. He gave the entire expanse of Admiralty Arch a final look before hurrying over.

"I thought I saw movement on the top of the arch, but it was only a flock of pigeons. Nonetheless, such birds are skittish and take to flight when a man approaches, which is the reason I studied the area so carefully."

"Leave not a stone unturned," said Lestrade, and gestured to my wife and me. "Major Von Ruden, you no doubt recall the Watsons from our earlier gathering at the Windsor."

"I do indeed," he replied, with a slight bow.

"They are joining our investigation at the request of the commissioner, and I should like you to provide them with all the details of the assassination attempt."

Von Ruden took a deep breath, seemingly not wishing to relive the event yet again. "All was in order while the Governor-General was paying an official visit to the South African High

Commission. My men were circulating amongst the crowd of tourists on the watch for any suspicious individuals, lookouts were posted on rooftops, and the perimeters secured. As the Governor was departing down the steps, one of the lookouts noted a glint of metal in the window of a surrounding building. He immediately focused in with binoculars and clearly saw the barrel of a rifle. He shouted out, 'Rifle!' Instinctively, my second-in-command, Adolph Smits, leaped in front of the Governor-General just as a muzzle flash occurred at the window." The major took another deep breath, his resolute expression fading for a moment and replaced by sadness. Collecting himself, he continued on. "The Governor was pushed into his waiting limousine, which sped away while we attended to Smits, who had taken a bullet to the chest and was grievously wounded. We had to secure the area before we could rush Dolphie to St. Bartholomew's Hospital, where he now lies close to death."

"Let us pray he recovers," said Joanna.

"There is little hope, with such a horrendous wound," Von Ruden opined frankly. "I have seen similar ones before."

"As have the fine surgeons at St. Bart's, where your lieutenant will receive the best of care," said Joanna. "In the meantime, I should like to speak with the lookout who spotted the rifle to make certain I have a complete picture."

"Of course." Von Ruden complied, and called out loudly for Paul Botha, who promptly came running across the deserted square. He was tall and broad shouldered, with close-cropped blond hair and pale blue eyes. There was dried blood on his hands, no doubt as a consequence of looking after the wounded Adolph Smits.

"Sir!" Botha said, assuming a posture of attention.

"Be at ease, Corporal," Von Ruden commanded, and waited for the man to relax. "The lady and her husband are associated with Scotland Yard and have questions for you."

"Yes, sir," said Botha, as his posture stiffened once again.

"Think back to the moment you saw the glint of reflected light in the window," Joanna began. "Had the sun come out?"

"It was intermittently showing through the clouds, ma'am," Botha replied without hesitation.

"And when you became aware of the glint, you immediately brought up your binoculars for a closer view. Correct?"

"Correct, ma'am."

"Pray tell us exactly what you saw, with as much detail as possible."

"There was the long barrel of a rifle protruding through the window."

"In clear view?"

"It was a rifle beyond any doubt, ma'am."

"Could you possibly tell us its make?"

Botha shook his head at once. "Not from the barrel alone, ma'am. Had I seen the stock I might have been able to do so."

"Then came the muzzle flash?"

"Bright as day, it was, and it seemed to last an inordinate amount of time," Botha described. "And when the flash had disappeared, the rifle barrel was gone from sight."

"I am curious about the rifle itself," Joanna probed further. "Could you determine if it was breech loaded?"

"I could not, for although the barrel was in clear view, its trigger mechanism was not in sight."

"Thank you, Corporal," Joanna concluded. "Your description was quite informative."

"Well then, if there are no further questions, Botha should now return to—" Von Ruden's instructions were interrupted by a shout from across the square.

"Major! We have located the assassin's room!"

Von Ruden and Botha dashed away, with Lestrade, Joanna, and I only a few steps behind.

"A tragedy about Smits," the inspector said sincerely. "He seemed like an entirely decent bloke."

"We found him quite helpful as well," Joanna added without going into detail.

"Would you care to share the purpose of his phone call this morning?" Lestrade requested in a low voice.

"What phone call are you referring to?" asked Joanna.

"Earlier today Smits stopped by Scotland Yard unannounced to see the commissioner, who was not present, for he had been called to a meeting at 10 Downing Street," Lestrade replied. "On his way out, Smits asked for your phone number, for he had obtained the important information you had requested."

"Do you recall the time when you spoke with Smits?"

"Shortly after eleven, I would say."

"Ah!" Joanna said, as if about to explain our failure to accept Smits's call. "We were absent from Baker Street for most of the morning."

"Was his information vital to our investigation?"

"It might have been," Joanna said evasively, as we approached the building where the assassin had housed himself.

Racing up the stairs, I allowed Lestrade to distance himself from us before asking Joanna, "What information did you request from Smits?"

"I made no such request," she replied sotto voce.

We reached the top of the stairs and followed Lestrade into a small office that faced Trafalgar Square. It contained a chair and simple desk, both of which were heavily coated with dust, indicating the room had been vacant for a considerable length of time. On the floor, halfway between the desk and window, was a spent cartridge shell that had a white chalk circle drawn around it.

Joanna carefully stepped over to the cartridge shell, with her eyes darting back and forth between the shell and the window. "Was this item moved at all?"

"No, ma'am," replied a heavyset detective. "We circled it to make certain it remained in place."

Von Ruden came over to the chalk circle and inserted a pen into the opening of the shell, so it could be lifted and examined without disturbing any fingerprints. "There is an inscription on its rear which is quite small and difficult to read."

Joanna reached into her purse for a magnifying glass and leaned in for a closer study. "It is inscribed with the letters *DWM* and the number nineteen-thirteen. The markings no doubt indicate the origin of the cartridge."

Von Ruden quickly glanced over to Paul Botha, saying, "You are our weapons expert, Corporal. Can you decipher it?"

"The letters stand for Deutsche Waffen und Munitionsfabriken, which is one of Germany's major producers of weapons and ammunition," he replied. "The number nineteen-thirteen tell us the year the cartridge was manufactured."

"So it all fits," Von Ruden concluded unhappily, as he again viewed the small office and its contents. "We have a German sniper using German weaponry, sitting in the very room as he waited for the opportune moment to assassinate our Governor-General. The dust has been removed from the seat of the chair, telling us that this is where he placed himself prior to making his move."

"The applause of the crowd when the Governor-General exited the South African High Commission was no doubt the assassin's cue that his target would now be in view," Botha added.

"Then he fires his shot and disappears into thin air," said Von Ruden, as a scowl crossed his face.

"Perhaps we will have the good fortune of discovering an eyewitness," Lestrade hoped. "We are now canvasing the area for observant individuals who might have seen a fleeing man carrying a case large enough to conceal a weapon."

"I would go about identifying the assassin in a different fashion," Joanna suggested. "You would agree that this dust-covered office has been vacant for a lengthy period of time, would you not?"

"Of course," Lestrade concurred.

"And that the letting agent for this building would be most eager to rent this space?"

"Surely."

"Then it might prove worthwhile to question the agent and determine who recently inquired and actually signed a lease to let this office."

"Capital!" Lestrade exclaimed. "The assassin must have inspected the office to make certain it suited his purpose."

"And even if he presented himself in disguise, there may have been other noteworthy features about him," Joanna appended.

"Thank you for that most excellent suggestion, madam."

"You are welcome, Inspector," said Joanna, hooking her arm into mine. "And on that note we must depart, for we have an important meeting awaiting us. Please inform us of any new developments at your earliest convenience."

"I shall, madam."

We hurried out and down the stairs, then exited into a nearly empty square where an eerie silence persisted. Our four-wheeler awaited us at Admiralty Arch, but it was now surrounded by curious onlookers, so we waited until we were securely inside the carriage before speaking.

"To St. Bartholomew's Hospital!" Joanna called up to the driver. "You must take the quickest possible route."

"Who are we to meet there?" I asked.

"Adolph Smits."

"But he has been grievously wounded and lies near death."

"Let us pray he has moments of consciousness, for the message he carries is the key to the entire mystery."

"How do you perceive that this message carries such importance?"

"Because he would only reveal its contents to the commissioner and me," replied Joanna. "And pray tell, dear John, what else does that rather dark observation tell us?"

"Good Lord!" I groaned, as the answer came to me. "There is a turncoat in Smits's unit."

"Beyond any doubt."

CHAPTER NINETEEN

The Message

The surgery ward at St. Bartholomew's consisted of dozens upon dozens of occupied beds that were situated side by side, with movable curtains between them, which allowed for some degree of privacy when required. At the rear of the ward was a single, windowless room that was reserved for critically ill patients in need of intensive care. As we approached, a young, handsome surgeon wearing a blood-spattered gown was emerging from the unit. His name was Harry Askins, and he was considered the most talented thoracic surgeon at St. Bart's.

He waved to us, having met Joanna when she had accompanied me to his wedding. Before he could speak to us, however, a sister rushed to his side and handed him a thick chart for his signature. After supplying it, Askins turned to us and asked cordially, "To what do I owe this honor?"

"We are here to see Adolph Smits," said I.

"Then you had better hurry, for he is not long for this world."

"Is there any hope?"

"Very little, despite our best efforts," Askins replied, and stretched an aching back. "The bullet wound not only caused a complete pneumothorax, but extensive hemorrhaging as well. He has received multiple transfusions, but we are unable to keep up with the blood loss."

"And the prospect for surgical intervention?"

"Virtually nil, unless we can stabilize his condition. Otherwise, he would never leave the operating table."

"Is he able to speak?" Joanna asked forthrightly.

"He lapses in and out of consciousness," Askins answered. "In his lucid moments, he utters words which are difficult to understand."

"Does he respond to questions?"

"Poorly, and then with the briefest of replies."

Another sister raced from the intensive care room and called out urgently, "Mr. Askins, please come quickly! The patient's blood pressure has fallen yet again and his pulse is irregular."

The surgeon hurried into the unit, leaving its door wide open. We could not help but look in and watch Askins adjust the rubber tube extending from the patient's chest, then increase the flow of a nearby hanging transfusion of blood.

"He is obviously in extremis," Joanna whispered to me.

I nodded as Smits coughed up frothy phlegm that was heavily soaked with blood. "I have seen chest wounds from high-powered rifles at autopsy, and the amount of damage inflicted is beyond belief. Large segments of the lung are destroyed and often a major vessel is severed."

"Such as a pulmonary artery?"

I nodded once again. "If that is the case here, there is no hope for survival."

Askins reappeared, his expression now dark and grim. "His

pressure is up a bit, but it will require multiple additional transfusions to remain so, and I have been told the list of donors is quite limited. "So I must hurry to the blood bank and alert them of the situation." He turned to depart and spoke a final word to us over his shoulder. "By the way, he is now complaining of pain, which indicates his senses are returning for the moment. Thus he may be able to converse with you."

He quickly exited the intensive care room as the sister stepped back to give us more room. Smits's grave condition became far more evident on closer inspection. His complexion was most pale and as white as the sheet he lay upon. There was a thick rubber tube extending from his chest, with bloody fluid being expelled from it and emptying into a large glass container. The tube moved up and down with his rapid, shallow respirations. His mouth was open, his eyelids closed.

Joanna leaned forward and whispered into the patient's ear, "Lieutenant Smits, this is Joanna Watson. Can you hear me?"

There was no response.

Joanna spoke again in a louder voice. "Lieutenant Smits, this is the daughter of Sherlock Holmes. Can you hear me?"

The patient's eyelids fluttered briefly, then closed.

"Lieutenant, try to open your eyes."

Smits's lids fluttered once more, but now remained partially open.

"Can you give me your important message?"

Smits's lips moved, but could make no sound. With effort, he tried again and uttered the word, "You . . ."

"Yes, yes," Joanna encouraged. "I heard the word *you*. Please continue."

"You . . . boat . . . ," he muttered.

Joanna nodded at once as she comprehended. "Yes! You are saying *U*-boat. Is that correct?"

Smits nodded ever so briefly.

Joanna rapidly turned to the sister who was trying to catch every word of the conversation. "It might be best for you to step out of the unit, for his message is meant only for my ears."

"Of course." The sister complied, hurriedly departing, closing the door firmly behind her.

Joanna returned to Smits's ear and asked, "What of the U-boat?"

"German . . . U-boat."

"Yes! We understand, but to what end?"

"For . . . stone."

"A U-boat for the stone?" Joanna queried before looking quickly to me. "I believe he is telling us a U-boat is coming for the blue diamond."

"But where and when?" I asked in reply.

She relayed the question to Smits in yet a louder voice. "Where and when is the pickup to be?"

"For . . . stone," he mumbled, as his eyes closed and his consciousness faded.

"But where and when?"

There was no response.

"Where and when?" Joanna repeated for the third time.

Again, there was no response.

Whilst we were pondering our next move, the door to the intensive care room suddenly opened and Major Von Ruden entered, with the sister at his side. "I am told that his condition has worsened even more," the major said dolefully.

"Sadly so," Joanna replied.

"His blood loss continues unabated," I added. "And apparently the list of suitable blood donors is quite limited."

"I shall alert my entire unit, and I can assure you that every man will step forward to donate as much as needed."

"Please do so at your earliest convenience."

"I shall," Von Ruden vowed, and looked over to the sister. "Has he shown any evidence of regaining consciousness?"

"Very little, sir," the sister answered. "Although he did mumble a few words when questioned by the lady."

"Oh?" Von Ruden asked, and turned suddenly to my wife. "Was it information I should be aware of?"

"I wished to know if he had actually seen the assassin, if only briefly," Joanna lied easily. "Unfortunately, he could offer no description, and repeatedly muttered the word *boat* for some reason."

"I see," Von Ruden said, showing an expression of bewilderment. "Are you certain it was *boat* he uttered?"

"Not entirely," Joanna uttered. "It might have been *Botha,* your man who first spotted the assassin."

"Possibly," Von Ruden agreed mildly.

"In any event, I know you will wish to call in the members of your unit to be blood donors at the earliest moment, for that is Lieutenant Smits's most urgent need."

"I shall attend to that immediately," said Von Ruden, and turned to the sister. "Where would be the nearest telephone?"

"At the front desk, sir."

"I shall return shortly," said he, and hurried away.

Joanna waited for a few brief seconds to pass before closing the door and inquiring of the sister, "I suspect the major wished to know every word of my conversation with Lieutenant Smits?"

"Oh, he was most interested," the sister replied. "He asked me to repeat every word several times."

"And what words were those?"

"*You* and *boat.*"

"Did he make any sense of it?"

"He did not appear to."

"Very good, Sister," said Joanna. "On that note we shall leave you, knowing that you will keep a most watchful eye on the good lieutenant."

"I shall indeed, madam."

We departed the intensive care room and, on exiting the surgical ward itself, happened upon Harry Askins, who was racing by.

"They are having difficulty matching the poor chap up for additional units of blood," said he unhappily.

"Perhaps the head of the South African security unit will be of assistance, for he is now calling in all members of his force to be prospective donors," I proposed.

"The more, the better," Askins said, and hurried on his way.

On leaving the busy, somewhat noisy surgical ward, we entered a quiet corridor where I remarked, "Let us hope Von Ruden comes through with the additional donors, good man that he is."

"He is a liar," Joanna said, with a scowl.

"In regards to collecting more donors?" I asked, taken aback.

"Oh, he will line up the donors."

"Then pray tell what is he lying about?"

"Everything else," Joanna replied, and left it at that.

CHAPTER TWENTY

The Turncoat

We returned to 221b Baker Street and found Dolly, the Alsatian, waiting eagerly at the door for us. Her tail was wagging furiously in anticipation of food, but she was to be momentarily disappointed. After Joanna gave the hound's head a brief scratch, we proceeded to the kitchen, where Miss Hudson was merrily applying a final basting to the well-cooked goose.

"I see your work on the fine bird is nearing an end," said Joanna.

"Another half hour should do nicely," Miss Hudson replied, closing the oven.

"I trust you have followed Dr. Watson's prescription to take frequent rest periods as you went about your tasks."

"Oh, poor Dr. Watson has tired himself out going up and down the stairs to look in on me."

"That is because he cares so much for you."

"And how well aware of that I am, Mrs. Watson."

Dolly began to whimper at the lack of attention being paid to her, now licking her lips to the side of her mouth, which was a sure sign she was expecting to be fed.

"The dog begs beautifully," Joanna commented, before asking Miss Hudson, "Do you have a tidbit for this starving hound?"

"More than a tidbit," Miss Hudson replied, and moved to the icebox to fetch a wrapped meat bone which she presented to my wife. "I know you very much enjoy doing the honors."

Joanna slowly unwrapped the thick bone that still contained a few generous strands of lamb. Dolly crept in silently, her eyes fixed on the meal as if it were prey.

"Stay!" Joanna commanded, and watched the hound come to an abrupt halt. My wife gave the dog's head a generous scratch and waited a moment before handing over the bone. Dolly's huge jaws clamped down on the prize; then she carried it over to a far corner to chew on it in private.

"You are spoiling her, Mrs. Watson," said Miss Hudson, with a hint of feigned exasperation.

"So it would seem," Joanna agreed. "And now up to our rooms so we can attend to Dr. Watson, who I am certain will be reenergized when you present him with your splendid goose."

My father awaited us at the top of the stairs, comfortably attired in a tattered maroon smoking jacket which he refused to

relinquish, for it was the last vestige of his happier, exciting days
with Sherlock Holmes. He wore the jacket when involved in a
most puzzling case, for he once confided to me that he believed
it brought good fortune.

"Thank you for sparing me yet another journey to look in on
the tireless Miss Hudson," he welcomed us.

"She seemed stronger than ever," said I.

"Let us hope she remains so."

Joanna took my father's arm and escorted him back into our
parlor that was pleasantly warmed with a blazing fire. "And now,
Watson, I should like you to enjoy a pipeful of Arcadia Mixture
while we apprise you of a most interesting sequence of events."

As we gathered around the fireplace and sank into our overstuffed chairs, Joanna went directly to the heart of the matter.
"We appear to have a turncoat in the South African security
unit."

"I say!" my father responded in surprise. "Is there solid proof
to back up this assertion?"

"Not as yet, but the circumstantial evidence is such that it can
bring me to no other conclusion," Joanna replied. "Let us begin
with the most important message meant for the commissioner's
and my ears only, but never delivered."

In detail, she told of Lieutenant Smits's unannounced visit to
the office of the commissioner, who at the time was engaged in
a meeting at 10 Downing Street. "When he was unable to see
the commissioner, the lieutenant obtained our phone number
from Lestrade, with the fabrication that he had acquired the important information we had requested. Of course no such request
was made. Smits called our number, but there was no answer, for
we were away at our appointment with Mr. Freddie Morrison,
while you, Watson, were in all likelihood looking in on Miss
Hudson. Hours later, Lieutenant Smits was grievously wounded
protecting the Governor-General during an assassination attempt.

Now, what do you make of that string of supposedly unconnected events?"

My father puffed gently on his pipe whilst he considered the question at length. Like her father before her, Joanna used Watson as a sounding board, for she often repeated Sherlock Holmes's very words that "Nothing clears up a case so much as stating it to another person." After a few minutes passed, my father concluded, "I take it you believe the assassination attempt on the Governor-General was a façade to cover the execution of Lieutenant Smits."

"Bravo, Watson!"

"But do you have concrete evidence, for this is a most serious allegation?"

"It is circumstantial, I must admit, yet more than strong enough to convince an old skeptic such as you." She arose from her chair to fetch a Turkish cigarette from the Persian slipper and, after lighting it, began to tread the floor at a rapid pace, which no doubt matched the speed of her thought process. "Let us establish the notion that the assassination of a most important political personage would require one to hire a highly skilled assassin. Agreed?"

"No doubt, and one that would command an exorbitant fee as well."

"And being accomplished, he would go to great ends to hide his presence, so that the deed and his escape could be carried out flawlessly."

"That is an entirely reasonable assumption."

"Then why did this skilled assassin not do so?"

My father sat up abruptly in his chair. "Are you saying he revealed himself?"

"In a manner of speaking, yes. Allow me to give you the particulars." Joanna clearly delineated the office with its open window overlooking Trafalgar Square, from which the assassin took his shot. "And he did so with the barrel of his rifle protruding out the window."

"Perhaps he was not so skilled, after all."

"Or perhaps he wished to be seen, for no assassin of any merit would ever do so," Joanna countered. "And he does so in broad daylight, with the sun peeking out in such a manner that it could produce a noticeable glint off the metal barrel. That is beyond foolhardy, for the target was only seventy-five yards away, which is an easy mark for an experienced marksman."

"Was the office cluttered to such an extent that it gave him little room?"

"To the contrary, Watson. There was only a simple desk and chair in that office, and the evidence shows he sat at the desk while waiting for the opportune moment."

My father gave the matter further thought as he pondered the assassin and his weapon, for he himself was a marksman who was experienced in the use of both rifle and pistol. He closed his eyes lightly, no doubt placing himself in the role of the assassin.

"It does not ring true, does it?" asked Joanna.

My father opened his eyes. "The shot should have been taken while seated at the desk, for such a position would have given the assassin's hands and weapon stability while in the act of firing."

"Spot-on, my dear Watson. And what if I added that the rifle produced a most prominent muzzle flash?"

"He evidently wanted to be seen, for such a flash could easily be seen a block away. Moreover, the blast lasted long enough for an observer to pinpoint its location."

"What sort of weapon produces a noticeable muzzle flash?"

"Many do, but none quite so striking as the short-barrel Mauser S Patrone rifle, which is a favorite of the German army."

"Which fits nicely with the spent cartridge shell we found on the floor near the window," Joanna appended. "It carried the label DWM, which is the abbreviation for Deutsche Waffen und

Munitionsfabriken, the firm which manufactures most of Germany's armaments."

My father squinted in puzzlement as another question came to mind. "But why leave the spent cartridge behind, where it was certain to be discovered?"

"It was his calling card," Joanna replied. "He wanted us to believe he was a German assassin."

"Do you believe otherwise?"

"I shall leave that question open for now, which brings us to the turncoat, who I believe to be Major Eric Von Ruden."

My father's jaw dropped, stunned by the shocking revelation. "Is there proof to show it?"

"Again, it is circumstantial, but I shall present you with the facts as they occurred and you may draw your own conclusion." Joanna described in detail our visit to the intensive care room at St. Bartholomew's and the dire condition of Lieutenant Smits. She then repeated the lieutenant's abbreviated, stammered response when asked about the message he carried. "He uttered the letter *U*, then the word *boat*, followed by what sounded like *for . . . stone*."

"So the thieves intend to transport the blue diamond across the Channel by U-boat," my father deduced immediately. "But that does not bring us any closer to the identity of the perpetrators."

"Oh, but it does," Joanna contended. "For a sister was present and overheard Smits's response to the questions. She was asked to excuse herself and did so, and while outside the intensive care room she encountered Von Ruden, who queried her over and over as to what Smits had told us. And he wanted it word for word."

"Did she disclose the lieutenant's answers?"

"Every syllable, yet when he entered the room he asked us the very same questions in an attempt to glean every shred of information."

"I do not see how that points to Von Ruden as the perpetrator."

"You must dig deeper, Watson," Joanna said, discarding her cigarette into the fire and watching it burn. "We have established that Smits was holding a secret message and that its contents were only to be revealed to the commissioner and myself. It must have been of vital importance, you would agree."

"Quite so."

"Then why did he not take Von Ruden into his confidence?"

My father grumbled at the obvious answer. "Because he realized that his major was a turncoat."

"And if his knowledge was discovered by Von Ruden, Smits knew it would result in his execution."

My father carefully assembled the new information before responding, "I am afraid, Joanna, that your conclusion is for the most part based on conjecture."

"You are missing the larger point, Watson."

"Which is?"

"How did Von Ruden come by the secret message? Surely, Smits did not tell him, which was the reason why the major tried to pry the lieutenant's words from us and the sister while the poor man was on his deathbed."

My father nodded slowly. "He believed that Smits now knew the identities of those involved in the theft of the blue diamond. But how did Von Ruden learn of the plot?"

"Perhaps from the same informant who passed on the particulars to Lieutenant Smits and who decided to play both sides of the street," Joanna surmised. "You will recall that Smits had remained in contact with the underworld sources he had gathered while serving as a detective in Johannesburg."

"So the informant in his greed demanded payment from both Smits and Von Ruden, separately of course."

"And the latter demand no doubt cost him his life."

"A bloody ruthless lot by any measure," said my father, as another thought came to mind. "Do you believe Von Ruden will attempt to have Smits murdered while he lies defenseless at St. Bart's?"

Joanna shook her head. "There is no need, for Smits will do the dying for him. But I am afraid, Watson, that it is we who now pose the greatest threat to Von Ruden and his well-constructed plans. For if we no longer exist, his path to success will be unimpeded."

"And like Smits had, we, too, have an assassin waiting for the opportune moment to strike," my father noted with gravity. "Thus we must double our precautions and limit our activities away from Baker Street."

"*Au contraire,* we must now expand our investigation and follow the trail of the blue diamond, for it will lead us to the precious gem and to the turncoat."

"How do you suggest we go about that seemingly impossible task?"

"We require the knowledge of a diamond merchant who is aware of all the ins and outs which are involved in successfully transporting a rare blue diamond from England to the Continent during wartime."

"It would have to be someone with a sterling reputation," I added. "Such a dealer would have to be an individual we could take into our confidence."

"Are we familiar with such a dealer?" asked my father.

"You are, Watson," said Joanna, as a hint of a smile crossed her face. "It is someone you are quite familiar with."

"Who, pray tell?"

"Your former comrade-in-arms, Albert Dubose."

CHAPTER TWENTY-ONE

Albert Dubose

It was late afternoon the following day before we could meet with Albert Dubose, for he was just returning from a business trip to the Netherlands. On entering his fashionable home in Kensington, we could not help but notice that the parlor itself and its fine furnishings were designed for an individual confined to a wheelchair. The room and its doorways were quite wide, and all of its cabinets and drawers placed at knee level so their knobs could be easily reached.

We were shown in by Bikram, his Sikh manservant, who had come to Dubose's assistance when he was gravely wounded at the Battle of Kandahar. It was there that an Afghan bullet had pierced his spine and caused a paralysis from the waist down. Were it not for Bikram, who fought by his side and carried Dubose back to safety, the young soldier would have surely perished in the Afghan desert. Since that sad day, Bikram had never left the jeweler's side.

"How good to see you again, Watson," Dubose greeted my father warmly. "And under much more pleasant circumstances."

"Indeed," my father agreed. "I take it your dreadful bedsore has healed well."

"Quite well, thanks to the treatment with those magnificent maggots."

I immediately thought back to our earlier visit with Dubose at St. Bartholomew's, where he was being treated for a large bedsore which reached the necrotic stage. All forms of therapy had failed until, as a last resort, his physician inundated the open wound with feeding maggots that promptly ate away the dead

tissue and left the healthy to heal. It was an archaic form of treatment which had been passed down through the centuries, but on
occasion still worked remarkably well.

"Mr. Dubose, I trust you recall me from our prior visit," said I.

"Of course I do, young Dr. Watson," replied he. "And it is
my pleasure to see you once again."

"Allow me to introduce my wife, Joanna, who unfortunately
could not accompany us before because of an ill child, who has
recovered nicely."

"Ah, the daughter of Sherlock Holmes," Dubose noted with
delight. "It is an honor to finally meet you, madam."

"The honor is mine, sir," Joanna returned the affable welcome.

"And would I not be correct in assuming that it was you who
brought about this unexpected visit, just as you had done with
the Watsons earlier?"

"You are most perceptive."

"Then let us begin, but first tea, if you would be so kind,
Bikram."

The tall, well-built Sikh had broad shoulders and dark skin
that was highlighted by the white turban and nicely starched uni-
form he wore. In an instant he silently turned and disappeared
through an exceptionally spacious doorway. His footsteps made
no sound.

Dubose wheeled himself over to a large mahogany coffee table
which rested in front of a marble fireplace with smoldering logs.
Above the hearth was a striking portrait of Dubose's brother, Felix,
a renowned London jeweler whose stores carried the finest gems
in all England. Yet it was Albert Dubose who was the bona fide
expert in diamonds, and it was he who determined the quality of
diamonds sold by Dubose Jewelers. His knowledge was so extensive that other London jewelers often sought his opinion when
they encountered a particularly rare or unusual diamond.

"I see where you successfully brought the case of *The Art of Deception* to conclusion," Dubose said, recalling the adventure in which valuable portraits were being defaced by a vandal for no apparent reason. It was during our investigation that we first encountered Felix Dubose, whose Cézanne had been savagely slashed. "We had the wonderful painting restored of course, but it never seemed the same."

"They never do when the damage is so large scale," Joanna remarked.

"That is one of the wonderful features of diamonds," said Dubose. "Despite their beauty and brilliance, they are naturally impossible to destroy."

"Which brings us to the purpose of our visit."

"So I presumed."

"And in particular, I require information on the transport of diamonds from London to the Continent."

"That I had not presumed," Dubose stated, now leaning forward with interest. "Are we speaking of legitimate or illegitimate transport?"

"Is there a difference?"

"There can be, especially during wartime."

"It is the latter I am interested in."

Dubose sat back and smiled to himself. "You are no doubt speaking of the blue diamond."

"What brings you to that assessment?"

"Oh, come now, madam. A famous diamond has been stolen and the daughter of Sherlock Holmes and the Watsons show up on my doorstep inquiring about the transport of diamonds to the Continent. What other conclusion could one reach?"

Joanna hesitated. "It might be in your best interest not to know."

"That dicey, eh?" Dubose asked, unmoved. "Nevertheless, your refusal to respond gives me the answer. So then, let us proceed with how to move diamonds across the English Channel."

Before we could continue, Bikram reappeared carrying a laden silver tray from which he served tea, then retired to a far corner where he stood motionless, like a statue in a museum. His eyes never left Albert Dubose.

"There is no difficulty moving diamonds out of an English port," the jeweler began once more. "For obvious reasons, they cannot be transported in merchant ships, for they well might become targets of German U-boats. But there are other civilian vessels, such as those used for fishing, which would do quite nicely. The difficulty is that one cannot simply sail such a boat into a foreign port without arousing suspicion and incurring inspection. Thus it is best to transfer the diamonds to a waiting vessel in the Channel, hopefully away from prying eyes, and then carry them on into a neutral port, such as Copenhagen or Rotterdam. But even under these precautions one has to be careful, for there are thieves and foreign agents situated on those docks waiting for a ripe opportunity."

"And there are eager buyers waiting as well, I would think."

"For diamonds, always, because they are without fail negotiable and untraceable."

"Would that still be the case for an immensely valuable blue diamond?"

Dubose shrugged his answer. "Once cut and polished into many pieces, it would be lost forever."

Joanna sipped her tea and studied the jeweler over the rim of her exquisite teacup. "But for such a procedure, it would no doubt have to go through Antwerp."

Dubose nodded quickly. "Only the Royal Asscher Diamond Company would be entrusted with such an immensely valuable diamond."

"And the Germans would surely be aware, would they not?"

Dubose nodded again. "As the occupying force, they keep

a keen eye on the diamond trade and would of course demand
their fair share. Keep in mind that war is a very expensive business and is believed to cost Germany several billion pounds a
year. Thus the Huns squeeze every shilling they can out of the
countries they occupy."

"What if the Germans were actively participating in the
transport across the English Channel?"

"Then it would be as easy as a walk across Hyde Park."

"But I suspect there might still be some difficulty moving
the blue diamond out of an English port on a reliable vessel."

"Not if it was done with guile. The best plan would be to
stay away from the busiest ports, which are always under careful
watch. One would find the somewhat less active docks at Dover
and Ramsgate more advantageous, and most importantly they
are close to London, which means less travel."

"And all such measures would have to be preplanned of
course."

"Only if one wishes to ensure success, for all it requires is one
slipup and your precious cargo is lost."

"Most informative," Joanna said genuinely.

"But not the sole purpose of your visit," Dubose went on.
"You could have obtained similar information from the Royal
Navy, yet you are here, which tells me your visit goes deep."

My father and I quickly glanced at each other, wondering
if Dubose was on the mark or simply attempting to match wits
with the family detective.

Joanna gave the jeweler a long, studied look before saying,
"What I am about to tell you must go no further than this room."

"Agreed," said Dubose, warming to the task.

"Some time ago—do not ask me when—I received a most
strange message which referred to a valuable diamond as a stone.
The term *stone* bothered me then and continues to do so. I wish

you to inform me how often the word *stone* is used as a substitute for *diamond*."

"Never by anyone who is familiar with diamonds," Dubose replied at once. "Calling a diamond a stone would be like referring to a Rembrandt as a painting. Both fall into their correct category, but each is so remarkable they demand their own distinctive name. Thus, only the uninformed would describe a diamond, particularly a blue diamond, as a stone."

"Would this hold true for thieves as well?"

Dubose answered with a shake of his head. "They use colloquialisms such as *ice* or *rocks,* but never *stones*."

"What of inspectors and constables?"

"No, nor does the ordinary man or the aristocrat who enters a jewelry store to purchase a diamond. Would he ever say that he desires to see a good selection of stones? I think not."

"So you would state conclusively that the word *stone* in the message did not refer to a valuable diamond?"

"And this individual was familiar with diamonds?"

"Quite."

"Then surely it does not imply or infer possession of the blue diamond."

"Most helpful," Joanna said, arising from her chair.

Dubose waved a hand in farewell. "Bikram will see you out, and Watson, I expect a return visit soon so we can speak of our old soldiering days."

"I shall look forward to it," my father replied.

Outside in the twilight, we carefully studied the street and footpath to assure ourselves that no one suspicious was watching us or even nearby. We saw only our waiting black taxi in front of the Dubose residence, with the driver promptly starting his motor as instructed. Although Kensington was an upscale, rather exclusive neighborhood, assassins were known to ply their trade in such places as well.

On opening the taxi door for Joanna, I asked in a quiet voice, "What did you make of our conversation with Albert Dubose?"

"Simply put, we have misread Smits's deathbed message," Joanna said starkly. "And that is much to our disadvantage."

Chapter Twenty-Two

The Spy

It was early afternoon the following day when the most unexpected telephone call came to 221b Baker Street. The caller was the director of MI5, who requested our immediate presence. An unmarked motor vehicle would shortly be at our doorstep to transport us to an undisclosed location. No further information was given.

We hurriedly reached for our topcoats and scarves, with my father checking the rounds in his Webley revolver before securely holstering it. Down the stairs we dashed, passing Miss Hudson, who was carrying a tray laden with roast duck that gave off a most appetizing aroma.

"Will you be returning for lunch?" asked she.

"Unlikely," Joanna replied.

"And what of the duck?"

"Refrigerate for sandwiches later."

A black sedan awaited us as we exited the front entrance. The driver remained behind the wheel, and it was of note that he was wearing a derby pulled down far over his forehead, which obscured much of his facial features. There was no greeting.

We sped through the Marylebone district, somehow managing to avoid the streets which had been badly damaged by the recent attack of German bombers. But this was to change as we entered Central London, where more careful driving was needed, for now the street was cratered with bowl-shaped cavities, with a number of the adjacent homes reduced to smoldering rubble. Ambulance workers were desperately searching for survivors.

Once we had cleared the heavily bombed area, our motor vehicle regained its speed and drove on until the Tower of London, with its massive brick walls, came into view. Now we could deduce the purpose of our summons, for here was the prison where spies and traitors were kept and later executed.

"The German spy must have been apprehended," I said, stating the obvious conclusion.

"And he must be talking or have in his possession important clues," my father added, then turned to my wife, who did not seem to be sharing our excitement. "What say you, Joanna?"

"I say it is most unlikely that our spy is imprisoned in the tower."

"Why so?"

"Because we are now racing by that hallowed place."

We continued on past several blocks of row houses before turning in to a narrow street that was within sight of the London docks. Down the way children were playing on the footpath, whilst nearby people were strolling about, some with dogs, all apparently carefree. We stopped in front of a row house with its shutters closed, and again our driver remained behind the steering wheel, and without saying a word gestured for us to leave the vehicle. As we departed, the door to the row house opened and we were led into a drawing room where Capt. Vernon Carter-Smith awaited us.

Skipping the amenities, he said, "We have located the German spy and need your assistance to bring him in alive."

The director of MI5 gave us every detail, speaking in a tone of voice devoid of zeal. He could have been reading from the telephone directory rather than telling a tale meant for spy novels.

"Using direction-finding radio equipment, we were able to intercept the German spy's signal and track his position to a modest hotel near the Thames. Yet again he was sending messages to what we believed was a U-boat in the English Channel. Our finder pinpointed the spy's location to a room on the third floor overlooking the river, which of course allowed us excellent transmission and reception. We are certain we have our man, for his last message again included the words *Backs to the Wall*. On questioning the hotel manager, we determined the agent registered under the name Lewis Marlowe and claimed to be a writer working on a historical manuscript. He wished to be undisturbed and would only leave his room to take an afternoon stroll. The charwoman was allowed entrance, but always under his careful eye, and all meals were to be brought to his room by a waiter.

"Now, one would think a capture could be easily accomplished by having an MI5 agent, disguised as a waiter, deliver the spy's food and simply overpower him when the door opens. But our spy is far too clever for that. He insists the waiter rap on the door to announce his arrival, then place the tray on the floor. The door will only open after the waiter has departed. And crashing our way into the spy's room will not do because that would give him time to bite down on a cyanide capsule, which all German agents carry and which brings instant death. We need him alive for obvious reasons. Thus our best chance for the grab is when he takes his afternoon stroll, and that is when Mrs. Watson and the two doctors come into play."

"I shall have my Webley revolver at the ready," my father volunteered.

"Which I implore you not to use," Carter-Smith said at once. "I stress again that we must take him alive, and gun battles, even the best planned, often go awry."

"Then what role are we to play?"

"A most important one, for we must be certain we have the right man when the capture occurs, and you shall so inform us."

The director of MI5 produced a sketch of the entire lobby of the hotel which showed the registration desk, a small shop, a separate dining room off to the side, and a quite large seating area, with couches, overstuffed chairs, and scattered coffee tables. "When the spy arrives in the lobby, he invariably stops at the desk to fetch a morning newspaper, then retires to a nearby chair for a read. He keeps his back to the wall and faces the entrance to view any arrivals. Being superb at what he does, the spy no doubt surveys the entire floor, searching for anything out of place. Staying in the hotel is a somewhat elderly gentleman in a wheelchair who is visited every afternoon by a young couple who are close relatives. They sit in a far corner where they are served tea." Carter-Smith gestured to us and said, "You three will take the place of that family."

"What of the elderly man in the wheelchair and his visitors?" asked Joanna.

"They will remain in his room enjoying lunch under the watchful eyes of one of my agents, while you and the Watsons are taken to the tradesman entrance of the hotel," the director went on. "Upon entering, the senior Dr. Watson will be provided with a wheelchair, and the three of you will proceed to the far corner of the lobby, where you will be served tea. There you will wait for a middle-aged man wearing a dark derby to approach the registration desk for a newspaper. Then the senior Dr. Watson will glance over, and if the registrar straightens his tie as the spy departs for his chair it will be your sign he is our man."

"Does he have any unusual features?" asked Joanna.

"He appears quite ordinary in every fashion, including height, frame, gait, and dress," Carter-Smith replied. "And the matter is further complicated by the fact that there are two other guests at the hotel who bear some semblance to the spy. That is the reason for this charade. We must be certain we have the right man."

"How do we signal that we have made a positive identification?"

"You will wait several minutes, then rise and kiss Dr. Watson's forehead, as if in farewell. Then proceed out of the hotel and ask the doorman to hail a taxi, which will appear instantly. Sometime later our spy will finish his newspaper and depart for his daily walk. As he exits, the doorman, who is one of my agents, will deliver a blow to the back of the spy's head and render him unconscious, thus completing the capture." The director of MI5 quickly checked his timepiece and gestured to an agent standing nearby. "We must set the pieces in play, for our spy will shortly be served his lunch."

We were driven to the hotel in the rear of a delivery vehicle so as to disguise our arrival, for the spy was often seen at the window of his room surveilling the footpath below. Despite the attention given to the smallest detail, I could not help but sense Joanna's concern as we approached the tradesman entrance.

"What so bothers you?" asked I.

"The plan," she replied.

"But it seems well conceived, without obvious flaws."

"Assuming everything goes as anticipated, which it rarely does when one has so many players in motion."

Our delivery lorry came to a stop and we entered a very busy kitchen where an MI5 agent awaited us. My father was quickly seated in a wheelchair, with a woolen blanket placed upon his lap and a thick scarf wrapped around his neck. He was instructed to slouch down in the wheelchair, which diminished his size considerably. He now appeared to be quite elderly and infirm. The kitchen workers made way as we wheeled my father into a half-filled dining room, then into the main lobby and over to a far corner well away from the registration desk. The lobby was for the most part vacant, with only a middle-aged couple opening their umbrellas as they departed into a light rain.

A waiter appeared and promptly served tea. The expression on his face and the brief stare he gave us indicated he was an MI5 agent in disguise. He disappeared into the dining room so that he would not be called upon by the spy. This unhurried activity was followed by an eerie silence in the lobby, the only sound being that produced by our muted conversation. We took turns glancing over to the registration desk whilst we waited.

"The silent, empty lobby is bothersome," Joanna spoke in a barely audible voice. "We are sure to draw his attention."

"What if he strolls over for a closer look?" my father asked.

"Ignore him."

"He may have become acquainted with this guest in the wheelchair earlier."

"That is most unlikely, for spies do not make acquaintances."

"But still, he may sense something is amiss and reach for his weapon."

"Then shoot him in the kneecap, which will produce such excruciating pain that he will have neither the time nor wits to swallow a cyanide capsule."

My father was indeed capable of such a shot, for he was a true marksman who visited a firing range twice a month to maintain his skill. And Joanna was absolutely correct in stating that the discomfort arising from a shattered patella was totally incapacitating and would bring the strongest of men to the ground, howling in pain. The only drawback of such a shot was that it could rupture the popliteal artery and cause a major hemorrhage. I loosened my tie a bit in the event it was needed as a tourniquet.

Suddenly, we heard the noise of a struggle originating from

the upper level of the staircase, followed by heavy footsteps coming closer and closer. Throwing off his blanket, my father jumped to his feet and assumed the firing position, with his revolver aimed at the base of the staircase.

"He is a madman!" a waiter screamed as he stumbled down the stairs, waving his hands wildly one moment and clutching his bloodstained white jacket the next. "A madman, I tell you!"

The injured waiter dashed across the lobby and into the dining room, where he was met by a chorus of shrieks from the diners. Then he bolted for the door to the kitchen and disappeared behind it.

The MI5 agent, disguised as a doorman, raced for the stairs with his weapon drawn. I quickly overturned a couch and secured my father and wife behind it. My father kept his Webley revolver pointed straight ahead, with his hand steady, but there was no way he could have been prepared for what came next.

The MI5 agent called out from the top of the staircase, "Dr. Watson, I need your assistance!"

My father holstered his revolver and hurried up the stairs, with Joanna and me a step behind. On the third level outside an opened door we found a dazed man, who was seated on the floor and holding a napkin to a gash on his forehead that was bleeding profusely. The injured man was obviously not the spy, for he was short, stout, and well into his middle years, with a spilled tray by his side.

My father rapidly attended to the wound by applying deep pressure with a clean handkerchief to stem the bleeding, then leaving the cloth in place to facilitate the formation of a clot. "That will suffice for now, but the wound will have to be closed with sutures."

"Thank you, sir," the injured man said gratefully.

"You are most welcome," my father replied. "But pray tell us how you came by this wound."

"I am not certain, sir, but I believe I was struck by the guest for no apparent reason as I delivered his lunch."

Joanna leaned in closer, and, using her own handkerchief, dabbed away the blood from the waiter's eyelids so he could see clearly. "We need to know precisely what happened prior to the blow being struck. Leave out no detail."

"Some water, please," he requested. I fetched him a glass of cool water from the room, which he thirstily gulped down. He then rested his back against the wall and took several deep breaths to gather himself before telling his story. "I rapped on the guest's door and announced that lunch was being served. It was my custom to place the tray down and depart, for only then would he open the door to fetch his food. But on this occasion, he chose to encounter me and ask why the service was late by fifteen minutes. You see, he demands his lunch be brought at exactly two without fail."

"And your response?"

"Why, the truth, madam. I told him that I was instructed to delay the service until a man in a wheelchair appeared in the kitchen. The guest then invited me in to receive a gratuity for my splendid work, and a moment later everything went black. I do not believe I tripped or—"

Joanna quickly interrupted as she looked up at us. "The delay for a man in a wheelchair alerted the spy and provoked the attack."

"Did I make an inappropriate statement?" the waiter asked anxiously.

"You only stated a fact," Joanna replied, downplaying the importance of the comment.

Carter-Smith was standing quietly in the background and had listened to every word of the injured man's tale. "The spy no doubt fled after the attack, but that was only minutes ago, so he may well be trapped in the hotel, for all entrances and exits are under heavy guard. Thus he will shortly be brought to justice, but in all likelihood dead, for he will choose cyanide over capture."

"He has escaped," Joanna said without inflection.

"Based on what, may I ask?"

"On the fact that the injured man is the waiter and he no longer has on his white jacket."

My father's jaw dropped. "The spy was the man fleeing down the stairs wearing a bloodied white jacket!"

"I am afraid so," said Joanna, with a nod. "He is a most clever fellow, and screaming about a madman was a nice touch."

The director of MI5 growled under his breath, showing a rare emotion. "So he has slipped from our grasp and with him goes our best chance to retrieve the war document before it sets sail for Germany." Then collecting himself, he paused and tapped a finger against his chin, rethinking the problem facing him. "But we have disrupted his schedule, which could delay his departure."

"Or hasten it," Joanna proposed. "Whatever the calculation, we have little time at our disposal."

"How much do you estimate?"

"Days at the most, for the longer he stays, the greater the chance he will be apprehended."

"Then we must redouble our efforts and trust that the spy will send further messages which we can track," he said, and led the way into the hotel room.

A thorough search revealed only a change of clothes, simple toiletries, and a stack of white sheets of paper on a small table. None of the pages had been written upon. On the floor was a wireless transmitter which looked as if it had been stomped upon and rendered useless. There was no sign of the war document.

I knelt down to examine the smashed wireless machine

which lay on its side. "I do not understand why he destroyed the transmitter, for now he has no way to send out messages."

"He could not carry it down the stairs," Joanna explained. "Had he done so, we might have recognized him as the spy. After all, bloodied waiters do not have wireless machines under their arms."

"Moreover, he may not have needed it," the director told us. "Spies often have additional equipment stashed elsewhere. I can assure you that if he wishes to send further messages, he will find a way to do so."

We departed without further discussion and, after instructing the registrar to have the injured waiter taken to a nearby surgery, we exited the hotel and hailed a waiting taxi. As we boarded the vehicle, a powerful thunderstorm broke loose and sent down a torrential downpour, which pounded on the roof of the taxi with such intensity that it was impossible for the driver to overhear our conversation.

Nevertheless, I spoke in a low voice. "I cannot help but wonder if the spy had sent a final message which arranged for the document to be delivered to a U-boat."

"It is best to assume such an arrangement has already been made," Joanna opined. "This clever spy has been one step ahead of us at every move, and it is wise to believe he remains so. And unfortunately we are now near the end of the chase, with time running out."

"Which places us at a major disadvantage."

"Thus it would seem."

"How shall we go about overcoming it?"

"By identifying the seller of the blue diamond as it changes hands," said she, resting her head back and closing her eyes in thought.

CHAPTER TWENTY-THREE

The Explosion

To clear our thoughts and not dwell on our setback, we decided on short notice to dine at Simpson's-in-the-Strand, which happened to be conveniently situated in nearby Covent Garden. We of course made certain we were not being followed by glancing periodically from the rear window of our hired taxi, as we rode along a circuitous route to my father's favorite restaurant. Nevertheless, on our arrival we took the further precaution of requesting a table away from the front door, and one that afforded a wall to our backs.

With our minds at ease for the moment, we enjoyed an excellent fare, with Joanna having the lamb, I the beef Wellington, and my father roast beef carved off the trolley. All was accompanied by Yorkshire pudding and washed down with a superb Médoc. We finished with Turkish coffee, and found ourselves enthralled by the exciting adventures of Sherlock Holmes, of which my father seemed to remember every detail.

"Tell me, Watson, was there ever a plot to assassinate my father?" asked Joanna.

"Three, and all were instigated by Moriarty," he replied at once, and proceeded to regale us with details of the failed attempts. "The first occurred just as Holmes was turning a street corner, alone and on a dark night. A carriage suddenly rushed toward him, and he was barely able to leap out of the way in time. The second attempt was closer yet. Holmes was walking along a footpath when a large brick fell from the roof of a house, missing him by only inches. And finally, on a stroll to my house, Holmes was attacked by a thug armed with a cosh. My friend managed to overcome his assailant and deliver him to the police. They were close calls in every instance, and he was most fortunate to escape unharmed."

"But I notice that you have not included his infamous fight with Moriarty at the Reichenbach Falls," said I.

"That is because I considered it a struggle between two equally matched adversaries, rather than one individual preying on another," my father clarified.

"Did my father revel in the death of Moriarty at the falls?" Joanna inquired.

"He showed no such emotion, for to Holmes it was simply a long-awaited fight with a worthy opponent, in which there would only be one victor."

"So he was not confident he would win?"

"I believe it was more a matter of him wishing to see if he would prevail over the cleverest opponent he had ever faced."

"And then he went into hiding for several years because he was of the opinion he would be in great danger from Moriarty's associates in London, who would seek revenge for the death of their leader."

My father nodded and added the finale. "Only when they were at last apprehended and imprisoned did Holmes return to our rooms on Baker Street."

"A most excellent ending," said Joanna, as a faint smile crossed her face and quickly disappeared. "And now, Watson, I have a closing question regarding my father, which only you can answer."

The sudden gravity in Joanna's voice drew my father's attention and caused him to lean in closer.

"It is quite straightforward," she went on. "I wish to know how you believe my father would have dealt with our assassin."

"In the very same fashion you plan to confront him," he

responded. "Holmes would seek him out and at the earliest opportunity destroy him."

"So be it," Joanna declared, pushing her chair back from the table.

We stepped out into a damp, dark night, with a heavy mist now covering the streets of Covent Garden. After glancing quickly to the sides, we hurried to our waiting vehicle and climbed in as our hired driver started its engine. The murky shroud made it difficult to determine if we were being followed, but it began to lift as we approached Marylebone, which gave us a better view of the traffic on Edgware Road. All was quiet until a large black vehicle suddenly sped by us and disappeared into the dimness ahead. Once again the street appeared silent and sparsely occupied, with hardly a soul on the footpaths. Yet we kept a sharp eye out and would continue to do so until we were safely ensconced in our rooms, for we knew our lives were in double jeopardy as long as Lieutenant Smits remained on the face of the earth. The perplexing message, I thought to myself, so much depended on the message he carried.

On arriving at the deserted footpath outside our residence, we dashed for the front entrance and heard Dolly barking a warm welcome. But as we reached the doorstep, a dark motor vehicle screeched to a halt on the opposite side of the street and a man abruptly appeared, waving a sparking light that flickered in the blackness. The illumination from a nearby lamppost brought the object into clearer view.

"Dynamite!" Joanna cried out, and pushed us through the doorway and into the foyer before landing on top of me.

Dolly flew past us into the street and lunged at the assailant with such force that the man crashed to the pavement. The lighted stick of dynamite seemed to float up into the air and be momentarily suspended there. Instinctively, Joanna somehow managed to lift a foot and kick the door shut, just as the assassin screamed in pain, which no doubt was caused by the giant hound clamping her massive jaws on some part of the man's anatomy. A mere second later came the explosion that rocked the entire frontage of 221b Baker Street. The door itself was dislodged from its hinges and tilted open by the blast, yet remained in an upright position.

Slowly rising to our feet, we took deep breaths and gathered ourselves, now aware of how close the hand of death had come. Evidence of the powerful explosion was everywhere, with the lamppost bent on an angle at its base, and beyond it a large lorry was lying on its side in the middle of the street. It was at this moment we realized it was more than the hound alone which had saved our lives. The large transport had blundered between the assassin and our door, and absorbed much of the blast, which accounted for it now being on its side, with a dazed driver standing next to it. We cautiously stepped out onto the pavement and around the bent lamppost, with its light fixture still intact and shining on the victims of the blast. The partially dismembered assassin was clearly dead, with a portion of his missing arm firmly clamped in the powerful jaw of Dolly, the Alsatian. The giant hound had been killed by the force of the explosion and would be sadly missed by the entire household at 221b Baker Street. The hired assassin would later be covered unceremoniously with dirt in a potter's field, which was far more than he deserved.

My father had hurried over to examine the stunned transport driver and then came back to report, "He is unharmed except for an obvious concussion. He, too, is somewhat fortunate in that the blast caught the very rear of his lorry, which was made of metal and gave him added protection."

"But it was Joanna who saved the day," I said. "Without her warning, we could have been blown to smithereens."

Joanna shook her head as she gazed down at the hound who had given her life to spare ours. "Had Dolly not attacked our assailant we would all be dead, for she gave us the time needed to close the door as well as the vital seconds required for the lorry to pass between us and the stick of dynamite." She sighed unhappily before adding, "It is remarkable how quickly dogs can distinguish between friend and foe, and act accordingly."

Miss Hudson appeared in her night robe and gasped loudly at the sight of the dead hound. "Oh, no!" she cried in a loud moan. "Not my sweet Dolly!"

"I am afraid so," said Joanna. "But you must be comforted in knowing she was the bravest of the brave, and died in the act of protecting us."

"What shall I tell poor Bertie who loved her so dearly?"

"How she died," Joanna replied simply. "I shall supply you with all the details at a more suitable time."

"And what am I to do with the piece of arm she has clamped in her jaw?"

"Pry it out and discard it," Joanna said coldly.

"I should take her inside out of the chill and dampness," Miss Hudson stated in a kind voice, then attempted unsuccessfully to lift the heavy hound. "I shall need a hand."

"Allow me to assist," my father offered, coming to her aid.

Once they had departed, I quickly leaned in to examine the dead assassin and search through his clothing. A leg and part of an arm had been blown off, but there was no evidence of great blood loss, indicating it was the blast rather than exsanguination which had caused his demise. His face was filled with terror, no doubt brought on by the knowledge his arm was about to be ripped off by a fearsome hound. In a vest pocket, I found a note which contained the identical, coded message carried by the initial assassin. I handed the slip of paper over to Joanna, who quickly read it.

221b Baker Street

+O +++

"And now the message is finally decoded," said she.

"How so?"

"The opening two lines instruct the three of us are to be killed in or about our residence on Baker Street," Joanna explained. "The multiple interrupted dashes on the third section do not represent some sort of natural decomposition, but rather the complete disintegration of our bodies by an explosive blast. It was their evil plan all along."

"But we were originally targeted at home by a marksman who shot, but fortunately missed me," I pointed out. "Was that simply an alternate plan?"

"I suspect so," Joanna replied. "For the conditions that stormy night were ideal for an execution, and the assassin found the opportunity irresistible."

"And he had a lorry in the alleyway ready to carry off our remains," I added.

My wife nodded, saying, "To a site where we would be certain to decompose."

"But all failed, and so he continued to lay in wait, knowing that another opportune moment to act would eventually arrive."

"We helped it arrive," Joanna corrected. "We put all the pieces in place for him."

"Intentionally?"

"Unwittingly," she went on. "I am of the belief he followed us to Albert Dubose's residence without being noticed, then to Simpson's-in-the-Strand, again without being seen. And he was behind us on Edgware Road before racing ahead, for he knew we were headed home. I suspect he carried the stick of dynamite with him everywhere, waiting for the perfect moment to light its fuse."

"It is rather poetic justice that the weapon intended to dismember us destroyed him instead," said I. "We should thus sleep a bit sounder tonight."

"That would be a mistake," Joanna cautioned. "You see, Von Ruden may well send another assassin, for we remain a threat to his grand design."

"But what if Lieutenant Smits dies?"

"It will not alter our eventual confrontation, for he realizes that I will not stop until he is brought to justice."

"So it continues to the very end, then."

"It will continue until one of us no longer breathes," said Joanna resolutely, and gave the dead assassin a final, dispassionate look.

Chapter Twenty-Four

The Disappearance

By noon the following day the door at our front entrance had been repaired and the bent lamppost straightened, and thus most of the evidence caused by the explosion had vanished. Only the blasted-out windowpanes on the ground floor remained and those were in the process of being replaced. All would soon be the same as before except for the constable now stationed on our doorstep.

"The commissioner insisted on the presence of the uniformed officer," Lestrade informed us, as he warmed his hands by the fireplace. "He believes it will dissuade any future assassins."

"I think not," said Joanna, puffing on a Turkish cigarette whilst pacing our parlor. "For this time around, I suspect they will send their very best."

Lestrade vented a frustrated groan at the menacing situation. "All this terrible mayhem brought to your very doorstep."

"By the evilest of men who intend to stop our investigation of the theft regardless of the cost in lives," said Joanna.

"With danger now lurking at every corner, surely you and the Watsons must become even more cautious."

"Excessive caution is a luxury we cannot afford, for it will impinge on the little time we have at our disposal."

Lestrade sighed resignedly. "The commissioner also believes that time is not on our side."

"Nor is it to the thief's advantage, for he has a timetable he must follow."

"I take it you are now speaking of Lieutenant Smits's utterance about a U-boat."

"Quite so, but where and when is the crucial information which unfortunately the good lieutenant failed to provide."

"Let us pray for his recovery."

"His chances to survive are rather dim," I interjected. "I spoke with Mr. Harry Askins, his surgeon at St. Bartholomew's, a few hours ago, and was told the patient had a prolonged episode of shock last night, which caused his kidneys to malfunction. This is a most ominous sign."

"And another setback," Lestrade said gloomily. "Even a brief moment of clarity on the lieutenant's part would be most welcome."

"You are hoping against hope," I stated frankly. "For such episodes of shock often damage the brain as well."

"So I will inform the commissioner," Lestrade said. "But on the off chance he awakens, Scotland Yard has posted a detective outside his hospital room."

"Which will give Lieutenant Smits added protection," I stated, then quickly added, "from curious onlookers."

"That, too."

After a soft rap on the door, Miss Hudson entered carrying a tray of freshly brewed tea, which she laid out and served without conversation. Our dear landlady remained distraught over the loss of Dolly, as evidenced by the redness in her eyes no doubt brought on by weeping.

"Will the inspector be joining you for lunch?" she spoke finally.

"You would be more than welcome, Lestrade," Joanna invited, tossing her cigarette into the fireplace.

"I wish that I could, madam, but I must shortly be on my way." Lestrade refused the offer in a kind way.

"Then it will just be the usual three of us," Joanna apprised the landlady.

"There is a possibility it will only be two this day, for Dr. Watson has departed to visit his personal physician," said Miss Hudson.

"Has he become ill?" I asked at once.

"He did not appear so," she replied, unconcerned. "The good doctor told me he was on his way to Harley Street and may not return until later in the day."

"His heart specialist," I noted.

Joanna's expression changed, with her brow now hanging over her eyes, but she made no comment.

"Well, then," Lestrade said, putting down his teacup. "I must take leave of you, for the commissioner awaits my return with a full report."

Once the inspector and Miss Hudson had departed and closed the door behind them, Joanna asked, "Has Watson been having symptoms again?"

I answered with an affirmative nod. "He detected a rapid,

irregular pulse last night and attributed it to anxiety from the explosion."

"But apparently it persisted."

"And became bothersome, for it is only under those circumstances does he visit his cardiologist to have his dose of digitalis leaf adjusted."

Joanna gave the matter more thought before requesting, "John, please be good enough to check Watson's nightstand and see if his Webley revolver remains in place."

I hurried into my father's bedroom and, after looking into the empty drawer by his bedside, hurried back. "He has taken the Webley with him."

"Good," Joanna said, as a hint of worry crossed her face.

"Are you concerned for his welfare?" I asked promptly. "Do you believe he may be in danger?"

"Probably not," she said, continuing to consider the situation. "It is less than a mile from here to Harley Street, and no doubt Watson's taxi picked him up at our doorstep and deposited him on the footpath outside the cardiologist's office. Thus there would be only the smallest window of opportunity for the new assassin to act, assuming one has already been set loose."

I nodded quickly at Joanna's assessment. "It would be quite difficult to hire a new, highly skilled assassin on such short notice."

"I am certain Watson factored that into his calculation."

"Yet he took his revolver with him."

"Better safe than sorry."

"Let us be certain he reached his destination." Out of concern I phoned the cardiologist's office and learned my father had already been seen and examined, then sent along his way. He had departed from the office ten minutes ago according to the secretary.

After hearing the report, Joanna said, "Then Watson should be home shortly, for it is a quick ride from there to here."

We waited impatiently as the minutes passed by, for my father was a man who valued punctuality and had adhered to a strict timetable all of his life. Had he definitely planned to be absent at lunch, he would have notified us, for the midday repast was always a gathering he so looked forward to. In addition, our worry was intensified by the lingering odor of exploded dynamite, which reminded us of how vicious and cruel our enemy was. It was not beyond them to harm my father as a way to distract us.

Joanna continued to pace the floor of our parlor, smoking one Turkish cigarette after another, whilst I glanced repeatedly from our window overlooking Baker Street, hoping to see my dear father approaching. All I saw were throngs of well-dressed shoppers entering stores which already had their inviting Christmas decorations in place. The festive scene did little to elevate my mood. As Big Ben struck one in the distance, a sudden thought came to mind which could explain my father's tardiness.

"It is quite possible that the cardiologist sent his patient elsewhere for other studies such as X-rays or blood studies," I suggested.

"Excellent!" Joanna approved of the idea. "Please call Watson's physician and determine if this has in fact occurred."

I immediately phoned the cardiologist and learned that no further studies were needed at the present time, which was disappointing news, and even more disappointing was the report that my father's condition had deteriorated somewhat and would now require a slightly increased dose of digitalis leaf, for which a prescription had been written. However, when told of my father's failure to return home, the cardiologist provided a most plausible explanation which gave me some comfort.

Placing the receiver down, I said hopefully, "My father may be at St. Bart's."

"Has he taken a turn for the worse?" Joanna asked at once.

"His heart rhythm is a bit more irregular, which can be

remedied by a larger dose of digitalis and does not necessitate hospitalization," I replied. "More likely, his visit to St. Bartholomew's was occasioned by the cardiologist mentioning that a lecture on quinine-resistant malaria was being delivered at the hospital this afternoon."

"Ah! A subject of keen interest to Watson," Joanna recalled. "This would be particularly so with the recent outbreak on the Balkan front."

"And even more recently amongst the Turkish troops."

"Who may I ask is delivering the lecture?"

"Stephen Marbury, a renowned expert on malaria, who has just returned from Paris with the latest developments."

"Watson would not miss that for the world."

"Nor should we."

We were able to quickly hail a four-wheeler and hurried to St. Bartholomew's, only to find that the lecture was scheduled for two thirty, which was an hour away. Rather than sit in a vacant amphitheater for a prolonged period, we decided to visit the intensive care room that housed Lieutenant Smits, with the faint hope that he was improving and could now verbalize. But our wish was soon dashed, for on our approach to the surgery section the double doors to the ward suddenly opened with a bang and out rolled a gurney transporting a deathly ill Adolph Smits. The mobile stretcher was being pushed forward by an orderly at the far end whilst being pulled by another at the front. A sister ran alongside holding up a unit of blood that was dripping the vital fluid into Smits's exposed arm. The surgeon, Harry Askins, followed through the door and stopped only briefly to give us an update.

"The patient's condition has gone from bad to worse," he said, pausing to catch his breath. "The poor man's chest is filling so rapidly with blood that he has a hemothorax, which leaves little space for air. Either we tie off the bleeder or he dies."

"Can he possibly survive the surgery?" I asked.

"We will find out shortly," Askins replied, and raced after the gurney.

I shook my head in despair as the gurney disappeared behind a second set of doors. "All continues to go against us."

"My father once said that there is nothing more stimulating than a case where everything goes against you," Joanna mused. "But I have doubts that he ever encountered a case such as this one."

"Indeed," I agreed, and turned for the corridor that led away from the surgical ward. "Let us rejuvenate our spirits with my father's appearance at the lecture."

Joanna quickly took my arm and redirected me in the direction of the intensive care room. "First, we should pay a visit to the detective who was assigned to guard Smits."

The sudden burst of activity had brought the surgery ward to life, with patients now moving about and filling the air with the hum of conversations. They seemed to ignore our presence except for a few who gave us only cursory glances. As we neared the intensive care room, the putrid aroma of stale blood and dead tissue came to our nostrils. The disagreeable odor had similarly affected Detective Sergeant Stone, who was wearing a surgical mask to ward against the unpleasantness.

He greeted us with a half salute and said, "Not a very good day, I am afraid, madam."

"So we see." Joanna peeked into the intensive care room, with its blood-splattered floor and used surgical instruments scattered about. "Did the patient speak at all in your presence?"

"Only briefly and I could not make much sense of it, madam," Stone reported.

"I need to hear his exact words," Joanna said, moving in closer so as not to miss a syllable. "And I want every sound he uttered in the order spoken."

Stone hesitated for a moment, thinking back in time. "A little over an hour ago he began moaning, and I wondered if he might be regaining consciousness. With that in mind, I hurried to the bedside and introduced myself as Detective Sergeant Stone from Scotland Yard. I spoke loudly and directly into his ear."

"Did he show any response?" Joanna asked.

"I believe so, for his eyelids began to flutter. It was then that I inquired about the message he had for the commissioner. His lids closed and he gave no answer, but the moaning started again, so I repeated my question even louder. That was when he spoke his first word, which sounded like *stone*. Initially, I thought he was uttering my name, but he continued to say it. Now I know this might sound strange, madam, but it was as if he was attempting to tell me, 'No! Not your name. Something else.' I have had that feeling before when questioning a dying witness. Rightly or wrongly, it is what I sensed, and the word which came out next made me think I was correct."

"And that word?" Joanna asked impatiently.

"It sounded like *wharf.*"

"*Wharf,* you say?" Joanna repeated, to be certain she had heard correctly.

"Yes, madam, that is what I believe he spoke."

"As in a dock or pier?"

"Yes, madam."

"Did the word *wharf* come before or after he had uttered *stone?*"

"It came after," Stone replied without hesitation. "But there was a pause between the two, and I wondered if he was trying to say 'wharf of stone' or something of that order."

Joanna furrowed her forehead in thought, as if concentrating on the combination of words. "While he was semiconscious, did you ask him about the site of the wharf?"

Stone shook his head. "Just as I was in the process of inquiring, blood began to gush out of the big rubber tube in his chest. It actually spilled out and splashed onto the floor. It was a most gruesome sight, madam."

"I would imagine so."

"The sister reacted quickly and was able to stem the hemorrhage somewhat before she called the surgeon in," Stone went on. "And shortly thereafter they all raced off for the operating room."

"So I gather the only words you heard clearly were *stone* and *wharf*?" Joanna asked. "Is that correct?"

"Yes, madam, except I do believe there was a gap between the two, where perhaps another word was intended."

"Very good," Joanna said, with a final glance into the intensive care room. "I have one last question for you to answer, which is of some importance to us. Did the senior Dr. Watson stop by this afternoon to see Lieutenant Smits? You may recall the good doctor from an investigation at the Windsor."

"I do recall the fine gentleman, but he did not visit during my watch."

Joanna nodded at the answer, then stared into space whilst she appeared to reconsider the problem we were facing. After a lengthy pause, she came back to the detective. "Sergeant, if and when the patient returns, I should like you to concentrate on one question and only one question, that being the location of the stone wharf. Were he to gain even a semblance of consciousness, repeat the words *location of stone wharf* over and over."

"And not the time?"

"That, too, but it is the precise location which is paramount, for once we have that we can cover every plank of the wharf for as long as we wish."

"Perhaps I should obtain a hearing horn which would amplify the sound in his brain."

"Do so at once," Joanna approved. "The louder it is, the more likely it is to be heard."

She reached for her personal card and handed it to the detective, with the request we be notified of any new developments regarding the lieutenant's responsiveness.

As we were turning to depart, we heard heavy footsteps approaching, then watched Major Von Ruden rush up to the door of the intensive care room and stare in. His eyes widened at the sight of the empty, blood-soaked mattress. "Has the worst happened?"

Joanna answered before Stone could. "We think not," she lied convincingly. "The surgeon is of the opinion that a window of opportunity has opened, which will allow for a procedure to stem the hemorrhaging."

I studied Von Ruden's reaction and saw no change in his expression. If he was either surprised or disappointed by the new information, he concealed it well. But then that is what one would except from a clever devil who arranged to have one of his own men shot under the guise of a botched assassination attempt.

"So there is hope," Von Ruden said, injecting a false note of optimism for our benefit.

"I do not believe the surgeon would operate unless he believed so," Joanna fabricated on. "And of course his postoperative care will be critical, with a sister at his bedside to provide careful monitoring."

"You seem quite familiar with the treatment of such patients," the major probed subtly.

"That is because I was once a surgical nurse at this very hospital," Joanna replied, then added, "and in light of my experience, the commissioner has requested I keep a close eye on the rather delicate situation at St. Bart's."

"I am certain Smits's family would be most grateful, for they fear the worst," said Von Ruden, now covering his nose against the stench. "Will the lieutenant be returning to this room postoperatively?"

"Yes, once it is cleaned, for it is here that he will receive the very best of care," Joanna answered. "And you can rest assured that no intruder will be allowed near the intensive care room, with Sergeant Stone standing guard at the entrance."

"You make it sound as if Smits needs to be protected."

"Quite so."

"From whom, may I ask?"

"From the press and news media," Joanna responded. "Smits's gallantry has caught the fancy of all London, and its newspapers would pay handsomely for a photograph of the intensive care room holding the critically wounded lieutenant."

"I can provide one of my men to stand guard and assist," Von Ruden offered. "They are particularly well trained in this regard."

Stone immediately stepped forward to respond. "With all due respect, sir, this is Scotland Yard's purview, not Johannesburg's, and it will remain so until I hear otherwise from the commissioner."

"As it should be," Von Ruden withdrew the offer graciously whilst checking his timepiece. "I must be off then, but should you require any assistance, all you need to do is call."

Joanna watched the head of the South Africa security unit hurry away and waited until he was out of sight before speaking. "Sergeant, you are to allow no one in this room other than medical personnel and those associated with Scotland Yard. There are to be no exceptions. Understood?"

"Clearly, madam."

"Carry on, then," Joanna said, taking my arm as we walked away. "Now let us find our Watson."

We moved at a rapid pace through the surgery ward and out into a wide corridor that was crowded with gurneys and wheelchairs and the uniformed orderlies pushing them. I was tempted to stop in at the nearby surgical amphitheater and learn how Lieutenant Smits was faring under the knife, but decided not to, for I was most anxious to set eyes on my dear father. Under my breath, I uttered a silent prayer for his deliverance, which was an act I rarely performed, for I was like most and only called on the Heavenly One when I needed him.

In the staircase heading down, we found quiet which allowed us to discuss our recent encounters in the intensive care room. It was our subtle confrontation with Major Von Ruden that pressed most on my mind.

"Von Ruden seemed eager to lay his hands on Lieutenant Smits," said I.

"Wouldn't you if you were in his place?" Joanna asked rhetorically. "He wants someone close by to inform him if Smits awakens from his coma and speaks, and what the message is. He would also like to know the moment the lieutenant leaves this world, for that event would remove a heavy burden from Von Ruden's shoulders."

"The major would be more than happy to help Smits make his final exit as well," I added.

"That, too."

"And what of the utterance *stone wharf*?"

"That is a puzzle within a puzzle and will require thought."

"Do you have any ideas?"

"A number come to mind, but until we have more clues, they are without merit."

On leaving the staircase, I asked a last question which, try as I might, I could not answer. "Why the emphasis on whether my father visited the intensive care room earlier?"

"Because on his arrival at St. Bart's, he would have been an hour or more early for the lecture and found a way to occupy his time," she replied. "Knowing our Watson, he would have stopped by the room to learn of Smits's condition, just as we had. But he did not, which is a most ominous sign."

My heart dropped, for I knew that Joanna's assessment was spot-on. What little optimism I had was rapidly disappearing.

We entered a large amphitheater and found its seats nearly filled, for quinine-resistant malaria was wreaking havoc the world over. At the podium below stood Dr. Stephen Marbury, a prominent expert on the disease, whom everyone turned to for the latest developments. I waved to him and, together with Joanna, descended the steps to have a few words with a colleague whom I was privileged to call a friend.

"John, what a pleasant surprise," he greeted. "And I see you have brought along your delightful wife."

"We are here at the urging of the senior Dr. Watson," Joanna prevaricated. "He insists we remain informed on the subject."

"I trust the good Dr. Watson will be attending, for I always enjoy our discussion on the history of the disease," said Marbury. "He has experience like no other when it comes to the ravaging effect on our soldiers in Afghanistan."

I nodded as I glanced around the amphitheater, hoping to find my father. I could not detect his presence in the seats, but throngs of physicians were still filing in from above.

Marbury noticed the movement of my eyes and reminded me, "Your father will be seated in the front row, where spaces are reserved for our elderly, retired physicians. They usually enter via a side door which allows them to avoid the narrow, steep climb down."

"Very good," said I, taking Joanna's arm. "We shall take our places and eagerly await your presentation."

Ascending the steps, we studied each row, seat by seat, without seeing my father. When we finally reached the top tier, we had a panoramic view of the entire amphitheater. Again, we scrutinized each and every row, and could not find my father. In particular, we studied the first row where the elderly, retired physicians were seated. John H. Watson, M.D., was not amongst them. Our concentration was broken by Marbury rapping on the wooden podium, which indicated the lecture was about to begin.

"What now?" I asked quietly.

"We hurry back to Baker Street and wait."

"For what?"

"The dreaded message to arrive."

CHAPTER TWENTY-FIVE

The Threat

We spent a long evening and sleepless night staring at the telephone and waiting for the message from my father's abductors, for we knew full well the instruction would not be delivered by hand. The latter method was far too risky in that the messenger might leave a trail that could be followed, and equally as important was that their list of demands would be lengthy and require a conversation to be had.

"Where do you believe they will hold him?" I asked the unanswerable question for the fifth or sixth time; the exact number I do not recall. "You must have some idea by now?"

"It is impossible to say with any degree of accuracy," Joanna replied. "We must take into account the rather disquieting fact that the abductors had a head start of several hours, during which time they could travel anywhere unnoticed. After all, an elderly gentleman in the rear seat of a motor vehicle would not arouse any suspicion."

"Not a carriage, then?"

"It would be too slow," Joanna said, reaching for yet another Turkish cigarette and beginning to pace once again. "They would wish to arrive at their concealed destination as quickly as possible."

"Which in all likelihood is in the greater London area," I surmised before adding, "but then again, I suppose a secluded cottage in the countryside would be more to their advantage."

"But a large motor vehicle arriving at such a location might draw the attention of the locals," she countered.

"What then about the wharf made of stone that Smits uttered?" I asked. "Could he be referring to a nearby hideout on the Thames?"

Joanna shook her head at the notion. "Their site of embarkation would be a somewhat smaller, congested port which would not be under careful watch. In such a place, a motor vehicle discharging passengers would not be unusual and the authorities would take little notice. However, we remain faced with the problem of what was meant by the term *stone wharf*. You will recall that the detective sergeant believed there was another word or syllable between *wharf* and *stone*."

I growled angrily in frustration. "I feel so helpless."

"One always has that sensation when in the dark with an absence of clues."

"We are not even certain how and where the abduction took place."

"I think otherwise," Joanna said, as she stopped pacing to extinguish her cigarette. "It would have gone as follows. When Watson departed Baker Street for his doctor appointment, he was seen to be alone and trailed to the Harley Street address where he would spend an hour or more. His followers then contacted the mastermind who quickly devised a plan in which a motor vehicle would be waiting near the cardiologist's office for Watson to exit."

"Perhaps disguised as a taxi?"

"Perhaps, but there was no need, for a passenger in the vehicle could approach Watson with a greeting and stick a revolver in the good doctor's ribs, then force him into the vehicle in a totally unsuspicious fashion."

"And thus leave no trail behind."

"I am afraid so."

After a brief rap on the door, Miss Hudson entered and immediately began choking at the dense cloud of cigarette smoke enveloping the parlor. Aghast, she covered her nose and hurried to the window to open it. "How can you possibly breathe such polluted air?"

"I am accustomed to it," replied Joanna, unconcerned. "And my brain functions best when stimulated by the vapors of nicotine."

"I am surprised Dr. Watson does not object," said Miss Hudson, as a draft of cold, fresh air began to clear the room. She glanced around the parlor, then to the chair which my father usually occupied. "Will Dr. Watson not be joining you for breakfast?"

"He is somewhat indisposed this morning with a touch of bronchitis from last evening's chill," Joanna lied easily.

"Perhaps he would enjoy a cup of freshly brewed tea, then?"

Joanna nodded. "Please bring up a kettle and I shall serve him when he awakens."

Miss Hudson took a long, deep breath and sighed sadly. "Poor Bertie and his wife return tomorrow from their journey to the Hebrides. I dread giving them the news of their dear Dolly, and have no idea what to say."

"Tell them the truth," Joanna said forthrightly. "And perhaps offer them some sort of compensation."

"And what might that be?"

"I will give it thought and come up with an appropriate gift."

"Very well, then," Miss Hudson said, and departed, closing the door quietly behind her.

Joanna returned to her worrisome pacing whilst I continued to be concerned over my father's health. His cardiac rhythm irregularities had worsened as of late and would no doubt deteriorate further with the greatly added stress of his abduction. And to compound the problem, he was without his heart medication, which was so vital in keeping his pulse steady and regular. A dreaded thought suddenly came to mind about my father's well-being. We would have to be certain he had survived the ordeal of his abduction. We would require proof of life.

The telephone rang loudly.

Joanna rushed to the phone and held its receiver in such a fashion that we could both listen to the caller.

"Yes?" she answered in a calm voice.

"This is Sergeant Stone at St. Bart's, madam," he replied. "I am sorry to disturb you, but you requested I notify you of any change in Lieutenant Smits's condition."

"Yes, of course," said Joanna, as our spirits dropped, for we feared we had lost our singular best source of information on the possible whereabouts of my father. "I should like all the details."

"The patient managed to survive the surgery and has now been returned to the intensive care room. According to the surgeon, the hemorrhaging has been stemmed, but the lieutenant remains in shock, with a dangerously low blood pressure."

"Is he still in a comatose state?"

"Yes, madam. The surgeon attempted to elicit a response on a number of occasions, but was unable to do so."

"Is he making any sounds?"

"Only a moan now and then, madam."

"If the patient shows any signs of awakening, please remember to do as you were instructed."

"I have a hearing horn at the ready and will employ it at the first opportunity."

"Keep a sharp eye, then."

"I shall, madam."

"Oh, and by the way," Joanna said quickly, as a last question came to mind. "Have there been any nonmedical visitors to the intensive care unit?"

"Only Major Von Ruden, who seemed relieved that his lieutenant had managed to survive the ordeal."

"Very good, Sergeant. Do keep us informed." Joanna placed the receiver into its cradle and commented with a sneer, "Von Ruden is only relieved that Smits remains comatose and is most unlikely to survive."

"Well, at least we know it is not Von Ruden who is watching over my father," I thought aloud.

"Which was never a consideration," said Joanna. "The sentinel would have to be someone permanently stationed there, and that someone is no doubt another member of the South African security unit."

"So you believe there is more than one turncoat?"

"There has to be, for the events that have occurred required coordination between several individuals," Joanna explained. "Take for example the attempted assassination. It could not be Von Ruden who spotted the glint of a rifle barrel, for that might have eventually cast suspicion on him. So he picked one of his cohorts to perform the act, which he could promptly respond to. And what of the marksman who fired the shot from the window?"

"Are you referring to the hired assassin?"

"How do you know it was a hired assassin?" Joanna challenged. "It could just as well have been a marksman from the South African security unit who conveniently left behind a spent German cartridge."

"The mire here becomes deeper and deeper."

"So it would seem."

The telephone rang again just as Big Ben was beginning to toll the noon hour in the distance.

Joanna reached for the phone and advised me not to interrupt until the abductor had listed all of his demands. She once more held the receiver in such a fashion that we could both listen to the caller.

"Yes?" said she.

"Listen carefully because I will not repeat myself. You are to desist from any further investigation, and you will be watched to make certain you do so. Any deviation whatsoever and you will never see Dr. Watson again. If we learn you have contacted Scotland Yard on this matter, we will consider it a deviation and Dr. Watson will suffer the consequences." The caller spoke in a muffled, hoarse voice which was impossible to identify. There was a prolonged silence other than the sound of Big Ben in the background and we feared the abductor had disconnected. Then, just before he came on again, a loud bell sounded at the other end of the line and quickly faded. "Did you hear every demand clearly?"

"Your words after *Scotland Yard* were drowned out by the passing bell," Joanna lied, obviously trying to keep the caller connected longer. "Please say again."

"If we learn you have contacted Scotland Yard on this matter, we will consider it a deviation and Dr. Watson will suffer the consequences," the abductor repeated.

"We require proof that Dr. Watson remains alive and unharmed," said Joanna.

"You have my word."

"Not good enough."

There was another lengthy pause before the caller said, "Hold."

Moments later my father spoke on the line in a somewhat infirm voice. "Yes?"

"Hello, Watson. This is Joanna," said she. "Are you well?"

"I am afraid my cardiac rhythm problem is acting up rather badly."

"Then you must adjust the dose of your heart medication."

"I do not have the digitalis leaf with me, for it remains in my drawer on Baker Street."

"We shall see that you receive your medication," Joanna said determinedly. "Give the receiver back to your abductor."

The caller came back on the line. "Dr. Watson will have to do without his medication."

"No, he will not!" Joanna spat out with fury.

"You are sadly mistaken if you think we will allow you to deliver the medication to him."

"He is a physician and can write his own prescription."

"I will consider it."

"You had better do more than consider it, for if any harm comes to Watson, I will chase you to the far corners of the earth and see you hanged from the end of a strong English rope. And do not believe your German friends will cover for you. For the war will end and you will find yourself being the hunted rather than the hunter. You will never know a peaceful moment."

After another prolonged pause, the abductor appeared to give in. "He will not be harmed."

"I require you to contact me again this evening to assure us that Watson has received his heart medication."

"The contact will occur between the hours of seven and eight," he agreed, and terminated the call.

"I believe he will follow your demands," I said optimistically.

"Oh, I am certain he will, but only until they have no further use for him."

I was shocked by the harrowing revelation which was totally unexpected. "Are you saying they will dispose of him?"

"They will have no other recourse, for Watson has seen their faces."

"Perhaps they were wearing masks."

"Even the man who abducted him in broad daylight on Harley Street?"

I nodded at the dire assessment which indicated my dear father's life was shortly to end. "Is there any way to persuade them otherwise?"

"I am afraid not, for once the U-boat appears, Watson becomes an overwhelming liability."

"Then we must find him quickly."

"And so we shall."

"But how do we go about it without even a hint of where their hideout is located?"

"To the contrary, John, I know now the area where they are holding Watson and, with a little good fortune, I may be able to actually pinpoint the address."

"How, pray tell?" I asked at once.

"You, like your dear father, have a grand gift for silence which renders both of you quite invaluable as companions," said Joanna, as a faint smile came and went from her face. "I now require absolute silence while I put together a plan which even Sherlock Holmes would applaud."

"Based on what?" I begged for an answer.

"The bells, my dear John, the bells," said Joanna, reaching for a Turkish cigarette and lighting it. "And now quiet, absolute quiet until all the pieces fall into place."

She began pacing yet again, head down, her brow furrowed in concentration. How? I pondered to myself, totally mystified. How could the ringing of the bells lead to a singular neighborhood and to a precise address within it? Big Ben, which sounded at the beginning of the phone call, could be heard throughout London, and the second bell at the end of the conversation was nondescript. The latter had a sharp, piercing quality, much like one elicited by a seagoing vessel making way in the fog. But then again, the sound was so commonplace and not likely from the Thames, which was miles away. I could not fit the ringing bells into any sort of meaningful pattern, yet Joanna's tone of voice seemed so confident, and if there was one characteristic I had learned during our marriage, it was my wife's deductive talents should never be underestimated.

Joanna abruptly stopped pacing and spun around on her heels to ask, "Did not Watson once complain of the odor of the digitalis leaf he was required to take?"

"He considered it rather sour, as was its taste," I recalled. "For these reasons, he often applied a drop of peppermint to the medication to conceal its unpleasantness."

"Good, very good," Joanna said, and, after lighting another Turkish cigarette from the one she was smoking, went back to pacing.

My confusion grew. As with any puzzle, I decided to examine all the individual pieces and see how they might fit together. We have two bells ringing almost simultaneously, with one clearly coming from Big Ben, the other commonplace and perhaps originating from a bell on a seagoing vessel. Now, how could these differing sounds somehow tie into the sour taste and smell of digitalis leaf, and render a worthwhile conclusion as to my father's whereabouts? I, like most mortals, had no answer.

Joanna hurried over to me with a request. "John, please be good enough to fetch Watson's vial of digitalis leaf."

"For what purpose, may I ask?"

"You shall see shortly."

I quickly went to my father's bedroom and returned with his nearly depleted vial of cardiac medication. "There are only a few tablets remaining."

"That will suffice," said Joanna, opening the small bottle and taking a measured sniff. "Perfect," she announced. "Its aroma is distinct, but not easily detected away from its container."

"Would it be too much for me to ask what the digitalis leaf is perfect for?"

"For setting a trap," she replied, screwing the lid back onto the vial, then taking a final draw on her cigarette before extinguishing it. "I do believe the tide is turning in our favor, as Major Von Ruden is about to discover."

"I am delighted to hear so," said I, becoming excited over the optimistic tone in her voice. "Might I learn of the particulars?"

"Of course, for you are to play an important role," Joanna responded. "Let us begin with the ringing of the two distinctive bells which we detected in the background of the caller. What do you make of them?"

"The first and longest came from Big Ben; of that we can be certain," I answered. "But its characteristic sound can be heard all over London. So that—"

"To the contrary," she interrupted. "The hearing radius of Big Ben reaches only about five miles, which for the most part covers only Central London."

"That does not begin to pinpoint the address where my father is being held."

"But the sound of the second bell we heard may well turn that trick for us."

"How so?" I asked, now more puzzled than before. "It could have been a loud warning from a seagoing vessel making way."

Joanna shook her head. "The sound of the second bell came and went too quickly. Ships making way on the Thames do not move that rapidly. Furthermore, the bells on the small vessels make a dull clang rather than the sharp tone of the bell we just heard, and such a sound would be too weak to carry from the river to our humble abode. And finally, although bells are sometimes used for that purpose, the larger vessels now employ foghorns."

"There was certainly no sound of a foghorn in the background."

Joanna reached for a metal poker and used it to stir the smoldering logs ablaze. "Watch them burn, John, and wonder what would happen if the fire spread to our parlor."

"Why, it could set the entire building on fire."

"Unless there was a prompt response by the Fire Brigade, which would announce their arrival by what mechanism?"

"A bell!" I exclaimed loudly. "The second bell we heard was made by an approaching truck from the Fire Brigade. And it came to a rather abrupt stop, indicating it had reached its destination."

"Very good, John. Pray continue."

I tried my best to think through the remainder of the puzzle, but no answer came. At length, I threw my arms up in defeat. "That fire truck could have been anywhere in London."

"Not so, for it had to be traveling within five miles of Big Ben."

"But that covers such a large area," I contended. "There is no way to pinpoint the location of that moving Fire Brigade truck. Even you, with your clever deductive mind, cannot do it."

"But Scotland Yard can," she said, reaching for the telephone.

CHAPTER TWENTY-SIX

The Trap

It required thirty minutes for the commissioner of Scotland Yard to respond to Joanna's request for the location of all Fire Brigade trucks which were racing to a fire within five miles of Big Ben at precisely high noon. The answer was most unexpected and provided an important clue, for there was only one fire truck that could have been in such a location at the noon hour, and its position was on Edgware Road just past Praed Street. And that placed it only a mile or so away from our rooms on Baker Street!

"Perfect," Joanna said, gleefully rubbing her hands together. "Now, as I recall, Watson would customarily stroll to the chemist's shop on Rossmore Road to obtain his medications."

I nodded without hesitation. "And only there, for he trusted the chemist to diligently measure the dose of all his medications. This is of particular importance when dealing with digitalis leaf." I gave the matter further consideration before adding, "I see where you are headed with the initial part of your trap. You expect to have my father write a prescription for digitalis leaf and insist it be taken to his Rossmore Road chemist."

"You are almost there," said Joanna. "But if Watson were to follow that path, it might well raise red flags for his abductors. Remember, they are a very clever lot and might see such an insistence as a ploy to make them expose themselves to a watchful eye at the chemist's shop."

"Are you perhaps overestimating their cleverness?"

"Not in the least, for I am merely placing myself in their stead and envisioning how I would respond to a desperate captive insisting on a given path," Joanna elucidated. "I would wonder if I was being lured into a trap."

"But surely my father has to write a prescription for his much-needed medication," I argued.

Joanna shook her head and reminded me, "Watson already has the prescription which was written by his cardiologist yesterday morning. Thus I believe Watson will simply beseech his captors to employ the chemist on Rossmore Road and explain the necessity of doing so."

"That makes it more believable."

"That is because it *is* more believable," Joanna went on. "But rest assured they will have a close eye on that chemist's shop to be certain they are not being watched or followed."

"Then how can we possibly hope to track the individual sent for my father's prescription?"

"By situating ourselves several blocks away in a nondescript four-wheeler."

"But we cannot follow his trail from that position."

"But Toby Two, with his keen nose, surely can," said Joanna. "Which brings us to a most important role you must play. It has to be carried out skillfully and in a casual fashion so as not to arouse suspicion."

"In some sort of disguise, then?" I wondered aloud.

"That will not work, for their watcher will know that you were the only man to enter this house since yesterday evening and will see through your disguise," she replied. "Thus you must be yourself in every way as you board a taxi to fetch Toby Two and return with her to Baker Street."

"I will be seen the moment I leave our doorstep."

"Well and good."

"And probably followed."

"Perhaps not, for it is me rather than you who they are most interested in," Joanna deduced. "But in the event they shadow you, all they will see is a man picking up a dog and bringing her back to Baker Street, where Miss Hudson will greet the hound as if it was hers."

"I take it Miss Hudson will be rehearsed."

"To a minimal degree."

"What then?"

"We involve Scotland Yard, for the trap will fail without their assistance."

"Has the commissioner agreed to participate?"

"He will once the plan is revealed to him," Joanna replied with confidence. "Now, be off while I make the necessary arrangements. And be quick, but do not appear to be in a hurry."

A taxi was summoned, which I boarded in a most relaxed manner, taking only a brief glance at the Christmas shoppers across the way, but seeing no one of suspicion. As we rode down

Baker Street, I appeared to be stretching my neck whilst stealing a glimpse from the rear window. Again, I saw nothing untoward. The fifteen-minute journey to Lower Lambeth gave me ample time to think through the design of Joanna's plan to rescue my father. The messenger for the abductors will in all likelihood arrive on foot, as do most of the visitors to the chemist's shop. In doing so, he would mix in and be nondescript, and in no way stand out. But shortly thereafter, a major problem would arise. How does the chemist notify us that the prescription has been filled and the customer is now leaving the shop? A phone call to Scotland Yard was out of the question, for it would take far too much time for them and us to respond. Moreover, the chemist cannot simply step out onto the footpath once the customer departs, for the abductors would surely be watching and immediately become aware of the trap. We of course would be blocks away and unable to see such a signal in any event. This problem required a most clever solution, and I wondered how Joanna planned to circumvent the dilemma under the watchful eyes of the captors.

Before I could come up with a solution, we entered Pinchin Lane, which was a row of shabby two-storied brick houses, all of which faced the street. I had to knock repeatedly on the door to Number Three before a blind on the second floor parted and Mr. Sherman looked out through thick, tinted spectacles.

"Go away!" he cried down. "Whatever you are selling I do not want any."

"It is John Watson, here for my wife, Joanna."

"Ha, the young Dr. Watson! I am on my way down, sir."

Moments later the door to Number Three was unbarred and opened. Before me was a quite odd-looking man who had changed little since I last saw him over a year ago. He was lean and lanky and very old, with a heavily lined face, stooped shoulders, and a humped back. His arms seemed far too long for his body.

"So, the good daughter is on the hunt again, eh?"

"Indeed she is, and in real need of Toby Two's keen nose."

"I am afraid the hound is beginning to show her age."

"How so?"

"She has become somewhat listless and is off her food a bit."

"Let us hope there is at least one more chase in her."

"This way, then." Sherman invited me in. "But keep clear of the Scottish wildcat. As you may recall, he appears tame enough, but every so often he pounces at moving targets."

We gave the wildcat a wide berth. Larger than a house cat, he had a bushy tail and long legs, and uttered a foreboding hiss as we walked by. Sherman led the way past a line of cages that contained a variety of cats and dogs and a mean-looking badger that clawed at its wire enclosure. The heavy, unsanitary smell of unwashed animals filled the air.

"Toby Two lives at number fifteen on the left," Sherman announced as we came to the end of the cages. The hound showed little interest in our arrival whilst looking out at us with droopy eyes. Slowly she began to wag her tail, now picking up my familiar scent. "Oh, yes, she is onto you."

He lifted Toby Two out and placed her at my feet, then stepped back. The hound once again struck me to be a most peculiar-appearing animal. She had many features of a long-haired spaniel, but the droopy eyes as well as the large snout were those of a bloodhound. Eyeing me warily, the dog sniffed at my outstretched palm and quickly detected Joanna's scent, for her tail began to wag vigorously, just as my wife had predicted it would. Sherman handed me a lump of sugar which Toby Two accepted after the briefest of hesitations. The alliance between the hound, Joanna, and myself was again sealed, and Toby Two eagerly followed me out and into my waiting taxi.

As instructed, I gave Toby Two a dog biscuit, which she happily bit into and devoured. It was only then that she stuck her head out the window to sample the air and savor the aromas contained in it. Every so often she would yelp pleasantly, giving the impression of having detected something familiar. Joanna had once commented that dogs had a sense of smell a thousandfold greater than that of man, and could easily distinguish between a hundred different scents at the same time. Toby Two would have no difficulty following the sour scent of digitalis leaf, which the messenger would carry out of the chemist's shop, but somehow we had to position the hound close enough to that particular customer. Then it struck me. She did not have to be that near, for the keen nose of a hound could track a moving scent a mile away. Yet the major obstacle remained. How do we single out the abductor from the multitude of customers as he departs from the busy chemist's shop?

On our arrival at 221b Baker Street, Toby Two was so eager to see Joanna that she leaped out of the vehicle's open window and into my wife's arms. Standing beside Joanna was Miss Hudson, who appeared to also celebrate the dog's homecoming. It was a picturesque scene that was perfectly acted and sure to fool the keenest eye.

Once inside, Joanna gave the hound's head a vigorous scratch whilst saying, "Well done, John."

"And to my surprise, we were not followed."

"But you were," said Joanna. "Shortly after your departure, a dark motor vehicle pulled away and into traffic, with a driver who looked much like a member of Von Ruden's security team."

"How could you discern his features from our window?"

"My Zeiss monocular came in handy," she replied.

We hurried up to our rooms, and Toby Two immediately began to sniff about our parlor, appearing to pick up more than a few interesting scents which obviously delighted her. She showed no signs of the listlessness Sherman had mentioned. Stepping around the hound, Joanna reached for her Zeiss monocular and went to the window, which had its curtains narrowly parted. She peered out for a full minute before declaring, "Aha! The vehicle that followed you has returned to its parking space, which is perfect timing, for now we are certain of the man sent to watch us."

"But will he not follow us when we depart on our mission to rescue my father?"

"Oh, beyond a doubt he will."

"Does that not concern you?"

"Not in the least," Joanna said with a mischievous smile. "His vehicle will not follow well with a flat tire."

CHAPTER TWENTY-SEVEN

Watson

At a distance of three blocks from the chemist's shop, we waited patiently in our carriage for events to unfold and bring the jaws of justice to my father's abductors. I was no longer concerned about identifying the individual sent to fill the prescription, for Joanna had constructed a simple yet foolproof plan to alert us upon his arrival. Once the prescription was given to the chemist, he would subtly signal the delivery boy to take the shop's Labrador retriever out to relieve itself. This of course was the cue that the abductor or his messenger was in the shop and would shortly leave. The hound would be seen by a detective with binoculars on a rooftop a block away, who would then use a reflective mirror to notify us and Scotland Yard that the target was now present and on the move. Despite the marvelous plan, I continued to worry about the motor vehicle which had so skillfully followed me to Lower Lambeth. Only Joanna's keen eye had detected the driver, and we were now depending on a tire becoming flat to prevent him from doing so again.

"How does this deflated tire take place?" I asked, breaking the silence with a question that had weighed on my mind. "The driver would surely become suspicious of anyone who loiters around the motor vehicle."

"It will not be done by a loiterer," replied Joanna.

"Then by whom?"

"Little Alfie, the cleverest of the Baker Street Irregulars."

My brow went up at the mention of the Baker Street Irregulars, a gang of street urchins that Sherlock Holmes had gathered up and employed to aid his causes. They currently consisted of a half dozen or so members, all streetwise, who could go everywhere, see everything, and overhear everyone without being noticed. When put to the task, they had a remarkable success record. For their efforts each was paid a shilling a day, with a guinea to whoever found the most prized clue. Since Holmes's death, most of the original guttersnipes had either drifted away or become ill. Only Wiggins, the leader of the group, remained and took in new recruits to replace those who had departed. We had used them in several cases much to our benefit, and I had no doubt they would perform admirably when it came to slashing a tire, but I wondered how they would go about it and be undetected. Yet I had another question which needed to be answered first.

"How did you manage to involve them so quickly?" I asked at length.

"Immediately after the motor vehicle began to follow you, I sent a message to Wiggins by taxi and urged him to find a telephone and contact me at once, which he promptly did," Joanna responded, pausing to gaze at a rooftop in the distance before continuing. "He was instructed to bring along Little Alfie and Sarah The Gypsy and have them dressed as upper-class young teenagers on their way home from school, while he was to be at-tired as a street sweeper. They were then to travel to Baker Street, where Wiggins would point out the motor vehicle whose rear tire was to be slashed by the two urchins parading by the target. Do you have the picture in mind so far?"

"Indeed," I said with a nod, for it was easy to envision the nicely disguised trio. The tall, pale-complected Wiggins, with his hollow cheeks, could effortlessly pass as a street sweeper, whilst the innocent-appearing Little Alfie and Sarah The Gypsy would no doubt pose perfectly as schoolchildren. But the mechanism by which they could cause a tire to go flat in broad daylight was beyond me.

"And now you are wondering how they planned to perform this task without being noticed," Joanna went on, reading my ex-pression. "I had to inquire as well, for the deflated tire must occur when the motor vehicle is some distance away from its parking space on Baker Street."

I nodded once more, now seeing the quandary. "If the flat tire happened suddenly while the vehicle was parked, it would be most suspicious."

"And give the driver time to repair or call for a replacement vehicle," Joanna added.

"So then, how does one ensure that the tire deflates, but only after the motor vehicle is well away?"

"Leave it up to the streetwise Irregulars to find the answer, which I did. Wiggins promptly provided me with a plan that I heartily agreed to. It will go as follows. Wiggins will slowly sweep the footpath just in front of the vehicle and nod respectfully to the driver, temporarily distracting him. At that moment, Wiggins will step aside to make room for the well-attired, sweet-appearing Sarah The Gypsy, who limps by, for she seems to be lame. Now the driver is totally distracted, which allows Little Alfie time to kneel down to adjust a shoe buckle. Alfie is now out of sight and will quickly pierce the tire with a sharp piece of metal, inserting it firmly into the rubber, but not deep enough to puncture it. When you and I depart, the vehicle will follow, and the farther it travels, the deeper the metal penetrates into the rubber until it pierces it altogether and one has a flat tire."

"Is Little Alfie confident of his method?"

"He has performed it a number of times in the past without failure."

"Is it not possible that the driver will rapidly hail a taxi and rejoin the chase?"

"That would be most difficult, for the moment he steps out of his disabled vehicle he will be arrested by Scotland Yard, who will be watching his every move."

"Nicely planned."

Suddenly, a mirror on a distant rooftop flashed twice, indicating the target was on the move and heading west. Joanna quickly reached for her parasol and rapped on the ceiling of our carriage. "Ha! The game begins!"

As instructed, the driver gently encouraged the horses to pull away, for we wished to give the abductor a head start of at least a block before we arrived at the chemist's shop and picked up the scent. Joanna allowed Toby Two to continue nibbling on a dog biscuit upon which her entire attention was focused. Like with other hounds, nothing superseded her stomach, but once put on the track of even the faintest scent she would follow it relentlessly. Now Toby Two was chewing on the last scrap of the biscuit and looked up to Joanna and whined for another.

"Later," she told the hound, who seemed to understand, for she rested at my wife's feet without begging further.

We approached the chemist's shop and slowed even more, for behind us was another carriage carrying Inspector Lestrade and Sergeant Stone, both armed and prepared to shoot on a moment's notice. They, too, slowed in order to provide abundant space between the two carriages and not arouse suspicion. When we were half a block past the shop, Joanna removed an airtight container from her purse and opened its top to give Toby Two a brief sniff of the digitalis leaf that it held within. Immediately upon closing the container, Joanna pointed to the window and ordered, "Go, girl! Go!"

In a fraction of a second, Toby Two leaped onto my lap and stuck her head, with its large, sensitive snout, out the window. She showed no response initially, but then she yelped with delight as her tail began to wag. I took a rapid, inconspicuous glimpse at the footpath in an effort to spot the abductor, but he was nowhere to be seen.

"We must be close," said I in a whisper. "Very close."

"Do not peer out again, and be prepared to pull Toby Two back into the carriage," Joanna enjoined. "Then position the dog to conceal your face."

Abruptly Toby Two stiffened, her tail no longer wagging and now straight as an arrow. A series of short yelps told us we had arrived at the site where the scent was the greatest. Our carriage was passing a detached two-storied brick house, with all its curtains closed. There was an alleyway, perhaps five yards in width, next to it, which allowed for entrance into a back garden. Joanna had hidden her face as well by holding up her parasol, which she gradually lowered. Toby Two let out an unhappy bark, telling us that the distinct scent of digitalis leaf was fading.

A block farther down our carriage came to a halt before a busy intersection where we were joined by Lestrade and Stone to discuss our best line of attack. The drivers were instructed to inspect the wheels of their respective carriages as if something were amiss with them. The façade was being performed in the event we were being watched from a distance.

"I think it is unlikely we are under surveillance," said Lestrade. "For we have been most careful at every step."

"There remains one step which concerns me," Joanna disagreed mildly. "As you recall, there was a motor vehicle which no doubt followed us when we departed from our rooms on Baker Street. The plan was to disable the vehicle en route and have the driver arrested, so he could not contact the others in his turncoat group. We need to be certain this was done."

"It was and in a most final fashion," Lestrade informed us. "The vehicle was stopped, but the bloody bugger decided to risk his chances with a shootout."

"I take it he lost."

"Permanently."

"Excellent," said Joanna, and pointed back to the house Toby Two had pinpointed for us. "That is where Watson is being held. You will notice there is an alleyway between that dwelling and the one next to it. It would be wise to have an observer slip into the adjacent garden and see what goes on in the house holding our dear Watson."

"I shall do it," Stone volunteered at once.

"All well and good, but you must be very careful, for if you are caught or noticed we will lose our advantage," Joanna warned.

"I am aware of that, madam."

"Then be off, keeping in mind there are two pieces of information which are of the greatest importance. Is Watson in fact housed within and how many men are holding him?"

Stone hurried away with quick, catlike steps that made no sound, which gave us encouragement that he might well be up to the task. We watched the detective slow his pace before abruptly disappearing into an alleyway that was located several houses before the one which held my father. It was obvious what his intentions were. He planned to enter that distant garden and silently make his way into the garden next to the house where my father was confined. Unless there was a fence between the two, I worried that Stone would be seen regardless of the care he took.

Furthermore, if the turncoats were as clever as we believed, they may have stationed a man on the rooftop, which would give him a panoramic view of the entire block.

The young detective returned in a matter of minutes, which was a bad sign, for the information we required could only be gathered after prolonged and careful observation. But then again, perhaps good fortune was on our side.

"Well?" Lestrade asked eagerly.

Stone paused to catch his breath before speaking. "It was impossible to even approach the house, sir, for there was no fence to hide behind and the only cover was a low hedge which for the most part had already shed its leaves."

"Could you hear any voices from within?" Joanna asked.

"No, madam, for I was too far away. And at that distance, one could not see through the windows."

"How many windows were there?"

"Four," he answered without hesitation. "Three of ordinary size, and one quite small which probably belonged to the loo."

"That is not of much help," said Joanna, her brow furrowing as she attempted to think through the problem.

"Perhaps our only option is to shout out a warning to the abductors, informing them that they are surrounded and offering them an opportunity to surrender," Lestrade suggested.

Joanna shook her head at the notion. "These men are stone-cold killers and will fight to the death, for they know a hangman's noose awaits them if captured."

"And such a warning would place us at a major disadvantage and put my father at even greater risk," I interjected.

Lestrade lifted his derby and scratched at his head in bewilderment. "I am open to other plans of action."

"Without the information we need, there is little hope, regardless of the plan," said Joanna, lighting a Turkish cigarette and now pacing back and forth on the footpath in front of us.

"The hedge and the window," she muttered to herself, as if the answer to our dilemma lay between the two. The pacing continued on and on until she suddenly spun around and came back to Lestrade. "Here is what you must do, Inspector. I would like you to instruct one of your men to immediately go to our address on Baker Street. Directly across the street from our rooms, he will notice two nicely attired young teenagers—a boy and a girl—moving back and forth amongst the shops. He is to approach them and, after identifying himself, tell the pair their presence is required by me and that I have a special task for them, which will be rewarded with an extra guinea. They may wish to be accompanied by their leader, a tall, slender chap named Wiggins, and this should be allowed."

Lestrade quickly gave the instructions to a young detective who dashed off to a nearby motor vehicle and sped away. Then the inspector returned to Joanna. "Pray tell who are these young teenagers and what role will they play in rescuing Dr. Watson?"

"They are the Baker Street Irregulars."

"I beg your pardon?"

"The Baker Street Irregulars," she repeated, before telling the fascinating story of the gang of street urchins gathered together by Sherlock Holmes to on occasion aid his cause, and in that regard his daughter was following in his footsteps.

"Are they truly that clever?" Lestrade asked.

"Remarkably so, as attested to by their high rate of success."

"And you say they go everywhere, see everything, and overhear everyone without being noticed?"

Joanna nodded, as a knowing smile came and went from her face. "The best of the lot is Little Alfie, who appears quite innocent, but who I do believe could snatch your wallet while shaking your hand."

"But approaching a house from an adjacent garden that provides no cover is quite another matter."

"So is inducing a tire to go flat three blocks after the motor vehicle has departed from its parking space, and performing this trick while the driver was keeping a close eye on everyone who approached and passed by his parked vehicle."

"I could not help but wonder how that feat was managed."

"So will the turncoats who are now holding Watson hostage," said Joanna. "Which brings us to another problem of immense gravity. No matter how skillful our line of attack, Watson will remain in great danger, for there will occur in all likelihood a fierce exchange of gunfire and the abductors may use their hostage as a shield."

"The only way to avoid that set of circumstances is to plan for a sudden attack and catch the turncoats by surprise."

"Too risky," Joanna said. "We have no idea of how many men we'll be facing and, most importantly, the position of Watson in the house. Without this information, I am afraid our rescue attempt will fail."

"We could wait them out and place a marksman on a nearby roof."

"And if they depart as a group, with their hostage in the center and a revolver pressed into his back?" Joanna challenged. "Furthermore, they may well decide to dispose of Watson just after seven this evening, which is the last time we will be allowed to speak with him by phone. If that be the case, your marksman will bring down the abductors, but we will lose our Watson."

"I see your point," Lestrade conceded. "So it would seem that no matter what plan of attack we take, poor Dr. Watson would be caught in the middle, with no way to defend himself."

"Unless he is prewarned," said she.

"And how would we go about that?"

"I have no idea," Joanna admitted. "But we had best come up with a mechanism to warn him, if we are to save his life."

"Perhaps the cunning, street-smart Little Alfie could think of such a mechanism," I chimed in.

"But how would he alert Watson to our presence?" asked Joanna. "First, the little urchin would have to have a good view of your father, which would be difficult enough, for that would require the lad to stand in view of the window for a prolonged period of time. Then he would have to send a signal that Watson could see or hear and understand. The signaling would present an even greater problem, for Little Alfie would have to make a noticeable sound that would certainly be overheard by—" She stopped in mid-sentence, with her face now showing an expression of deep concentration. Tapping an index finger rapidly against her chin, my wife began muttering to herself, which was a sign the pieces of the puzzle were beginning to fall into place and that an answer would be forthcoming. At length she said, "It has to be a sound that both Watson and his captors hear, but only Watson perceives as a signal that we are here and coming for him. Thus he could take cover at the first sign of our attack."

"That is a large order, madam, for any unusual sound would alert the vigilant turncoats," Stone posed for consideration.

"That depends entirely on the source of the sound," Joanna countered, and turned to me. "John, here I must ask you to think back over the years and try to recall any song or music which Watson truly enjoyed. A song would be best."

I shrugged my shoulders. "My father was not musically inclined, as you know."

"I am aware, but in the past were there not concerts or musical plays he particularly enjoyed?"

"He would only attend those at my dear mother's insistence, and he frequently dozed off within a matter of minutes after taking his seat."

"When you were a lad, did he ever sing to you?"

I had to smile at the pleasant remembrance. "When I was quite young, I would awaken from a bad dream and have difficulty falling back to sleep. It was then that my father would massage my back and sing an old military song."

"A military song, you say?"

"In every way," I replied. "For it was and remains to this day the regimental song of the Northumberland Fusiliers, with whom my father gallantly served in the Second Afghan War."

"Do you remember the song?" Joanna asked at once.

"It is called 'Blaydon Races.'"

"No, no. I meant the words themselves."

My mind went back in time to my father's voice gently singing me back to sleep. "I can recall the first verse or two, for the song was sung at a recent Fusiliers' reunion, which I attended with my father."

"Please recite those verses for me."

"I shall have to paraphrase some of the words."

"Do so."

I cleared my throat and sang poorly:

"Oh, me lads, you should have seen us gannin
Passing the folks along the road just as they were stannin."

With a shrug of my shoulders, I said, "I am afraid that is all I can remember."

"It is perfect," Joanna lauded.

"To what end?"

"To save your father's life."

A Scotland Yard motor vehicle came to a halt beside our carriage, and Little Alfie and Sarah The Gypsy alighted, followed by the always watchful Wiggins.

"Here we are, ma'am," the leader of the Irregulars said. "And

I must say this is the very first time I've been given a lift by Scotland Yard."

"Let us hope it is the last," Joanna quipped. "Now, you must listen carefully to my instructions, for a man's life hangs in the balance. An error on your part and the hostage dies."

"Hostage, eh?" asked Wiggins. "Might we know who?"

"The famous Dr. Watson whom you know by sight," replied Joanna. "And we mean to rescue him from his captors unharmed."

"Then we shall need the particulars, ma'am, down to the smallest detail."

The three Irregulars moved in closer, with expressions as calm as though they had been asked the time of day. But it was Little Alfie and Sarah The Gypsy who drew my attention. They had grown since last year and appeared to be young teenagers approaching puberty. Both had the look of innocence, but more so Little Alfie, with a lock of his brown hair hanging over his forehead. The dark-complected Sarah The Gypsy seemed a bit older than her mate and was turning into a real beauty. But appearances were deceiving, for in an instant they could transform themselves into street urchins capable of snatching your timepiece long before you realized the item was gone.

Joanna laid out the problem for the Irregulars, detailing the individual obstacles they faced and how each had to be overcome without being noticed. Again and again she emphasized the two critical pieces of information which had to be obtained. And she sweetened the task by offering a guinea for each piece brought back to us, then pointed to the dwelling to be surveilled.

She concluded by asking, "Are there questions?"

Little Alfie stepped forward and inquired, "How far is the hedge in the adjacent garden to the house?"

"Five yards," Stone replied.

"Too far," Little Alfie said at once. "One must be in the alleyway to grab a peek in those windows. We need an excuse to be there; otherwise, we will stand out like a turkey parading across Trafalgar Square."

"You must think of a clever reason," Joanna demanded. "And it has to be one which will not arouse the slightest suspicion."

"That presents a difficult problem, ma'am, particularly with no concealment," Wiggins opined.

"And just loitering there would draw the attention of even the laziest of coppers," said Sarah The Gypsy, absently scratching her armpit. "A neighbor might also complain and cause a ruckus which would upset the entire cart."

We all turned to Little Alfie for a solution, for the youthful-appearing lad was a quick thinker who at his early age was already a master of deceit, which accounted for his incredibly high rate of success. My mind went back to the case of *The Disappearance of Alistair Ainsworth,* in which Little Alfie managed to steal a look through a dusty window in a posh neighborhood, which explained why a commander in the Royal Navy, who was supposedly at sea, was meeting secretly with his wife and a high-ranking admiral at an expensive residence in Knightsbridge.

Little Alfie snapped his fingers and smiled mischievously. "I've got it!"

"Details, we need details," Joanna insisted.

"It goes this way, ma'am," he replied, reaching into a trouser pocket for a half-eaten apple, from which he took a generous bite. After a thorough chewing, he continued on. "Sarah and I will give the impression of being boyfriend and girlfriend, who have slipped into the alleyway for a kiss. That should give us time to peek in the window and hopefully see where your Dr. Watson is located. We might also be able to tell if he is being watched by one man or more."

Everyone nodded at the plan except Joanna, who stated, "A

quick kiss will not suffice, for it will limit your viewing to a single window which may have its curtains drawn. Instead, I wish you to do the following, understanding we have only once chance at this. You are to kiss firmly, then laugh and kiss once more. At this juncture you will be embracing and smiling, which allows for you to whirl around past several windows. Thus each of you should have a proper look into the house."

"Easily done," said Little Alfie.

"But if we see Dr. Watson, how do we signal our presence?" Sarah The Gypsy asked. "Any untoward noise and they will be onto us quicker than a hiccough."

"Not if the noise is a song," Joanna said, as I saw the final pieces of the adventure fall into place. "You will do exactly as I say, without deviation. First, you are to circle back two blocks, and return to the chemist's shop on Rossmore Road. You are then to continue on to us, holding hands and singing the following song at the top of your voices as you pass the house holding the hostage. Here are the verses, which I will recite and you are to memorize.

"Oh, me lads, you should have seen us gannin
Passing the folks along the road just as they were stannin."

"Now let me hear the words and put them to song."

It required multiple attempts, but by the third try they had learned the verses by rote, and I must say their voices were rather pleasing.

"Sing loudly," I reminded them, "for my father must hear the song, perhaps while deep into the dwelling. But do not shout, for that might arouse some degree of suspicion."

"Not to worry, guv'nor," said Little Alfie. "And to further draw your father's attention, we'll have a good, loud chuckle between verses."

"Most excellent," I approved.

"Once you are approaching the house, I want you to glance around and see if there is a guard posted," Joanna instructed. "Then, holding hands and singing, you are to dash into the alleyway and begin kissing while taking secret looks into the windows. Spend no more than a minute or so before hurrying to the far end of the passageway and circling back to us. You are to follow these instructions to the letter, if you wish to claim the extra guinea."

Little Alfie smiled. "Have your purse at the ready, ma'am."

"Then be off."

The pair slipped away in a carefree fashion, holding hands as would be expected of adolescent lovers. I was not concerned for their ability to follow Joanna's plan, but for how my father could signal he had received our message and, if he did, how he would find a secure position out of harm's way when the gunfire exchange began.

"I see worry on your face, John," said Joanna.

"Your plan is well designed, but even the smallest misstep could result in disaster," I admitted. "I keep thinking of Robert Burns's poetic words that 'the best-laid plans of mice and men often go awry.' And this holds true in particular for my father's safety."

"It is Watson's reactions which concern you the most," said Joanna. "Correct?"

I nodded slowly at her accurate perception. "Under ordinary circumstances and in his younger days, I have no doubt he would respond in a clever manner, and easily match his abductors step by step. But he is not nearly as agile as he once was, and his heart illness has slowed him even more. Then, add in that he slept little last night and remains under dreadful stress, and all seems to go against him."

"I believe you are underestimating your father," said Joanna.

"For it is not his body which will save him, but his quick mind that I am convinced will rise to the occasion."

I reached for my wife's hand and gave it a gentle squeeze. "I am of the opinion that you are trying your best to assure me."

Joanna returned my squeeze with a soft, feminine touch before replying, "I am simply reminding you that our dear Watson was a fine physician with over thirty years' experience and it is instilled in such individuals to respond quickly under the greatest of pressures."

"I must say I find some comfort in your assessment," said I. "But he will be in the line of fire regardless."

"Do you not believe he will be aware of that danger?"

"But how can he possibly avoid it?"

"By using his quick wit to find a secure position."

"And suppose he is tied to a chair?"

"That will complicate matters."

On that unhappy note, Lestrade hurried over to inform us, "Using binoculars, one of our spotters has detected the pair of Baker Street Irregulars returning, and they are taking their time about it."

"If they are walking slowly, there is a purpose to it," said Joanna. "You must have your men prepared to act now, for we will not have a minute to spare."

"They are, madam," Lestrade replied. "We shall take our four-wheeler, with myself, Stone, and two additional detectives slouched down in the carriage. When we arrive at the house, we will pounce."

"Even if we lack the critical information so needed for success?" I asked concernedly.

"It is now or never, and we can only hope that surprise is on our side," said Lestrade, and turned as the duo of Irregulars came into view. He reached for his revolver and checked its rounds before replacing it in its holster. The inspector looked up as the youngsters abruptly broke into a run and raced over to us.

"Well?" Joanna asked quickly.

"Easy as pie," Little Alfie responded. "We sang your song loud and clear, then made our way into the alleyway for a kiss and embrace, placing ourselves in front of the side windows. I managed a sly peek into the parlor and saw the elderly gentleman up and walking toward us."

"Was he able to see you?"

"Most unlikely, for we were too far from him."

"Could you tell if he was going yet into another room?"

Little Alfie shook his head. "We had to look away, for at that moment another man appeared directly behind him. He was following the elderly gentleman, no doubt."

"Only one man?"

"Only one we could see," said Little Alfie. "So as not to cause suspicion, we moved on a bit past the large window."

"So the elderly gentleman did not see you and thus did not send any sort of signal," Joanna concluded.

"I did not say that, ma'am, for I believe the gent did signal us," Little Alfie corrected. "It was quiet enough, but Sarah picked it up and we thought it best to scurry away."

"Back up a moment!" Joanna commanded. "Tell us every detail about the signal which was sent."

Sarah The Gypsy stepped forward to answer. "My hearing has always been quite sharp, ma'am, and has gotten me out of more than a few tight spots. So when I heard the rap on the window, I glanced over and saw the elderly gentleman, who waved briefly."

"Which window?" Joanna asked at once.

"The small one, ma'am."

"Watson is in the loo and telling us he is secure for the moment," Joanna said in a rush. "Now is the time!"

The detectives dashed into their four-wheeler, which immediately pulled away, with our carriage a safe distance behind. Our destination was only a block away and could be reached in under a minute.

"How long can my father remain in the lavatory without arousing suspicion?" I asked.

"Long enough, let us hope."

"Certainly the turncoat guarding him would not stand at the opened door to watch my father relieve himself."

"A clever guard might well do so."

The carriage in front of us came to an abrupt halt, and the four detectives rapidly climbed out and sprinted for the entrance to the house where my father was being held captive. A burly detective, at least six feet tall and weighing over two hundred pounds, smashed the door off its hinges with one mighty blow from his shoulder. Then he kicked it down and stood aside as Lestrade and Stone raced in, weapons drawn and ready to be discharged. There followed a barrage of gunfire, with one shot finding the young detective who was stationed on the footpath and guarding the perimeter. He fell to the ground, clutching his bloodied upper arm. We waited impatiently in our carriage, and each of us said a silent prayer for my father's welfare. There were no further shots as anxious seconds ticked by in the eerie stillness.

Our prayers were answered when Lestrade stepped out of the entrance and shouted, "All is well and Dr. Watson is unharmed!"

We alighted from our carriage and ran for the house, with the broadest of smiles on our faces. Passing the wounded detective, we could determine the injury was not severe, for he was now standing and no longer clutching his bloodstained shoulder. Joanna reached my father first and gave him the tightest of embraces.

"Oh, Watson, we were so worried," said she, her voice cracking.

"I am fine, my dear," my father assured. "A little fatigued perhaps, but otherwise quite fit."

As Joanna stepped aside to give me my turn, I noticed a small tear of joy forming in the corner of her eye. She made no effort to hide her emotion and brushed the teardrop away with a fingertip.

I, too, embraced my father and was never so glad to feel his touch. "It is wonderful to see you unharmed, Father."

"I am equally delighted," he quipped, thus telling us that his mind and spirit were entirely intact. "But pray tell, how in the world did you know to send the children singing 'Blaydon Races' to alert me?"

"It was Joanna's idea," said I.

My father nodded and smiled happily at the reply. "It was a plan that only Sherlock Holmes or his daughter could have devised on such short notice. The words were not exact, but close enough to ring true." His smile grew as he clapped my shoulder; then it disappeared as he looked down at the dead turncoat who had one bullet wound in his forehead and another in his upper chest. "You no doubt recognize this scoundrel."

"Paul Botha," Joanna responded. "I suspected he would be one of the turncoats when it was he who conveniently noticed the glint of the rifle barrel at Trafalgar Square. The timing was too good, the shot which nearly killed Smits too accurate for a moving target."

"Will there be yet more turncoats, other than Von Ruden?" Lestrade asked.

"I think not, for three would be all that was required," Joanna answered.

"I am tempted to arrest the bloody major," Lestrade growled. "But the evidence at this point is altogether circumstantial."

"And would never stand up before a hard-nosed British jury."

"Perhaps we should put a tail on him," the inspector suggested.

Joanna shook her head. "Let him roam free for now, and allow him to believe he has outwitted us."

"It would seem that he has."

"The game is not yet over, Lestrade."

Our conversation was interrupted by Stone, who came over to inform us, "The house is clean and unfurnished except for the parlor. We did discover a stack of maps on a table by the fireplace."

"Did you touch them?" Lestrade asked quickly.

"No, sir, for they might contain valuable fingerprints."

"Such as those belonging to Von Ruden," Lestrade said hopefully. "Which would place him in the house where the good Dr. Watson was being held captive."

Joanna waved away the notion. "It would never hold up in a British courtroom, for a clever barrister would simply claim that the maps were taken from his office without consent."

"And so we would be outwitted again," Lestrade grumbled.

Joanna reached for the maps with gloved hands and opened each separately. They were quite large and showed a considerable amount of detail. One illustrated all of Europe and had a thick line drawn upon it that began in the middle of the English Channel and extended up through the North Sea and into the Baltic Sea until it stopped at the German port of Hamburg. "This line of ink reveals the journey the U-boat will take back to Germany."

"Carrying the turncoats with the war document," Lestrade interjected.

"No doubt," Joanna said, and studied a second map which showed the entire Eastern Hemisphere. Upon it was drawn another thick line which went from Hamburg through Germany and Austria, then on to Portugal, from whence it continued out into the Atlantic Ocean and down the coast of the African continent to South Africa. "This is the route by which they return home, probably aboard a merchant ship."

"Still carrying the diamond?" the inspector wondered aloud.

"Unless they entered into some arrangement with the Germans, which is altogether likely," Joanna replied, and went to the third map that depicted southeastern England, with London at its center. There were no markings to indicate where the U-boat would surface for the turncoats.

"A blank," Lestrade remarked dispiritedly.

Joanna reached for her magnifying glass to carefully study the area of London and the surrounding ports, searching for hidden markings or signs.

"Nothing," she declared, refolding the maps and placing them back on the small side table. "Has the body been searched?"

"It has, with no findings whatsoever," Lestrade replied. "There was no wallet or papers of identification."

"Well then," Joanna said, stifling the start of a yawn, "it has been a long day for all, but particularly for Watson, who I believe would welcome a fine dinner and a comfortable seat in front of a cozy fire at 221b Baker Street."

"I do indeed look forward to both," my father agreed.

The detective who had been guarding the front perimeter stepped into the parlor and was again clutching his bloodied shoulder. My father, forever the physician regardless of the circumstances, rushed over to lend his assistance. Lestrade hurried over as well.

Joanna watched intently before turning to me and instructing, "Please move between the detectives and the small table, so I can snitch a map."

"But that is crime scene evidence," I objected mildly.

"Which will only gather dust in a file at Scotland Yard."

I positioned myself so the theft of the map would be unnoticed, and observed my father as he examined the young detective's shoulder. Although there was a fair amount of blood, I could see that no significant arteries or veins had been severed.

My father seemed to share that opinion, for he soon announced, "It is a superficial wound which will only require a suture or two and you will be on your way."

"Thank you, sir," said the young detective gratefully.

"It is I who should thank you, young man, for participating in my rescue."

"I was honored to do so," he replied, as the body of the turncoat was being prepared for transport.

"And now to Baker Street," Joanna directed.

Outside, the Baker Street Irregulars had positioned themselves on the footpath, no doubt awaiting payment for their invaluable service. They were rewarded with two guineas, and a bit more to cover their taxi ride back to Whitechapel.

On approaching our carriage, I whispered to my wife, "What is so important about the map of southeastern England?"

"If my assumptions are correct, it should tell us where the U-boat will surface to pick up the blue diamond."

"But the map showed no markings."

"That is what is so telling," Joanna said, and helped my father into our carriage.

CHAPTER TWENTY-EIGHT

The Unmarked Map

We received a warm welcome from Miss Hudson on our return to Baker Street. Toby Two was particularly happy to see our dear landlady, for she was spoiling the dog with repeated treats, and thus the hound was eager to follow her into the kitchen. Once in our parlor, we settled in our comfortable, overstuffed chairs and sipped from glasses of fine Madeira. My father seemed much at ease as he packed his cherrywood pipe with Arcadia Mixture, but his face was now illuminated by a glowing fire and showed the deep lines that no doubt were magnified by the ordeal he had just endured.

"I know you must be quite fatigued, Watson," Joanna remarked, "but now might be the best time to tell us of the abduction, while your memory is still fresh. If you do not feel up to it, I would understand."

"Now is indeed the most opportune time," my father said, lighting his pipe and taking a few gentle puffs. "I can recall every moment most vividly and can describe the entire adventure in detail."

"I take it that all began on Harley Street."

My father nodded as his face hardened briefly. "As I was departing the cardiologist's office, a gentleman waved and approached me, like we had encountered one another in the past. He smiled and promptly placed a partially concealed revolver against my ribs and herded me into a waiting motor vehicle."

"Did you recognize the abductor?"

"Not at first," my father replied. "I was to later learn it was Paul Botha, one of the turncoats. Apparently, he had followed my taxi from Baker Street to Harley Street."

"And I suspect he realized you were visiting your cardiologist because it was Harley Street and there was a brass plaque at the entrance to his office."

"Most likely, for he could not have known of my appointment in advance," my father agreed. "In any event, we ended up at a sparsely furnished home on Rossmore Road where I was handcuffed to a radiator in the parlor and only released for visits to the lavatory. I was told to remain silent and if I made any noise whatsoever I would be gagged."

"Was the driver of the vehicle known to you?"

My father shook his head. "I had never seen him before, but his accent was South African and I assumed he, too, was a turncoat."

"Your assumption is correct, for I believe he was the driver who attempted to follow us to the chemist's shop where the rescue plan was to be put into play."

"I trust he was interrupted along the way."

"By Scotland Yard, with whom he had the misfortune of engaging in a gunfight, which cost him his life."

"Good riddance, for he was the nastier of the two and seemed to enjoy telling me that my days on earth were limited."

Joanna reached for a Turkish cigarette and, after lighting it, began pacing the floor of our parlor, apparently gathering her thoughts. "So just prior to the rescue we have Botha guarding you and the driver quite dead. Who then went to the chemist's shop to have the prescription for digitalis leaf dispensed?"

"It was Botha," my father answered. "Before departing, he forced me into a spare room and onto the floor, where he tightly bound me hand and foot with a thick rope. I was then gagged and handcuffed to a radiator, making certain I was immobile and would remain silent. It was most uncomfortable to say the least."

"Thus we can conclude that the turncoats were a group of three and only three, with two now dead."

"So it would seem."

"I hope that Botha did not leave you in such an uncomfortable position any longer than absolutely necessary," said I, envisioning the torment of being bound, gagged, and immobile on a hard floor.

"He was in no hurry to release me, but when I feigned cardiac symptoms he thought it wise to release the ropes and allow me to take the prescribed medicine."

"How did you arrange to ingest the digitalis leaf in the lavatory?" Joanna asked. "You must have realized an attack was imminent."

"It was the children singing the song which alerted me," my father replied. "They could have only learned it from John, which meant he, you, and Scotland Yard were nearby and primed for attack. Thus I had to somehow convince my abductor to allow me to take the medicine in the lavatory, where I would be out of the line of fire. Fortunately, the answer came quickly."

I leaned forward, ears pricked, for Joanna was most accurate in her assessment that my father's body may well be aging, but his mind remained sharp as ever. "Please go through it step by step, Father."

"It was quite simple when I recalled that one of the major side effects of digitalis leaf was nausea, at times followed by vomiting. I informed Botha of the unpleasant symptoms induced by the drug and implored him to allow me to ingest the drug in the bathroom, for the nausea could arise very rapidly, yet be abated by gulping down copious amounts of water."

"Most clever," said Joanna, with a nod, and tossed her cigarette into the fireplace, then went back to pacing. "But I would have thought that Botha would have insisted the door to the loo remain open, so he could watch your every move."

"He did, but I suddenly began to retch and actually managed to bring up a bit of gastric fluid," my father described. "Apparently, Botha does not have a strong stomach, and elected to retreat to the parlor, which gave me the opening I required."

"Bravo, Watson!" Joanna praised, and applauded briefly. "And that is when you glanced out the window."

"And fortunately saw the children, at which time I retched again to cover the sound of me rapping on the window," my father recounted. "Your timing was spot-on, for had you waited another minute longer I would have been forced back into the parlor and handcuffed to the radiator."

"Other than the discomfort of being bound in a most uncomfortable position, I trust you were neither harmed nor abused," said I.

"There was no need for them to do so, and they even talked freely in my presence, for they knew I was to be disposed of prior to their final departure," my father replied. "They seemed to take great joy in regaling how the money garnered from the blue diamond would aid their cause."

"What cause?" I asked.

"The coming rebellion, which would deliver a severe blow to the Crown," he answered, as his expression again hardened. "The blue diamond was to be cut and polished in Antwerp and the majority of the gems given to the Krupp family, whose factories supply the German army with most of their weapons of war. In return, the Krupp industries would send a million pounds' worth of such weaponry to South Africa where the last remaining Boers will launch a major attack and attempt to overthrow British rule."

"Much like the Maritz rebellion of 1914," Joanna noted.

"Except this time around, they will be far better armed and joined by seasoned troops from neighboring German East Africa," my father went on. "Such an attack would divert South African soldiers to their home front away from the European continent and, if successful, would stop the flow of vital raw materials to England's factories. It would greatly aid Germany's war effort and be a disaster for Britain."

"They must be stopped!" I shouted my thought aloud.

"And we have only twenty-four hours at our disposal," Joanna said, reaching for the map of southeastern England and tacking it to the wall next to her writing desk. "Again I must implore you, Watson, to think back to all the conversations the turncoats had, and whether their port of embarkation was ever mentioned."

"Never," my father replied promptly. "For I listened carefully in hopes they would mention it, well aware of how important that piece of information was. They spoke only of their journey through Germany and Austria and on to Portugal, where they would board a ship at Lisbon. They chatted quite excitedly, like individuals who would be visiting those countries for the first time."

"But no talk of an English port, eh?"

"Not in my presence."

Joanna studied the large map at length, moving her magnifying glass up and down the extended coastline of England. "It must be a sizable port within easy driving distance of London."

"Based on what, may I ask?" my father inquired.

"The lack of markings on the map," Joanna responded. "They saw no need to make any, for I suspect the route to the port was straightforward and required no deviation from the main roads that surround London. As our American colleagues might say, it would be a straight shot."

"But why a sizable port?" my father asked. "It would seem a smaller, out-of-the-way port would better serve their purpose."

"You must place yourself in their stead, Watson, and think as they do," Joanna explained. "In particular, how would they manage to reach the U-boat from an English port?"

"It would require a launch."

"A large vessel of some note. Yes?"

"One would think."

"Of course one would, for you are venturing into the English Channel where the sea and current are most unforgiving and a rowboat will not do," she went on. "Thus they would use a larger vessel, which would be noticed by all at a small, tranquil port but by few at a busy one."

"But there are dozens of such ports within easy driving reach of London," I countered.

"Which complicates matters," said Joanna, and returned to studying the map with her magnifying glass. "But that number can be substantially reduced."

"How so?"

"By contacting their harbormasters and determining which of the ports have stone wharfs."

Our conversation was broken by Miss Hudson, who, after a brief rap on the door, entered with a tray laden with food that gave off a most delectable aroma and immediately whetted our appetites. We dined on nicely prepared roast beef, potato spuds, and Brussels sprouts wrapped in bacon, which we consumed with delight, particularly my father, who had been denied food during his captivity.

After dinner we settled in our comfortable chairs in front of a crackling fire and enjoyed snifters of brandy, all of which intensified our postprandial lethargy. I was forced to stifle a yawn, for the excitement of the day had worn off and a deep fatigue had set in, which was made worse by our nearly sleepless night before. My eyelids were closing and I endeavored to keep them open, but it was a futile attempt. My father's exhaustion was also obvious, for he had no doubt slept little whilst held captive and was denied the comfort of a simple bed. And I could not help but wonder if the stressful event had caused his cardiac condition to worsen.

"You appear done in, Father," said I. "Which I pray will be remedied by a sound night's sleep."

"You are also concerned with how well your father's heart held up to his dreadful ordeal," Joanna observed.

"How could you have possibly known that?" I asked, impressed as always by my wife's ability to read my mind.

"Because you were staring at the bottle of digitalis leaf, which he had placed on a nearby side table rather than in his night table where he usually secured it," she elucidated. "The look of worry on your face told me you were wondering if he required yet another dose of his medication, which would indicate his cardiac condition was worsening."

I found myself nodding at Joanna's accurate deduction, which was derived from subtle clues that most of us would have overlooked. "As you can see, Father, I am helpless at keeping secrets from my wife."

"Not to worry, John," said my father. "I placed the digitalis leaf in plain view to remind me to take the next prescribed dose, for I could not do so while retching for my captor's benefit."

"Nicely done," I said happily. "And on that note, we should retire early for a well-deserved good night's sleep."

As I helped my father to his feet, he advised my wife in his kind voice, "You should take a respite as well, my dear, for a solid slumber will greatly refresh your mind."

"The answer will not come in my sleep, Watson," said Joanna, and raised her magnifying glass to again study the map, which she was certain held the secret location of the port from whence the war document would make its final exit.

Chapter twenty-nine

The Pursuit

My father and I slept soundly through the night and entered the parlor midmorning, and much to our surprise found it free of tobacco smoke, which suggested Joanna's search was over and the secret of the map revealed. But this was not to be the case, for the window was cracked open to clear the air, which indicated Miss

Hudson had made her customary appearance to serve breakfast. Yet the dishes of bacon and eggs on the dining table were untouched, for Joanna was of the opinion that ingested food diverted the circulation to one's stomach and away from the brain, which by nature would impede the thinking process.

"No luck, then?" asked I.

"None," Joanna replied, continuing to pace. "But I feel the answer is close at hand and requires only a final piece of information to bring it to the surface."

"And this conclusion is all based on their failure to mark the map of southeastern England?"

"It is out of place," said she. "And it is the out-of-place items which often provide the best clues."

"I fail to see the connection between the unmarked map and the other two which were marked in excitement over their upcoming journey back to South Africa," I admitted. "And why leave all three behind?"

"They did not intend for them to be discovered," Joanna explained, pointing to the cold ashes in our fireplace. "You will recall we found the maps on a small table near their hearth, which I believe was a reminder to dispose of them prior to the abductors' departure. They planned to leave nothing behind except perhaps for Watson's body."

"But why did they not line the map of England if it was to be burned?"

"Because that portion of their journey was uninteresting, for it took a direct route to a nearby port."

"You are convinced of this?"

"There is no other explanation."

My father raised a hand holding his pipe and interjected, "There is yet another possibility. Perhaps the map remains unmarked because they plan to travel by train."

"I considered that mode of transportation as well, but believed

it most unlikely," said Joanna. "The turncoats must have realized their carefully devised scheme might be uncovered and, if so,
all of England would be on the lookout for them. The very last
place they would wish to be was Paddington or Victoria station,
which would be closely watched by Scotland Yard. Furthermore,
a train would be quite confining and if the turncoats were recognized they would be easily surrounded and apprehended." She
redirected her pacing to the Persian slipper that held her Turkish
cigarettes and lighted one. "I must remind you to always think the
way the criminal does, if you hope to trap him. Otherwise, you
will remain a step behind."

"But a motor vehicle has its disadvantages as well, for it can
develop mechanical difficulties or perhaps run low on petrol," I
argued mildly.

My father sat up abruptly. "They will be traveling by motor
vehicle. I am certain of it."

"What convinces you so?" asked I.

"Because I overheard my captors mention petrol in one of
their earlier conversations," my father replied.

Joanna quickly discarded her cigarette into the fireplace and
hurried over. "Tell us the exact words they spoke, Watson, and
please be precise."

My father furrowed his brow and thought back in time before speaking. "The nasty fellow asked if they had enough petrol
or should they add to the tank, and Botha responded that a half
tank should suffice."

"Most important, Watson!" Joanna cried out. "For I believe
we can say without fear of contradiction that the motor vehicle
they were referring to was the four-seater Wolseley they have been
employing for all their missions. Now we have to learn how far
that vehicle will travel on a full tank."

"One hundred and sixty miles," I answered.

"How do you know this?" Joanna asked at once.

"Because last month I considered buying a four-seater Wolseley and actually visited the dealership. I inquired how far the vehicle would travel on a full tank and was told one hundred and sixty miles."

"Which tells us a half tank will allow for a journey of eighty miles," Joanna calculated, and raced to the map on the wall and quickly read its legends. Then she reached for a ruler and began drawing straight lines along the coast of England, with London being the central point. "An inch equals a hundred miles, and thus eight-tenths of an inch is the equivalent of eighty miles," she went on. "So now we know the major port we are seeking is within that radius on our map."

"How many of them fit that profile?" I inquired.

"At least ten," Joanna replied, and began reading off their names. "To the north are Southend-on-Sea, Clacton-on-Sea, and Harwich. South of London are the larger ports, which include Margate, Ramsgate, Dover, Hastings, and Folkestone, and Folkestone being only—" She stopped in mid-sentence and shouted out, "Folkestone is the secret port! That is what Smits was attempting to tell us. But we only heard the word *stone* and before it the syllable *for*, which we misinterpreted as *for stone* or *for the stone*. What he was trying to convey was the port of Folkestone."

"Perhaps the lieutenant was also attempting to say the wharf at Folkestone."

"No doubt, Watson, for earlier this morning I phoned the harbormaster of London, who was most familiar with the ports surrounding his city. He related that virtually all their wharfs were constructed of wood and stone, but that Dover and Folkestone were in particular heavily made of the latter." She promptly admonished herself, saying, "I overlooked the clue regarding Folkestone, and that blunder has cost us valuable time which we can ill afford to spare."

Joanna dashed for the telephone and dialed the number of the commissioner of Scotland Yard, which she knew by rote memory. It required several long minutes for the call to be put through, during which time she impatiently tapped her foot on the floor and muttered words we could not understand. Finally, the connection was made.

"Listen carefully, Commissioner, for we have much to do in very little time," Joanna said urgently, and began listing instructions.

There were two quite long piers at Folkestone, which were connected at right angles to each other. Our Scotland Yard launch was positioned at the end of the seaward wharf, which gave us a panoramic view of the entire harbor. Twilight was beginning to set in, and the activity at the port was limited to a few fishing boats returning with their catch from the Channel. This observation, together with the last rays of the sun now disappearing, lessened our confidence in Joanna's prediction that Folkestone would be the port of exit for the blue diamond.

"Perhaps your timing was off a bit," my father predicted, as he sought to explain the failure.

"You must be patient, Watson," said Joanna. "In all likelihood they are simply waiting for a heavy mist to cover their departure."

"That moment is almost upon us."

"And so is their exit."

"Pray tell how can you be so certain of their timing?"

"You must take into account that today is Saturday, and there will be no launches for hire tomorrow when all shops are closed," Joanna explained. "Von Ruden is now on the run, for he knows that you have been rescued and two of his fellow turncoats are dead. Thus we are onto him and he has no choice but to make a hasty escape. Every hour he spends in England places him at greater and greater risk, and he must therefore rush to depart with his precious diamond and war document."

"But the U-boat must be signaled and somehow given the exact time to surface," said Lestrade. "That is no easy task for a man in hiding."

"There must be a coconspirator involved, who may well be a German agent stationed in London," Joanna went on. "I suspect it was he who sent the radio signal and hired the launch which will take them to the U-boat."

"And that launch will be abandoned at sea once Von Ruden and the German agent board the U-boat."

"Undoubtedly so."

"But I continue to worry about the timing, now that the last of the sun has disappeared beyond the English landscape."

"Our major concern should not be the exact timing, but whether Scotland Yard's launch can keep up with the one Von Ruden has hired."

"I believe it will hold its own."

But the tone of the inspector's voice caused me to wonder how confident he was of the launch's speed. To be outrun by the enemy at the very last moment would be most disheartening. I gazed down at the stokers and the engine now purring in low gear, and hoped their performance would not let us down.

An eerie quiet overtook the entire harbor, with all boats secured to the piers and gently bobbing in the calm water. We heard a ship's bell clang in the distance from an incoming vessel, but the sound rapidly faded and the stillness returned. Minutes dragged by as our ability to view the sea itself diminished further. The evening mist appeared to thicken, with beams from the moon barely able to shine through. Then we heard it. A ship's engine suddenly came to life at the far end of the opposing pier. We hurriedly brought our binoculars up and watched a launch, approximately the size of ours, pull away from its mooring and start out to sea. The moon momentarily broke through the mist and afforded us a more distinct picture of the vessel. Now, on second looks, it seemed larger than ours and no doubt more powerful. Our eyes remained fixed on the enemy's launch as it cleared the confines of the harbor, then abruptly sped out to sea.

"The chase is on!" Joanna cried out to the pilot. "Follow the ship which has a green light starboard!"

We rapidly moved out of the harbor, with our launch's engine now roaring to full power. At first, it seemed we were closing the gap between ourselves and the enemy, but this advantage lasted only briefly, as the launch ahead no doubt became aware of our presence and laid on more steam. They were at least a hundred yards ahead and clearly increasing their distance from us. The green light, which was to be our guide, was gradually disappearing from view.

"Pour it on, men, pour it on!" Joanna shouted down to the stokers in the engine room. "Give us every pound of steam!"

Our speed increased noticeably, but we were not able to close the gap, and remained a good hundred yards or more behind the enemy. A late-returning fishing vessel suddenly blundered in front of us and we had to swerve mightily to avoid a collision. This maneuver put us even farther behind, and in the dimness our hopes began to fade, and then faded further as we watched the monstrous hull of a U-boat come to the surface.

"Be careful here," Joanna warned loudly. "Most U-boats have a powerful deck gun and we are totally defenseless against it."

The pilot slowed our speed to a near standstill, but with the enemy now stationary, we drifted closer than we wished to be. Again we brought up our binoculars and watched Von Ruden and his coconspirator hurriedly securing their launch to the U-boat. Our presence was apparently unsettling to the Germans, for they rotated their deck gun and fired off a shot which whizzed by overhead and landed harmlessly behind us, yet still caused a mighty explosion which rattled our launch stem to stern. A second round came even closer and set off an earsplitting blast that momentarily lifted us out of the sea. It was now clear our lives were in dire jeopardy, for in our current position we were well within their range and the next round was certain to find us. Joanna and I embraced, as if for a final time.

But in the blink of an eye all changed. Out of the mist appeared HMS *Courageous,* the mightiest of the Royal Navy's battle cruisers, with its powerful deck guns now rotating so that they would be trained on the U-boat. In desperation, the Germans attempted to turn their auto-cannon on the British warship, but their efforts were slow and in vain. The HMS *Courageous*'s quick-fire guns boomed aloud, and seconds later found their mark, which caused fingers of flame to appear and dance around the U-boat's conning tower. The light from the blast illuminated the entire submarine, which allowed us to watch two figures frantically climbing from the launch onto the deck of the U-boat. The German gunners fired two consecutive rounds, which fell just short of the British destroyer and caused a large wave to bounce off its bow. Despite our closeness to the epic sea battle, we chose not to take cover, but rather to steady ourselves and face the obvious danger.

"I will say this for the Royal Navy," Joanna remarked in a calm voice. "They do know how to keep to schedule."

I looked at my wife oddly, wondering if I had heard her words correctly. "Are you telling us you arranged for the warship to show up at precisely the right moment?"

"Actually, it was the commissioner who followed my advice and placed an immediate call to the Admiralty," said she, then added, "the commissioner of Scotland Yard's voice appears to carry considerable weight."

The deck guns of HMS *Courageous* fired a final volley, all of which seemed to find their target simultaneously. By every account, the rounds must have penetrated deep into the hull of the submarine and struck its large fuel tanks, for there followed a massive blast which tore the vessel apart. As the wreckage of the U-boat sank into oblivion beneath the cold waters of the Channel, the seamen to a man aboard the *Courageous* broke out into a prolonged, deafening roar. It was the roar of victory. We happily joined in.

CLOSURE

Nearly five full days passed before all the pieces of the puzzle came together and brought the case of *The Blue Diamond* to its final conclusion. It was difficult to believe so much time had flown by, but then again, I was consumed with a backlog of duties at St. Bartholomew's and scarcely had a moment to glance at the calendar.

After a long afternoon's work that went well into evening, I returned to our rooms at 221b Baker Street to find Joanna and my father seated in front of a blazing fire enjoying snifters of brandy. Outside, pellets of rain and slivers of snow were being blown about, some of which were forming icicles on our large window.

"Thank goodness you are safe and sound," my wife welcomed me. "A heavy storm from the North Sea is sweeping into London and will in all likelihood render the streets impassable. I should not like to think of you spending the night in an uncomfortable room at the hospital."

"Particularly with the saddest of events, which occurred only hours before my departure," said I. "I am afraid the news is quite heartbreaking."

Joanna quickly rose and motioned to the fireplace. "Warm your hands while I fetch you a brandy, then give us the unpleasant details."

"And most unpleasant they are."

"What has transpired?" my father asked, obviously concerned.

"A patient has died."

"Lieutenant Smits?"

I shook my head. "Anika Hopkins's baby boy."

"Which was to be expected."

"But nonetheless tragic."

I accepted a snifter of brandy from Joanna, then told of the sad event. "Late this morning the baby went into congestive heart failure and was rushed to the Hospital for Sick Children, with his mother by his side. Little could be done for the toddler, so he was transported to St. Bart's for immediate consultation with one of our staff cardiologists. Unfortunately, the child expired on arrival before he could be seen by a consultant. I was in Lieutenant Smits's room when I received news of the baby's demise, which brought the lieutenant great distress, for he was particularly fond of the lad. He insisted on joining me in the emergency area so that he might comfort his dear friend, Anika."

"Was Smits in any condition to do so?" my father asked. "When last seen he was near extremis."

"But he has made a miraculous recovery following surgery and multiple transfusions, and is now sitting up in bed ingesting a soft diet."

"Yet he no doubt remains in a most weakened condition."

"Indeed, it is difficult for him to even stand, yet he demanded I accompany him in his wheelchair to the grieving mother's side. I had no choice but to do so, for I believe he would have crawled on hands and knees to reach her. When the lieutenant saw Anika Hopkins holding the dead baby, he wept and did his best to comfort her by promising to join Anika on her sad journey home. Once there, her departed husband and baby would be laid to rest in the family plot outside Johannesburg."

"What a sorrowful scene that had to have been," my father noted in a soft voice.

"I must admit my eyes moistened up a bit as well," I said, and decided to change the topic of conversation to a happier one. "But there is one spot of good news for you, Father, for I happened upon your fine cardiologist, who told me of a new, more purified form of digitalis leaf, which could be of much benefit to you. Because of its purity, the dose of the medication can be more accurately adjusted, thus allowing for it to calm down your erratic heart rhythm nicely, without inducing the drug's toxic effect."

"Jolly good!" my father approved.

We were interrupted by a gentle rap on the door and Miss Hudson entered, followed by a short, thin man in his middle years whom we did not recognize. He wore a heavy topcoat and shuffled his feet nervously about, with cap in hand.

"This is my friend Bertie, who has just returned from his journey to the Hebrides and has come to fetch his sweet Alsatian. I of course told him of Dolly's tragic ending, but thought you might wish to have a word with him."

"Indeed I would," said Joanna, stepping forward at once. "But first, may I offer you a drink to ward off the chill?"

Bertie shook his head ever so slightly. "No thank you, ma'am. I am fine."

"Then let us simply tell you that if it were not for your valiant hound, the three of us in this room would not be alive today. She gave her life for ours, and I can assure you we shall never forget her. Please inform us if there is any way to compensate you for your loss."

"That will not be necessary, ma'am, for we shall take great pride in knowing she took a bloody Hun with her."

"Were medals handed out to hounds, Dolly would surely deserve one."

At that moment, Toby Two, who had been carefully eyeing the visitor, came over to sniff his shoes, tail wagging in the process. The dog went toe to heel and seemed to relish every whiff.

"She is detecting the scent of the Alsatian, which is ingrained in all my clothes," Bertie explained, and reached for a dog biscuit in his coat pocket. "I always kept one on hand for my dear Dolly."

Toby Two chewed on the biscuit, with all of her attention on the treat. Once it was finished, the hound whined pitifully for a second helping, her tail now straight as an arrow.

"Still hungry, are you?" Bertie asked, and leaned down to scratch Toby Two's head, which caused her tail to wag again.

Joanna's eyes suddenly lighted up. "The hound seems to take to you."

"I get along with all dogs, ma'am."

"Would you consider taking Toby Two home with you?"

"Oh, I could not accept your gentle dog, ma'am."

"She is not mine, but borrowed from a somewhat unpleasant kennel which she will be pleased to see the last of."

"But will the owner not be upset?"

"The owner of the kennel has suffered a stroke and will no longer be able to offer his animals," said Joanna. "You shall be doing both him and us a favor by providing the dog with a new home."

"I should pay something, ma'am."

"I shall see to that," Joanna assured. "Now be on your way and give that gentle dog the life she deserves."

"She will spend her nights by the fire and her days romping around in our back garden, finding new scents to sample and track."

"Then we wish you a very pleasant good evening."

Toby Two hesitated to follow the visitor out, but rather looked to Joanna for instructions, which came with a silent flick of her wrist to the door. The dog still hesitated, but when my wife uttered a soft, "Go!" the hound with the keenest nose in all London trotted out behind her new master.

"And now for a last piece of business before we refill our snifters and settle down to one of Miss Hudson's sumptuous dinners," I announced. "The body of Eric Von Ruden has finally washed up on the shore of Dover. His remains were brought to St. Bartholomew's for postmortem examination, but nothing was found either on or inside of him."

"The traitor!" my father spat out derisively.

"Who will be buried in an unmarked grave in the far corner of a potter's field."

"It is a shame to contaminate such good English soil."

"I am of the same opinion," said I. "But that decision is not ours to make."

Joanna stared into the fire to contemplate the matter further, for there was something of concern still on her mind. "Is there any possibility that the war document survived the blast?"

"Not according to the commissioner of Scotland Yard, who believes the war document, along with the blue diamond and Ming vase, are buried deep beneath the soft mud on the floor of the English Channel, well away from German eyes."

"I take it that is the belief of MI5 as well?" Joanna queried.

"And of Vernon Carter-Smith in particular, who is of the opinion there is no chance the items can be recovered."

"And who disappeared into the shadows before any further questions could be asked."

"He did indeed, but only after handing me a message meant for the three of us," said I, and reached into my coat pocket for an unaddressed envelope which I passed on to my wife. "It is to be destroyed once read."

Joanna opened the envelope and removed an unmarked card upon which there was a single handwritten sentence. It read:

All England is in your debt.

Our hearts were warmed, the message tossed into the fire.

The following summer the British Expeditionary Force gathered seventy-five miles north of Paris to set in motion the Backs to the Wall plan, and with precise timing were to later spring a deadly trap which inflicted devastating losses on the German army. It was the British victory in the Battle of Amiens which marked the turning point that eventually led to the end of the Great War.

ACKNOWLEDGMENTS

Special thanks to Peter Wolverton, for being an editor par excellence, and to Scott Mendel, for being such an extraordinary agent. And a tip of the hat to Danielle Prielipp and Hector De-Jean, my superb publicists, and to David Rotstein, for his wonderful cover designs.